Jason Dean spent much of his professional life as a graphic designer before deciding what he really wanted to do was write the kind of international thrillers he's always loved reading. The James Bishop series was the result. He is now working on the next book in the Korso series. Jason lives in the Far East with his wife and their dog.

Also by Jason Dean

Korso Thrillers

Tracer
Sanctum
Prototype

PROTOTYPE

JASON DEAN

CANELO

First published in the United Kingdom in 2023 by

Canelo
Unit 9, 5th Floor
Cargo Works, 1–2 Hatfields
London SE1 9PG
United Kingdom

A CIP catalogue record for this book is available from the British Library.

Print ISBN 978 1 80436 152 8
Ebook ISBN 978 1 80436 151 1

Look for more great books at www.canelo.co

Printed and bound in Great Britain by Clays Ltd, Elcograf S.p.A.

1

For Jeevan Rai,

fellow film aficionado

ONE

'Do you know what's about to happen to you, Darian?' the man with the small eyes asked. 'Specifically, I mean?'

Darian Yanev shook his head in mute terror. It was the only part of his body he could move. Naked from the waist up, his arms, torso and legs were strapped tightly to a steel gurney that was angled slightly downwards, with his head at the lower end. Underneath his head was a large plastic bucket, full of water. Yanev's puffy face was still bleeding from the beating he'd just taken, the left eye swollen up until it was almost completely shut, while a kaleidoscope of bruises covered his chest and stomach area.

'Well, I'll tell you,' his interrogator said, grabbing a thin towel from a nearby table. Another older man, dressed in a dark, expensive three-piece suit, stood in one corner or the small, windowless room, watching the proceedings. 'First thing we do is place this damp towel over your face, and then I fill that jug over there with water and slowly pour it over your nose and mouth. You'll try holding your breath, but adrenaline will take over and your heart will be pumping a mile a minute, so you'll be forced to let it out, and then when you inhale you'll be taking in pure H20. The wet towel will clamp tight against your nostrils and mouth, and you'll choke uncontrollably. You'll get spasms in your larynx and won't even know if you're breathing in or out, which will feed your panic even more.'

'Please…' Yanev began.

'Now they say waterboarding simulates the effects of drowning, but that's wrong. You actually *are* drowning. With your medical background you must know how painful that is, with your lungs heaving violently as they try to take in oxygen that's no longer there. So my question is, are you really going to force us to go through with this, or can we just cut straight to the part where you give us what we want?'

Yanev's breathing was becoming short now. He also looked terrified. 'My pills…' he mumbled in a thick voice.

'That's right, Darian,' the other man said. 'Just give us the formula for those pills of yours and all this will be over in seconds. We'll untie you and treat your wounds, and then we'll draft up a legal agreement whereby we can all profit from this. I'm a fair man, and that's all I've ever wanted, so why not make it easier for yourself and just tell us?'

'My pills,' Yanev said again. He took a deep breath, and swallowed. 'My pills…'

'Christ, this is useless.' The older man gave a weary sigh. 'Okay, get on with it.'

'Yes, sir,' the first man said, and carefully arranged the damp towel over Yanev's face until it was completely covered. Yanev whimpered helplessly underneath, his breath still coming in short rapid gasps, while the interrogator grabbed the empty jug from the table and filled it with water from the bucket on the floor. Then he raised the jug eight inches above the man's head and began to pour.

The effects were immediate. As soon as the liquid made contact with the man's nasal cavity, Yanev's chest hitched violently and he arched his body off the gurney as far as it would go. He gagged and coughed and spluttered, his head twisting from side to side in a pointless effort to escape the onslaught, while the other man continued pouring water onto the shroud over his face. As the seconds passed, Yanev's struggling became more strenuous, and his hacking more violent.

Finally, after another twenty seconds, the man in the suit said, 'Enough.'

The first man stopped pouring, and yanked the drenched towel from Yanev's face. His back still arched, Yanev's chest continued to jerk and hitch as his lungs tried to take in the necessary oxygen. It took another two minutes before his breathing became even close to normal.

'Well?' the interrogator asked. 'You ready to talk now?'

'My pills,' Yanev said, in a hoarse voice. 'My—'

'Again with this.' The interrogator shook his head. 'Looks like we'll have to take another dip.'

'Wait.' The other one stepped forward, leaned in closer to Yanev. 'He keeps saying the same thing. What about these pills, Darian? Are you saying you've already taken the next step and synthesised some, that you've actually developed prototypes?'

Yanev nodded his head. He coughed again, and said, 'Yes, but—'

'I knew it.' The man in the suit turned to his subordinate with wide eyes. 'I just *knew* it. The answer to all our problems and it's right here in front of us.' He turned back to Yanev. 'Forget about the formula, Darian. Just tell me where you hid those pills, and this will all be over in seconds.'

'My pills,' Yanev croaked. 'Please…'

'*Just tell me where you hid them, godammit.*'

Yanev opened his mouth, as though about to speak, and then his eyes widened and his body suddenly started jerking spastically as he frantically tried to take in air again.

'What the hell?' the interrogator said, backing away.

'Dammit, he's having a coronary,' the other one said. 'That must be what he was talking about. His heart pills.' He quickly patted Yanev's trouser pockets, but found nothing. He turned to his subordinate. 'His shirt and jacket. *Where are they?*'

'The room at the end of the hall.'

'Get them. *Move.*'

As the interrogator dashed from the room, the man in the suit held Yanev down as he struggled frantically against his bonds, his head twisting from side to side, his eyes bulging from their sockets. Spittle flew from his mouth as his movements quickly became even more frenzied. The interrogator returned in less than half a minute, out of breath, and holding two small tube containers.

'Found these,' he said. 'Digoxin and beta-blockers.'

'Give them to him. *Quick.*'

The interrogator unscrewed the cap of the first tube, and was dropping several pills into his palm when Yanev let out a long, piercing scream that sounded anything but human. He froze for a moment, every muscle stretched to its limit, and then suddenly collapsed back onto the gurney like a rag doll. He didn't move after that.

'No, no, no, no.' The man in the suit placed his fingers against Yanev's carotid artery, then pressed his ear against the man's chest. He stayed there for at least twenty seconds. Finally, he rose up again, and shook his head. 'No pulse at all. He's gone. *Shit.*'

'You're sure?'

The man in the suit just looked at him with contempt. 'A man with a weak heart. I don't suppose you thought to check his medical history before putting him through all this?'

The interrogator looked pained. 'Things kind of escalated before I had a chance to think about it.'

They looked down at the corpse on the gurney. The seconds passed in silence.

'So what now, boss?' the interrogator asked finally.

'Now?' The older man gave another deep sigh. 'We keep going, of course. This is far too big to let go. It just means we'll have to do things the hard way. The formula's died with Yanev, but those samples of his have to be somewhere. And nothing's going to stop me from finding them. Nothing.'

TWO

Korso carried the man's body into the small cubicle and set him down on top of his unmoving partner, who was already slumped over the toilet seat. They were both big men, and Korso was starting to sweat under his tuxedo from all the heavy lifting. But nothing in life came easy. If you wanted something bad enough, you had to make the effort.

Straightening up, he checked each man's pulse one more time. Slow, steady, regular. The propofol dosage he'd used would keep each of them out of action for the next couple of hours or so. More than enough time. Through the thick walls, Korso could hear the muffled tenor of the legendary José Balotelli as he scaled the high peaks of '*Que dit-il?*' from Act III of Verdi's '*Don Carlos*'. Even muffled, the man's voice was incredible. Pity he couldn't enjoy it like the rest of the audience out there. But Korso knew this particular performance was also being recorded for posterity. He'd buy the digital version so he could listen to the whole thing later, but it wouldn't be the same.

The little cubicle was very cramped now, and it took some manoeuvring until Korso was able to shut and lock the door from the inside. Stepping onto the chest of the man he'd just brought in, Korso hefted himself up and over the left-hand partition and dropped down into the adjacent cubicle, and then out again.

The restroom was still otherwise empty, and would likely remain so until the next intermission in twenty minutes time, but Korso didn't want to push his luck. Anybody could come in at any moment, and the fewer people who saw him the better.

Korso stepped over to one of the mirrors and checked his reflection, straightening the creases in his tux jacket and making sure the bulge under his left armpit wasn't too noticeable. Satisfied, he opened the door and the orchestra instantly became clearer and more forceful. He stepped out into the lushly carpeted corridor and looked both ways. Still nobody else in sight. Korso turned left and followed the curved hallway until he was standing in front of the door to Box 9 again. No guards, this time.

He turned the handle, gently pushed the door open a few inches, and then sidled in through the gap, quickly closing the door behind him. The box was dark, the only light coming from the stage out front. There were eight seats inside, but six were empty. A man and a woman sat in the two front seats, completely engrossed in the performance two tiers below them. It seemed neither had noticed him enter.

Reaching under his tuxedo jacket, Korso felt the weapon in his inside pocket. Eyes still on the two in front of him, he walked forward and slipped into the chair directly behind the man. His name was Gianni Accetta, and he was one of the most ruthless and successful arms dealers in all of southern Europe.

Korso waited. When there was a brief lull in the music, he coughed lightly.

Accetta turned at the sound. So did the girl. Wearing a backless designer dress, she looked to be in her late teens or early twenties, and was stunningly attractive, with long silky black hair down to her waist. The man was in his fifties, with a precisely trimmed goatee beard and dyed black hair artfully swept back over his head to cover the bald spot. He was also wearing a tux, just like every other man in the Teatro di San Carlo tonight.

'*You*,' Accetta said in perfect English. 'What are you doing here? How did you get in? Where are my men?'

'Occupied.' Korso jutted his chin towards the performers down below. 'Good to see Balotelli still on top form, isn't it? He should never have retired.' He turned to the girl. '*Vi divertite, Francesca?*'

'*Sì, molto.*' She gave him a puzzled smile. '*Ti conosco?*'

'No, but Mr Accetta here knows me well enough, right?'

'Okay, I'm impressed,' he said. 'You know my girlfriend's name, you found out where we'd be tonight, and you even found a way past my bodyguards somehow. Where are they, by the way?'

'In the restroom.'

'Both of them? How?'

'Trade secret.'

It hadn't taken too much effort, really. Korso had simply waited in one of the cubicles until one of the bodyguards decided to take a quick bathroom break while everybody else was enjoying the second act. Since '*Don Carlos*' was Verdi's longest opera at four hours, Korso felt confident it would happen sooner or later. And he also knew how to move silently. A quick jab in the carotid artery and the first guard went out like a light. Inevitably, when he failed to return to his post, his partner soon came to investigate. Thirty seconds later, he was unconscious too.

'It seems I'm going to have to find better help.' Accetta furrowed his brow when he saw Korso's right hand inside his jacket. 'Or is too late for that?'

Korso just looked at him, and said nothing.

'*Gianni,*' the girl said, clutching her lover's arm, '*che succede? Chi è questo uomo?*'

Accetta ignored her, and watched transfixed as Korso slowly pulled the weapon from his inner pocket. No doubt preparing himself for the worst. But before it was even halfway out, he could see it wasn't meant for him. Or rather, it was, but not in that way. Korso gently laid the thing on the armrest and carefully unwrapped the protective cloth wrapping until the asset was displayed in all its glory.

'*Oh Dio.*' Accetta's eyes widened at the sight. '*Magnifico.* Absolutely incredible. And it's really…?'

'…the fabled *Arctic Wolf*?' Korso finished for him. 'The one and only.'

Started in secret by the acclaimed American knife maker, Buster Warenski, during his final years, and completed by his most talented student, Cable Wrightson, after his death, the knife was a true sight to behold. Intricately embroidered on both handle and sheath, the dagger contained 15 ounces of 18K gold, 29 ounces of 95% pure platinum, and 77 diamonds totalling eight karats. It had always been planned to be the fourth in Warenski's much-celebrated *Legacy Knives* series. The first, a faithful reproduction of the gold dagger found in Tutankhamen's tomb, had taken Warenski five years to make. The second, *The Gem of the Orient*, took twice that, while the third, *Fire and Ice*, took another seven years. Each one was an absolute masterpiece of craftsmanship, and would easily reach seven figures if put up for auction. Possible eight.

The fourth knife was in the series was never named, but Warenski gave a few hints as to what it might look like once completed. He died before it could be finished, but rumours soon circulated that he had given Wrightson, his very first apprentice, verbal permission to complete the work according to his detailed specifications. In honour of his mentor, Wrightson never once revealed its existence to the public, not even after he finished it. In 2011, the dagger was allegedly stolen from a safe in Wrightson's house and never seen again, although the legends surrounding it grew all the same. Nobody knew where the *Arctic Wolf* title originated, but it fitted the chilly appearance of the dagger perfectly. Under natural lighting, one could make out an almost bluish tint to the blade when it was tilted a certain way. It really was a work of art.

Since the *Arctic Wolf* wasn't a 'pure' Warenski piece, it was hard to gauge how much the thing was really worth. And what with it being stolen property, the Warenski estate was unlikely to ever give it their official seal of approval either. But Korso knew there were a handful of collectors around the world who'd still pay through the nose for the knife should it ever materialise on the open market.

Accetta moved to touch the prized item.

'Not so fast.' Korso said, and covered it again with the cloth.

Accetta made a fist of his hand as he pulled it back, clearly embarrassed at exhibiting such blatant hunger. He glared up at Korso. 'What are you doing here anyway? We were due to meet up in Milan tomorrow night for the exchange. Or did I get my dates mixed up?'

'I decided to bring things forward a day instead. You'd be amazed at how many of my clients suddenly decide, once the salvaged item in question is physically back in their hands, that it would be far simpler to erase me from existence rather than pay me my agreed thirty-three per cent. It's become an occupational hazard. That's not to say you'd be anything but honourable, but I've found it's better to prepare for the worst. I've a number of workarounds for any given situation. In this case, using the backdrop of a charity comeback performance by the most accomplished opera tenor of our age, at Naples' historic Teatro di San Carlo no less, was too good an opportunity to pass up.'

'*Gianni, chi è?*' Francesca asked her man, more forcefully than before. Without looking at her, Accetta told her to be quiet and watch the show. She turned away in a huff.

'She'll make you pay for that later,' Korso said.

'Not if she knows what's good for her. Tell me, where did you find the dagger?'

'In the home of a very shady but highly influential businessman in Buenos Aires. He probably hasn't noticed it's missing yet. But then, I know for a fact he's got a lot of other things on his mind at the moment. I made sure of it before I left.'

'And would I know of this man?'

'I dare say you've had business dealings with him in the past.'

'Interesting. And he was the one who stole it from Wrightson's safe in America?'

Korso shook his head. 'He was at least two steps removed. I did discover that he stole it from the man who arranged the original robbery, though. After having him killed first, of course. But it's here now, one step away from changing ownership again. Once we complete the financial arrangements, that is.'

'And can I assume the original amount we agreed upon is still in effect? Or have you decided to get greedy now that you're once more in the driver's seat?'

'A contract's a contract, Mr Accetta, and I always keep my end of the deal. That's why I'm always in demand. $1,500,000 was the agreed figure, which makes my percentage half a million. I assume you can transfer it to my account immediately?'

'Of course.' Accetta pulled a phone from his trouser pocket and began swiping the screen.

Meanwhile, Korso pulled his own phone from his jacket and went straight to the password-protected website of his private Lichtenstein bank. After keying in his account number and fourteen-digit password, he went to his account page and waited. As he watched Accetta play with his own phone, he listened to Balotelli sing the final few notes of '*Que dit-il?*' before the orchestra segued seamlessly into '*Ce jour heureux est plain d'allégresse!*' This would allow Balotelli to get his breath back before Act III's final ensemble piece, '*En plaçant sur mon front,...* *Sire, la dernière heure,*' which would immediately be followed by the second intermission. Korso aimed to be long gone before then.

He noticed the girl had quickly rebounded from her earlier rebuff and was once again happily entranced by the performance below. Which showed a strength of character rarely seen in someone so young, and especially in one so beautiful. It seemed Accetta had better judgement in women than Korso gave him credit for.

'There,' Accetta said. 'The money's been deposited.'

Korso looked down at his own phone. After a few seconds, the figure of US$500,000 appeared in his credit balance. Almost immediately it disappeared again, having automatically been split into seven random amounts and wired to seven other untraceable accounts he held around the world. He logged out, pocketed the phone, and slid the asset across the armrest.

Accetta took the dagger and slowly removed the protective cloth again. Seemingly forgetting Korso was even there, he just stared down at his prize in a state of awe.

'Small word of advice,' Korso said.

Accetta looked up at him. 'Yes?'

'You may want to keep your ownership of this particular knife a very close secret. And I mean from *every*body. I prefer live clients to dead ones, and this is starting to look like one of those artefacts that brings bad luck to anyone who possesses it. Like a Judas Coin.'

'I'm surprised. You don't strike me as someone who believes in luck, bad or otherwise.'

'I don't, but I do believe in circumspection where certain items are concerned.' Korso shrugged. 'Your choice. Do as you will.'

He smoothed down his tuxedo as he stood up. '*Francesca*,' he said, and waited until she turned his way, '*è stato un grande piacere conoscerti.*'

She smiled at the compliment, and said, '*Il piacere è mio,*' before turning back to the show.

Korso looked down at Accetta. 'And if you want another piece of advice, you should hold onto this girl. It'll be worth it in the long run.'

At the door he turned back to see Accetta whispering something in Francesca's ear, Stepping out into the still empty corridor, Korso shut the door and left them to it.

THREE

Korso pressed his key card close to the reader, waited for the click, and pushed open the door to his third floor hotel suite. Locking it behind him, he stepped into the modern living room and set his vinyl bag down on the glass coffee table.

Out the windows, he could see the April sun slowly setting on the cityscape outside. He went over to open the French doors and stepped out onto the small balcony. The lukewarm breeze against his face felt refreshing, and he let the snatches of amiable chatter from the pedestrians and tourists below wash gently over him. He was currently staying at the five-star Hazelton Hotel, set in the heart of the leafy, upscale Yorkville district of Toronto. He had to admit it was an excellent hotel, with no shortage of amenities and first-class service all round. But the main reason he was staying there was its close proximity to the Thomas Fisher Rare Book Library on St. George Street, where amongst other treasures they had a very rare copy of Shakespeare's first folio on display.

Published in 1623 by two of Shakespeare's friends and fellow actors, John Heminge and Henry Condell, *Mr William Shakespeare's Comedies, Histories, & Tragedies* was the earliest collected edition of the bard's works, and has since become one of the most sought-after items in world literature. Only 750 first folios were printed, and just 233 of those are known to have survived today.

One could only view the Thomas Fisher Library's copy on request, under very strict supervision, and there was a very long waiting list. But Korso needed to visit in person so he could compare their first edition to his own notes taken over a decade ago from a similar edition. To complicate matters further, proofing corrections continued to be made during the initial printing process and no pages were discarded, meaning each copy was unique with its own typographical errors, and no copy contained all pages in their final state. This obviously meant that those copies that came at the end of the print run had far fewer typos than the very earliest printings.

It was all very confusing, but that was part of the challenge.

In between salvage assignments, Korso spent a good portion of his time tracking down some of the world's rarest first editions for a select roster of clients. Since he'd always loved the written word, this was less work to him than it was a hobby. Also a very lucrative one, since he commanded a finder's fee for any successful transaction between buyer and seller. But more than anything else he took pleasure from the detailed investigative work involved, and could lose himself completely for days when he was deep into the hunt.

Currently, he had a very rich Asian client who was considering purchasing a first folio from a private collector in Oxford, England, whom Korso had met at an exclusive invitation-only sealed-bid auction six months previously. This collector had told Korso he'd only consider selling if the right offer came along. Korso had managed to view the folio himself and was fairly sure it was the genuine article, but 'fairly sure' wasn't good enough in these instances. Hence, this trip to Toronto only five days after the completion of the Italian job, followed by today's visit to the library, which he'd actually arranged two months previously.

But the wait had been worth it, since he now knew beyond doubt that the collector's copy was genuine. And since it contained more typos than usual, that meant it had come fairly early in the printing process – somewhere in the late seventies was Korso's estimate.

Grabbing a Coke from the mini-bar, he unscrewed the cap and took a long swig from the bottle. Then he removed his laptop from his bag and sat down at the small office desk by the window. He logged onto the hotel's Wi-Fi network and went straight to check his highly secure email account.

Since Korso rarely used a phone more than once before destroying the sim and trashing it, email remained his principal means of contact. He had a wide range of forwarding services to guide incoming and outgoing messages so that none could be traced to his IP address. And he also used a very exclusive proxy VPN – designed for him personally by MD Dog, a skilled hacker whose services he employed on a fairly regular basis – which added that extra level of security.

In Korso's line of work, one could be never be too careful.

Once the page loaded up, he saw a new message in his inbox. It had been sent the day before. The sender was *IVOSEC*, his secure mailing service in Lichtenstein. They were very expensive, but completely trustworthy in all matters. With the kind of exclusive clientele they attracted, reputation mattered more than anything else, which meant they had to be above reproach. So far they'd never let Korso down.

He opened the email. The message was brief and to the point:

'Dear sir – We have just taken possession of a package addressed to you.
　　Please advise at the earliest opportunity. Kind Regards, IVOSEC.'

For all its brevity, it was an interesting communiqué. For a start, he wasn't expecting any package. Added to which, he knew of only three people who were even aware of this particular mailing address. And in each case, he'd advised the person in question to only use it as a last resort.

From his bag, he pulled out one of the prepaid phones he'd picked up at Toronto Pearson Airport two days ago and keyed in a number from memory. After four rings, a male voice said in perfect English, 'Good afternoon. May I take your account number?'

Korso gave it to him.

'Thank you, sir. Ah, yes, we emailed you yesterday about the arrival of a package under your name. Would you like me to give you the details over the phone?'

'Not yet. What kind of package is it?'

'A postcard.'

'Any message on the back?'

'No, but there *is* a 21-digit number written there.'

'Can you scan each side at a high resolution and email the PNG files to me?'

'Certainly, sir. They've already been scanned in readiness and I'm sending them as we speak. Is there anything further?'

'Yes. If I don't call you back within the next hour, I want you to shred the postcard and delete the scanned files.'

'Of course. I'll take care of it personally.'

'Thank you. Goodbye.'

'Goodbye, sir.'

Korso saw a new message had arrived in his inbox. As before, there was no header. He opened it up, downloaded the two untitled PNG files to his hard drive, and logged out again. He double-clicked on the first file, and the image opened up.

The front of the postcard showed a shot of the Kuala Lumpur skyline at sunset, with the Petronas Twin Towers as the main centrepiece. Which immediately told him who'd sent it. Of the three people he'd given this mailing address, there was only one who'd worked alongside Korso in the Malaysian capital before. It had been a long time ago, and Cole Ashcroft had helped Korso out of a very sticky situation when it would have been far more sensible to just walk away. Korso had given Cole the Lichtenstein mailing address and told him that any time he needed the favour returned, just send word.

It seemed today might be the day to repay that debt.

He closed the image and opened the second file. On the right-hand side of the postcard was the Lichtenstein mailing address, written by hand in neat caps. There was a US postage stamp in the upper right-hand corner, with a California postmark dated a week before. On the left side of the card was a handwritten line of numbers:

099518515453930259017

He remembered the simple code sequence. It wasn't hard to crack, but it wasn't meant to be. Korso picked up the phone again. Ignoring the second digit, the fourth, the sixth, and so on, left him with *09155 590507*. He keyed in the number, made the call and waited. It was finally picked up after the seventh ring.

'So you're still using that mailing service,' the familiar voice said, the faint East Coast accent still recognisable after all this time. 'I was hoping you would.'

'Hello, Cole.'

'Good to hear your voice again. Uh, what do I call you now, by the way? Or are you still using your old handle?'

'No, I discarded that one shortly after the Malaysia thing. These days I go by Korso.'

'Korso, huh? Though I doubt it's your real name, right?'

'Not even close. It's just a brand, as good as any other.'

In fact, Korso hadn't used his actual birth name in over twenty years and probably never would again. To prove the point, he possessed three completely 'genuine' passports under different aliases, two of which were currently housed in separate safety deposit boxes – one in Helsinki, the other in London. Each passport had cost him somewhere in the mid-six figures, although he would have willingly paid twice that amount if necessary. The peace of mind they brought him simply couldn't be measured in financial terms.

'Answer a question for me,' Korso said.

'Shoot.'

'You remember that civil engineer you bribed in Kuala Lumpur? We found out he had a serious allergy to something. What was it again?'

Cole snorted. 'Jesus, that guy. Couldn't stand the smell of fish, could he? Didn't matter if it was cooked or raw, the slightest whiff would send him into a major panic attack. Even talking about it brought him out in hives. That satisfy you?'

'It does. So what's the purpose of this call? You finally calling in that favour?'

'Kind of. What it is, I been out of play for the past few years and I need a stake again. To make things worse, I got in hock to some people recently and they're not the kind of folks you wanna owe for very long, not if you value your health. And they're starting to put some real pressure on me to pay my debts, like fast. Now you know my skills are kind of specialised, so I'm looking for a certain kind of job with a payday that'll wipe out my debts *and* tide me over for the foreseeable future. And there aren't many of those around for someone in my field, at least not semi-legit ones. And I was never much of a planner, so it's not like I can dream something up from scratch like you can.'

Korso sat back in his seat, looked out the window. 'So either the perfect job's come along, or you're hoping I've got something going with a space in it for you.'

'It's the first one. Now I won't say the job's perfect since I don't know too many details about it yet, but I've been assured the payday's somewhere in the high six-figure range, and that's enough for me. It's also as close to being legit as these kinds of jobs ever get, which is a real bonus.'

'And where do I fit in?'

'Well, that's the interesting part, see. The only reason I even got to *hear* about this job was because of my past association with you, even though it was just on that one project, which barely lasted a week. But while I been away, it seems you've built up a solid rep as the number one go-to guy for finding things that can't be found. The embassy guy who contacted me said you call yourself a "covert salvage specialist" now. That right?'

'It's close enough. What guy? Which embassy?'

'The American Embassy in Bulgaria. The guy's name is Todd Belmont. He's some kind of high-flyer over there, more likely chief assistant to one of the bigwigs in the place. But he's got something major in mind, and he can't go through normal channels. So he contacted me because he heard that I knew you. Apparently, you're not an easy guy to get hold of. Anyway, whatever this thing is, he wants you in on it. Me too, but only if you're part of the equation. So now you see why I connected with you after all this time.'

Korso picked up the Coke bottle and took another slug. Placing it back on the desk, he gently turned it between his fingers as he mulled over Cole's words. Something he'd said was still niggling at him.

'Hey, Korso, you still there?'

'When you say you've been away, Cole, what do you mean by that? Where exactly?'

'Just… away.'

'You mean prison.'

There was a pause. 'Yeah, okay. If you must know, I drew a seven year stretch for armed robbery, got out in four for good behaviour.' Cole sighed. 'I was part of the backup crew on a bank job that went sour.'

'They usually do.'

'So one of the crew turned states', and I was one of the unlucky ones who got sent down. Anyway, what difference does it make? I did my time and I'm out now, free as a daisy.'

It could make all the difference, Korso thought. A man fresh out of prison was often too hungry to be smart. Cole's judgement could be faulty, his good sense taking a back seat to the lure of a quick payday. But he couldn't say any of that. At least, not at this stage.

'So I assume this Belmont wants to set up a meet with us.'

'Right, and as soon as possible. So what do you think?'

'I think I still owe you that favour, so the least I can do is meet the man and discuss it. But it'll be completely on my terms, and I get to choose the playing field.'

'Yeah, Belmont figured as much. So what have you got in mind?'

FOUR

Korso sipped at his chilled grapefruit juice and pretended to play on his phone as he sat back in his comfortable armchair, though his eyes remained constantly alert to the travellers and airport staff constantly passing through the place. He watched everyone, missed nothing.

It was two days after his phone conversation with Cole. Korso had landed at Terminal 5 of Heathrow Airport two and a half hours before, and once through immigration he made his way to the highly prestigious first class lounge, the Concorde Room, ostensibly to wait for his connecting flight. The lounge was so exclusive you could only gain admittance if you actually held a first-class ticket for a BA flight. Otherwise you had to make do with one of the other lounges in the terminal. He'd been sitting there for the past ninety minutes, purposefully choosing this spot as it afforded him the best possible view of the lounge area.

Despite its modern design, the Concorde Room still retained the look and feel of an extremely luxurious living room, with plenty of comfortable settees and armchairs, daybeds, and even the odd walled fireplace – fake, of course – dotted around. From his central position, Korso had a perfect view of the main entrance to his left, as well as the central hallway containing the spas and washrooms, staff quarters, and the three private cabanas at the end. Directly ahead was the Concorde bar and a communal business suite, while to his right was the faux outdoor terrace, suspended over the main departure concourse below. Behind him was the main dining area, where he'd had lunch. The large room was busy without being packed. There were no tannoy announcements allowed in this terminal, so all he could hear was the pleasant buzz of light chatter around him.

Adjusting the flat cap he'd picked up from the BOSS duty-free store, Korso checked his watch and saw it was now 2.50 p.m. He'd already noted the shift change at 2 p.m., although the attractive BA stewardess who'd served him still remained on duty. He watched as she led a female traveller to the second cabana and unlocked the door, and then they both disappeared inside. Seconds later the stewardess exited, and she unlocked the third cabana door, right at the end. She entered this one, and two minutes later she came out again holding a tray containing two empty wine glasses, which she took into the employees' room.

Korso was polishing the tinted lenses of his spectacles when he saw Cole enter the lounge, carrying a duty-free bag. It was 2.56 p.m. Korso put his glasses back on and studied the man without being too obvious. Cole was about five-ten and slope-shouldered, with short brown hair combed forward and a deeply lined face that made him seem older than he was. It was clear that prison hadn't been good to him, but he still looked healthy enough. On the surface, at least.

Looking around, Cole spotted the bar and after a quick check of the time, went straight to the one empty stool. He ordered a scotch and ice from the bartender, downed it one go and quickly ordered another. He took a small sip, and then took his drink with him as he approached a steward. They chatted briefly. This steward then led Cole to the third cabana, and they both went inside. The steward exited a few seconds later, closing the door after him.

Those private cabanas were the main reason Korso had chosen Heathrow's Terminal 5 for the meet. A couple of days earlier, Korso had reserved a two-hour slot for the cabana at the end, starting from 3 p.m.

At 3.02, a forty-something man in a well-tailored navy-blue suit stepped through the main entrance. He had thinning blond hair and dark eyes, and carried a small attaché case in his right hand. As he glanced around the lounge, Korso lowered his head to his phone. When he looked up again, the man was marching down the hallway towards the cabanas. He knocked on the last door, paused, and then disappeared inside.

Korso waited for several more minutes, watching for anything that might give him pause. But other than the single anomaly that he'd already accounted for, nothing else pinged on his radar. Pulling his cap down low, he grabbed his light carry-on bag and stood up and made his way down the well-lighted corridor to the cabanas. He knocked on the door. Somebody said, 'Come in,' and Korso opened the door and entered the room.

The private cabana wasn't large, but it didn't feel cramped even with three adult occupants. There was one lounger, one large ottoman, two more chairs, a coffee table, and a large plasma TV on the wall. The TV was showing a Champions League match replay, with the sound off. A private bathroom and shower took up the rear half of the room, with a frosted glass partition separating it from the rest area. Cole perched on the ottoman, while the other man sat on the lounger as he pulled a thin laptop from his case.

Cole was smiling as he placed his empty glass on the floor and got to his feet. 'Hey, man, it's been a while. You haven't changed much.'

'You have,' Korso said, shaking his outstretched hand.

'Yeah, well, there's a reason for that...'

'I know.' Korso turned to the other man. 'And you must be Belmont.'

'Call me Todd,' he said without getting up. 'Good to finally meet you, Mr Korso.'

'The title's not necessary. And I'll stick with Belmont, I think.'

'Whatever you say. Put down your bag, take the weight off. How was your flight in?'

'Fine.' Korso dropped his flight bag, but remained standing.

'There's a call button on the table there,' Belmont said. 'You mind pressing it for me? I could do with something cool and wet right now. Anybody else want anything?'

Korso looked down and pressed the button, while Cole said, 'I could go for another scotch. They serve the good stuff here.'

'As well they should for these prices,' Belmont said. 'Not that I'm complaining, Korso, but is there a particular reason why you chose this location for our meet?'

'Airports are completely neutral ground, and thanks to the numerous body scanners and metal detectors, almost all of my security concerns are taken care of as a matter of course. As for this private room, it was a choice between Heathrow and the Cathay Pacific lounge in Hong Kong, since they're the only airports that have them. But as you were paying both our travel expenses, I figured a first-class trip to the Far East might be asking too much.'

'I appreciate it.' There was a light knock on the door, and Belmont said, 'Come in.'

The door opened and the same stewardess who'd unlocked it earlier stepped into the room. She was holding a small tablet. 'Good afternoon,' she said, offering Cole and Korso a radiant smile. She barely noticed Belmont. 'Can I bring you gentlemen anything from the kitchen, or maybe something from the bar?'

Cole ordered another glass of scotch and a steak sandwich. Belmont asked for a Tiger beer. She touched the tablet screen a few times, and turned to Korso. 'And for you, sir?'

Korso was studying her carefully. 'What's your name?'

She blinked at him. 'Samara.'

'Nice name. Take a seat, Samara. And maybe close the door while you're at it.'

'Excuse me? I'm not sure I under—'

'Wait a second,' Belmont interrupted. 'Am I missing something here?'

'Let's stop with the act, Belmont. She's with you. Admit it, or I leave right now.'

Belmont opened his mouth, and quickly closed it again. Finally, he sighed and said, 'Better do as he says, Sam. Korso, meet Samara Graynor.'

Korso waited until she clicked the door shut, then said, 'Okay, where are they?'

She turned back to him, her brows drawn together. 'What are you talking about?' she said, reverting to her own American accent. West Virginia, probably.

'A short while ago I watched you unlock this room and step inside. Two minutes later you came out holding a tray with two empty glasses. And it doesn't take two minutes to pick up two glasses, which means you must have been doing something else in here instead. My guess is you were busy planting a miniature spycam somewhere, probably two. Along with a hidden microphone, of course. So my question is, where are they?'

She raised a single eyebrow, then gave a small shrug. 'I placed one cam at the top of the TV screen, with a small mic next to it. The other camera's set into the handle of the bathroom door behind you.'

'And the footage to be transmitted and saved to your little tablet there, no doubt.'

A wisp of a smile. 'No doubt.'

'Remove them please, and delete all footage so far.'

She removed the three devices and stuck them in her skirt pocket. She then showed him her tablet screen as she used a special app to deactivate both cameras and delete the few minutes of transmitted footage. 'There, no more Big Brother. I promise.'

'How did you even know?' Belmont asked. 'There has to be more than just seeing Samara spend two minutes inside a cabana.'

'I've been here a couple of hours, and so I witnessed the change of shift at two p.m.' Korso removed his cap and tinted

24

glasses, dropping both on the coffee table as he took a seat on one of the chairs. 'But Samara here was the only staff member who remained on the floor, which suggested to me she might not be genuine. I also noticed she never spoke to any of her BA colleagues, although that didn't necessarily mean anything then. But when she took my drink order outside I also heard a slight mid-Atlantic twang on certain words, which told me she wasn't even British either. So those were two red flags right there, and two wrongs rarely make a right. The extra time she spent in this room was just added confirmation, that's all.'

'Uh, somebody mind telling me what the point of all that was?' Cole asked, looking quizzically around the room.

'I always like to know who I'm dealing with, Mr Ashcroft,' Belmont said, 'and your colleague's the very definition of a riddle wrapped up in an enigma.' He turned to Korso. 'No photos exist of you anywhere and very few people have met you, or even seen what you look like. So I thought I'd break the trend and see if I could turn anything up of interest.'

Korso stared at him. 'Curiosity's fine in certain situations, but this is not one of them. I'm half-considering ending this conversation right now.'

'Don't do that.' Belmont held up both hands in surrender. 'It was an error of judgement. You have my apologies, it won't happen again. But on the plus side you've proved that you're not only worthy of your rep, but the right man for the job I've got in mind. *If* you're still interested, that is.'

'I'm as yet undecided.' He watched as Samara passed by, smoothing out her skirt as she took a seat on the other chair. 'You played your part very well, by the way. You melded in with your surroundings like you really belonged.'

'Not well enough, apparently.'

'Don't take it badly. I tend to focus on the little things most other people miss.'

'Still, one of my specialties is dialects,' she said, removing her hairpin and allowing her shoulder-length black hair to fall free, which emphasised her high cheekbones all the more. 'I really thought I had my King's English down pat.'

'You just neglected to crop your *r* at the end of a couple of words. I barely noticed it myself. But you enunciated your consonants, especially those hard *t*'s and *l*'s, which most Americans forget to do. They teach you that in the CIA?'

'The CIA? What makes you say that?'

'Belmont here represents one of the US embassies in Eastern Europe; he even looks like a state official. You look anything but, yet you're here working alongside him, and on equally foreign ground. So call it an educated guess.'

She snorted. 'Sounds more a wild stab in the dark to me.'

'Korso, how long do we have this room for?' Belmont asked.

'Until five p.m.'

'More than enough time.' Belmont turned to Cole. 'Mr Ashcroft, would you mind getting yourself a late lunch in the restaurant outside? The food here's supposed to be excellent, and I'd prefer to speak with Korso alone. No offence, but I want as few witnesses as possible to hear what I'm about to say. Assuming Korso here accepts the assignment, he can then fill you in on the details himself.'

'Fine by me,' Cole said. He got up and turned to Korso. 'Come grab me once you're done, whatever you decide.'

'I will.'

Cole left the room, gently shutting the door behind him.

'Good,' Belmont said. 'So let's get down to the—'

'Before we start,' Korso said, 'I'd like some clarity as to why there's three people in this room instead of two. Now I've got no objections, but it seems clear to me that Samara's here for a reason. And while I've got a pretty good idea what that might be, I'd still like to get it out in the open.'

'Okay, you've got me curious,' Belmont said. 'Why do *you* think I want Samara here?'

'I'm sitting right next to you,' she said. 'You can address me directly. I won't blush.'

'Okay.' Korso turned to her. 'I think that this whole stewardess masquerade was basically a demonstration put on partly for my benefit. I think you wanted me to see you in action so that I'd be less likely to object when Belmont here tells me you're also coming along for the ride, whether I like it or not. Am I getting warm?'

Samara smiled. 'Something along those lines. Although it would have been that much more impressive if you hadn't revealed me before I wanted you to. You kind of ruined my moment, you know.'

'I doubt that. You could have easily planted those spy cameras twenty-four hours ago without me being any the wiser. But instead you chose to do it minutes before our designated meeting time, knowing that I'd be out there checking out my surroundings before I committed to anything. Which means you were hoping I *would* reveal you.' He turned to face Belmont again. 'So did I pass your little test?'

Belmont gave a single bark of laughter. 'With flying colours, I'd say. It's always good to know you're dealing with a professional. And with something like this we had to be absolutely sure, you understand. So now we've got that out of the way, should I go on?'

Korso motioned with his hand. 'The floor's all yours.'

FIVE

'It all began three weeks ago,' Belmont said, 'when I received at a call at my office from a guy named Darian Yanev, who said he was a chemist at Vercogen, a mid-sized pharmaceutical company located in Sofia's downtown district. He wanted to come in and see me for a preliminary meeting to discuss a scientific discovery he'd recently made that would be extremely beneficial to my country. And himself, of course. He didn't give me any clues over the phone, but he did say that if I wasn't interested in seeing him there were plenty of other embassies in town that would. Naturally I was very curious, so I told him to come to my office that afternoon to talk about it further.' He paused, and looked over at Samara.

'What?' she asked.

'I'm just thinking now's maybe a good time to get a real stewardess in here to take our drinks orders. I'm still pretty dry after my flight. Anyone else feel the same?'

'Why not?' Korso pressed the call button a second time. He turned to Samara, silently pointing at her BA uniform as he jutted his chin towards the bathroom area. She understood straight away, and got up and disappeared behind the frosted glass partition. No sense in risking embarrassing questions from the genuine airport staff if it could be avoided.

The service was always good in first class. It only took thirty seconds for the inevitable knock on the door. Belmont got up and opened it, revealing a male steward this time. He briefly glanced into the room as he took Belmont's order, and then went away. Less than two minutes later he returned with a tray containing a bottle of Tiger Beer and two bottles of Evian. Belmont took the tray, and the steward left.

Samara emerged from the bathroom and sat down again in the same seat. Once they'd each parched their respective thirsts, Belmont opened up his laptop and navigated to the place he wanted. 'So Yanev was brought to my office early that afternoon, right on time. He wasn't exactly an impressive specimen: a bony guy in his early-forties, wearing the kind of ill-fitting suit you might pick up in a thrift store, and his hair was greasy and all over the place. But when he took a seat and spoke for the first time, I suddenly lost all interest in his physical appearance. I've heard some pretty effective opening gambits in my career, but this one was a real doozy.' He took another sip of his beer.

Korso just waited patiently. If Belmont wanted to stretch things out for dramatic effect, it was easy enough to let him. It was his story.

Once Belmont realised Korso wasn't about to bite, he put down the bottle and continued, 'So what he said was that he was recently put in charge of developing a new pill to treat glaucoma.' He narrowed his eyes to read something off the laptop screen. 'Acetazolamide tablets. Don't know if I pronounced that right. Says they're a "*carbonic anhydrase inhibitor that reduces intraocular pressure by reducing the secretion of aqueous humor.*"' He looked up at them again. 'Quite the mouthful. Anyway, these things usually come in eye drop form and this new pill was supposed to replicate the effects, plus add a few more that would put it two steps ahead of the competition. And Yanev said he eventually came up with a new formula that did just that, except this one came with one additional side effect that the previous ones didn't.' He paused again for effect.

This time, Korso bit. 'And what was that?'

Belmont grinned. 'It also gave the user perfect night vision.'

He let that one lay there, percolating, while he watched Korso's reaction.

'*Perfect* night vision,' Korso said, raising an eyebrow. 'Seriously?'

'Okay, maybe not 100 per cent perfect, but according to the pill's creator, it comes pretty damn close. So what do you think of that?'

'I can think of a few immediate possibilities,' Korso said.

'I bet you can. The effects on the optic nerve are only temporary, of course, and generally last between six to eight hours before the user's eyesight gradually returns to normal. But we're talking about something that in the right – or wrong – hands could shift the global balance of power pretty much overnight. Forget night–vision goggles, they're history. We're talking *natural* night vision in tablet form, where night actually becomes day, with everything in crystal clarity. The military applications alone for such a pill are almost incalculable. You can get a headache just thinking of the potential, especially if its use was initially confined to one country.'

'Such as the United States, perhaps?'

'Sure, why not?'

'How many other people knew about this discovery of his?'

'Well, he said for his own security he'd mentioned it to the only other person he could trust, his brother, Teodor. And he'd also committed the complete formula to memory and made sure there was no written record of it anywhere. In addition, he said he'd been very careful about keeping the latest test results from his employers at Vercogen, since he knew they'd claim complete credit for his discovery as well as the lion's share of the profits, while the best he could hope for would be a nice little bonus in his end–of–year pay packet. But he worked as part of a team consisting of other chemists and lab technicians, and at least one of them *had* to know that something interesting was happening. You can't develop something as revolutionary as this in a complete vacuum.'

'And as it turns out,' Samara said, 'he didn't. But we'll get to that in a moment.'

Korso nodded his head. 'What did Yanev want in return for his formula?'

'A US green card, for starters,' she said. 'He also wanted a house in the Florida Keys, a lump sum of $20 million to be deposited in a Swiss account of his choosing, and exemption from paying US taxes for the rest of his natural life.'

'The usual,' Belmont said. 'All of which the State Department would have happily given him, assuming his claims for the pill were true.'

'So this is still only theory, then.' Korso furrowed his brow. 'Or do you know for sure that these pills work as advertised?'

Belmont grimaced. 'I never got the chance to sample one, unfortunately. As far as Yanev was concerned this was only a getting-to-know-each-other meeting, so he could gauge our interest and see what we could do for him in return. He told me he'd personally synthesised and manufactured fifteen prototype pills on the sly, tested two on himself, and secreted the other thirteen in a place where nobody could ever find them. Apparently, they're fairly generic in appearance, except for a crescent moon symbol on one side. He even came up with a catchy name for them: *White Nights*. It wasn't until the follow-up meeting that he was going to bring one of these samples for me to try myself.'

'Let me guess: there was no follow-up meeting. Or I wouldn't be here.'

Belmont gave a weary sigh. 'We arranged that he'd come and see me first thing the next morning, a Tuesday, but he never showed. I learned from the police that Darian Yanev suffered a fatal heart attack in the early hours of Tuesday morning. His body was discovered in a side street in Orlandovtsi, in the city's northern sector, which isn't a recommended place to visit at night. And before you ask, his medical history confirms he suffered from a mild form of dilated cardiomyopathy for much of his adult life. That's a genetic form of heart disease where one chamber of the heart is weaker than the rest, so it's unable to pump blood as efficiently to the rest of the body.'

'Strange that he died from it on that night, of all nights.'

Belmont gave a thin smile. 'Isn't it? I had the same thought at the time, so I did a little checking with my contacts in the police, and found out that he'd been found with bruises all over his face and body, and the medical examiner also found traces of water in his lungs.'

'Most likely beaten and tortured,' Korso said. 'Water in the lungs suggests waterboarding was used.'

'That's what we think, although the police are currently treating it as just another mugging that went wrong, which is fine by me. But I think somebody high up at Vercogen found out about Yanev's discovery and decided he shouldn't keep it to himself, only they miscalculated badly as to how much pain he could withstand, and his heart simply gave out before he could tell them anything useful.'

'What makes you think he didn't spill everything before he died?'

'Well, for one thing, the medical examiner estimated Yanev's time of death at approximately one a.m. on Tuesday morning. And it just so happens that one of Yanev's neighbours called the police at five fifteen that same morning when she heard somebody break into his apartment next door. When they arrived they found the perpetrators had upended the place from top to bottom, as though searching for something.'

Korso reached for his Evian bottle. 'Like a pill container, for instance?'

'Exactly,' Samara said. 'And you don't waste time searching for something that you've already got. Anyway, Yanev is unlikely to have hidden them in so obvious a location. He was too smart for that.'

'I get that impression,' Korso said, 'which raises another interesting question.'

Belmont leaned forward. 'Which is?'

'He was due to see you the next morning, right? Only this time, he'd be bringing along a sample pill for you to try.'

'That was the plan.'

'So how were you supposed to test it in broad daylight? Because I can't believe Yanev would hand over one of these White Nights and just trust you to take it at nightfall. The first thing you'd do would be to get a sample to your top scientists and instruct them to reverse engineer it, and get the formula that way. And he'd know that. Yanev would want to physically give you the tablet himself, know for sure that you'd swallowed it and watch the effect it had on you.'

'He's right,' Samara said. 'That part's always bothered me too.'

Belmont was frowning at the ceiling. 'Yeah, I see what you mean.'

'It's likely he did plan on giving you a sample,' Korso said, 'but only under his strict supervision, and at a time and a place of his own choosing. At the second meeting, I expect he would have given you further instructions to meet up later that very evening, at a location where he could know for sure you'd come alone. All academic now, of course.' He took another sip of water. 'You definitely think somebody at Vercogen was behind his death?'

Belmont nodded. 'Got a pretty good idea who it was, too. The CEO is a fellow named Andrey Deleva, and as you'd expect for a man in his position he's got a fairly chequered past. He's well educated, and fluent in three other languages, including English. Word is he started out loan-sharking on the streets in his teens, and from there he gradually worked his way up into the legit business world through a combination of fists, brains, and sheer ruthlessness. He bought Vercogen twenty years ago for a song, and thanks to his exploitation of several minor drug patents already on their books, was able to rapidly expand it into a respectable-sized business that generated a decent profit, year in, year out.'

'But…?' Korso prompted.

'But those original patents weren't enough to keep a business of that size going forever, and the few commercial drug patents Vercogen applied for in recent years never amounted to anything much. All of which means the company's currently operating in the red, and sinking fast. So it's not too hard to imagine Deleva's reaction when he found out about this miracle discovery of Yanev's. Since Yanev was an employee of his, he'd feel quite rightly that anything the chemist developed on company time and on company premises would automatically become the property of Vercogen. Clearly, Yanev felt differently and paid the price as a result.'

'If what you say is true,' Korso said, 'then a man in Deleva's position wouldn't have even tried handling Yanev alone. Somebody else must have done the real dirty work.'

'Well, there's a guy called Simov who fits the bill,' Samara said. 'He works at Vercogen under the title of Operational Consultant, but he's essentially the head of security. Deleva hired him shortly after he bought the company and he's been in that same role ever since. If Deleva trusts anybody, it's him.'

'What was this Simov before?'

'He was a cop, police inspector, third grade, with the kind of record most criminals would envy. Twenty years ago he was facing three separate investigations for corruption, manslaughter, and the sexual assault of eight female prisoners, when Deleva came on the scene and somehow got all the charges dropped. Simov immediately quit the police and Deleva took him on as his security chief. They've been thick as thieves ever since.'

Korso leaned back in his chair and looked at a spot on the wall. 'And still no signs that they've found the samples?'

'None that I can see,' she said. 'I've been watching the Vercogen building off and on for the past week, and Deleva's still got Simov running around the city like a maniac as he frantically chases up leads, usually accompanied by a couple of his associates.'

'So the job, as I see it, is to find and recover the samples before Deleva and Simov do, and then hand them over to you, so you can get them reverse-engineered and patented.'

'Couldn't have put it better myself,' Belmont said.

'I assume they don't know about this brother, Teodor?' Korso lowered his gaze to the man sitting in front of him. 'Or put another way, they *know* about the brother but they're unaware that Yanev confided in him before he died, is that right?'

'That's right. And that just happens to be our little ace-in-the-hole.'

'I was hoping there was one. So where is this brother of his?'

Belmont took a deep breath. 'Well, he's not hard to find. He's currently serving a ten-year sentence for counterfeiting at Tsentalen Sofiyski Zatvor Prison, in central Sofia.'

Korso blinked. 'I see. I take it he and Darian were still close?'

'A lot closer than most siblings,' Belmont said. 'Both their parents died when they were children, and after a distant aunt took them in Teodor assumed the role of breadwinner for the three of them. According to the police records, he was only thirteen when he joined a gang and started working the streets. He might not have been much of a good citizen, but he turned out to be the kind of big brother a boy dreams about, basically supporting the kid out of his own pocket. He was also intelligent enough to see his younger brother had far more book smarts than him, so he paid for his education and made sure he went to the best schools, and even paid all of Darian's university tuition fees after he graduated.'

'Nice guy. So I take it he got in touch as soon as he got word of his brother's death, and let you know of his interest?'

'Correct.' Belmont scratched the side of his neck as he took another sip of beer. 'Teodor Yanev got word to his lawyer, who contacted one of our consular agents, who then brought it to my desk. But since I couldn't risk visiting this Teodor myself, even on an unofficial basis, it was at that point that I brought Samara into the picture and updated her on the current situation. She and I have worked together on a few things in the past, and so I knew I could trust her discretion.'

'You mean CIA things?' Korso asked.

'If you say so,' Samara said. 'So I went and visited Teodor in prison instead, and after a lot of feeling each other out, he finally admitted that Darian had told him exactly where he'd hidden the sample pills, and that he was willing to give us their location. For a hefty fee, of course.'

'Of course.'

'Except before all that, he said we also had to something else for him first.'

'And that is…?'

'To break him out of prison.'

SIX

Korso had to smile. He couldn't help it. 'Now why didn't I see that coming? Somehow, you neglected to mention that this assignment would come in two parts. What else haven't you told me?'

'There *is* only one part to this thing,' Belmont said, frowning. 'Once you break the brother out, he leads you straight to the White Nights. That's it. Simple.'

'Nothing's ever that simple where humans are involved, Belmont. You know that. But at least now I understand why you contacted Cole as a first step, since one of his specialties is finding ways into hard-to-access places. And the state prison of a major East-European country certainly qualifies.'

'And we hear he needs the work, which also helps.'

'Not always.' But Korso let that one pass, and glanced at Samara. 'And I assume you expect to be part of the crew I end up putting together for this? *If* I accept the job, that is.'

Samara shrugged. 'I have a few specialties of my own, you know. I'm very versatile.'

'That I can believe.'

'Wait a minute,' Belmont said. 'Let's backtrack a bit. What kind of crew are you talking about here, Korso? Because the fewer people who know about the existence of these pills, the better.'

'Look, you want me to plan and orchestrate this thing, and Cole's already on board to help me get into that prison if need be. That's two already. In addition, I'd also need a reliable hacker and an even better driver. That makes four.'

'Five.' Samara smiled. 'Don't forget me.'

'Perish the thought.'

'Hold on,' Belmont said, 'why do you need a driver? Or a hacker, for that matter.'

'We're living in a digital world, Belmont, and a good hacker can do things for me that nobody else can. Fortunately, I've got someone I use on a fairly regular basis, so that's not a problem. But a prison breakout invariably means a quick getaway will be required, and for that I'd want a professional driver. There's simply no other way.'

Belmont puffed his cheeks and blew air from his lungs. 'Okay, if that's the way it has to be. So does this mean you'll take the job?'

Korso considered the question seriously for a moment. He'd come along in the first place in order to repay a favour to Cole, but he was under no pressure to accept the job itself. Added to which, he'd only just come off one, and that had taken a fair amount of time and effort to complete. Almost three months, in fact. Yet he had to admit the more he heard about these White Nights and what they could do, the more intrigued he became. Most of his assignments, once reduced to their basics, were pretty simple when it came down to it. This one looked anything but, which only made it stand out all the more. Sometimes a new challenge was its own reward.

'I'm interested,' he said, finally, 'let's put it that way. But there are a few other matters to iron out still.'

'Such as?'

'Samara, for one.' Korso turned to her. 'Am I to assume that her inclusion on the team is part of the deal?'

'It kind of is,' Belmont said. 'For something this important I have to have somebody on watch who I can absolutely trust, and Samara happens to be that person. Is that a problem?'

'That depends.'

Samara leaned forward. 'On what?'

'On whether we can agree as to who's the conductor on this trip. You or me?'

'What's wrong?' she asked, a slight upturn at the corners of her mouth. 'Does the thought of taking orders from a woman scare you?'

'Gender doesn't enter into it. I don't take orders from anyone. Not any more.'

'Meaning you did once?'

'We all did once.'

She sat back in her seat. 'Korso, as far as I'm concerned, once you accept this assignment whatever you say goes. In all matters to do with business, that is. That's why we approached you in the first place. That answer your question?'

'It does. Now how sure are you that this Teodor knows the location of the White Nights? He could just as easily be leading you on so you'll break him out of prison, after which he'll make a run for it and disappear into the crowds.'

'That's always a possibility,' Belmont said. 'I'm afraid I don't have any guarantees to give you, and there's no way to know for sure Teodor's telling the truth until we get him out. However, I *did* get someone to check the prison visitors' log, so we know for a fact that Darian visited him on five separate occasions during the last month of his life, whereas he only visited once a fortnight up until then. From that, I can only assume Darian was taking advice from his more streetwise brother on how to handle himself during the various negotiations to come. Then there's the fact that Teodor knows all about the pills and what they can do. If he knows that much, it follows that Darian also told him where he hid them.'

Korso nodded his head slowly. 'So what else does he want? Money, I presume?'

'What else? He's asked for $5 million to be wired directly to an overseas account, yet to be set up. $500,000 once he's out of prison, the rest to be paid on delivery of the goods. I agreed to his terms.'

Korso raised an eyebrow. $5 million was an interesting figure. If Darian told his big brother about the samples, then he would surely have also told him how much he was going to demand for them. Yet Teodor, the tough streetwise one, was only asking for a quarter that amount. Very strange.

'Something wrong?' Belmont asked.

'That's a very low asking price. Comparatively speaking.'

'It is, but on the other hand he also needs us to commit a major felony on his behalf, so it's not like we can get official funding for this. Teodor's far from stupid, and he understands the practicalities of the situation better than anyone.'

'I'll have to take your word for that. Other than him and the three of us in this room, who else on your side knows anything about this?'

'If by "our side" you mean the US State Department, then nobody at all. Everything we've discussed today is completely off-the-record. Naturally, had Darian made that second meeting, I'd have gone through normal channels all the way down the line, and it's my guess the whole thing would have been fast-tracked down to a matter of days, and he'd already be soaking it up on the Keys as we speak. But without him, anything we do from our end has to remain completely unofficial, and therefore totally deniable. Let's face it, we're already talking about a major prison break here.'

'Still, that leads us on to a far more important question. Maybe *the* most important.'

Belmont smiled. 'You mean, how much will *you* get paid?'

'You took the words out of my mouth. You're aware that I generally take thirty-three per cent of the salvaged item's market value?'

'Ashcroft told me, although I don't that would really work in this case, do you? Also, you're not working alone this time.'

Korso shrugged. 'So what figure have you come up with? I'm curious to see if it matches mine.'

'$5 million US. In cash. That's payment on delivery.'

'Okay. First point, how is that even possible?'

'What do you mean?'

'I mean if this is all supposed to be off the books, how is it possible for you to gain access to that much cash? You got it stashed in a cupboard somewhere?'

'Actually, you're not too far off the mark. We do have a vault in the embassy sub-basement, and amongst other things it contains a slush fund of sorts. Unofficial, of course. The United States government has got very deep pockets, and you never know what kind of sudden emergencies can crop up in foreign territories in these troubled times. Friends can suddenly turn into enemies at the flip of a coin, so every embassy has to be prepared for any and all contingencies. And we've learnt from decades of experience that cash tends to solve most problems that crop up.'

'So the urban legends are true. And you're able to gain access to this vault?'

'Not easily, but I can find a way. Besides, it'll only be a temporary withdrawal of funds. Once the current administration understands what's landed in their laps, they'll be only too happy they got it for the price they did.' Belmont offered his open palms. 'So there it is. Five million to be divided in whichever way you see fit. Take two for yourself if you want, split the other three million between the others. We won't tell.'

Korso shook his head. 'Equal risks, equal shares.'

'That's what Ashcroft told us you'd say, but it's your choice.'

'That was the first point,' Samara said, 'what was your second?'

'The second point is: the figure in my head was six million. It still is. Not including expenses.'

'*Six million?*' Belmond said. 'Forget it, Korso, that's not what's on the table. You've got to understa—'

'I don't care what's on the table, Belmont. You approached me, not the other way around, and that's because you know I've got a reputation for completing whatever I set out to do. I could ask for twice that amount and you'd still be getting it cheap, and you know it.'

'So why don't you?' Samara asked.

'One of the secrets of my success is I never get too greedy. And I might require a favour from you people in the future. A good businessman builds bridges, he doesn't burn them.' He faced Belmont again. 'So is it a yes or a no? I didn't come here to haggle.'

'You're saying you'll take the job, then?'

'If the price is right.'

Belmont thought for a moment, then nodded. 'You've got yourself a deal. Six million it is.'

'Fine. I take it you brought the preliminary expenses, as I requested?'

'Right here.' Reaching into his attaché case, Belmont pulled out a bulky manila envelope and passed it over. Korso opened the flap and saw two thick wads of used hundred-dollar bills inside, each one wrapped in a thick rubber band.

'Forty thousand,' Belmont said. 'All in non-sequential notes. Enough to get you started. If you need any more, just let Samara know and she'll get in touch with me.' He closed his laptop and placed it back in the attaché case. 'Anything else you need from me while I'm here?'

Korso grabbed his carry-on bag as he got up, and dropped the envelope inside. 'Nothing that can't wait.'

'Good. So we're both heading back to Sofia now. What about you?'

'I'll be there soon enough. There are details I have to sort out first.' Donning the flat cap and tinted glasses again, Korso pulled a phone from his pocket. 'Let me have your number, Samara. I'll give you a call once I've set up a base of operations.'

She recited a number, and he keyed it into his phone as he walked towards the door. 'Please don't forget,' she said. 'I'd hate to have to come looking for you.'

'I never forget anything,' he said, and exited the room without looking back.

SEVEN

Cole Ashcroft sipped at his scotch as he gazed at the couple sitting at the table across the way. They'd only just arrived in the lounge, and were studying the menu before they ordered. He saw they each wore a platinum wedding band. The husband wasn't much to look at. He looked to be well into his fifties, with a pot belly, almost no chin and even less hair. His wife was on a whole other level, though. She looked about half his age, and was so good looking she could have walked straight out of a fashion magazine.

That's what money got you in this life, regardless of your appearance. And that's what Cole wanted more than anything. Money, and all that came with it.

Ever since he'd walked out of Limefields Corrections Facility in Huntsville, Alabama four months previously, the acquisition of a big score had been at the forefront of his mind. Especially after he got in some major trouble at the racetrack, forcing him to borrow some large sums from some very disreputable people. The very worst people, in fact. So when he'd been contacted by that Belmont guy a few days ago, and told that there might be something for him if he could persuade a past associate to come and listen to a proposal, it had seemed like an answer to his prayers. And being supplied with a first class ticket from LA to London was just the icing on the cake. The food on the flight had been great, but the fillet steak he'd just finished was absolutely the best meal he'd had in years. He could get used to this kind of treatment very easily, and only hoped he'd be allowed the chance.

43

His thoughts were suddenly interrupted by motion in front of him, as Korso sat down on the chair opposite and placed his bag on the floor.

'How was lunch?' he asked.

'Fine,' Cole said. 'You were gone a while. I don't mind admitting I was starting to get antsy there. So is it good news or bad?'

'We're now on the clock. I accepted the job.'

Cole grinned and slammed the tabletop with his palm. 'Now *that's* what I'm talking about. Man, I knew things would turn around once you were involved in this. I just *knew* it. So what kind of payday are we talking about here?'

'On the successful completion of this assignment we'll receive a total of six million dollars, in cash.'

Cole's mouth actually fell open at this news. He wasn't sure he'd heard correctly. Korso looked amused at his reaction. A stewardess chose that moment to approach the table and ask if either of them wanted anything else. Cole quickly downed the rest of his whisky and requested another, while Korso asked for a tonic water and ice.

Once she'd left them, Cole leaned forwards and whispered, 'You did say *six* million, right? In US dollars?'

'To be split four ways. The nature of the job necessitates it be a team effort.'

'Four ways, huh? And would, uh, that be equal shares?'

'I don't work any other way.'

Cole sat back in his seat, still unable to really believe it. One and a half million apiece. Tax-free. And if Korso said the money was to be split fairly, it would be. He was as solid a guy to have on your side as anyone could hope for. 'So what's the job?'

'The first part entails breaking a man out of Tsentalen Sofiyski Zatvor Prison, in central Sofia, most likely in broad daylight. That's where your particular know-how will come in handy.'

Cole blinked. 'One man, and he's worth six million bucks? What is he, the pope?'

44

'Just a man, but it's what he knows that's important. Part of the deal in getting him out is that he'll then lead us directly to the asset Belmont's after.'

'And what's that?'

'It's complicated.' Korso paused as the stewardess returned with their refreshments. Once she'd gone, he said, 'I'll explain it once we're all together in Bulgaria. By the way, Samara Graynor will be joining us on this. Part of the package, apparently.'

Cole frowned as he took a sip of his scotch. 'What? So it's a five-way split now?'

'No. Whatever she's making on this is completely separate from us.'

'In that case it's fine with me.' Cole looked into the main lounge area and saw Belmont approaching the exit. 'There he goes now.'

Korso turned his head and watched Belmont leaving the Concorde Room via the main doors. Once he was gone, Korso faced front and drank some of his tonic water.

'You think he can be trusted?' Cole asked.

Korso gave a small shrug. 'As much as anyone in his line of work can be. I'm sure he's already held back certain information from me, even though being candid would benefit everybody in the long run, but that's par for the course in these situations.'

'What about these other two you mentioned? I assume one of them's a cyber-ops specialist, am I right?'

Korso nodded. 'There's a hacker I use fairly regularly, goes by the handle of MD Dog. I'll make a phone call later, but I'm certain they'll be on board for this. And we'll also need a good wheelman. There was an American I worked with on a job a few years back, name of Dominic Ripley, but I've no idea if he's still working. You know of him?'

'Yeah, I heard of him, but I think he died about three years ago. Cancer of the colon.'

'Pity. Do you know of anybody as good?'

Cole smiled and pointed a finger at him. 'It just so happens I *do* know of somebody. You ever hear the name, Lucian Aviles?'

Korso furrowed his brow in thought. 'Isn't that the Venezuelan driver who raced Le Mans a while back, managed to win it three years in a row?'

'That's the one. Except a serious crash put an end to that career, and ever since Lucian's been working the outer fringes of the NASCAR stock car circuit to make ends meet. Sometimes as mechanic, sometimes as driver. Also does occasional getaway work to pay the bills, but only if the money's right and the set-up's solid. We worked together on a job once, and everything went like clockwork.' Cole looked at him. 'What do you think?'

'Sounds ideal, but I'll check some of the more recent NASCAR races out on YouTube, just to make sure. Have you got a contact number?'

'Not any more, but I'm sure I can get someone who'll dig one up for me. You want to make the call, or should I?'

'You do it, and the sooner the better. Make it clear that Lucian will have to be prepared to drop everything and get on the next flight out to Bulgaria, or we'll find someone else.'

'I can't see that being a problem, not once I mention the amounts involved.'

'Good. Assuming things go well, give me a call and I'll arrange necessary transport for both of you. No first class this time. We'll all be travelling separately, but I still want our arrivals into Bulgaria to be as low-key as possible.'

Cole grinned. 'Flying coach after this might be the toughest part of this job, but I'll try and get over it. What are you going to do?'

'I'll stay in town tonight. I've got calls to make, details to take care of.' Korso reached down into his bag, and brought out some folded hundred-dollar bills. He handed the notes to Cole. 'Living expenses for the next couple of days. My advice is to go easy on the nightlife here. London's an expensive city for the unwary.'

'Way ahead of you, pal.'

Korso grabbed his bag and stood up. 'See you soon,' he said, turning round. He began walking towards the exit.

Cole just sipped some more of his vintage scotch, and thought about what he was going to do with all that money to come.

Once Korso received confirmation that the funds had been transferred successfully, he logged out of his online account and erased the browser history, and then emptied the cache as well. Eternal vigilance was a hard habit to break. But nobody had ever died from being too careful.

He closed the lid of the MacBook Air and set it on the bed. He'd gotten a single room at a modestly priced two-star hotel, set in a Victorian property on a little side street in Paddington. The rooms weren't much to write about, but the place had complimentary Wi-Fi and a kitchen that stayed open till late. He'd just used up over half of Belmont's expense money in one go, but at least now they had a base from which to work. Along with a few other add-ons.

For various reasons, Korso had set up a number of dummy corporations around the globe over the years, and one of those happened to have its registered office in Bulgaria. He'd visited the country a few times on business, and had always thought it would make a good location for a tax shelter, should he never need one. But now he'd just utilised the corporate name and official address to secure a three-month lease on a semi-furnished house in the Pavlovo district, a mixed residential and business neighbourhood in the southern part of the capital. The detached two-storey house was located on a quiet, tree-lined street with plenty of natural cover from neighbours, and it even had its own double garage. He could move in as soon as he picked up the keys from the real estate agent. The whole transaction had been surprisingly smooth from start to finish.

So that was one task dealt with. Still a few more to go yet, however.

Stretching his arms, Korso went over to the mini-bar and pulled out a bottle of mineral water and untwisted the cap. The prices the hotel charged were ridiculous, but it wasn't his money. Korso grabbed his phone from the worktable, keyed in a brief text message and sent it off. It was the first step in a process they each knew by heart. Putting down the phone, he then took a long drink of the sparkling water as he walked over to the window. Parting the drapes a little, he looked out into the night and saw the rear of a neighbouring apartment building, and not much else. He was closing the drapes again when the phone trilled at him. He picked it up and took the call.

'Hey, K,' the caller said. It was the croaky voice of an elderly man, but Korso knew better. 'Been a few months since we last talked. So how's things with my fave client?'

'Hello, Dog. Is it really necessary to keep using that thing when you talk to me?'

'With you, specifically? No. But you never know who might be listening in, even on a super-encrypted line like this one. Better safe than sorry, I say. Especially after certain recent events.'

Up until recently Dog's identity had always been a very closely guarded secret, as it has to be with all the best hackers. Anytime they spoke on the phone, Dog always used a sophisticated voice modulator for added security. The voice could be male, female, or even a child's. But now that Korso had actually seen Dog in the flesh, there didn't seem much point to the facade. A face-to-face meeting was part of the price he'd insisted on to help keep Dog out of jail a while back, and he'd gotten it, but not in the way he'd imagined. But it meant he now knew Dog was female, and an attractive female at that. As-part payment for that assignment, he'd also requested the use of Dog's professional services – completely gratis – for the next few years. Dog had kept up her end on that part as well. So far.

'So what's up?' she asked.

'I've got a job, and I thought of you.'

'As loquacious as ever, I see. And what kind of job might this be?'

Korso gave her the basic gist in as few sentences as possible, but without going into specifics about the White Nights themselves. That could wait until a more opportune time.

Once he'd finished, Dog gave a low whistle. 'Prison break, huh? Okay, that's kind of unexpected.'

'What do you mean?'

'Well, we've known each other a long time, K, and other than the occasional partner you've always preferred to work solo whenever possible. Yet here you are, busily getting a crew together. I gotta say it's highly atypical of the man I thought I knew.'

'Whatever the job requires. There are a couple of additional wrinkles to this one, though. One you'll like, and one you may not.'

'Well, don't keep me in suspense. Give me the good news first.'

'You won't be working for nothing on this occasion. The total fee is $6 million, to be split equally four ways.'

There was a pause on the line. 'Whoa, that's quite the surprise. A very nice surprise, I have to admit. I guess you better hit me with the bad news now, and I bet it's *really* bad.'

'I think I'll need you on-site for this one, Dog. Or close by, at least. Some things I might need from you, I don't think you'll be able to do remotely.'

Dog gave a weary sigh. 'Yeah, okay, that does kind of suck. But on the other hand it gets me out of the house, which is something I'm trying to do more of these days, so it's not like it's the end of the world.'

'That's a very healthy attitude, Dog. I'm impressed.'

'Hey, I'm a healthy gi… person at heart. I thought you knew that. So when do you need me there?'

'As soon as possible. I'm in London right now, and I'll be flying out in the morning. I've rented us all a place there, but

I know that's not your style so you're free to stay wherever you want, as usual.'

'*Muchos gracias*. Anything else?'

'Yes. The principal for this one is a man named Todd Belmont, who holds some kind of senior position at the US Embassy in Bulgaria. I want to know as much about him as you can find. The same goes for a person called Samara Graynor, who seems to have some long-term connection with Belmont.' He spelled both names, and said, 'She's joining us on this one at the client's request, Dog, and I think she might be either CIA or ex-CIA, but I'd like to know for sure. And anything else you can dig up, of course. I don't have much else to give you other than her name, but you can probably get started by checking through the recent British Airways arrivals at Heathrow and go on from there. I'll be using this number for the duration, so you can call me on it tomorrow when you've got something.'

'Will do. Is that it?'

'Not quite.' Korso then asked her if she could bring along some very specific pieces of kit that he might end up needing, if only for backup purposes.

'Yeah, I think I've got exactly what you want,' she said, 'and they're also about five times smaller than the ones currently on the market, which is a bonus.'

'Good. Now I've already got a private mailbox at one of those self-storage places in Sofia, so put five or six of those things into a jiffy bag and once you've landed, head on over to the storage place and drop it into my mailbox. I'll text you the address and box number after this call.'

'No problem. Well, I better get moving now if I'm gonna catch my flight. *Ciao*.'

Dog hung up. Korso looked down at the phone display and saw that somebody had tried calling a few minutes before. He clicked on the number. After two rings the call was accepted, and Cole said, 'You okay to talk?'

'What have you got?'

'I just finished speaking with Lucian, and we're all good to go on that front. The money on offer was just too sweet to turn down.'

'Excellent.'

'You manage to check out those YouTube videos?'

'I did. Very impressive skills on display. And I've just spoken to that other colleague I mentioned, so that now makes four of us. I've also rented us a house in the city. I'll be flying out in the morning to collect the keys.'

'Sounds good. Uh, about transport...'

'Just text me Lucian's details and email address, along with yours, and I'll arrange plane tickets for each of you within the hour.'

Cole promised to send the details over ASAP, and Korso ended the call. After another sip of mineral water he moved onto the next item on his to-do list...

EIGHT

At 8.15 p.m. the next day, Korso was in the main living area of their new house in Sofia, using Google Maps Street View to navigate the roads and junctions surrounding Tsentalen Sofiyski Zatvor Prison, when he saw Samara finally descend the stairs to join them.

The first floor was mostly open-plan, with a huge living room at the front, adjoining a largish dining area and a sizable kitchen at the rear. There was a downstairs bathroom opposite the utility room, both of which were situated next to the large double garage at the side of the house. Korso's hired Infiniti was in there at the moment, with enough space for one more vehicle. Possibly two. Upstairs consisted of four bedrooms and two more bathrooms, one of which was an en-suite. There was also a sizeable cellar, which might come in useful, depending on the circumstances. In addition a six-foot high wooden fence surrounded the entire property, shielding them from the neighbours on either side, along with any casual pedestrians that might pass by in the street.

Upon landing at Sofia Airport, Korso had collected the house keys from the agent and then spent the next couple of hours stocking the kitchen with a selection of dried and tinned food purchased from a nearby supermarket. Although he expected they'd be ordering meals from one of the local restaurants most of the time. There seemed to be a wide and varied choice. He also had three extra keys cut for the others.

Cole had arrived at three in the afternoon, while Samara showed up four hours later, wearing a t-shirt and tracksuit bottoms and carrying a medium-sized knapsack. They'd each picked a bedroom for themselves already. Korso didn't particularly care where he slept, and would settle for whichever room was left after the last member of their team arrived. Cole was now sitting at the dining table, playing solitaire while he sipped some of the whisky he'd bought at duty-free. Korso was keeping an unobtrusive eye on his alcohol intake. So far, it didn't look like it might be a problem, but you never knew.

Samara took a seat on the L-shaped settee adjacent to Korso. 'So when do we meet this mysterious hacker of yours? What's his name again, Doctor Dog?'

'MD Dog,' Korso said, still staring at the laptop screen as he clicked the trackpad, 'and I wouldn't hold your breath. I've never actually met Dog in person, so even I don't know what gender pronoun to use. For all I know Dog could be male, female, or even trans.' The lie came easy to his lips. He knew just how seriously Dog took her anonymity, since he felt exactly the same way about his own affairs. And he wasn't about to reveal her secrets just for the sake of polite conversation.

'So if we can't even meet him, or her, how do we know they're as good as you claim?'

'I guess you'll have to take it on faith. Anyway, it's not your concern.'

'Really? If we're all supposed to be working together on this, don't you think it should be everyone's concern?'

Korso sat back and looked at her. He also noticed Cole had stopped his game to watch them both. Samara was staring straight back at Korso, although he noticed the hint of a smile at the corners of her mouth.

'I'm not sure what point you're trying to make,' he said. 'We're well past the decision-making stage now. That part's done and dusted. All that remains is acceptance or withdrawal. Because if you *do* want to withdraw, this is the time to do it.'

She tilted her head. 'You trying to get rid of me already?'

'No, I just think it's best we get any issues you have out in the open before—'

Korso paused at the sound of his ringtone. He picked his cell up off the coffee table and took the call without looking at the display. 'Hello?'

'Hey, K. You free to talk?' This time the voice on the other end resembled that of an adolescent boy's. Korso hated it when Dog did that. Dog knew that too.

'Not really,' he said, his gaze still on Samara, 'but that needn't stop you.'

'Okey-dokey. So you'll be glad to know I'm here now, and not a million miles away from your current location. That's not a bad neighbourhood, by the way. Good choice.'

'Thank you.' Korso got to his feet and began moving towards the kitchen area.

'I assume you've got a Plan B, just in case?'

'And a C.'

'Ha. Same old K. Anyway, on to the point of this particular call. Let's start with the slightly less interesting of the two, shall we? So your Mr Todd Belmont started out as a salaried government clerk as soon as he left Law College, and quickly got transferred to the Foreign Service while he was still in his early twenties, initially as a junior consular agent. His old man was pretty high up in the Office of Policy Planning at the State Department before he retired, so he probably called in a few favours to get his boy fast-tracked. From there, Belmont began steadily rising up through the ranks, first as a junior cultural attaché, and then as a Foreign Service Specialist in the role of Information Resource Officer.'

'Whatever that means,' Korso said. He was standing next to the kitchen counter and peering through the window at the rear garden, although it was too dark to see very much.

'Yeah, when you think about it, that title could almost cover what *I* do. Anyway, over the years he's been stationed at various mid-level embassies and consulates around the world, and taken up a number of specialist roles, such as Facilities Maintenance Officer and General Services Officer and so on. They sure like their titles, don't they? But currently he's Second Secretary at the Embassy in Bulgaria, where he's been for the past three years.'

Three years was a long time for someone like Belmont. Korso imagined he must be getting itchy feet by now. 'Is he married?'

Dog chuckled. 'Not our Mr Belmont. He definitely likes the ladies, and he's usually got two or three on the go wherever he happens to be stationed, but never anyone permanent. He's got a sweet three-bedroom apartment in the centre of town, all paid for by the State Department. According to his psychological profile he's known to be highly ambitious and ruthless with interdepartmental rivals, which comes as no surprise at all. His record is pretty clean for the most part, although I found he *was* involved in a spot of bother when he was stationed in Cairo a few years back.'

Korso had been filling the kettle while Dog talked. He switched it on. 'I'm still here.'

'Well, it seems someone at the embassy was suspected of smuggling out diamonds and a few other odds and ends in the diplomatic pouch, on a semi-regular basis. Belmont's name comes up a few times in the internal investigation reports, although nothing was ever proved. After a few weeks the invest-igation came to a sudden halt without the culprit ever being discovered. Reading between the lines, it looks to me like someone higher up swept the whole situation under the carpet. It might have nothing to do with Belmont at all, but it's kind of intriguing when you consider how influential his old man was, don't you think?'

'I do.' Korso emptied a teaspoon of instant coffee into a mug. 'Anything else?'

'Only once we get to your Samara Graynor, and that's where things get a little more interesting.'

'In what way?'

'Well, for a start, she doesn't actually exist.'

'Explain that.'

'Well, she obviously uses that name because she that's what it says on her passport, but she's got no social security number, no credit history, no history of tax payments, or any other kind of history you can think of for that matter. Nothing. She's basically a ghost. Sound familiar at all?'

Korso watched the water in the kettle as it came to a boil. 'I can't believe you hit a dead end and just gave up. You've got something. What is it?'

'Well, I found the germ of a clue in her original passport application from two years ago, and did a little backtracking from there. To cut a long story short, it turns out there used to be a Petty Officer First Class in the Navy SEALS named Samantha Greenford, who's military mug shot very closely resembles the passport photo of this Samara Graynor. Unfortunately, I couldn't access much of Greenford's military record as most of her file's been redacted with black bars everywhere you look, which kind of tells its own story. But it seems she resigned from military service five years ago, at which point Samantha Greenford ceased to exist, at least on paper. Now what do you think of that?'

Korso poured hot water into his mug and began to stir the coffee. 'Spook,' he said quietly.

'Yeah, that's my guess too. She could belong to any one of those three-letter outfits: the CIA, the NSA, or even the DIA. And whatever she's doing for them, she does it under a variety of identities, of which Samara Graynor is probably just one. You want my advice, K, I'd say this one definitely requires watching.' Dog paused. 'So what are you going to do?'

'Keep her close.' Korso took a sip of the coffee. Not exactly restaurant quality, but it would do. 'Did you manage to get those plans and blueprints I wanted?'

'Yeah, I emailed the files over to you ten minutes ago. As you'd expect, the plans for that prison were the toughest to crack, but I finally got hold of them from a nasty little corner of the deep dark web. There's a highly secure message board there for ex-cons, and two of those guys verified the plans as accurate and up-to-date.'

'Good. Anything else?'

'Not yet, but I'll keep checking. Now you can do something for me.'

'Which is…?'

'Which is to tell me the real reason why we're all here. If we're going to all this effort to simply break some guy out of jail, then it's because he's got something or he knows something valuable to our principal. So what is it?'

'Before I answer that, I need to know how secure this line is.'

'Well, as you can guess, after my recent unwanted encounter with Interpol I've tightened up my internal and external security by about the power of ten, and that goes treble for all mobile communications. Believe me, the algorithms I use to encrypt outgoing and incoming transmissions are so complex nobody's ever going to crack them. We can talk freely, and you can take that to the bank.'

'Okay, I believe you.' Korso then explained about the White Nights, and what they could actually do. It only took him three sentences to get the relevant points across. Afterwards, there was a lull on the line.

Finally, Dog said, 'You're serious? No, don't answer that. I know better than to ask.' She let out an audible breath. 'But, Jesus…'

'Kind of a game-changer, isn't it? And now you know as much as I do.'

'Wow… Okay, plenty for me to think about there, K, so I best let you get back whatever you're doing. Speak to you soon, okay?'

'Right.' Korso ended the call, and took his coffee back to the living area.

Cole looked up at him from his cards. 'Who was that?'

'The other member of the team. We've now got plans for the prison, along with much of Sofia's public sewer network. I'll download them so you can take a look for yourself.'

'Cool.'

Korso went over to his laptop and logged onto his email account. After opening Dog's email and downloading the seven enclosed attachments to his desktop, he took the MacBook over to Cole at the dining table and set it down. Cole swept up his cards and put them to one side, then double-clicked on the first PDF file and peered closely at the laptop screen.

Korso left him in peace and resumed his place on the settee, where Samara was still sitting in the same position. 'So what else did the invisible Dog have to say?' she asked. 'Five minutes seems a long time just to tell you to go check your emails. You wouldn't be checking up on me, by any chance? Or am I just being paranoid?'

'I like to cover all angles, that's why you approached me. And you're quite the blank slate, Samara.' Korso furrowed his brow. 'Or is it Samantha? I'm a little confused.'

A faint smile began to emerge on her lips. 'Well, well, well, maybe I need to give this Dog its day. I thought I'd covered my tracks pretty comprehensively, but it turns out I'd left a few crumbs behind after all. Round of applause for our mysterious hacker.'

'Out of interest, which particular acronym do you belong to?'

She gave a playful shrug. 'If I said none of them, would you believe me?'

'Probably not.'

'Then why ask?'

'Never hurts to try. So, Petty Officer First Class. If I've got my official rankings correct, that's fairly high up in the chain of command, especially for such a young recruit, which implies you were very good at your job. Didn't fancy going all the way?'

'To what? A lifetime of paperwork, policy meetings, and endless glad-handing?' She gave a snort. 'Not really my style, Korso. I'm sure you can understand.'

He was just taking another sip of his coffee when three loud knocks echoed through the house. All heads turned to the front door in unison. Korso went over and opened it.

Facing him was a petite, attractive woman wearing a baseball cap, jeans and denim jacket. He judged her height as maybe five feet two inches at most. She was carrying a large bag that was almost as big as her.

'Hello,' he said. 'I recognise you from your TV interviews. Come in.'

She didn't move. 'And you are?'

'Korso. Cole's already inside. You're the last to arrive.'

Lucian gave a brief nod, and passed by Korso as she entered the house. Cole waved from the dining table, and said, 'Hey, Luce. Good to see you again. How you doing?'

'Dying on my feet.' She removed her cap to release her long, frizzy black hair. 'The flight was a bitch. I feel sore all over.' Turning to Samara, she said, 'Who are you?'

'My name's Samara. And you must be the driver.'

'That's me. Anytime, anywhere, any kind of vehicle. So what do you do?'

'Lots of things.' She smiled. 'I can make up a list for you if you like.'

Lucian gave her a pretty grin back. 'Maybe later, when I'm not so whacked out.' She turned to Korso. 'Cole tells me you're the man with the plan. What's the plan for tonight?'

'Rest. Eat, if you want. We'll get started first thing in the morning. For now, grab yourself one of the two remaining bedrooms and get unpacked.'

She dropped her bag on the floor. 'Let's discuss a few things first. Cole told me the payday for this is *seis millones de dólares. ¿Es eso cierto?*'

'*Si, es cierto.*'

She narrowed her eyes at him. 'You speak Spanish.'

'*Un poco.*' Considerably more than a little actually, but that wasn't information he needed to share.

Lucian glanced pointedly at Samara on the settee, before turning back to Korso. 'And that's split how many ways?'

'Four. You, Cole, Dog, and me. And before you ask, that's equal shares.'

Lucian smiled again. 'Yeah, Cole mentioned that part on the phone. I just wanted it confirmed. What about expenses?'

'To be provided as and when,' Samara said. 'Why, what are you thinking of?'

'Vehicles, mostly.' To Korso, she said, 'Unless you want me to just pluck them off the street, that is. I can do it, but I prefer to avoid that kind of thing if I can help it.'

'I agree. No sense in bringing unnecessary attention to ourselves. We'll go the legit route wherever possible. What else is on your mind?'

'That coffee, mainly. It smells pretty good right about now.' Lucian put a hand over her mouth and yawned. 'Make me a cup?'

'I'll make us two,' Cole said, and got up and walked over to the kitchen area. 'Come on over. We can catch up.'

'Sure,' she said, and went over to join him.

Korso sat down again, and took a few more sips of his own coffee. Samara said, 'Cute little thing, isn't she? Also, a lot shorter than I imagined.'

'As long as she can do what she claims, I don't care what she looks like.'

'So what prompted you to pick her?'

'Cole recommended her. They've got history. But let's talk about you.'

'Tell you what, let's not.' She smiled out of one corner of her mouth as she pulled her phone from her pocket. 'How about I order us all some food instead? What do you fancy, Chinese or Indian? I'm buying.'

NINE

'First, the good news,' Korso said, setting down his glass of orange juice. It was 8.27 the next morning, and they were all sitting at the dining table, having already finished their respective breakfasts. 'Sofia's one of the poorer European nations, with no new prisons built here in over eighty years, and the ones currently standing haven't received any investment at all from the government. Any funding for improvements generally comes from private donors, who've usually got better things to invest in than state prisons. All of which means we can count on weak spots, both in the matter of security, as well as in the actual structure itself.'

'That's right,' Cole said. 'And Sofia Central Prison's one of the oldest, dating back over a hundred years, so you can expect plenty of natural rock erosion to have taken place over time, especially below ground level. Korso and I went over the schematics Dog supplied last night, and we both agree it looks promising for our purposes. Samara, you visited this Teodor Yanev about a week ago, right? Give us your impression of the place.'

Samara shrugged. 'Well, the guards don't exactly give visitors a guided tour of the joint, you know? But what little I did see looked pretty rundown and ragged. That goes for the guards, as well. They didn't strike me as the best of the best. If it wasn't for the uniforms, I might have mistaken some of them for inmates themselves.'

'You would have been in the west wing then,' Korso said. 'According to the plans, that's where visitors get processed before they're led to the visitors' room.'

She nodded. 'That's right, the west wing.'

'How many wings has this place got?' Lucian asked.

'Four in total,' Korso said, 'if you're looking down, the prison is basically in the shape of a cruciform, with the four separate wings all connected by a wide central corridor. There are two main courtyards, a smaller one between the south and west wings, and a much larger one between the north and east wings. The south wing is where most of the administrative offices and buildings are located, along with the political department, whatever that is. And the whole prison is surrounded on all sides by a five-metre-thick stone wall, with a guard tower at each corner. Plus razor wire and motion sensors, of course.'

Samara said, 'Guess that means we're not going in through the front, huh?'

'There's also a huge police station one kilometre to the south,' Korso said, 'which further limits our options. Now we've marked two potential entry points into the prison, although one looks a lot more promising than the other. But either way, it means we'll be making use of the city's sewer system, which is the not so good news.'

'*Sewers?*' Lucian's expression was one of pure disgust. 'Forget it. No way am I going down in that shit, not for any amount of money.'

'You won't have to. You'll have other responsibilities above ground.'

'Good. Just as long as we understand each other.' She drank some more of her coffee.

'She's got a point,' Samara said. 'The sewer system *is* particularly bad here, I know that much. The government keeps promising structural improvements, usually around election time, and then nothing happens for another four years.'

'That's something we can be grateful for,' Korso said. 'If the authorities don't care what happens under Sofia's streets, I'm happy to keep it that way. Unfortunately, the city employs a mixed sewer system that collects rainwater runoff, industrial wastewater and domestic sewage all in the same pipe, with the main effluents running along the city's riverbanks until they reach the municipal sewage treatment plant in Kubratovo. So it *will* stink to high heaven down there, which means at least two layers of protective gear each, along with gas masks or respirators. It's also a real labyrinth, made up of a confusing network of passageways and tunnels, some of which are over a hundred years old. And since it'll be as dark as space, we'll need some industrial-strength flashlights to get around as well.'

'Uh, I have a question,' Samara said. 'If Lucian isn't going underground, who is?'

'Cole, you, and myself. We'll have plenty of tools and gear to take along for the job, and two people just aren't enough for that. And we'll definitely need you there for the actual extraction itself.'

She sighed. 'I'd prefer not to be down there at all.'

'Join the club,' Korso said with a shrug. 'Though you must have handled worse conditions back when you were in the service.'

'Sometimes, although that wasn't out of choice.'

'You were in the armed services?' Lucian turned to her. 'What? Air Force, Army?'

When it seemed she wasn't going to answer, Korso said, 'Maybe you should just tell her. After all, we're all working together on this, aren't we?'

Samara smiled. '*Touché*. Okay, if you must know, I was a Navy SEAL back in the day. But I left all that behind a few years ago. I'm now just a normal citizen like you guys.'

Except normal citizens generally don't usually walk around with multiple identities, Korso thought with amusement.

'Whoa, Navy SEAL.' Lucian made an impressed face. 'Badass. Don't tell me. Special Ops, right?'

'You're right, I can't tell you.'

'Ha. So, what, they got you working at the US embassy now?'

Samara sighed, clearly not happy at still being the centre of conversation. 'Not officially. I sometimes get called in for certain specialist or consultant work, that's all.'

'But you live in these parts, right? You obviously know the country pretty well.'

'I reside here for now, yes. And I can also speak enough of the language to pass as a native, if people don't listen too carefully.'

'That particular skill set will come in very useful,' Korso said. 'Not everyone here speaks English.'

'Tell me about it,' Lucian said. 'I practically had to use sign language with my cab driver yesterday.' She turned back to Cole. 'So how do you plan on getting into the prison?'

'I've got a few ideas rolling around my head,' he said, 'but it all depends on which entry point we decide on. If we go with the northwest option we can make as much noise as we want, as there's a public park directly above with plenty of insulation between us and it. But the other entry point's under a heavily built-up area so we'd have to go in with the minimum of noise, which presents a whole new set of problems I don't even want to think about yet.'

Samara turned to Korso. 'Which one looks the best option?'

'The second one, naturally. But we've still got a few things to check before we make the final decision. Lucian, there's a Nissan Infiniti rental in the garage. The keys are on the kitchen counter. Once you've dropped each of us off at our respective destinations this morning, I want you to take it out for a spin. Concentrate on the immediate vicinity of the prison to start with, and gradually spread out from there. Just drive through Sofia and see as much of it as you can, so you can get a feel for the place and find the best routes, especially those to and from the main airport. There are also several airstrips once you get out of the city, and I want you to check those out as well. It's always good to know all the exits.'

'*No hay problema.*' Lucian took another sip of her coffee.

'Where are *we* going today?' Samara asked. 'Or is it a surprise?'

'Cole will be picking up most of the gear necessary for traversing the sewers, while you and I will take a walk around the streets surrounding the prison, looking like your average couple out for a stroll. Google Maps can only show you so much. I always like to see the site in question with my own eyes.'

'Sure, we can do that.'

'And wear a baseball cap. There'll be security cameras at each of those guard towers and I don't want to risk anyone recognising you from your previous visit. Or your next one.'

'My next one?'

'Teodor will need to play his part in the breakout, and he'll have to know exactly what's required of him beforehand. What was the official reason you gave for visiting him last week?'

'I just told them I was his late brother's fiancé. Nobody questioned me about it.'

'Good. You can use that same reason when you see him again.'

'When might that be?'

'Tomorrow, or maybe the next day, once I've finally figured out the details.' Korso turned to Lucian. 'I've also got one or two ideas about possible getaway strategies I need to discuss with you before we leave. These are worst-case scenarios I'm thinking of, but I like to be prepared. One would involve almost perfect synchronisation for it to work, but it should be possible with enough prep. You'll have to tell me what you think. Also, yesterday you mentioned you drive any kind of vehicle. Would that include the flying kind?'

'Sure, I own a private pilot's licence for single-engine aircraft, and I can handle most small choppers without a problem. Why?'

'I just like to know what options are available to me. Depending on the circumstances having someone who can fly could make all the difference between success and failure.'

Lucian nodded vaguely, and then shared a meaningful glance with Cole, who said, 'Uh, Korso, before you said that getting this guy out is only *part* of the deal, that once he's free he'll tell us the location of the asset our employer's really after. So what's this asset?'

'Samara here can tell you better than I can, so I'll give her the floor. But I'd wait until she's finished before asking questions.'

'Thanks.' Samara leaned forward in her seat, and then began summarising everything Belmont had told Korso at Heathrow Airport. It took her a few minutes to cover every point, but she had Lucian's and Cole's complete attention throughout. There were no interruptions.

Once she was done, there was silence in the room. Cole's mouth was partially open. Looking quizzically down at her coffee cup, Lucian picked up a teaspoon and started tapping it lightly against the tabletop. Finally, she said, 'A see-in-the-dark pill. And it's genuine? There are actual prototypes of these babies hidden somewhere?'

'That what Darian assured Belmont before he died,' Samara said. 'That he'd secreted a pill container with the prototypes in a place nobody could ever find them. His brother Teodor confirmed it when I went to see him recently. So there you have it in a nutshell: we get the brother out of jail and he'll show us where the tablets are.'

Cole snorted. 'Out of the pure goodness of his heart, right?'

'And a huge payoff, don't forget,' Samara said. 'Five million in cash isn't exactly chump change.'

'Except if this Teodor knows what these pills can do,' Lucian said, 'then he has to know five million's a fraction of their real worth.'

'That part bothers me, as well,' Korso said. 'In fact, it's my guess Teodor's already thinking up various ways to screw us over once we get him out.'

Samara frowned at him. 'You think?'

'You know it as well as we do. Had Darian lived there's every chance he'd have kept to the deal he made with Belmont, but Teodor's a horse of a different colour. He's a born hustler, has been since he was a kid. He knows the world and what he can get out of it. And he knows that once he gets his hands on those pills he can essentially name his price, so why hand them over to us if he doesn't have to?'

'Okay, fair enough. But short of chaining the guy up in the cellar, which would be counter-productive on almost every level, I don't see what we can do about it.'

'Let me worry about that. I'm sure something can be worked out.'

At some point, Cole had pulled a pack of Marlboros from his pocket and extracted a cigarette. As he played it between his fingers, he said, 'So, once the pills *are* in our possession, what's stopping us from shopping around for other prospective buyers ourselves? Assuming these things can do what you claim, the six million bucks Belmont's offering us seems like so much small change. I mean, it's just a thought, but maybe we should set our sights a little higher?'

Samara began to rise from her seat. 'Now wait a min—'

'There's a small problem there, Cole,' Korso cut in. 'Two, actually. First, I was the one who accepted this job, which means I take the blame if it goes south. Now I've spent the last few years building a rep for seeing a job through from start to finish, and I'd prefer not to throw it all away in the hope of grabbing a quick payday from some interested competitor. Then there's the fact that it's Belmont's money that's financing this whole job in the first place. Since he officially represents one of the most powerful nations on earth it wouldn't be too hard for him to make public enemies out of all of us with a few well-placed memos if he really wanted to. And I much prefer to stay in the shadows where I belong, as I'm sure you do. When you make a deal, you're better off keeping up your end. It's kept me alive this far, and I want to keep that record going. Anyone got a problem with that?'

Cole slipped the unlighted cigarette between his lips. 'Hey, I'm with you, pal. It was just a thought.'

Lucian asked, 'And if Belmont goes back on his word...?'

'Then that opens up a whole new playing field,' Korso said, 'with a whole new set of rules. But let's stick to the original plan, shall we? We've got enough problems ahead without needlessly creating more.' He looked at each of them. 'Anybody got any other questions?'

Nobody did.

'Good. Finish your coffees and we'll get going.'

TEN

'See you both later,' Korso said, and slammed the car door shut. He and Samara watched as Lucian sped off down Mayor Georgi Vekliski Street before taking a left at the end, towards the city centre, where she'd drop Cole off. Korso had been impressed with her driving thus far. She handled the car expertly while keeping within the speed limit, and always seemed to have total awareness of every other vehicle around her.

'Which way?' Samara asked. 'North or south?'

'You choose,' Korso said.

With a shrug, she adjusted her baseball cap and began strolling north. Korso kept pace alongside her.

Although the day was sunny there was a slight chill in the air, and they each wore a light jacket over their clothes. The street they were on was on the western side of the prison. Immediately to their right was an imposing twenty-foot-high brick wall, with at least three layers of razor wire at the top. Beyond the wall, Korso could just make out the topmost floors of three large windowless buildings inside. To their left, the first of many run-down-looking apartment buildings rose into the sky, partially blocking out the sun. The road on either side was lined with parked vehicles of all shapes and sizes, none of them new.

'Definitely not one of the upmarket neighbourhoods.' Samara was looking up at the tower block next to them.

'So much the better.' Korso watched a man exit the building, led by a greyhound on a leash. 'Residents in these kinds of areas usually know how to mind their own business.'

'Yeah, there is that. So are we searching for anything in particular, or just looking?'

'Just looking for now, but shout out anytime you spot something that looks like a manhole cover. There should be some located a little further out from here, although I couldn't find any of them on Google Street View.'

'Ah, the penny drops. Will do.'

They walked unhurriedly, Korso making mental notes of everything within his vision. He knew none of the nearby manhole entrances were of any real tactical use to them, as Cole had told him that those surrounding the prison had been soldered shut years ago, to deter possible escape attempts. But he still wanted to know where they were located. All information relevant to their mission was helpful, whether he ended up using it or not.

They'd been walking in silence for a minute or so, when Samara said, 'You don't trust me, do you, Korso?'

'I wouldn't take it personally. Trust's a hard thing to come by in my business.'

'But you trust Cole.'

'To a point. We worked together once and he was solid, but that was then. People change over time. Also, he's only recently gotten out of prison himself, and that can have an adverse effect on a man's better qualities. But you're still a huge question mark to me at the moment, and I've learnt never to accept people at face value.' Hoping to change the subject, he said, 'You've seen this Teodor character up close. How much do you know about him?'

'Well, I've done a lot of research on the guy's life over the past couple of weeks, so probably a lot more than I want to.'

'Give me your opinion of him.'

'He's a lowlife, but a highly intelligent one. And I don't just mean street-smart. I get the feeling he was the brainier brother of the two, but he didn't have the patience to focus that intelligence on anything tangible or long lasting. On the other hand, he was forced into making a life decision when he was practically a kid, but he doesn't seem too broken up with regrets now that he's pushing fifty. In my opinion, he seems content to be what he is: the eternal outsider.'

'I can empathise. Will Belmont keep his word and pay him off?'

Samara turned her face to him as they walked. 'What you're actually asking is, will Belmont keep his word with you?'

'No, I'm not asking that. I always get my fee, one way or the other. I play fair with those who play fair with me. If they don't...' He shrugged and left it at that. There was no point in making unnecessary threats so early in the game. 'But Teodor's another matter, and five million's still a huge amount of money.'

'Belmont will pay what he's agreed to pay,' she said. 'He and I have worked together before, and he's always kept up his end.'

Korso looked up to his right. 'We're approaching the prison boundaries. There's a guard tower coming up. I see two CCTV cameras, one aimed this way, so keep your head down as we go by.'

'Right.'

There was a narrow access road just past the edge of the prison wall. Korso made note of it as they passed. He saw the cul-de-sac ended outside some kind of warehouse. In addition to the No Entry signs on either side of the road, there was a pair of unmanned automatic arm barriers preventing vehicles from entering unless the driver had a key card. Once they passed it, the cobblestone street they were on soon widened into a proper thoroughfare with traffic, and Korso saw a huge Kaufland hypermarket with its own two-storey car park coming up on their right. It took up the rest of the block. Running down the left side – into the distance – were more apartment buildings, all carbon copies of the ones they were passing now.

'We'll make one complete circuit,' he said. 'Then once we're back where we started, we can branch out a little for a wider look at the area.'

'Okay. We can also grab some lunch at the food court in Kaufland's later.'

Korso nodded as he watched the traffic ahead, though there wasn't much at this time of the morning. He said, 'Back at Heathrow, Belmont did a nice job of skimming over your initial involvement in this enterprise. I'm interested to know what made you join up.'

She snorted. 'Come on, Korso. Genuine night-vision pills for the masses? Given the chance, who'd want to miss out on something that monumental?'

'I understand that. But assuming we succeed, what do *you* personally gain from their discovery? Is it money? Glory? Political influence? Or is it just the thrill of the chase?'

She stared ahead as she walked. 'Maybe I'm simply here under orders.'

'You mean from Belmont?' Korso shook his head. 'I don't see it.'

'No? Why's that?'

'Because back in London, he treated you as an equal rather than as a subordinate. I could tell just from his body language, and yours too. He asked you to come in on this and you accepted. It was your choice.'

'Well, you're right about that, at least. Belmont's far from stupid, and he knows I can do things he can't. So here I am.'

When she didn't add anything more, Korso said, 'So you're not going to tell me what you're getting out of this?'

'Maybe. I don't know yet. Let me think on it.'

Korso shrugged and said nothing. He knew better than to push. He clearly wasn't going to get the whole story from her at this early stage, so better to be patient. That was something he was very good at. And there were other ways to gain information.

They continued strolling alongside the large Kaufland building. He couldn't see any sign of a main entrance anywhere, so the store was probably only accessible via the car park they'd already passed. At the end, they turned right into Skopie Street, where they walked another three blocks until they reached the next road that would lead them back. He hadn't seen any manhole covers at all yet. Maybe they were all further out. He also noticed there weren't many other pedestrians in this part of the city, but then the prison probably had something to do with that. He kept his eyes and ears open all the time, on the alert for anything out of the ordinary. They were walking alongside the south wall of the prison when something began pinging on his internal radar.

When they finally made it back to their original starting point on the west side of the prison, Korso just kept on going, as though about to do another circuit.

'I thought we were going to branch out from here,' Samara said.

'We were. But a few minutes ago I noticed a car following us. Don't look back.'

'No need to insult me.'

'My apologies.'

'Did you get a good look?'

'Just a brief glance when I turned my head to talk to you a few minutes ago. Looks like a Honda something or other. It was still there in the corner of my vision when I checked a minute later. And moving at a snail's pace too, which isn't natural. I couldn't tell how many were inside. Please assure me Belmont's not keeping tabs on us, because that would make me very angry.'

'Definitely not,' she said, slowing her pace to match his. 'So what are you thinking?'

'That it's logical to assume more than one party might be interested in Darian's wonder pills. Other than Deleva and his people, I mean. If word somehow got leaked to the higher ups at Vercogen, it could easily have reached the ears of others too. You said it yourself. Darian wasn't working in a vacuum. And if these people know that much, then it's not beyond the realms of possibility that they might know you're also involved somehow.'

'Or even you.'

'Unlikely, I'm not a known face. Although we can't discount any possibility at this stage.' He sighed. 'It's troubling, nevertheless.'

She frowned. 'What do you think? The Russians?'

'Could be. Maybe even the Chinese. At this point it's anyone's guess.'

Korso came to a stop and turned to Samara. To his left, out the corner of his eye, he saw the black Honda near the southwest guard tower as it turned into this street. It was about two hundred feet away.

'There it is,' he said. 'Same car as before. And I think now would be a good time for you to kiss me.'

'Say what?'

'How else are we going to get a better look without giving ourselves away? We're supposed to be a couple, after all.'

Samara breathed a long sigh. 'Seriously, the things I do for my country.' As she put her arms around Korso's neck, he noticed somebody getting out of the car and start to walk slowly in their direction. The vehicle continued moving at the same pace as the walker.

'One of them just got out,' he said, and leaned forward and kissed her lightly on the lips, although his eyes were still on the man in the distance. He was shaven-headed with a short beard, and wore jeans and a leather jacket. 'He doesn't look Asian.'

Samara returned the kiss, her eyes moving in the same direction as Korso's. They each watched the man stop and pull a pack of cigarettes from his coat pocket. He put one in his mouth and took his time lighting it. Clearly playing for time. The car had also stopped.

As Samara nuzzled Korso's neck, she whispered, 'We could lead this guy into the multi-storey car park, say, then grab him and see what's what. It's always useful to know who you're dealing with.'

'Not always.' He brushed his lips against her warm cheek. Despite the circumstances he found the sensation not unpleasurable, and she also smelled very nice. 'Given the choice, I'd prefer it if we all remained strangers at this point.'

'So what do you want to do?'

'Split up. You make your way into one of these buildings and find yourself a good hiding place. Make use of your CIA training and break into an empty apartment if you have to, just don't let yourself be caught. Meanwhile I'll continue on to Kaufland and lose whoever decides to follow me there. I'm sure I don't need to tell you to use as indirect a route as possible when heading back to the safe house. If that place gets discovered, then this whole job's over before it's even begun.'

'Not necessarily.'

'It is as far as I'm concerned. We'll meet back there later. Give me a goodbye peck, and then make your exit.'

Samara brushed her lips against his cheek, and said, 'I'm gone.' She turned away and began walking towards the apartment building directly behind her.

Without looking back, Korso turned north again and began walking. Logic dictated that the follower would go after Samara, while the vehicle would stick with Korso. But human beings were rarely logical, and it was easy enough to check. Pulling his phone from his pocket, he opened the camera app and switched it to the front-facing mode. Since he was in motion the image quality wasn't great, but past his left shoulder he could see the Honda still back there, along with the walker. He thought he could see two people in the car. The walker had a phone next to his ear, probably asking what he should do. Korso kept watching them both as he walked. There were no other pedestrians, no other vehicular traffic.

After a few more moments, the man on foot pocketed his phone and continued on in the same direction as before. As did the vehicle. So they weren't interested in Samara at all. It was Korso they were really after. That was bad. Very bad indeed.

75

Passing the access road adjacent to the prison, Korso picked up his pace and kept moving north. Within seconds, the walker had lengthened his stride to match Korso's, and the car began picking up speed as well. He kept his eyes on the phone display as the vehicle began to close in on him. Then out the corner of his vision, he saw it pass by him at a languid twenty miles per hour. A navy Honda Civic, with two men in the front. He couldn't see their faces. He also noticed the man behind him was walking a lot faster now. Fifteen feet ahead the Civic came to a gentle stop under a conifer tree, just at the point where the narrow cobblestone street ended and the real road began. He put the phone back in his pocket.

Then he suddenly sprinted towards the car.

When he was less than five feet away he saw the passenger door opening, but Korso had already swept past before he could see who was inside. He waited for shouts from behind him, but there were none. All he heard was a revving engine and the slam of a door. He kept running, and within seconds he was on the main part of the street again, with other vehicles entering the Kaufland car park coming up on the right. Korso switched direction and entered the car park area on foot, just missing a station wagon as it was pulling out. The driver honked his horn in anger, but Korso ignored him and kept on going.

He glanced behind him and saw the man about a hundred feet away, just turning into the car park and still running after him. There was no sign of the Honda Civic. Korso faced front again and saw the entrance to the ground level car park just up ahead. Inside, he could see at least a dozen shoppers of various ages walking back to their vehicles, either carrying large shopping bags or pushing trolleys. The place already looked about half full. On the left were two sets of double doors leading to the hypermarket itself. As Korso ran towards the doors, he spotted a young couple and a middle-aged woman coming the other way, the latter pushing an empty trolley. He reduced his speed to a fast walk, and walked ahead of them into the large store.

As soon as he was inside, Korso removed his navy jacket while he checked his surroundings. The place was cavernous, with aisles and aisles of products straight ahead and a huge food court area on the right. Pop music played from speakers in the ceiling. The place wasn't exactly packed, and he counted only thirty or so shoppers in his immediate vicinity. Turning to his left, he saw a pharmacy, a small newsagent selling magazines, tobacco, and other odds and ends, and then a hallway that led to the toilets. In front of the newsagents was a spinner rack, displaying cheap casualwear such as sunglasses and baseball caps.

Korso walked over to the rack. There was one girl behind the till, currently serving a customer. Korso quickly grabbed a dark green baseball cap from the stand and affixed it on his head, then walked towards the hallway leading to the toilets. He found the men's room on the left and went inside. There were eight urinals at the end and four cubicles on his left. No windows. One man was standing in front of one of the urinals, while another elderly man washed his hands at the sinks to Korso's right. None of the cubicles were currently occupied.

Korso stepped behind the entrance door, pulled out his phone and pretended to key in a message. Once the elderly man finished drying his hands, he gave Korso a brief glance before exiting. The other man zipped himself up and went over to the sinks to wash up. Korso ignored him and continued to look down at his phone. Once he'd left, Korso placed his jacket on a hook in the closest cubicle and took his place behind the entrance door again.

He felt there was a fair-to-evens chance the guy in the leather jacket would check the toilets before checking the rest of the store. He hoped so. That was why Korso had ducked in here, it being the most obvious place to hide. But what was obvious to him might not be to the guy outside. All he could do was wait and see.

Korso strained to listen, hoping to hear the sounds of rapid footsteps outside. But all he heard out there was the same muffled pop song that had been playing when he arrived. He continued waiting. The seconds passed slowly.

Without warning, the door was suddenly pushed open, blocking him from the person on the other side.

As the door began to close, Korso saw part of a leather sleeve. That was enough. If he was wrong, he'd apologise. Korso dropped his right shoulder and pivoted on his right foot and as his body followed, he swung his left leg up and round in a classic roundhouse kick. He felt his instep and shin smack into the man's stomach like a battering ram. There was a startled *woooff* sound, and the man fell back against the door. Quickly regaining his balance, Korso came around and saw it *was* the same one who'd been chasing him. The man's body was bent forward as he tried to pull air back into his lungs.

Before he could regain his wits, Korso kicked the door shut and at the same time slammed the tip of his elbow into the guy's right temple. The man grunted as his head rolled to the side with the punch, and Korso grabbed hold of his jacket lapels before he could fall. Using all his strength, Korso yanked him round in a tight semi-circle and threw him at the nearest cubicle. The man tottered back against the door and fell into the cubicle itself, Korso following a split second behind him.

The man's body crashed against the toilet seat, arms and legs splayed out wide. As Korso moved in, he suddenly kicked out with both feet, his left boot striking Korso in the right thigh. Ignoring the sudden jolt of pain, Korso leaned in close, grabbed the man's head with both hands and slammed it against the porcelain cistern. Hard. The man stopped kicking him. Korso did it again, even more forcefully, and the man's eyes rolled up in his head as he lost consciousness.

Korso took a deep breath as he stepped out of the cubicle. Only a few seconds had passed, so they were still alone. He returned to his downed pursuer who now lay spread-eagled on the toilet seat, and shut and locked the door behind him. Inspecting the man's face carefully, Korso judged him to be somewhere in his late twenties, with high Slavic cheekbones and deep set eyes. He was sure he'd never seen the guy before today. He searched the man's jacket pockets, both inside and out, and found nothing at all. Trying the jeans next, he found a basic phone in the front left pocket, and a small wad of 50 leva notes in the right. He kept the phone, left the money. Pulling the man up to a seated position, Korso checked the rear pockets and found nothing there. But he did find a pistol sticking out of the man's rear waistband.

He pulled the piece out, and saw it was a compact Walther PPS M2 9mm semi-automatic, with a seven-round magazine. It looked almost new. Very handy. He stuck the gun in his own waistband. Often the best way to arm yourself on foreign territory was to simply take a weapon off the nearest lowlife. After carefully positioning the man's body so he wouldn't slip off the toilet seat, Korso took one last look at him. The fact that he hadn't been carrying any identification meant he was a pro. But a professional what? That was the question. Maybe he could get some clues from the phone, although he wasn't holding out much hope on that score. Shaking his head in frustration, Korso hefted himself up and over the partition and dropped down in the next cubicle, just like he'd done in Italy.

Grabbing his jacket from the hook, Korso lowered the bill of his baseball cap and exited the men's room. Outside, the store was pretty much as he'd left it, with shoppers going about their business without a care in the world. He couldn't see anybody waiting for him, but that didn't mean they weren't. There had been two more men in that Honda Civic. Either one of them could have entered the store as backup. Maybe both of them.

Noticing some empty shopping baskets nearby, Korso went over and picked one up. He placed his jacket inside. Now he looked just like everyone else. He started walking towards the other end of the vast store, keeping an eye for some kind of employees' entrance. He didn't waste time looking for either of the other two men, since he had no idea what they looked like anyway.

When Korso reached the back of the hypermarket, he saw a set of double doors next to the delicatessen section that could only lead to the warehouse area out back. There was a sign above the doors in Bulgarian. Since their Cyrillic alphabet was very similar to Russian, he was able to decipher it easily enough: *Employees Only.*

He mulled around the bread racks until he saw a young guy in the standard red Kaufland polo shirt approaching, pushing an empty Yorkie cage. The double doors opened automatically when he was less than five feet away, and he pushed on through without stopping. Korso put down the basket, grabbed his jacket and was about to follow the guy inside when he noticed another employee stacking shelves nearby. She was looking his way with a frown on her face. Before she could say anything, Korso tapped his watch apologetically and said in Russian, '*Moj pervyj den. Za opozdanie.*'

She shrugged disinterestedly and returned to her work. It was always somebody's first day in these kinds of places, and it would also explain why she didn't recognise him.

Korso entered the warehouse confidently, looking as though he belonged nowhere else. The large stockroom was lined with heavy duty racking, all filled with pallets and crates of various sizes. A mini forklift moved along one of the aisles, carrying a fully loaded pallet, while other employees pushed hand trolleys around as they collected various stock from their checklists. There were about a dozen workers in view. Half of them wore the standard polo shirts, while the others wore general work clothes or dark coveralls, so Korso didn't feel out of place. Everybody was busy. Nobody paid him any attention.

He turned to his right and noticed a pallet on the ground nearby. It contained a dozen cardboard boxes, each one with the *Mizo Coffee* logo on the side. Korso went over and picked one up, and carried it down one of the empty aisles towards the rear of the warehouse. He could see two of the shutters at the end were open, and a truck was currently parked in front of one of the loading docks, its rear trailer doors open to reveal a half empty interior. A Kaufland employee was already in there, loading cartons onto a hand trolley. The other dock was empty.

Just before he reached the end of the aisle, Korso placed his Mizo Coffee carton on top of some other boxes on the rack to his right and just kept on walking. He walked out onto the empty dock and jumped the three feet to the ground. There was a small staff car park back there, with a small access road to the left of the building. The navy Honda Civic that had been following him was not among the parked vehicles. Just past the cars were four industrial sized dumpsters. The only other person in sight was the truck driver, who was casually leaning against his cab and smoking a cigarette while he played on his phone. He barely glanced at Korso.

Korso kept on walking past the parked cars running along the side of the building. He'd just passed the last dumpster and was about to turn into the access road when a man's voice said, 'Stop right there, my friend.'

ELEVEN

Korso halted in his tracks, groaning inwardly. So much for the stealth option. And that voice had sounded all too familiar for his liking. Keeping both hands at his sides, he turned slowly to face his challenger.

The man was standing in the shadows behind the dumpster closest to Korso, completely out of view of the truck driver. Wearing a dark windbreaker and black trousers, he stood about five-ten and had a fairly athletic build. He was also holding a pistol aimed at Korso's midsection. When he stepped into the light, Korso saw a heavily lined face under a thick thatch of greying hair that was receding at the temples. The deep-set eyes were pale blue and as hard as stone. Korso still recognised them after all these years.

'Balakin,' Korso said. 'I might have known. And there I was, hoping I'd never have to see your craggy face again.'

'That's not friendly, Korso,' Balakin said, his deep frown adding even more lines to his brow. 'Korso, that *is* your name now, yes? You change it so often, it's hard to keep up.'

'That's the whole point. And stop pointing a gun at me and I'll be as friendly as you want. Or maybe you should just pull the trigger, finish what you started all those years ago. You want me to make it easier for you and turn my back? I know that's more your style.'

'Now, now. It's not good to be bitter, my friend. Besides, that's all ancient history. I simply did what I had to at the time. You would have done the same, given the chance.'

'I had every chance, and I still didn't.'

He and Balakin had been forced to work together on a recovery job eight years earlier, back when he was just branching out in the 'salvage' business. The clients for that one were a pair of shady Algerian businessmen desperate to retrieve an accounts book stolen from their company safe, which contained enough evidence to put each of them away for five lifetimes. Each man had a particular agent in mind for retrieving the book. One wanted Korso, the other preferred an ex-KGB manhunter named Anton Balakin. In the end they enlisted both men's services, in the hope that two like-minded specialists working together would produce far quicker results.

The theory worked, to a point. Although neither liked the other very much, Korso and Balakin respected each other's abilities and agreed to put their personal differences aside for the sake of the assignment. They finally located the asset in question four weeks later, having chased the perpetrators responsible across three separate continents. The problems began when Korso led Balakin to the trio's hideout in Mexico City. Korso had planned for a furtive entry and minimal bloodshed, with Korso entering via the rear and Balakin acting as the diversion at the front. But Balakin had simply gone in guns blazing instead, killing the two male members of the group before Korso had even gotten into position. When Korso emerged from the kitchen, he'd sensed movement and quickly ducked to avoid a gunshot from the living room that would have taken his head off. When he got there he saw an armed Balakin standing over the female leader of the trio, who was lying on the floor, bleeding badly from a gunshot wound in her side. Although there was a pistol still in her hand, Korso could see there was no way she could have shot at him from her position. And since the other two members of the crew were already dead, that left just one culprit.

Balakin had seen Korso's expression change and was already bringing up his own gun to try again, but Korso was faster, and clubbed him on the back of the head with his own piece. The

Russian dropped to the floor, unconscious, while Korso tended to the woman's wound and stemmed the bleeding. Promising to let her go if she gave up the book's hiding place, she took him at his word and gave him the exact spot in the rear yard where they'd buried it. Once he'd safely retrieved the item, he watched the woman stagger into her clapped-out Fiat and drive away to parts unknown.

When Balakin regained consciousness some time later, a calm Korso explained how he'd already mailed the book to an anonymous PO Box he'd rented weeks before in Algiers, and that if Balakin ever wanted to get paid he'd better make sure Korso reached their clients in one piece. If Balakin only disliked Korso before, he loathed him after. That Korso was the one who presented the asset to their very satisfied clients only made it worse.

They each got paid in full, though.

'You should have killed me that day in Mexico City,' Balakin said now. 'Why didn't you? I've always wondered.'

'Killing's a bad habit to get into, and it wasn't necessary at the time. Anyway, I'd already planned ahead for your double-cross, so it didn't exactly come as a surprise.'

'So I gathered. Still, one other thing puzzles me...' Frowning, Balakin reached into his jacket pocket with his free hand and pulled out a phone. He pressed a quick key and raised it to his ear. The moment he heard the ringtone coming from Korso's pocket, he gave a thin smile. 'And that answers *that* question.' Pocketing his phone again, he said, 'Toss it over to me, will you?'

Korso pulled the other guy's phone from his pocket, and lobbed it underhanded to the Russian. Balakin just looked back at him, patiently. With a shrug, Korso used his left hand to slowly pull the little Walther PPS from his waistband and then tossed that over too. It landed at Balakin's feet with a loud clatter.

Balakin picked up the Walther and stuffed it in his jacket pocket. 'And what of my colleague? Is he still breathing?'

'He was when I left him. But he'll have an aching head when he wakes up.'

'My congratulations; you've just made yourself another enemy. And a nasty one at that. Vlad collects grudges like a philatelist collects stamps.'

'I'm already quaking in my boots.' Korso nodded towards the gun in Balakin's hand. 'Are you planning on using that?'

'Of course not.' Balakin stuck the pistol back in his shoulder holster. 'Now that you're unarmed we can converse like responsible adults. Believe me, harming you is the farthest thing from my mind.'

'Then why are you here?'

'You know why.'

'I don't know what you're talking about. I'm between jobs and came out here to visit an old girlfriend. When I saw three dangerous looking men shadowing me, I told her to head back to her apartment and lock the door while I made a run for it. I thought I'd made it until you showed up.'

That thin smile returned. 'And said with such a straight face too. You would have been a fine actor had you gone down that road, Korso. Now, let's stop all the dickering and cut to the heart of the matter, shall we? I know you're here for certain tablets supposedly secreted by a Darian Yanev before he died. Since your specialty is recovering the unrecoverable, it came as no surprise when I spotted a man who closely resembles someone I once knew strolling around the prison walls this morning. And I also have it on good authority that Darian Yanev's brother, Teodor, is currently holed up in that very same prison. Now isn't that a remarkable coincidence?'

Korso thought it best to say nothing.

Balakin pulled out a pack of Gitanes and took one out before offering it to Korso, who just shook his head. 'Oh yes, I forgot. You don't.'

'Still got the same expensive tastes, I see.'

'What's the point of money if you don't spend it on the good things in life?' Lighting his cigarette with a gold Zippo, Balakin pulled out his phone and pressed another number. When the other end picked up, he told his other man to collect Vlad from the toilet and to be at the staff car park in ten minutes to pick him up. He said all this in Russian, so Korso understood everything. Not that Balakin needed to know that.

Pocketing the phone, Balakin took another drag of his cigarette as he looked at Korso. 'Now why would you be poking around Sofia Central Prison, I wonder? Could it be that this Teodor might have an inkling where these pills are hidden, and could it be that he's willing to tell you if you were to somehow break him out? Please don't feel the need to answer. Consider these rhetorical questions.'

'Let me ask you something then: how did you gain this information?'

Balakin shrugged. 'Let's just say that I have access to reliable sources in all manner of places and institutions, which is one of the main reasons my services continue to be in such high demand. Does that answer your question?'

'More or less. Mostly less. So what do you want?'

'For you to be successful in your task, of course, whatever that task may be. But I think you should be aware that there are other parties who are extremely interested in purchasing those pills, should they be recovered, and for prices that would make any sane man's eyes water.'

'What kind of prices?'

'How does eighty million Euros sound?'

Korso made sure to look impressed. 'That's fairly extravagant. And these other parties, might they also have Russian accents by any chance?'

Balakin shrugged. 'They might, or they might not. Does it really matter?'

'Not particularly. Money's money after all.'

'My sentiments exactly. So can I take it the idea of passing over your current client in favour of one who pays significantly better doesn't fill you with disgust?'

'I'm a businessman, and if I *were* involved in what you're suggesting, then I'd have to take an offer like that very seriously. Let's say I'm very interested. Theoretically, that is.'

Balakin blew out smoke. 'Excellent. I was hoping you'd see the bigger picture here. Naturally, the money would be split right down the middle.'

'Even though I'd be doing the lion's share of the work? Doesn't quite seem fair, does it?'

Balakin shrugged. 'Very well, I can lower it to sixty-forty in your favour, but that's as far I'd be willing to go. I'm the one with the necessary contacts, remember.'

'As long as you remember that I haven't actually agreed to anything yet, Balakin. And I don't like being pressured either. Maybe you recall that about me, as well.'

Balakin held up both hands in mock surrender. 'No pressure at all, my friend. I'm simply making overtures that will hopefully lead to further negotiations between us. You still have free reign, as always.' He reached into his inner pocket and pulled out a small card and a pen. He wrote something down and passed the card to Korso. 'I can be contacted on that number at any time, day or night. Any time at all.'

Korso looked down at the phone number and quickly memorised it. As he was placing the card in his back pocket, he turned to his right and saw a car approaching along the small access road. It was the same Honda Civic as before. As soon as the driver pulled to a stop a few feet from the dumpsters, the rear door was pushed open and the one called Vlad emerged, glaring at Korso as though he might tear him apart with his hands.

Speaking in Russian, Balakin ordered him to get back in the car before he embarrassed himself further. Clenching and unclenching his fists, Vlad gave Korso one last murderous glare, and then did as he was told and got back in.

'See what I mean?' Balakin dropped his cigarette butt and ground his heel into it. 'Now thanks to you, he'll be in a rotten mood for days to come.'

'Is he ever in a good mood?'

'Hmm, you may have a point there.' Balakin opened the front passenger door. 'Anyway, I'm very glad we had this talk, Korso. I hope we can do it again. Can I offer you a lift anywhere?'

'I'll make my own way back, thanks.'

Balakin grinned as he got in the passenger seat. 'Of course.'

'But maybe hold off on returning his gun to him until I'm out of view.'

'Be assured of it. *Do svidaniya*, my friend. And do stay in touch.'

'Until then.'

Balakin shut the door, and Korso watched the driver make a U-turn and slowly go back the way he'd come. Once he was out of sight, Korso returned to the empty loading dock and did the same.

TWELVE

'Are you serious?' Lucian asked, her fork paused an inch away from her mouth. '*Forty* million Euros? And you didn't bite the guy's hand off?'

'You don't know him like I do,' Korso said.

The four of them were back at the safe house. It was just after five in the evening, and they were making their way through a variety of Chinese dishes that had just been delivered from a restaurant nearby. Open cardboard takeout containers littered the dining room table. Korso dipped his chopsticks into his chicken chow mein, lifted out some egg noodles and bean sprouts, and popped them into his mouth.

As he munched on his food, he said, 'I worked along-side Balakin eight years ago, and once was enough. He's ex-KGB, and the art of treachery and double-dealing is as deeply ingrained in his DNA as the workings of a combustion engine is in yours. He tried to kill me at the conclusion of that job, and would have tried again if I hadn't made the necessary preparations beforehand. So the amount he's offering now is meaningless, since nobody but him would ever see a penny of it.'

Cole grabbed a spring roll from one of the containers. 'So why are you telling us?'

'To make a point. This was just one instance. If Balakin and his contacts know about the pills, then there's every chance that other interested parties are also privy to this information. And if that's the case any one of us could be approached with a similar outrageous offer, maybe even coupled with a threat or two.'

Samara was nibbling on some crispy duck and rice, and not saying very much. But she was frowning deeply at what was being said.

'That's just your opinion, though, right?' Cole said. 'I mean, any offer that comes our way doesn't *have* to be a snow job. It could be genuine.'

'Ordinarily, I'd agree. But with these White Nights you're talking about potential profits in the billions, and that sort of money brings the very worst people out onto the playing field. The kind of people who consider a bullet in the head the ideal solution to any given problem. First and foremost, you have to assume whatever amount these parties are offering is a lie, and then go on from there.'

'So what did you tell this Balakin?' Samara asked.

'That I'd give it serious consideration, which should keep him out of my hair for a while. At least until we get Teodor out. But that's not what bothers me most. The four of us have to consider ourselves under the microscope now, when I was banking on us being able to work completely in the shadows from start to finish. Balakin himself admitted he's got spies everywhere, and I can only assume one of them is currently working out of the same embassy as our client, Belmont.'

Samara turned to him. 'What makes you say that?'

'By the fact that Balakin and his two goons completely left you alone and focused on me instead. I told him you were an old girlfriend I was visiting, but he knew I was lying right off the bat. That tells me he already knows you're involved in this thing, which implies he's already got someone in the embassy feeding him info.' He turned to look at Lucian. 'I'm just hoping that they don't know about you or Cole.'

She gave a loud snort. 'Nobody followed me today if that's what's bugging you. I go on full alert mode every time I get behind the wheel, and nobody ever creeps up on me unless I want them to.'

'What about you, Cole? Can I assume you employed some basic evasive manoeuvres on your route back here?'

Cole grinned as he bit into his spring roll. 'If I was paranoid before, it's only gotten worse since I got out of prison. I used two different cabs on the way back, and then finally ducked through one of the bus stations to catch an Uber I'd booked beforehand. And each time I was looking out the rear window so much I started getting a crick in my neck. There was nothing back there, I'm sure of it.'

Korso just nodded noncommittally.

'You don't look convinced,' Samara said.

'I'm just naturally wary. Because if I don't know who all the players are before we even start, then what else don't I know? I do know that his job would have been difficult enough with just the five of us involved. But now...?' he shrugged.

Cole leaned forward, looking anxious. 'Hey, Korso, tell me you're not thinking of calling the whole thing off. We can still do this, man. You know we can. We've got the financial backing, we've got access to all the intel we need thanks to Dog, and we've got the manpower. As far as I'm concerned, everyone else can go get screwed.'

Korso turned to Lucian. 'What about you? You feel the same way?'

'Hell, yeah. Look, you brought us all in to do a job, *amigo*. So let's do the damn job.'

He turned to Samara, who just shrugged. 'You already know my answer. I'm in, all the way.'

'Okay, that's settled then.' Korso popped some more noodles in his mouth. That's all he'd wanted to hear. 'Cole, you want to show us what you picked up today?'

Cole's good humour returned in a flash. 'Let me go grab the stuff from the garage. Wait here.' He got up from the table and disappeared into the utility room, where a connecting door allowed entry into the garage annex. He returned moments later, carrying some full-body work coveralls and a large bag of equipment.

Holding up one of the pale grey coveralls, Cole said, 'So what we've got here is the current top-of-the-line Tyvek body suit used by most government sanitation workers in this part of the world. They sure ain't cheap, I can tell you that. This thing's waterproofed all the way to the neckline, and comes with its own built-in rubber waders and gloves. I've also got us some hi-vis overalls to stick over them, they'll add credibility in case we're unlucky enough to be challenged by anyone else down there. Although if anyone starts asking questions we're screwed anyway, since I don't speak a word of the local lingo.'

'Samara does,' Korso said, 'and I know enough Russian to back her up if need be, so that shouldn't be a problem. What about respirators?'

'In the bag. I got us some full-face respirators with filter cartridges, as well as hard hats with built-in flashlights. Also, in the garage I got us four spare pairs of wellington boots, some additional heavy-duty flashlights, gas detectors, along with a couple of portable oxygen tanks in case we face a gas leak down there. I've also got us some portable diamond drills with extra-long drill bits, three combo chipping hammers, an air compressor, and a few more goodies besides. But they were too heavy to bring back with me, so I'll need Lucian to help me pick those up in the morning.'

'I'm impressed,' Samara said. 'You seem to have thought of everything.'

'Hopefully. Although there's still a few more pieces to get yet.'

'And on that subject,' Korso said, 'I think I've found us a decent panel van online. I've already texted you the weblink, Samara. The seller lives about fifteen kilometres away so I want you to call him up and arrange a viewing after we've finished eating, and take Lucian with you to give the engine a proper inspection. If the vehicle ticks all the boxes, just pay the guy in cash and bring it back here. We can start prepping it tomorrow.'

Samara nodded. 'Will do.'

'I'll give it the full works,' Lucian said. 'Poor guy won't know what hit him.'

'One more thing, Samara,' Korso said. 'How hard would it be to get your hands on a couple of pump-action shotguns for us? Just as a precautionary measure, but it's better to have a weapon and not need it than the other way around.'

'Well, I could probably find us something. You got a particular model in mind?'

'The Mossberg 500, or the Remington 870.'

She nodded. 'Both good choices. I'll look into it.'

Cole put down the body suit and took a pull of his beer. 'Korso, what about getting us down into the sewers in the first place? You manage to locate us a prime access point yet?'

'I was about to get to that.' Korso went over to the living area and retrieved his laptop. He set it down on the dining table and opened up a PDF file. 'I put Dog to work on the problem, and they managed to find me schematics of all the major car parks located within a three-kilometre radius of the prison. There are nine in total, but only three of those are actually state-owned.'

'Car parks?' Samara looked from Korso to Cole, and then back again. 'Did I miss a meeting? What's the relevance?'

'It's very simple,' Korso said. 'As you know, the only way to gain access to the sewer network is via one of the primary manhole entrances dotted around Sofia. Like most capital cities, you can easily spot them on most sidewalks or right in the middle of the streets, but those are all far too exposed and therefore no good to us. Having your vehicle break down over the manhole entrance might work in the movies, but real life's a little more complex. All it would take is one overly curious cop for the whole thing to fall apart in seconds. Besides, we need to be in total control of our entrance and exit for the entire duration, regardless of how long it takes.'

'Right,' Cole said, nodding. 'But fortunately, you can also find manhole entrances on other government-owned land, such as municipal car parks, and those are the kinds of locations we can have more control over. Especially if we happen to park directly over the manhole in a specially modified panel van.'

Samara began to smile. 'Okay, now I see it. And you say Dog's found something we can use?'

Korso nodded. 'There's a small three-storey car park one kilometre south of the prison, on Vazrazhdane, that looks almost perfect. I've got the plans here.'

The other three gathered around to look at the schematics on the screen, while Korso zoomed in on the relevant sections as he spoke. 'Now there are actually two manhole entrances on the premises, and both of them lead directly to the city's central sewer network. There's this one here, for example, but as you can see it's far too close to the spiral ramp that leads to the second floor, which means a constant stream of vehicular traffic passing by. The other one looks far more promising, though.' He zoomed in on another section. 'It's situated in a no-parking spot at the other end, about twenty feet away from the main stairway entrance, see? There's also a steel barrier there to partition it off from pedestrian traffic, so anyone parking there would still have some degree of privacy.'

'How do you know about the barrier?' Lucian asked. 'You checked it out yourself?'

'Not yet, I'll take a look tomorrow. But Dog was able to source a few photos of the building interior from one of those weird niche websites that caters to car-park enthusiasts.' Korso opened up another folder and double clicked on a handful of jpeg files. The first shot showed a line of parked vehicles in a dimly lit indoor car park that could have been taken anywhere. But the second was a mid-range shot of one end of the car park. In terms of content and composition it wasn't a very good photo, but it was all he had. Set into the wall at the end was a door marked EXIT, with two more unidentified doors to the right. There was part of a yellow steel barrier to the left of the exit, and then more parked cars on the far right.

'This is the area I'm talking about,' Korso said. 'You can't see it in this shot, but there's an open space to the left of this yellow barrier, where the manhole's located. Obviously the site's far from perfect, but it's an enclosed location, which means it's far easier to control. Now the car park's pretty small and only holds a maximum of one hundred vehicles, and the building itself was built back in the sixties and hasn't been modified since then, so it's pretty run-down compared to others in the area. Even better, there are no CCTV cameras anywhere.'

'You're kidding,' Cole said.

'Not according to Dog. The place is about as vanilla as they come. Apparently, there are long-range plans to demolish the building and build a conference centre on the site, but that's years away. Dog says there are only two attendants on the premises at any one time, and there's just a single automated barrier to get in and out, with one ticket machine to each floor. No lifts, no ramps for the disabled, just one set of stairs. It's really considered an overflow car park to its nearby larger brother, so it's not used anywhere near as much, which is another major point in its favour. But the good news ends there.'

Samara snorted. 'Yeah, I could see that coming. So what's the bad news?'

'The bad news is it's situated one hundred and fifty feet from the Capital Directorate of Interior, on Antim Street. That's the police headquarters building I mentioned earlier.'

Lucian slowly turned to stare at him, wide-eyed. 'You're saying this place is right in the cops' back*yard*?'

'Wonderful,' Cole said in a gloomy voice. 'So this car park handles their overflow?'

'I'd say more in theory than in practice.' Korso went to the satellite view of Google Maps to show them the car park's short distance from the main police building, which took up almost a whole block by itself. A main thoroughfare separated the two buildings, but the police headquarters was still far too close to the parking lot for comfort. He pointed to a flat-roofed annex at the south of the seven-storey metro building. 'The police have got their own underground parking in here, so they don't really use the other one much. It's essentially a cheap public car park used by employees working at nearby businesses.'

Cole sat down next to him, took another pull of his beer. 'But you say this place is staffed, right? What makes you think they're gonna just let us park in a no–parking zone for however long we want?'

'Money always talks. Once we've got the van, Samara and I can head over there and make them an offer. I'm sure they'll be happy to oblige.'

Samara was nodding her head. 'I've already got an idea about that.'

'Good.' Korso took a sip of his Coke. 'Now about getting into the prison itself. Cole and I talked it over earlier, and we both agree the entry point on the southeast side is the only realistic option for us.'

Lucian frowned. 'Why?'

'Lots of reasons. We already know that part of the prison was built a long time before the rest, so the concrete foundation will be substantially weaker in that section. Also the outer walls are only twelve inches thick, while the walls for the other wings are almost twice that. And best of all, much of that east wing has been closed off for the past decade, mainly for safety reasons. Apparently there was a collapsed roof that took out three prisoners outright, and put two guards in intensive care. Ever since then the administrators have blocked off most of that wing as unsafe, even for prisoners. The only areas still used are the isolation cells, the prison library, and a few offices.'

'It also means,' Cole said, 'we're less likely to come face to face with a bunch of armed guards on the other side. And we don't have to worry too much about any noises we make from drilling either. Best of all, because the stone's that much weaker it means I won't have to use C4 on the walls. Using even minute amounts of plastic explosive underground makes me nervous, so if I can find other ways to gain access I like to use them instead. C4's also deafeningly loud, which is exactly what we don't want.'

'So what will you use for this?' Samara asked.

'I ain't about to give away all my secrets yet. But it'll do the job with the minimum of noise, I guarantee it. We'll still need to do some drilling, but not as much as you might think. The only downside is it takes about twelve hours for the effects to work.'

Samara raised an eyebrow. 'You expect us to wait around in that stink all day?'

'That won't be necessary,' Korso said, who already knew what Cole planned to use on the walls. 'If we time it so we start in the afternoon, we can get everything ready and then all go up to the van and sleep in there overnight. Then we go back down the next morning and break through, and do what needs to be done.'

'Just like that,' she said. 'I like how you make it sound so easy.'

'That's one thing it won't be.'

'So how bad will it be down there?'

'It won't be pleasant, but I've done this kind of thing before and it's bearable as long as you've got the right equipment. The respirators will block out ninety per cent of the smell, but you get acclimatised to it after a while anyway. As for the route we'll be taking…' Korso opened another PDF file, which showed a basic plan of the sewer network in the centre of the city. 'This gives a pretty good idea of what we'll be dealing with.'

'*Madre de Dios*,' Lucian said. 'It looks like a maze down there.'

'That's exactly what is it is,' Korso said, 'although this map does cover a large section of the city. What we want is here.' He zoomed in on a section, which looked a lot simpler when seen up close. Tracing his finger along the screen, he said, 'This is the actual area of the sewer system we're interested in, called the eastern low-level outfall. Now from our point of entrance here, we'll proceed north along this tunnel until we hit this junction here, where we'll turn west. Halfway along there's a weir, or low dam, which shouldn't affect us as it's only used during times of heavy rainfall. But it means hefting the equipment over before we can progress to this smaller tunnel here, where we'll continue west...'

'How much smaller?' Samara interrupted. 'Look, I don't know about you guys, but this is not making me happy. In case you're interested, I suffer from mild claustrophobia.'

'You're not the only one,' Cole said. 'But all it basically means is that tunnel's six-feet high instead of sixteen. Some of the old pipes down there you can drive a truck through. Even the smallest have to be big enough for technicians to walk down. It'll be fine.'

'Six feet high.' She nodded. 'Okay, that's not so terrible.'

'So we continue west along here,' Korso said, 'all the way to this junction, where we'll turn north into this wider tunnel here. Now this is the tunnel we want, since it puts us right next to the sub-basement of the prison, which is also twenty feet below street level.'

Lucian was frowning. 'What's the sub-basement used for?'

'Solitary confinement, mostly,' Cole said. 'They've got twenty four cells down there where they keep the very worst prisoners, sometimes for days, sometimes for months.' He gave a dramatic shiver. 'When I was in that shithole in Alabama, I heard a lot of horror stories about the isolation block they had there. I expect the ones here are ten times worse.'

'Anyway,' Korso said, 'after comparing the plans of the prison with those of the sewers, Cole and I have managed to calculate the best possible entry point, exactly thirty-three feet along that wide tunnel I just showed you. Once we get through that outer wall, it'll put us deep in the closed-off section of the wing, in an empty room that previously housed the prison refectory. From there we should be able to access the rest of that east wing, and specifically the solitary cells, without too much trouble.'

'In theory,' Samara said.

'Pretty much everything's theory at this point,' Korso said, turning to her. 'But from that, you can probably guess where we'll need Teodor to be at the specified time. You'll need to be at your most persuasive when you go visit him.'

Samara rubbed a hand across her forehead. 'Christ, I'm not looking forward to that conversation.'

'Don't blaspheme,' Lucian said, still looking at Korso. 'I like that backup getaway plan of yours, by the way. But it does mean we'll need to get hold of two very specific vehicles at short notice, so they'll have to be new, or close to it.'

Korso nodded. 'Talk to Samara here. She'll arrange for the necessary funds to be transferred over to my business account here, and then I can wire it to whichever dealer you end up using.'

Samara nodded her head in agreement.

'Cool. So when are we doing this?'

'Today's Tuesday,' Korso said. 'My plan is to start work on the sub-basement wall on Thursday, and ideally get Teodor out the next day, on Friday. But it all depends on the weather forecast, on whether you can get the vehicles we need, and whether we can convince our boy to be where we want him at the specified time. We'll know more tomorrow. Is there anything else?'

When nobody replied, he said, 'Good. Samara, it's time you made a call to a guy about a van.'

THIRTEEN

Samara reached out her side window and pulled the ticket from the machine, then waited patiently for the steel barrier to slowly rise before driving them inside.

It was almost nine on Wednesday morning. The previous evening, she and Lucian had driven out and inspected the van for sale: a ten-year-old silver VW Crafter with over 150,000 miles on the clock. After a thorough inspection and test drive, Lucian had deemed it perfect for their needs and Samara had paid the man in cash. Lucian wasn't the easiest person to get along with, but she sure knew her vehicles. The diesel engine was a lot louder than they'd expected, but it always started first time and hadn't stalled once.

'Office over there,' Korso said at her side, pointing to their left.

'Uh-huh.'

Samara steered them straight ahead, passing parked cars on either side. The ground level was still less than half full, which meant the two upper levels were likely to be almost empty. That was good. Two hundred feet away, she could see the far end of the building matched the photo Korso had shown them perfectly. There was the clearly designated exit door, along with the yellow steel barrier to its left. As they got closer she could see a clear area next to the barrier, with cross-hatched yellow markings on the ground and enough space for maybe three vehicles. There were no signs to denote its purpose, but right in the centre of the markings was a square manhole cover.

'As advertised.' Samara came to a stop in front of it. 'Looks like Dog was right again.'

'Dog usually is.' Korso was looking in all directions, but there was no one else around at all. He got out of the van and took some close shots of the manhole cover with his phone camera. He got back in, shut the door. 'It looks good. Let's check that office now.'

Samara backed up and retraced their passage before coming to a halt next to the kiosk in question. There was no sign outside. Through the kiosk window, she saw a dark-haired man in dirty overalls sitting inside, tinkering with something she couldn't make out.

'You're the powerful American producer,' she said, switching off the engine, 'so say as little as possible. If you do speak, be brash.'

'I'll do my best.'

As they exited the van, she looked over at Korso again. He was wearing a navy pinstripe suit he must have brought along in his luggage. Samara had to admit it fitted his athletic physique as though it had been moulded to him. He was a strange guy, that was for sure. She could size most people up pretty fast, but after a full day together she still found him hard to read. He never seemed to act the way she envisioned. Since their pseudo-lovers act at the prison yesterday she'd been half waiting for him to make some kind of follow-up move towards her, but he'd barely glanced her way at all, except to talk shop. She'd seen how Cole looked at her, for instance. That was something she was used to. But Korso clearly couldn't care less, which was both refreshing and annoying at the same time.

Brushing the thought aside, she entered the small office and got into character. When the man looked up, she said in Bulgarian, 'Morning. You the man in charge here?'

'One of them.' The attendant dropped what he was doing and came over, looking each of them up and down. Samara clearly held his interest the most. 'Help you?'

'I hope so. My name's Anna. This here's my producer, Mr Richard Bauer. You may have heard of him. We represent a major US studio, and we're over here doing some location scouting for a big budget action movie currently being developed. What's your name?'

'It's Ivan. Hey, is this for real? A movie? Who's gonna be in it?'

'We're still waiting for signatures on contracts, Ivan, so I can't say. But we think this particular area has got great potential for a high-speed car chase we're storyboarding. Now it appears this lot is right in the middle of everything we want to see, so we're hoping you'll let us use it as a base of operations for the next couple of days. The van behind us holds all our equipment, so we'll be needing access to it at all hours, day and night.'

Ivan frowned as he rubbed an earlobe. 'Sure. We've got a third guy works the night shift, so that's no problem. You can park anywhere you want.'

'Good.' Samara pointed behind her. 'We want that spot back there with the yellow markings on the ground, right next to the exit door. You know where I mean?'

The frown grew deeper. 'That area's a no-parking zone.'

'We understand that, but we still want that space.' She reached into her jacket pocket and pulled out a fat roll of notes. 'How much do you take home a month, Ivan?'

He gaped at the roll, practically salivating. 'Uh, just over 1500 leva. Before tax.'

Samara counted off thirty 100 leva notes and offered them to him. 'There's two months' pay. Tax-free, no questions asked. Now do we get that space or not?'

Ivan looked over at her 'boss'. Korso just looked back at him impatiently, and then made a twirling motion to Sam.

'My boss is in kind of a hurry, Ivan,' she said. 'What's your answer?'

'Two days, you say?'

'Three at the most.'

Ivan took the notes from her. 'Lady, the space is all yours. But you'll have to pay the same to the other day guy, Vassil. He's on the second floor at the moment, cleaning a customer's vehicle. Same goes for the night guy too.'

'Not a problem. Give this Vassil a call and get him down here, but tell him to hurry, will you? We've got places we need to be.'

Ivan pulled out his phone and made a brief call, while Samara peeled off another thirty notes and put the rest back in her pocket.

Ivan finished the call. 'He'll be right down.'

'What's the night guy's name?'

'Boyan. He usually comes in around six, just before we quit for the day.'

'Fine. When he arrives, let him know the situation and that we'll come see him tomorrow night and give him the same amount. Think there'll be any problem with him?'

'None at all. He's always broke.'

When Vassil showed up a minute later, she let Ivan explain the situation to him. Once he was finished Samara handed over the cash, and Vassil tucked it into his overalls pocket. 'Pleasure doing business with you,' he said. 'Anything else you want, just ask.'

'All we ask is that you leave us alone whenever we're here. Deal?'

'Whatever you want,' Ivan said. 'You're the boss.'

Samara showed him her ticket. 'In that case, maybe you can validate this for me too.'

'Sure.' Ivan turned and grabbed a small book of coupons from the desk. He ripped one out and passed it to her. 'Just scan that against the reader and you'll be let out.'

'Come on, come on,' Korso said in a loud American accent. 'Let's wrap it up. We've got that meeting with the financiers at ten, and we're already running late.'

'Yes, sir.' Samara followed Korso back to the van, got in the driver's seat and started the engine. 'Well, that went better than expected.'

'You were at your charming best,' Korso said. 'Good practice for when you go and visit Teodor. Maybe you can try and—' He stopped at the muffled sound of a ringtone. He took his phone from his pocket, checked the display and took the call. 'Lucian. What's up?' He listened for a while, then said, 'Right. I'll meet you back at the house in about fifteen minutes and we'll go check them out.' He ended the call, smiling faintly.

'Good news?'

'Promising. After collecting Cole's equipment from the supplier, Lucian was on her way back to the house when she noticed a BMW dealer along the way and pulled in for a closer look. Apparently they've got two used silver E90 sedans on the forecourt, one a 2009 model, the other one from 2010. Lucian says they look practically identical, which would make them perfect for our needs. You heard the rest. We'll need some funds transferred over to my account, so you better call Belmont to arrange it.'

'Will do.' Samara put the van into gear and steered them towards the parking lot entrance. She inserted the ticket, and then placed the coupon's barcode against the reader. The barrier rose up and she drove through. 'You need me to come with?'

Korso shook his head. 'Now things are starting to come together the sooner we can get Teodor locked into position, the better. What time are visiting hours at the prison?'

'Generally two p.m. to four p.m. on weekdays.'

'In that case, arrange to visit Teodor this afternoon and let him know exactly what we need from him, and when.'

After checking left and right, she pulled out into the quiet street. 'He won't be happy, I can tell you that.'

'Freedom always comes at a cost,' Korso said, and looked out the window. 'He'll get over it.'

FOURTEEN

Balakin logged out of his Caymans account, then erased the browser history before shutting the laptop. The money had finally been deposited as promised, which meant one less thing to worry about. He allowed himself a small smile. It always paid to keep your options open; that's why he'd lasted as long as he had.

The room he was in was large and mostly empty, just like the others in the rented industrial unit, with the exception of the kitchenette and the bathroom. Three of those rooms also acted as sleeping quarters for his men, though Balakin had his own quarters elsewhere. Whenever he was on an assignment Balakin usually set up his HQ at a mid-level industrial estate on the outskirts of town, often with cash. Once you found the right person, there were always vacant units available for short-term rental, no questions asked. He'd found that industrial parks were about as anonymous as you could get; none of the other business tenants ever paid the least bit of attention to your comings and goings. It was the perfect way to hide in plain sight.

He looked over at Vlad, who was sitting in a chair glaring at whatever was playing silently on the large TV. He barely paid it any attention at all.

'Stop brooding,' Balakin said. 'When a man lets his emotions dictate his actions he's no longer of any use to me. And if you allow your anger towards Korso to affect my business here in any way, I'll make you regret you were ever born. Do you understand me?'

Vlad turned to Balakin and nodded. 'I understand, sir.'

'Make sure you do. Now where are the others?'

'Alexei went to get something from the garage, and Viktor is listening to today's phone recordings. He said that—'

Balakin raised a hand to cut him off as his phone vibrated on the table. He checked and saw it was for a video call. He made a brief hand signal to Vlad, who immediately switched off the TV and left the room without a word. Balakin waited for him to close the door behind him before taking the call.

The stern face of his current client immediately filled the screen. It looked as though he was calling from his office.

'I got your text,' Andrey Deleva said in perfect English, 'but couldn't talk until now. You have news?'

'I do.' Balakin lit a Gitanes and then recounted his meeting and conversation with Korso, holding back the more sensitive details that Deleva didn't need to know.

Once he'd finished, the CEO almost smiled. 'This all sounds very promising. And you feel sure this Korso is planning to break the brother out of prison?'

'I wasn't before, but I am now. Don't forget I worked alongside him before, and he never does anything without checking all the angles first. Like me, he's meticulous in his methods. If he was out there checking the prison grounds himself, that can only mean one thing. He's going to try and get Teodor Yanev out, and that can only be so he can then lead Korso to the prototypes. He didn't exactly deny it when I suggested it, either.'

'Not exactly surprising. Would you in his place?'

Balakin shrugged and took another drag from his cigarette.

'So just how competent is this Korso?'

Balakin hated to promote a competitor, but he also knew that being honest about Korso's skills would also benefit himself in the long run. So he said, 'He's right up there with me, if that's what you're asking. I've heard enough stories about him from some of my previous clients. He's very picky about the recovery assignments he takes on, but whenever he accepts a job he generally brings it to a successful conclusion. And he's not a man to be underestimated either. I did only once.' *And it almost cost me my life*, he didn't say.

'And what about this woman who was with him? Another member of his team?'

'Without a doubt. She had that professional look about her. Possibly ex-military. If I'd had an extra man with me I would have had her followed, but I deemed it best to focus on Korso at that point. We did manage to get some shots of her, though only in profile. But if we spot her again we'll know it.'

Balakin watched Deleva get to his feet and begin pacing around his office. 'I still think my original idea of calling in some favours and getting the brother temporarily released into our custody would be a better solution. It would cost, but it could be arranged. Then it would just be a matter of making him talk to us.'

'You mean like you talked to Darian? That turned out really well, didn't it?' Balakin tried not to laugh. It was always the same with amateurs, especially ones who sat behind desks all day. They always thought they knew better than the pros in the field. 'Besides, you and I both know the more people you involve in this thing, the more chance there is of it leaking out. Whoever you dealt with to get him released would be sure talk to somebody else, and by this time tomorrow the whole world would know about the prototypes.'

Deleva sighed. 'I suppose you're right. So what's your plan now?'

'Keep a close watch on the prison and the US Embassy as before, and basically leave Korso and his crew to get on with it. Once they get him out, we'll follow them to their hideout and keep it under surveillance.'

'And then?'

'And then we'll know who the other players are, and we'll see what kind of opportunities present themselves. One thing I know for sure: it doesn't matter how good a crew you put together, there's always at least one weak spot. So that's what we'll concentrate on.' Balakin blew out another plume of smoke. 'After that the rest will be easy.'

'I hope you're right, Balakin, I really do. For both our sakes.' Deleva ended the call.

I'm always right, Balakin thought. *That's why I'm still at the top of the heap.*

He leaned back in his chair and stared up at the ceiling as he took another drag of the cigarette. Deleva probably wouldn't have been smiling though, had he known the exact nature of the deal Balakin had offered Korso. And it had been a genuine offer too. Or almost. Just yesterday, Balakin had made contact with a senior minister at the Chinese Embassy in Sofia, and had a long discussion with him about the White Nights' existence and Balakin's current role in recovering them. The minister had then contacted his superiors back home, and when he came back thirty minutes later he assured Balakin that his government would guarantee him a payment of eighty million Euros on delivery of the pills. *If* they worked as claimed.

And now that the Chinese had deposited the agreed two hundred thousand Euros into his account as a retainer, Balakin was satisfied that they were serious. Whether he honoured their deal or not was another matter, of course. He rarely put all his eggs in one basket. Though he had to admit that eighty million *was* a vast amount of money, enough to last several lifetimes. But on the other hand his current deal with Deleva was just as enticing in its own way. After all, fifty per cent ownership of the White Nights patent once the pills were in their hands was nothing to be sniffed at. Take the quick payout now, or be patient and a wait for a much larger payout later? Or maybe there was a way to achieve both ends.

It definitely required further thought.

As did the matter of Korso, of course. The man had shown interest in Balakin's offer of a temporary partnership that morning, but had he been sincere? It was so hard to tell with

Korso. Balakin's instincts told him Korso was just telling him what he wanted to hear, but then again people could change a lot in eight years. It could be that Korso had finally come to realise that there were no sides in business, only self-interest. And half of eighty million dollars was still a fortune by anyone's standards.

Not that Korso would ever see any of it, of course. But that was something he could deal with later. There were plenty of other details to sort out first, such as locating Korso's current base of operations. Possessing that information would simplify his job greatly, and knowing the location *before* the jailbreak would be even better. Which reminded him… He had plenty of feelers out in the city already, but there was always room for more.

He picked up the phone again.

FIFTEEN

The prison guard led Samara to a table next to one of the barred windows and told her to wait, then gave her one final leering glance before walking back the way he'd come. Samara wasn't offended, having purposely changed into a low-neckline blouse for that very reason. Anything to keep the guards' attention distracted. She'd also had to suffer an extensive body frisk before being let into the west wing, just like last time. But that was also to be expected. Men were so pathetic and predictable, always thinking with their dicks. Most of them anyway. She pulled out a plastic chair and sat down.

Samara glanced around the modestly sized room. As before, about half of the tables were occupied by inmates on one side, with relatives, girlfriends, wives, or lawyers on the other. The hushed sound of whispered conversations buzzed all around her. Two more guards constantly patrolled the area, making sure nobody made physical contact with a prisoner. There wasn't a single moment that passed when Samara didn't feel eyes on her.

Eleven minutes later she saw the stocky Teodor Yanev being led into the room, wearing the same grubby navy tracksuit he'd worn during her previous visit. This time there was a purplish bruise around his right eye. The guard pointed Samara out to him, and Teodor made his way over to the table, nodding at several compatriots along the way. He took the seat opposite Sam, and stared unashamedly at her breasts before raising his eyes to her face.

'*Haresva li vi gledkata?*' she asked in a weary tone.

'Sure I like view,' he said, grinning as he rubbed a palm across his close-cropped scalp. 'I stuck in this bastard of a place with only other stinking men all around me, and you a sexy lady. So what you expect? And speak English, yeah? Ears in walls here.'

'You mean the walls have ears.'

'Yeah, what I said. Not so many people in here speak English good like me, so they don't know what we say.'

She pointed at the discoloured bruise above his eye. 'What happened to you, Teodor?'

He shrugged. 'Some asshole thinks he teaches me lesson over old business deal, so I teach him lesson instead. He with doctor now. No big thing. Happens in here all the time.' He crossed his arms and leaned in a little closer. She noticed part of a chest tattoo peeping out the top of his vest. In a low voice, he asked, 'So you got good news for me, or what?'

'Very good news. We're making the final preparations as we speak. We're planning to break you out two days from now, on Friday afternoon.'

Teodor's eyes widened. 'Two days? Hey, great. But why not night? Is better at night.'

'Because sounds travel further at night, and we'll be making a lot of noise with our drilling. This way, the general rush hour traffic coming from above should help drown out what we're doing below.'

Teodor gave an appreciative nod. 'Okay, I get it. So who plans this? You?'

'No, a man named Korso. He's done this kind of thing before.'

'Korso? What kind of name is this? He Russian or something?'

'Possibly. Or maybe Spanish, or Portuguese. Maybe even American. Nobody knows his true nationality, or his real name. Korso's just an alias he uses.'

'Sure, I know all about alias. Got a few myself. So what you want from me?'

'That's the tricky part.' She pointed down at the tabletop. 'We'll be coming in via the sewer tunnels and entering through the sub-basement in the east wing, where the outer walls are at their thinnest and weakest. Which means you'll need to be down there as well, all ready and waiting for us.'

Teodor stared back at her, his previous enthusiasm waning by the second. Finally, he said, 'East wing is solitary, lady. The Hole. Some guys go in, they don't come out ever. Others come out, they not the same as guy who went in. Bad place down there. No light. Only black. You know this, right?'

'We know it. But that's where you'll have to be if you want to leave this place. What's the least serious offence a prisoner can commit to be sent to the Hole?'

'Hey, you think there's rulebook in here? Prison not like world outside. All depends on mood of senior guard at the time. *Govno.*' He shook his head in disgust, looked out the window. Samara let him think it over. With someone like Teodor, she knew better than to press. He had to make the decision himself.

Finally, he turned back to her. 'Prisoner hits guard, he get sent to the Hole. Hurt guard bad, he get a month down there, maybe a year. But just a tap' – and he flicked a finger here – 'maybe he get a week. I hope.'

'So you'll do it.'

He snorted. 'What, you think I like it here? Maybe I trip and fall against guard so he knocks head against wall. Accident, yeah? Not so bad for him, so maybe not so bad for me.'

'Maybes are no good to us, Teodor. You have to—' Samara stopped as she spotted one of the guards approaching their table. Once he was within hearing range, she switched to Bulgarian, and said, 'You see, Darian only left me a little money when he died and that's all gone. I don't know what I'm going to do next, Teo. I guess I'll have to find a job?'

Teodor just shrugged. 'So get a job. What do you want from me? I can't help in here.'

They both watched as the guard moved on to another table. Switching back to English again, Samara said, 'Now you have to be sure you'll be sent to the Hole, and we have to be certain you'll be there when we arrive. We can't contact each other again after today, and we'll only get one chance. If we get inside and you're not where you're supposed to be, we'll have to leave empty-handed. And we won't be coming back any time soon.'

'And you forget all about special pills, huh? Only I know where Darian hid them. I stay here, nobody gets them.'

'That's how it goes sometimes.' She gave a casual shrug. 'Win some, you lose some. The world keeps on turning regardless.'

One corner of his mouth turned up. 'Yeah, around and around. Don't worry, lady, I be there on time.'

'Fine. You know how many guards are in that section, and what their routine is?'

'Sure. One big steel door before solitary, okay? Two guards stay outside steel door. They leave cons alone, only go in to deliver meals, or maybe bust some heads for fun or if cons are screaming too much. Your Korso, he might have to bust heads too, you follow? Like those two guards.' He smiled. 'I like to see that. Your boss got my money waiting?'

'The initial down-payment's all ready to be transferred to an account of your choosing. Five hundred thousand dollars, as agreed.'

'Good. You got place for me to hide out?'

'We've got a place for all of us to hide out. A large house. Very secluded and out of the way. You'll like it.'

'I like anything after this shithole. Maybe you and me could share room, yeah? Get to know each other some more? I show you some things.'

She smiled with one side of her mouth. 'There's very little you could show me that I haven't seen already, Teodor. Besides, you're not my type, and I'm definitely not yours.'

'Yeah? Maybe I change your mind about that, lady.'

'Best you put all that out of your head,' she said, sliding her chair back. 'You've got far more important things to worry about right now, like getting yourself put in the Hole. Arrange it today if you can. Tomorrow at the very latest.' She stood up.

'I know what to do, lady. You make sure you do your part, yeah?'

'Why else would I be here?' She gave him her sweetest smile. 'See you Friday,' she said, and gave a small wave as she turned and walked out of the room.

SIXTEEN

Andrey Deleva leaned back in his leather executive chair and watched his PA silently pick up her phone, diary, and legal pad from his desk. Sonja gave him that secret little smile he liked, and then sidled past an impatient Simov as she passed through the door to the outer office. She had the most beautiful ass and she knew it. Just one of the many things Deleva liked about her. That she was also good at her job was just icing on the cake.

Once the door clicked shut, Deleva said, 'So what have you got for me, Simov? Good news, I hope.'

'Better news, at least.' Simov walked past the imposing abstract tree sculpture that dominated the third floor corner office, and stepped over to the window. 'One of my sources at the prison just told me that Teodor had another visit this afternoon. The same woman who visited him last week, claiming to be Darian's fiancé.'

'Well, well, well.' Deleva extracted a Cuban from the humidor on his desk. Opening his desk drawer, he reached in and took out his cutter and carefully snipped the end of the cigar. 'It seems our chemist had a love life nobody knew about, least of all Darian himself. What name did she use?'

'Same as before: Katerina Petrova. It's a fake. I've already checked.'

'How long did she stay this time?'

'Not long. Ten minutes, maybe. But what's interesting is that this time she and Teodor both talked in English.'

Deleva looked up with raised brow. 'And you know this how?'

'My source is one of the guards on duty in the visitors' room. He said as he approached Teodor's table he could hear the two of them speaking in English, only for them to suddenly switch to Bulgarian as he passed by.'

'Did he hear anything useful?'

Simov shook his head. 'It wouldn't have made any difference anyway, since he doesn't speak the language. But I'd say this confirms what you've thought all along, that Teodor is the key to finding the prototypes.'

Deleva nodded in agreement. It also confirmed everything Balakin had told him earlier, which was surprising. And while he couldn't be sure this Petrova was the same woman Balakin had seen with Korso outside the prison, he thought it highly likely. Taking a box of matches from his drawer, he took one out and struck it against the side. He lit his cigar evenly, drawing the smoke into his mouth without inhaling. 'They're going to break him out, of course.'

Simov nodded. 'It's the only answer that makes sense.'

'I still wish I'd listened to my first instincts, though, and gotten you to go see Teodor yourself and offer him a similar deal.'

'It wouldn't have worked, boss. If Darian revealed to him where he hid the samples, then he would have also filled him in him on Vercogen's financial status as well. And he probably gave Teodor detailed descriptions of you and me too. Even if I *could* break into that stone fortress, Teodor would have seen through me in seconds. He's no dummy.'

Deleva could see all that plainly enough. He was just enraged with the whole situation, that's all. He couldn't help it. To think that he was so close to a revolutionary discovery that could save his company and make him a billionaire ten times over, *and* it legally belonged to him too. That was the worst part of all. As Darian's employer, it was a legally binding fact that everything the chemist produced on Vercogen's time and using Vercogen's resources automatically became the company's intellectual property. And so, armed with that knowledge, the little bastard had decided to steal it away from its legal owner and line his own pockets instead. Each time Deleva thought about it, the red mist descended and he visualised himself torturing the little shit to death all over again.

Except this time, *after* he revealed the pills' whereabouts.

Returning to the present, he quickly briefed Simov on his earlier video conversation with Balakin, and added, 'He seemed fairly confident that once this Korso broke Teodor out he'd be able to follow them all back to their hideout. But he was pretty vague on how exactly, and that troubles me. I don't like the idea of relying solely on that man's word, especially when the stakes are so high.'

'I got to tell you, boss, I don't trust that ex-KGB bastard at all. I still don't know why you brought him in on this in the first place.'

'Because he gets results,' Deleva said. But Simov was right. Balakin was a distinctly untrustworthy character, and the mere thought of giving such a man fifty per cent ownership of the pharmaceutical patent for the White Nights was almost more than he could bear. It would be so much better if they could get their hands on Teodor without his help, thus allowing Deleva to keep the exclusive patent rights for himself. Taking another drag of his cigar, he said, 'I don't suppose there's any way we could beat him to the punch and get our hands on Teodor ourselves?'

'I've been wondering the exact same thing myself, boss,' Simov said. 'And I think I might have something. It's a long shot, but who knows?'

Deleva leaned forward, suddenly alert. 'Tell me.'

'Well, during this past week I've been researching Teodor Yanev's life and habits before prison. I've had a few quiet talks with some of his past associates and discovered all kinds of things about our boy. And one thing they all agree on is that Teodor's a major sex addict. They say that there were few lengths he wouldn't go to in order to get laid, often three or four times a day. He even had a favourite part of town he'd go to, where the more downmarket brothels are located. Apparently, he was on very friendly terms with each of the owners, so that he could always get service at any time of the day. And if sex was pretty much all he thought about on the outside, it's a good bet he's only gotten worse since being locked up. I'd say the very first thing Teodor will demand after he gets sprung is female company.'

Deleva nodded, already seeing where this was going. 'And since he's the only one who knows where the pills are, he'll have the bargaining power to get whatever he wants. That particular area of town that he likes, where is it?'

'It's a little side street off Pencho Slaveikov Boulevard, near the Petrovska University Hospital. There are three brothels still operating in that particular street, all with local mafia protection, and they're the ones he always liked to visit most. There's also a bar there called *The Icicle* where he used to drink, along with one or two others. Some of the pros like to go when they're off-duty, often to pick up extra johns on the side. Now if we assume this crew successfully break Teodor out of prison, I think he'll find a way to contact one of his three favourite whorehouses at the first opportunity and get them to send over a girl.'

A smile began to slowly spread across Deleva's lips. 'That's not bad, Simov. Not bad at all. You've already made preparations, I assume.'

'I've waved some money around to some of the girls, and told them that if Teodor shows up at any point over the next few days, they only have to give me a call to receive a huge bonus on top. Every one of them was happy to oblige. I've also placed some of my men in the vicinity on watch, just in case Teodor actually shows up in person.'

'We couldn't get that lucky.'

'You can never tell, boss. But I thought it best to be prepared, just in case.'

'I agree. Well done, Simov.' Deleva took a long drag of his cigar, and blew out a long plume of smoke. Now they had a definite plan of action, tenuous though it might be, his mood had brightened a little. 'So now all we do is wait for them to make their move.'

SEVENTEEN

Lucian waited for the entry barrier to rise all the way up before stepping on the gas and steering them into the parking lot. It was three minutes past four on Thursday afternoon. The weather forecasts promised clear skies and sunny spells for the next three days, and far more importantly, no chance at all of rain.

Korso was in the Infiniti's front passenger seat, with Cole and Samara in the back. Nobody spoke. During the last twenty-four hours, Korso had gone through it all step-by-step, over and over again, until they had everything memorised to his satisfaction. Now it was time to put all that theory into practice. Korso had led enough of these kinds of operations to know the adrenalin was probably starting to kick in at this point, with everyone eager to get started on the task at hand.

The car park was almost filled to capacity today, with only a couple of empty spaces visible on this floor. Korso also noticed at least five of the parked vehicles were police cruisers, and they were just the ones he could see. But as before, there was nobody else in sight. Two hundred feet away, he saw their VW panel van was still parked in its designated spot. Cole had finished working on the van interior the previous afternoon, and once he'd packed it with all their gear, equipment and supplies, Korso and Samara had driven it out to the parking lot and placed it in the agreed spot. There were still a few other details to finalise up top, but Lucian could handle them while the others were down below.

She parked a few spaces away from the van, and left the engine idling. As Korso reached for his backpack by his feet, he said, 'You've got the spare keys for the VW?'

'Got 'em,' Lucian said. 'I'll also come out here whenever I can, and check if anyone's getting too curious about this van. Those cops across the way give me the creeps, being so close and all. I suppose you noticed the cruisers in the parking bays we just passed?'

'I noticed them. But in a city of this size the cops have got plenty of other problems to busy themselves with. We'll do our thing and let them do theirs. Everybody ready?'

Without a word, Samara and Cole each opened their respective doors and got out. As they carried their own packs to the van, Lucian gave Korso a final good luck salute. He gave her a single nod of acknowledgement and got out on his side. Slamming the door shut, he watched as she pulled away and drove back towards the exit.

Samara had unlocked the VW's side door, and both were already inside. With a final glance around the mostly empty car park, Korso joined them in the van and slid the door across, locking it behind him. He reached up and pressed the switch in the roof, activating the interior light.

One of the reasons Korso had picked the Crafter was for its more than ample cargo space. At fifteen feet long by six feet wide, there was enough room for the three of them and all their tools and equipment. The cabin was also completely self-contained with no direct access from the front, meaning nobody on the outside could see in. Arranged neatly along the side of the van were three mattresses and two air compressors, a number of shoring props and aluminium planks, as well as canvas workbags containing spare oxygen tanks, flashlights, portable camping lanterns, blowtorches, drills, jackhammers, cutters, pickaxes, shovels, and more besides. There were also two collapsible hand trolleys to transport it all. Cole checked each bag again to make sure everything was present and correct.

In addition, there was a brand new portable toilet in one corner, along with a concertina style privacy screen. Answering the call of nature wouldn't be much of a problem when they were down in the sewers, but since they'd all be sleeping in here later on these last two items would very soon be worth their weight in gold.

While Samara silently put her body suit on over her own clothes, Korso tested the newly installed single pulley system in the ceiling of the van. It was still solid. Grabbing the length of rope on the floor, he carefully attached it to the bottom of the overhead wheel, and then looped it down through the wheel on the moveable lower pulley before looping it back up through the top one again, making sure the rope was firmly seated into the grooves. Now they had a working compound lift system.

Cole came over, holding two cast-iron manhole lifting keys with extended D-shaped handles. 'Give me some space, guys.'

Korso and Samara moved back out of the way while Cole reached down and peeled a section of the carpet from the floor. Underneath, set into a black rubber frame, was a rectangular steel panel with bolt locks on all four sides. Cole had spent most of yesterday working on it. He unlatched each of the bolts, then pulled the plate up and placed it to one side. Through the hole in the floor, they could all see the manhole cover directly beneath them. Cole passed Korso one of the lifting keys, and then knelt down and inserted his into the side of the manhole cover. Korso knelt down and did the same on his side. Yesterday, he and Samara had spent over fifteen sweaty minutes loosening the cover, making sure the thing wasn't stuck fast into its housing. Korso didn't want any last minute surprises. On the count of three, he and Cole heaved up at the same time. This time the process was a lot faster, and the cover came away smoothly. Korso slid the thing across the concrete until the manhole opening was completely clear.

'Lamp,' he said. 'And flashlight.'

Samara grabbed one of the flashlights and a waterproof LED camping lantern with a length of rope already attached, and passed both over. Korso made sure the lantern was at its lowest setting before switching it on. At its highest setting the lamp was capable of giving off 1500 lumens, the equivalent of 100 watts, which would be enough to light up the whole tunnel. He slowly lowered the lantern down into the shaft, and it didn't take long before it reached the floor of the sewer. Korso let the rest of the rope fall after it, and then looked up at Samara and nodded.

Already dressed in full body suit, Samara carefully pulled a respirator over her face and then placed one of the hard hats on her head. Activating the lamp on the front of the helmet, she draped her legs over the hole while Korso aimed the flashlight directly at the shaft. They could clearly see the vertical iron rungs bolted into the side of the shaft, leading down. Samara dropped down to the surface of the car park, and placed one foot onto the top rung before descending the rest of the way down the shaft.

As soon as her head disappeared from view, Korso and Cole began fastening the two hand trolleys to the pulley system. Once they were ready, Korso called down, 'All good with you, Samara?'

She answered immediately. 'I don't think "good" is the best word to use, but it could be worse. The sewage is only ankle deep at the moment, and there are no rats in sight. This lantern's amazing, by the way.'

'It should be at that price. You ready for the rest of it?'

'Sure. Send the trolleys down.'

'On their way.'

Korso let Cole lower the two trolleys while he got busy putting on his own gear. Once he was fully dressed he took over from Cole, who had just finished attaching three of the bags to the pulley. It took another ten minutes before everything was below ground, of which the air compressors took the longest. Then Cole squeezed through the hole in the floor and descended the shaft himself. When he was halfway down, Cole stopped and aimed the beam of his flashlight up at the van.

After one last look around the rear cabin, Korso killed the interior light and slowly lowered himself through the hole. Once his foot touched the top rung, he grabbed hold of the rectangular steel panel and pulled it down with him, then pulled the carpet back across the opening. With only his head protruding from the shaft, and using Cole's flashlight to see with, Korso patiently affixed the steel panel to the bottom of the van and latched all four bolts against the frame.

Korso slid the manhole cover towards him until most of the shaft was covered. After descending two more rungs, he used both hands to slide the heavy manhole cover the rest of the way until it sank into its housing with a solid *whump*.

Then he descended the ladder all the way down to the bottom.

EIGHTEEN

While the other two finished loading the equipment bags, shoring equipment and air compressors onto the hand carts, Korso looked around their new surroundings. Samara had tied the lantern to a ladder rung. It was now at its highest setting, and the whole tunnel was illuminated for a hundred feet in each direction. Korso judged the chamber to be about ten or eleven feet in diameter, with plenty of room to move around. He noticed the sludgy liquid lapping against his rubber waders was currently at just over two inches high, while the wheels on the trolleys were about almost four inches in diameter, so no problem there either.

Korso activated the light on his hard hat, and pulled his respirator away from his face. He took one sniff and immediately wished he hadn't. The stench of the hydrogen sulphide in the air was noxious enough to make him gag. He quickly fitted the mask back over his face and pulled his cell from his pocket and switched it on. He'd already downloaded the sewer plans to his phone yesterday. He would have much preferred to upload them to his GPS and use them as a directional tool, but with no phone signal underground this was the only other alternative. Also attached to his wrist was a palm-sized camping compass, which would be essential in the hours to come. He slid it into his palm and checked the needle.

'Looks like it's back to basics again,' Samara said, nodding at the little compass.

'The old ways are still the best.' Korso pointed right. 'We want north. This way.'

He walked over to the trolley Samara had loaded up, grabbed the long handle and began pulling it along behind him. Despite the heavy weight, it moved fairly smoothly through the shallow waters. Samara walked at his side, while Cole was at the rear pulling the other cart. Their sloshing echoed loudly throughout the chamber as they waded through the liquid.

'How far to the entry point?' Samara held the lantern high like a beacon, the harsh light bouncing off the circular walls and casting rippling shadows over the oily water at their feet. 'You said it was only a kilometre from the car park, right?'

'As the crow flies,' Korso said. 'But we won't be moving in a straight line, so it's more like a kilometre-and-a-half. And because of these hand trucks we'll be moving at a much slower pace than usual. I figure we should probably reach our destination in about half an hour. Barring any sudden complications.'

'Bite your lip. We don't want any of those down here.'

'I'm with you there,' Cole said from behind them. 'Christ, it's hot under all this gear.'

Korso stayed silent. He figured now probably wasn't the time to mention the smallest tunnel ahead wasn't six feet high, as Cole had claimed in the briefing, but five. Possibly less. And at half a kilometre, it was by far the longest tunnel on their route as well.

They continued walking at the same slow-but-steady pace, each of them taking extra care not to slip on the silt-covered floor of the sewer. Korso constantly checked their route on his phone, mentally counting off the metres as they went. After a couple more minutes the light from the lantern picked out a T-junction up ahead, exactly where it was supposed to be.

'We turn left up there.'

'You're sure?' Samara asked.

'Well, we can turn right if you want, but it'll only take us to the waste treatment plant five kilometres east of here. Left is better.'

She sighed. 'A comedian. Just what I need right now.'

When they reached the junction, Korso led them into the westward tunnel and they kept on going. This tunnel was a little narrower, but not by much. The next one would be worse. When they were about halfway along, Korso slowly came to a stop and looked at the walls to his left and right. The others halted as well.

'What's wrong?' Cole asked.

'According to the plans there's supposed to be a small weir around here. I don't see it anywhere.'

'Let me take a look.' Samara aimed the light to their left. Carefully inspecting the wall, she took a few steps forward before coming to a halt. She knelt down. 'Here's something. Just under the water there's the remains of four bricks protruding out of the wall. Nothing else though. Maybe the rest of the dam just corroded over time.'

Korso came over to where Samara was kneeling, and saw she was right. Time had gradually smoothed over what was left of the bricks sticking out of the wall. He ran his boot over the floor where the dam should have been. It felt a little more uneven than the rest, but that was all. 'I guess nothing lasts forever,' he said. 'But at least it shows we're still on the right track. Let's keep going.' He grabbed hold of the cart handle and started off again. Samara and Cole followed suit.

After five more minutes of walking in silence, Korso finally spotted the next T-junction up ahead. It was more a fork really, and branched off into two separate tunnels – one leading north-west, and the other going east – that were significantly narrower than the channel they were traversing. Nobody said anything, but Korso could already see the lantern starting to wobble more than before, and Sam's breathing was becoming shorter and more laboured. He had the distinct feeling she was a little more than 'mildly' claustrophobic, as she'd previously claimed.

'We want that left hand tunnel there,' Korso said. 'Then it's just a straight line till the final junction. Shouldn't cause us any problems.'

'Don't jinx it,' Cole said.

Samara said nothing at all, although the light from the lantern continued to judder.

Korso had to lower his head and slouch in order to enter the northwest tunnel. He was just over six foot tall, and judged this tunnel to be just over four feet from floor to ceiling. He'd never been too bothered by small spaces before, but even he felt crammed in and constricted. He looked over his shoulder and saw Samara tentatively step into the channel behind him with her head lowered, lantern leading the way.

'Good,' he said. 'Keep that light as high as you can.'

She didn't reply. Nor did Cole at the rear. But the light was shaking quite badly now. Korso kept moving forward without commenting on it, knowing it was the worst thing he could do. With so little room to manoeuvre, the light couldn't travel anywhere near as far and it felt as though the walls really were closing in on them. Their walking pace was a lot slower too, which only made it worse.

Over the sloshing sounds of their steps, Korso said, 'About five years ago I was emailed by a man named Alain. He wrote that he and his partner owned a computer software company that catered for the aviation market, developing apps and software for 3D product design, simulation, manufacturing, and so on. They were very successful, and he quoted me an average yearly net income of two million Euros. I did some research and discovered that quote was somewhat on the low side. Most years they took in close to three million. They had offices in Nice, Frankfurt and Madrid, and were thinking of setting up additional offices in the US and Canada in the near future.'

Korso stopped speaking for a moment, and just concentrated on putting one foot in front of the other. He noticed the light coming from behind him was now steadier than before, and smiled to himself. It was working. After a few moments, Samara said, 'Let me guess. This Alain guy got screwed over by his business partner, big time.'

'Got it in one. When Alain came back from a fortnight's vacation in Barcelona he discovered his partner had completely emptied their bank account of seven million Euros, cashed in the negotiable bonds they'd kept in the safe, which amounted to another four million, and then disappeared. And to add insult to injury, this guy had also taken a Picasso still-life that they'd previously picked up at auction and put on display in their shared office. It was a relatively small piece, measuring just ten inches by six, but it was from the artist's popular surrealist period so they knew how lucky they were to own it.'

'Worth how much?' Cole asked from behind them.

'It cost them €2 million five years before, and it was worth double that by the time of the theft. It had been a while since I'd taken on a job, so I checked out this Alain's bonafides and then called him up and arranged a meeting at a small anonymous café in Nice, where I asked him what he wanted from me. I reminded him I wasn't a private detective, and that even if I was his partner would surely have sent the stolen funds to a variety of offshore accounts around the globe, and that it would be close to impossible to get it all back.'

'Except he didn't want the money,' Samara said. 'He wanted that Picasso back.'

'You've heard this story before?'

The echo of Samara's chuckle sounded good in the enclosed space. 'Money's replaceable, but art's one-of-a-kind,' she said. 'Plus this is Picasso we're talking about.'

'Well, you're right again. Alain knew the embezzled funds were gone for good, but he wanted that artwork back and he wanted me to get it for him. I told him I'd do it for a third of the painting's market value: €1,333,000.'

'Meaning he'd have had to sell the painting in order to pay your fee?'

'No—' Korso paused as the cart's front wheels caught on something below. He yanked the trolley over the obstruction, and kept on going. 'No, Alain was too smart to put all his eggs into one basket. Amongst his real estate investments were three beachfront properties on the Côte d'Azur, and he'd just sold one of them for over three million, so he wasn't exactly struggling. Once I knew he had the money I got to work locating the Picasso. It took me a fair while, but I finally discovered where the partner had stashed it.'

'Where?'

'In a safety deposit box located deep in the sub-basement vault of a private Paris bank. I rented one of their boxes for myself and took a good look around the place, but it was clear that the bank's security was far too formidable for a direct assault. I had to think of another way in, and approaching via the sewer tunnels was the only other feasible alternative, which naturally meant assembling a team to help me get in and out.'

'Okay,' she said, 'I'm starting to sense parallels here. So how did it all go?'

'Logistically, it was a lot tougher. The Paris sewers date back to the fourteenth century and are almost like a second city mirroring the one above, even down to the street signs. Much of it's been turned into a tourist attraction by the city, but there are still hundreds and hundreds of small spurs and detours that are rarely visited, or even used, to this day. And one of those little-used spurs actually led to within ten feet of the base of the vault itself, resting on a two-foot-thick concrete foundation with reinforced steel bars, which in turn rested on a pair of thick concrete pilings. So we'd have to use jackhammers to get through the clay of the piling until we reached the concrete base, shoring as we went along, and then we'd then have to blast our way through the floor itself in order to get inside the vault.'

'Tough job,' Cole said. 'What did you use, C4 or semtex?'

'Semtex. We also had to time it perfectly so the traffic above would cover the noise of the blast. It was tricky, but manageable.'

'What about the pressure alarms inside the vault? Doesn't matter which way you come in, they'd activate the second you set foot inside there. That bank would have been swarming with gendarmes in seconds.'

'Which is what happened. But I'd planned it over a public holiday so the time lock wouldn't open for another forty-eight hours, and there were no exterior signs of forced entry. The police just assumed it was a fault in the system, which is a fairly common occurrence with bank alarms.'

Korso was still looking ahead as he spoke, still counting off the yards they'd covered. Further ahead he could just make out the next junction, dead on schedule. Time to wrap this up. 'As it turned out, I was in and out of that vault within three minutes, with the Picasso safely in my hands. We were out of the sewers and back on dry land within thirty. Alain was very pleased at the handover, and paid the agreed fee in full. But I'll never forget that long tunnel spur we had to travel down to reach the vault. It was only two-feet high in some places, and we had to crawl most of the way while hauling all our equipment behind us. You can probably imagine the kind of effluent we had to negotiate. It was like being buried alive. So this tunnel is easy-street by comparison. The next junction's just up ahead, by the way.'

'Well, all right,' Samara said.

Once Korso reached the T-junction he waited there until the others caught up. When Samara saw the sizes of the two tunnels leading off from it, she smiled at Korso for the first time since they'd descended. Both tunnels looked to be around ten feet high.

'This tunnel on the left is the last one,' Korso said. 'We're directly under the prison right now. Who's got the tape measure?'

'Over here.' Cole unzipped one of the equipment bags on his trolley and reached inside. He pulled out a 50-metre tape measure and handed it over.

'Samara, you go ahead with the lantern, but not too far.' As she moved further into the chamber, Korso placed one end of the tape measure against the wall at the opening. 'Cole, hold this here for me. Keep it steady.'

Cole took the end and held it tight against the wall. At the same time he took an opened pack of Marlboros from his overalls pocket, and pulled a cigarette out with his lips.

Korso immediately removed the stick from his mouth and snapped it in two. 'You know better than that. No naked flames down here.'

'Shit, I forgot. Sorry.'

Shaking his head, Korso let the rest of the tape unwind itself from the large spool as he followed Samara into the wider tunnel. When Korso reached thirty-two metres exactly, he stopped and took a long piece of chalk from his overalls pocket. Samara moved in with the light as he etched a large cross onto the curved brick wall at his left.

'Okay,' he called out to Cole, who joined them moments later. Korso pointed at the chalk cross. 'There's our point of entry. Now let's get everything set up.'

NINETEEN

Korso dropped his pickaxe and carefully backed out of the man-sized hole in the sewer wall, dragging as much rubble and debris back with him as possible. They'd taken turns to dig over the preceding four hours, starting with the jackhammers and pneumatic drills before eventually switching to manual tools. To prevent possible cave-ins, he and Cole had made sure to fortify the sides and ceiling using the shoring rods and units and the aluminium planks they'd brought with them. So far, they'd performed exactly as advertised. As soon as Korso's feet touched ground again, he moved out of the way while Cole hauled the rest of the rubble out by hand. He then used a shovel to even the debris out until it began to drift down the tunnel along with the rest of the sewage.

Thanks to the four lanterns hanging from the walls, the tunnel was now as bright as day. Samara came over and handed Korso a bottle of water. Pulling up his respirator, Korso downed half of it in one go. H20 had never tasted so good. Close quarters digging was hard, hot and tiring, especially with all the extra layers of clothing they wore.

'How close are we?' Samara asked.

'I broke through the sewer tunnel wall twenty minutes ago.' Korso paused as he took another gulp of the cool water. 'I'd say we've got about another three feet of centuries-old mud and crap to get through before we get to the sub-basement wall of the prison itself. But once we've gotten all that out of the way we should have ourselves a decent-sized chamber from which to work. Or one of us will, anyway.'

'That prison wall's made of natural stone,' she said, taking the water back, 'meaning it's gonna be a lot tougher to get through than brick.'

'Which is why I'm here,' Cole said, joining them. 'And my bag of tricks, of course. Don't worry about it. We'll get through it all right.'

'Can't argue with a confident man,' she said, and turned back to Korso. 'How you doing? Want me to take over?'

Korso appreciated the offer. He knew how hard it was for her to go into such an enclosed space, yet she never complained when it was her turn. 'It's still my shift,' he said, pulling down his respirator. 'I just needed a breather, that's all. What's the time?'

Cole checked his watch. 'Just coming up to nine. Thirty more minutes until supper.'

Korso nodded. They'd brought plenty of pre-packed sandwiches and snacks along with them, but all three had agreed to eat them no earlier than nine thirty. Right now, Korso was really looking forward to that twenty-minute snack break. He had no doubt Samara and Cole felt the same. But it meant they'd be lucky to be done by 2 a.m. at the very earliest. It would be a long night. Still, it was no less than any of them had expected.

After tightening his gloves, Korso grabbed one of the jackhammers leaning against the wall and made sure it was still connected to the air compressor, and also pulled out an extra-long chisel attachment from one of the equipment bags. Taking both tools with him, he climbed back into the hole in the wall and resumed work.

—

By the time they'd finally cut through the mud, clay and rock separating them from the prison, and then cleared all the rubble and debris out of the hole and safely shored up the chamber, it was already 2:20 on Friday morning. They were all very tired. The work had been slower going than Korso had hoped – the space between the sewer and the prison had been over four feet deep, not three — but at least the hard part was mostly over. He hoped.

The last remaining barrier was the reinforced stone wall of the prison itself, and that was Cole's task. The chamber they'd cleared for him was barely four feet by four, and shored on both sides and ceiling with the last of the aluminium plates, but the lantern Korso had put in there helped dispel the oppressiveness.

Korso was crouched down in the sewer, watching Samara as she used the jackhammer to drill through the sub-basement wall. Like him, she was wearing ear protectors. Even so, the noise from the drilling was thunderous in the enclosed space of the tunnel.

Finally, the drilling stopped. Samara placed the jackhammer on the floor of the chamber and carefully crawled through the hole, taking the hand Korso offered before climbing out into the tunnel. She removed her ear protectors and respirator, and then blew out a long exhausted breath.

'All done?' Cole asked, still stirring his slurry in the plastic bucket. Instead of the respirator, he was wearing thick rubber gloves, safety goggles and a dust-proof mask.

'Just as you instructed,' Samara said. 'So what the hell is that stuff anyway? It looks like cement, but I'm assuming there's more to it than that.'

Cole smiled as he worked the paddle. 'And then some. You're looking at what's known as non-explosive hydro-expansive demolition grout. It's basically a chemical agent that fractures rock, stone, and even reinforced concrete. I've heard it called Chinese Dynamite in the trade, but I couldn't tell you why since it wasn't even invented there. All you have to do is combine half a gallon of cold water with five kilos of this dried cement-like powder and then stir it into a semi-liquid mixture like I'm doing now, making sure there are no lumps. Then once it's ready, you simply pour or squeeze the concoction into the pre-drilled holes in the concrete you want broken up, and then you wait.'

'For roughly twelve hours,' Korso said.

Cole nodded. 'Ideally, yeah. Although it could be sooner, depending on the outside temperature and how porous the rock is that you're trying to break though. But in our case, I'd say we'll need twelve hours minimum. As the name suggests, the chemicals in the grout will cause it to slowly expand until cracks start appearing in the surrounding rock. Those cracks will keep getting wider and deeper until, after twelve hours or so, the rock will just break apart naturally. We might need to drill some more tomorrow, but it won't be much. The chemicals in this shit do much of the work for us.'

Samara looked at the hole in the wall. 'If this grout is supposed to be so good, how come we didn't we use it on the sewer wall too?'

'Mostly for reasons of time,' Korso said. 'Doing it that way would have added at least another day to the whole job, and that's time we can't afford to lose.'

'More than a day,' Cole said. 'It would have been easy enough to drill holes into the sewer wall, but we'd have to wait twelve hours and come back and do the same thing with all that clay and dried mud after. Then another twelve hours goes by before we can go start working on the prison wall itself. That's a day and a half already, not counting sleep time.'

Korso nodded. 'And we've already got Balakin on our trail, and possibly others we don't even know about.'

'There, that should do it.' Cole stopped stirring, and pulled out the plastic paddle. 'Okay, somebody want to pass me a bottle?'

Korso stepped over to the first cart. From one of the equipment bags he grabbed a plastic squeezy bottle with a fifteen-inch tube protruding from the top. He passed it to Cole, who unscrewed the cap and then poured some of the viscous solution into the container.

'Okay, while I start squeezing this mess into the holes, you two can prepare some more bottles for me. By the way, this stuff is seriously toxic so make sure you put on your safety goggles first. And don't hang around; this'll start to solidify after fifteen minutes.'

While Cole crawled through the hole in the wall, Korso returned to the equipment bag and pulled out the rest of the squeezy bottles, along with two sets of safety goggles for himself and Samara. Then they started filling the empty bottles with the rest of the grout. It was easy work, and didn't take long. Korso passed the five full bottles down to Cole in the chamber.

It was almost two forty when Cole finally emerged, smiling, from the hole. He tossed the last bottle into the sewage at their feet. 'All done. Even had some left over.'

'Good,' Korso said. 'Now back to the van.'

'Not a moment too soon,' Samara said, collecting the camping lanterns from the walls. 'I just wanna be able to breathe though my nose again.'

With no equipment to carry back other than the lanterns, the return trip was a lot less stressful than their arrival. Even that long narrow tunnel didn't seem to bother Samara too much. Or if it did, she didn't show it. Nobody talked much on the way back. Korso came away mostly satisfied with the night's work thus far, although something at the back of his mind kept niggling at him. Maybe it was the fact that things had gone more smoothly than expected. He'd learned through painful experience that no matter how carefully you planned, problems invariably arose at some stage or other. And usually at the worst possible moment. But he thought it probably best to keep these vague misgivings to himself, especially as they might well come to nothing.

It was just after three in the morning when they reached their original starting point, whereupon they did everything in reverse. Korso went first up the ladder, and used his shoulders and arms to carefully push the manhole cover out of its housing with the minimum of noise. Once he'd slid it to the left, he unlatched the four bolts of the steel panel on the underside of the van and removed the plate, and pushed the section of carpet above out of the way. Then he hauled himself up into the dark interior of the van.

Once the other two had joined him, Korso pulled off his respirator and overalls and placed them in the corner of the cabin. Meanwhile, using just a single lantern for illumination, Cole used the lifting keys to manoeuvre the manhole cover back into its original position underneath them.

'Man, fresh air never tasted so good,' Samara said, removing her own overalls. Like Korso, she was wearing just jeans and a t-shirt underneath. 'I am well and truly beat.'

'We all are.' Sitting cross-legged on the floor, Korso pulled his phone from his pocket and switched it on. Straight away, he saw that he'd received thirteen missed calls since they'd lost the signal in the sewers. They all came from Lucian. The first had been logged at 7.34 the previous evening, while the latest call had been just forty minutes ago. Meaning whatever the snag was, it looked to be a big one.

Korso called Lucian, listened to the ringing tone. It was picked up after six rings.

'So you're back,' Lucian said, sounding wide awake. 'I been trying to get hold of you for hours.'

'I just found that out,' Korso said. 'What is it?'

'We've got problems.'

TWENTY

'I figured as much.' Korso held back a sigh. As ever, he'd been right to be wary. 'What kind of problems?'

'You know that police building across the way, the one you advised us not to worry about? Well, after dropping you guys off yesterday, I was exiting the car park when I passed a couple of blue-and-whites coming in, one right after the other. So I decided to drive past the front of the precinct building and see what's what, and that's when I saw the emergency bollards and sawhorses blocking their underground entrance. That immediately got my radar up, so I found a place to sit and just watched for a while.'

The van's interior light came on suddenly. Korso shielded his eyes from the glare, and saw Cole had fixed the floor plate back into place. He and Samara were watching him, each aware that something was afoot. Korso put the phone on speaker and placed it on the floor.

'Now we can all hear you, Lucian,' he said. 'Go on.'

'Okay, so I'm watching the front of the precinct after dropping you off, and for half an hour all I see is workmen in hi-vis jackets going in and out of their car park entrance, and various work vans and cement delivery trucks coming and going, but hardly any police cruisers. Now I figure if they've barred entry into their own car park, then they have to be doing some major renovations down there, you know? And if that's the case…'

'…then the cops will have to start using the overflow car park instead,' Korso finished for her.

Samara groaned aloud. Cole sat down on the floor, and mumbled, 'Shit on a stick.'

'Tell me the rest,' Korso said.

'So I drove back to your car park, and watched the entrance to that one for a while. And sure enough, it wasn't too long before I saw another blue-and-white go inside, and then another one came along, and then another after that. I tried calling you then, but you must have already entered the sewers by that point 'cause I couldn't get a signal on my cell. Couldn't you have gotten us some decent walkie-talkies, at least?'

'Wouldn't have done any good,' Korso said. 'They still need radio signals in order to work, and the only way to access those underground is to piggy-back off an already existing leaky feeder antenna system, and tune into their specific radio frequency. Which means everyone else on that frequency would be able to eavesdrop on us.'

'Well, it was just an idea. So, anyway, I stuck around for another half-hour and saw at least a dozen more cruisers enter the place. It was like a cop's convention in there, police uniforms everywhere you looked. It must have been the end of a shift or the start of the next one, so I decided to drive back to the safe house before anyone took an interest in me.'

'So the police vehicles are still parked here?'

'That's what I'm saying. I drove back at about nine p.m. for another look, and I calculate at least half of the first floor was made up of cop cars. I'm not exaggerating.'

Korso shook his head slowly. The longer this conversation went on, the worse it got. 'Was anyone showing particular interest in this vehicle?'

'Not as far as I could see, although I was only in there for fifteen minutes or so. But you know it's only a matter of time before one of those uniforms decides to poke his nose around that generic looking van parked in the no-parking zone, and then what?'

'Then we're screwed,' Cole said.

'I don't see how,' Samara said. 'Even if they do break in here, all they'll find is what's left of our equipment and three bare mattresses. Depending on their timing they might even find us in here, sleeping. Sure it's suspicious, but we're not likely to get arrested for that.'

'That's not what I'm worried about,' Korso said, 'It's not difficult for the police to get inside a vehicle if they really want to, and if one of those cops does decide to take a closer look inside this van when we're not here, then all he has to do is pull up the carpet and he'll see that panel in the floor. Once he removes that and notices the manhole directly underneath it, he'll easily put two and two together and then we're really in trouble. And with no phone signal underground, there'd be no way for Lucian to warn us a bunch of cops are up here waiting for us. We come back with a recently escaped convict in our custody, they'll slap the cuffs on us in seconds, and there's no lawyer on earth who can get us out of that one.'

'So what the hell do we do now?' Cole asked.

Korso thought for a moment. 'We get some sleep as planned. Tomorrow we'll continue with the prison break as before, with the only change being our exit route. Before we head back down to the sewers we'll have to wipe our prints off every surface in here, because we won't be coming back here again.'

'Good thing we had that backup getaway plan of yours,' Lucian said.

'Speaking of which, is everything set up at your end?'

'Almost. I've tuned up the engine of the first Beamer until it's about ready to take off. The other two vehicles I'll take care of at first light tomorrow. Everything will be ready.'

'Good. You best get some sleep yourself. I'll call you again late morning.'

'Right.' She clicked off, ending the call.

Nobody spoke for a while, all three remaining lost in his or her own thoughts. Korso accessed the sewer plans on his phone again, and rechecked the alternative underground route he'd gone over with Lucian yesterday.

Finally, Samara breathed a long sigh and said, 'For a brief moment there, I was thinking we'd come straight back to the van with our prisoner in tow, and then just cruise on out of here and back to the safe house without a care in the world.'

'Nothing's ever that easy,' Korso said. 'At least not in my experience.'

'Or mine,' Cole said. 'Maybe one of us should take a look-see.'

'I'll do it,' Korso said. 'Kill the light first.'

Once Samara had clicked off the interior light, Korso gently slid open the van's side door and stepped outside. The car park was as quiet as a tomb, not even any traffic noises coming from outside. Looking around, he saw about sixty parked vehicles on this floor alone, all spaced out in random fashion. Well over half had visible police markings on the sides. When he heard vague sounds coming from the direction of the main entrance, Korso got back into the van and slid the door shut. A second later, Samara switched the light back on.

'Well?'

'Lucian wasn't exaggerating,' Korso said. 'The place is packed with police cars, even now. And the ones that aren't could still be unmarked police cars for all I know. I'd say that pretty much settles it.'

'Great.' Samara pulled a mattress from the wall, and used it as a seat.

'So once we've gotten Teodor out,' Cole said, 'which route do we take?'

'You remember that last T-junction after the narrow tunnel,' Korso said, 'where we turned north into the final tunnel instead of south? This time we'll have to take the south route instead, and then go on from there. According to the plans it's just over a one-kilometre journey along three connecting tunnels, so it should take us less time to walk it. Especially as we won't have to lug any equipment back with us.'

'And we'll end up where exactly?' Samara asked.

'Under the visitors' car park at the National Hospital of Cardiology, located less than one klick southwest of the prison. The only problem is, this time the manhole exit we want is right out in the open where anyone can see us. According to Lucian, it's a fairly busy car park too. Busier than the one we're in now.'

Samara furrowed her brow at this. 'But she'll be there waiting for us, right?'

'She'll be waiting for me, Cole and Teodor,' Korso said. 'You'll no longer be with us by that point.'

Sam's frown lines grew deeper. 'Please explain that.'

So Korso explained.

TWENTY-ONE

Korso, Samara and Cole returned to their entry point in the sewer at 3.12 p.m. on Friday afternoon. Samara positioned three of the four lanterns on the walls, while Cole took the fourth with him into the hole and then set the light down in the tiny chamber beyond. Korso stood by the opening, waiting for Cole's verdict as he inspected the effects of the grout on the sub-basement wall.

In the van, they'd all had a decent, if fitful sleep, while the portable toilet had proven to be worth every penny Korso had paid for it. More importantly, no curious policemen had attempted to gain access to the vehicle while they were in there. After a cold lunch made up of ham and egg sandwiches, yoghurt, orange juice and fruit, they'd wiped their prints off every surface and then geared up as before. The thirty-minute journey through the sewers had been just as straightforward as the previous two times.

Cole was busy doing something in the chamber now, but Korso couldn't see what. 'How does it look in there?' he asked.

'It's all good,' Cole said, grinning back at them. 'That grout's really done a job on this whole section of wall. It's practically in pieces already. I won't know if we're all the way through until we get all this compact hardcore and rubble out of the way.'

'Start passing it through to us then,' Korso said.

'Right.'

Korso crawled halfway into the hole and noticed the opening caused by the grout was about three feet square. He took the large slab of misshapen rock Cole placed on the ground, then shifted his body a little and passed it back to Sam, who disappeared with it into the main part of the sewer. Korso turned back and took the next piece Cole had laid down, then passed that one back to Sam, who was already waiting at the sewer opening.

For the next twenty minutes they all became focused on passing large slabs of rock from one end to the other. It was hot and tiring work in such an enclosed space, but there was no way around it. Korso watched the square-shaped hole in front of Cole get bigger and bigger as the obstructions were removed piece by piece.

Finally, Cole said, 'Okay, I think we're close to the finish line here. Let me check.'

Korso watched him grab the pickaxe from the ground, and then start to jab the sharp end repeatedly into the hole. After a minute of this, he emerged and turned to Korso. 'Still not there yet. I'd say there's another couple of inches of solid stone to go before we break through to the other side. You wanna pass me one of the pneumatic drills?'

'I'd prefer we use just manual tools. If we're as close as you say, then I don't want to risk using the drills unless we really have to. The sound of hammering can always be explained away as something else, but a drill always sounds like a drill. And we still don't know for sure what's on the other side of this wall.'

Cole shrugged. 'We've gotten this far, so I guess we can get by on brute strength for the rest. But it'll take longer.'

'That's something I can live with.' Korso swivelled in the other direction. 'Samara, hand us another pickaxe and one of the sledgehammers.'

'Right.' She disappeared from sight. Moments later, she returned with the two tools and passed them along to Korso, who handed them to Cole.

'You want to start,' Korso asked, 'or shall I?'

'I might as well get working on it, since I'm here already.'

'All right. Call out when you want to switch.'

Cole didn't answer, but ducked into the opening and began attacking the remains of the wall with the pick. Korso watched him for a moment, and then carefully backed out of the small passage to join Samara in the sewer.

She was facing away from him, looking past the lights at something further down the tunnel.

'What is it?' Korso asked, straining his eyes through the mask. All he could see was the glare of the lanterns on either side, and undefined darkness in between them.

'Not sure...' She suddenly aimed a finger at a point in the darkness. '*There*. At the water line. See them?'

Korso saw. An ugly flash of two yellow eyes, set close together. Then another pair appeared beside them. Rats. He was only surprised it had taken this long for them to appear. He heard squeaking sounds, and took a few heavy steps towards them, making as much noise as possible. The squeaks suddenly grew shriller and then he heard splashing sounds as the rodents quickly scampered away, scared off by the unknown threat to their domain.

'More afraid of us than we are of them,' he said.

'Don't kid yourself, Korso,' Samara said. 'I've seen genuine footage of sewer rats that gave me goosebumps for days. They grow them big down here.'

Korso had nothing to say to that, so he remained silent. They each stood there listening to the sounds of metal hitting rock coming from the chamber. After a while, Samara said, 'Korso, about that Paris job you mentioned.'

'What about it?'

'Well, I was just wondering...'

'Hey, somebody wanna take over for a while?' Cole's voice echoed. 'My arm's just cramped up on me. Jesus.'

'Come on out,' Korso called back. 'I'll take over.'

Cole slowly emerged from the hole, feet first. Korso helped him out and watched him gently rub the tendons of his upper left arm. 'I'll be okay,' he said, grimacing. 'Guess I must have pulled a muscle or something.'

Korso entered the hole and crawled through to the little chamber at the end. He saw Cole had made decent progress on the sub-basement wall already, especially around the centre. Whole areas of rock had come free, and there was a small mound of debris on the ground directly underneath. Korso pushed the rubble to the sides to give him more room to play with. Positioning himself so he wasn't blocking the light, he grabbed the pickaxe with both hands and then struck the sharp end at the centre of the wall. Large cracks immediately appeared that hadn't been there before, as more pieces of stone came loose and landed on the muddy floor. He pulled his arms back and struck the wall again. And then again. And then again, until it simply became nothing but routine exercise…

It took Korso by complete surprise when he finally broke through.

He judged about ten minutes had passed since he started, and it was only now that he noticed the sharp ache in both shoulder muscles. The hole caused by the pickaxe was only about two inches in diameter, but he thought it was one of the beautiful sights in the world. Removing his respirator and mask, Korso placed his left eye against the hole, but saw nothing but darkness beyond. Which was exactly what he'd hoped for. According to the plans, before the cave-in this room was supposed to have been a commissary for the staff and guards. Now it was just an empty space. Long unused, and hopefully long forgotten.

'Okay,' he called out. 'I'm through the wall.'

He heard a loud whoop from Cole, and Samara hollered, '*Yesss.*'

'Another five minutes more and I should have an opening big enough for us to crawl through. Somebody want to pass me a flashlight?'

Without waiting for an answer, Korso retrieved the pickaxe and attacked the wall again, his aching muscles all but forgotten. At some point he sensed a human presence behind him, but he carried on swinging the pickaxe regardless, striking the stone with all his strength as he slowly and steadily enlarged the diameter of the hole. Rock crumbled and fell into the room beyond. When he felt he'd made a space big enough for them to crawl through, he put down the pickaxe and leaned his back against the wall of the chamber. He rubbed his shoulder muscles gently while he got his breath back.

'Nice job, Korso,' Samara said, watching him from the other passage. She passed him one of the flashlights. He switched it on and then carefully crawled through the opening in the wall until he was back on solid ground again.

As he got to his feet, he took off the respirator and was pleased to find the stink of the sewer not so pervasive in here. The air felt damp and cool against his face, while the place smelled mostly of mildew, mixed in with old oil, damp wood, wet plaster, and drainage.

Moving the light around, he judged the whole room to be about sixty feet by a hundred. There were no furnishings left to signal its previous life as a prison canteen, just piles of old rubble and huge slabs of broken concrete everywhere you looked. Here and there he spotted some rusted steel piping poking out from the crumbling walls. It looked like the after-effects of a gas explosion. To the right, part of the ceiling and wall had also collapsed from the previous cave-in, leaving a steep mountain of rubble and rock. Korso could see clearly into the room above, and saw it was just as dark and dilapidated as the one he was in.

Hearing movement behind him, Korso turned to see Samara helping Cole up from the ground. As he got to his feet he switched on his own flashlight, and moved it around for a better look. Samara did the same with hers.

'Whoa,' she whispered. 'It's like a mausoleum in here.'

'So this was the refectory, huh?' Cole aimed the beam of light at the ruins above them. 'What's that supposed to be up there?'

'It was an admin office once. Cole, there should be an exit door up ahead that leads out to the main corridor. See if you can find it, will you?'

'Right.' Cole moved off down the room, stepping gingerly between the large slabs of stone lying on the ground.

'If this was supposed to be a canteen,' Samara said, playing the light around, 'where's the kitchen? Shouldn't there be old ovens and steam tables somewhere around here?'

'I imagine everything of value got salvaged before this whole area was closed off for good.' Korso shone the light on the steel pipe remains protruding from the wall to their left. 'That was most likely the cooking area over there.'

'Man, what a shithole.' She turned back to Korso. 'So where are we in relation to the isolation cells?'

'I'll show you.' Korso brought out his phone and activated the display, noticing there was still no signal down here. He went straight to the prison plans he'd downloaded and zoomed in on the western section of the east wing at the sub-basement level. Using his finger to scroll across the map, he said, 'We're here in the old refectory. The door at the other end of this room should lead to the main corridor, which by rights should still be in use. As you can see there's a toilet and some utility rooms on the other side of the corridor. At the end of the passage is this T-junction here. Right eventually takes you to the stairwell to the ground level, while left takes you to the Hole.'

'Along with the two guards at the door.'

'Or maybe more than two. We've only got Teodor's word on that, and he could be wrong. I won't know for sure until I'm there.'

They each turned at the approaching footsteps and bobbing beam from the third flashlight. 'I found the door,' Cole said. 'Come take a look.'

'Locked?'

'Better if you see for yourself.'

Korso and Samara followed Cole's light, stepping carefully between or over the obstructions on the floor. Finally, they saw Cole's light land on the top part of a door. Above it, more of the ceiling had started to collapse, and Korso saw that large blocks of fallen masonry and concrete completely blocked the rest of the exit. The blockage was about four feet at its highest, and more than ten feet wide.

'This'll take more than one of us to clear,' Cole said.

Korso placed his flashlight on the ground, and aimed the beam at the obstruction. 'So let's get started.'

TWENTY-TWO

With all three of them on the job, it didn't take too long to clear the debris. The smaller pieces were easy enough to carry, while the larger and heavier concrete slabs they simply pushed along the floor until they were out of the way. After another fifteen minutes of labour, they finally had clear access.

The door was made of thick hardwood and had a rusted iron pull-handle on this side, along with an equally rusted lock underneath. Cole knelt down and aimed his flashlight at the lock, then placed an eye against the hole. After a few seconds, he pulled his eye away. 'Can't see much though all the gunk, but the lock itself looks fairly basic. Shouldn't take me long.' He reached into his work belt and pulled out a small canvas tool pouch.

'Wait.' Korso placed a hand on Cole's arm before he could unzip it. 'That door could be alarmed.'

'After all these years?' Samara asked.

'I'm not about to take anything for granted in this place.' Korso aimed the flashlight at the bottom of the door and nodded to himself when he saw a tiny gap there. 'You two wait here a minute.'

Returning to the sewers, Korso grabbed the equipment bag that had held the squeezy bottles. He took it back to the others at the door, and opened up the bag. Korso rummaged around inside until he found the items he needed and placed them on the floor.

There was a hand taser, a telescopic baton, a folding knife, and a small tin carrying three syringes, each containing 10 mg of Diprivan. The final item was a Medit flexible fiberscope with a metre-long, two-millimetre-diameter insertion probe at one end, and an intricate-looking eyepiece at the other. He made a point of taking this with him on every assignment, along with its slightly larger brother. He'd lost count of the amount of times they'd helped him out of a hole.

After unwinding the cable, Korso crouched down and inserted the thin probe partway into the gap under the door. He looked through the eyepiece and saw a high-definition fish-eye view of a corridor. The light source coming from above indicated this part of the prison was still in use. With his other hand he slowly manoeuvred the cable around until he saw a barred steel security door directly ahead. Beyond this was another empty corridor. He carefully rotated the probe until it was pointing upwards, towards the refectory door itself. He moved the cable around, but couldn't see an alarm box above the door, nor any kind of wiring near the ceiling.

'How's it look out there?' Cole asked.

'So far I don't see anything that could be an alarm. Still checking.' Korso panned the camera slowly to the left until he had a good view of the rest of the corridor. It looked to be about a hundred feet long, with four doorways running down the right sight. But more importantly, there was nobody else in sight. Finally, he pulled the thin fibre-optic cable out of the gap, then got to his feet again.

'Okay, we're clear. Cole, do your thing.'

Cole opened up his tool pouch and pulled out his lockpick tools. Korso rolled the scope up and held it out to Sam. 'You mind looking after this for me?'

Samara nodded, and stuck the scope in her work belt. It was an expensive piece of kit, and Korso didn't want to risk dropping it if he had to run through the sewers. Kneeling down, he opened the equipment bag again and pulled out a spare respirator, a hard hat, and an extra set of overalls. After placing them on the floor, he got to his feet and took off his own protective gear. Underneath, he was wearing black nylon workpants, a black button-down shirt with epaulettes on the shoulders, and rubber-soled boots. After Dog had found out where the prison guards got their uniforms, Korso had paid a visit to the same outlet and picked up a full set for himself. Reaching into the bag again, he pulled out a set of working handcuffs, a black cap with a thin chevron strip above the visor, and a black zip-up jacket with more epaulettes on the shoulders. The cap he placed on his head, while the cuffs he attached to his belt, along with the taser gun and the baton. He placed the tin containing the syringes into his left trouser pocket, while the folding knife went into his right.

Donning the jacket, he adjusted the plastic name badge on his left breast until it was straight. The name on the badge read *Ivanov*, the most common surname in Bulgaria. The jacket even had an embroidered patch on the left arm with the official Central Prison logo. That patch had cost more than the clothes themselves.

He faced Samara. 'Think I'll pass muster?'

She shone her flashlight on him, tilting her head as she looked him over. 'A set of keys and a two-way would complete the picture, but otherwise you look the same as the guards I met. As long as nobody looks too closely.'

'Good enough. And now it's time for you to leave us. You know the route?'

'Back to front. Even if I do get lost, I've still got the plans on my phone.'

'You won't get lost. You're better at navigation than either one of us.'

Samara smiled. 'Flattery will get you everywhere.'

Korso turned at the sound of a metallic click behind him.

'That's it,' Cole said. 'We're in.'

'Right,' Samara turned to go. 'Good luck, and I'll see you later.'

'Kill some rats for me,' Cole said.

Both men watched Samara as she made her way back to the sewer tunnel. Once she was gone, Korso turned and gripped the door handle. He shared a glance with Cole, and then pulled open the door. It was stiff at first, but he managed to open it all the way without it creaking. He poked his head out and looked left, then right. Still nothing and nobody on either side. The corridor directly ahead was still deserted too.

'Start making preparations,' Korso whispered, and stepped out into the prison's sub-basement. He approached the steel door in front of him, gave it a gentle shove. Locked, of course. Korso turned towards the hallway at his left. Fluorescent lighting ran the length of the corridor, while the dank and dirty walls on either side were riddled with vertical cracks from the ground up. There were bigger cracks running along the ceiling too, which was worrying. This place was due for another cave-in at any time. He heard faint muffled shouting in the distance, but couldn't tell from which direction it came. Other than that, all was quiet.

He began walking slowly towards the T-junction at the end, all his senses on high alert. Passing the first door on his right, he saw no markings to signify its purpose. But fifteen feet further on was the second door, and this one bore the universal male toilet symbol. He kept on going, treading slowly and carefully, making as little noise as possible. He passed by the other two unidentified doors and when he was still twenty feet away from the end, he could hear a man's exclamation coming from around the corner.

Korşo stuck to the left wall, and when he reached the corner he peered round.

The open area on the left was about fifty feet square, with a large steel door set into the brick wall at the rear. It looked about a hundred years old, and was made of solid steel with a barred window at chest height. Below a metal handle were a large keyhole and a thick steel latch. Set against the left-hand wall of the room was an open cage with space enough for five.

Inside the cage were three seats and a bench, as well as a long work desk with two computer terminals. Sitting in front of one of the terminals, with his profile to Korso, was a prison guard. His uniform matched Korso's almost exactly. He was wearing earbuds, while his right hand moved a mouse around on the desk.

He suddenly raised his left hand in the air in frustration. '*Govno.*'

Korso knew what that word meant. So the guard was probably playing a video game, and probably getting beat. As long as the man was occupied, that was fine with him. He peered to the right and saw a dimly lit hallway with a set of stairs at the end, leading upwards. There was nobody else in sight, which gave him pause. Korso turned back to the guard in the cage. According to Teodor there should have been two men on duty in this part of the prison. So where was the other one? He began to reach for the taser gun at his back, thinking this was almost too easy, when he heard the sound of a door opening behind him.

He lowered his hand from his belt and turned to see a figure emerging from the toilet he'd passed, zipping up his fly. The man was dressed identically to Korso, but the similarities ended there. This guy was huge. Korso estimated his height at around six-four, and his weight at around 260 or 270 pounds. Most of it was muscle, and much of it above the waist. If anything, Samara had played down her description of the prison staff. If not for the uniform, he could easily have been mistaken for one of the inmates.

After straightening his waistband, the guard looked up and spotted Korso standing there. He frowned deeply, said something Korso didn't catch.

Korso thought fast. With the first guard currently occupied by whatever was playing through his earbuds, the more distance he could put between the two men the better. Especially with what he knew was coming. Seeing no other alternative, he began walking towards the big guard, his facial muscles relaxed in order to look as bored as possible. He made a note of the equipment on the guard's utility belt: a set of keys, a two-way radio, a stun gun, a police riot baton and what looked like a Mace pepper spray.

The big guard spoke again, more impatiently this time. Korso still didn't understand the words, but it was clearly a question, so he said, '*Az Ivanov. Pervyj den.*' The 'first-day-on-the-job' excuse had worked back at that hypermarket, so it seemed worth another try.

'*Ivanov?*' the guard said, still frowning. '*Kavko iskash?*'

Korso had an idea that one meant *what do you want?* So as Korso closed the distance between them to just a few feet, he held up one finger while his right hand reached for something at the back of his belt. He grabbed hold of the taser, turned off the safety, and as he brought it around he lunged at the guard and pressed the plastic trigger. There was a loud crackling sound as the two prongs at the end sparked with electricity, and before the guard had a chance to react, Korso jammed it into the side of his neck.

There was a brief sizzling sound as the guard's muscles suddenly contracted, his hands curled into claws as fifty thousand volts surged through his nervous system. Korso kept the taser pressed against the man's thick neck, counting the passing seconds, while his other hand reached for the telescopic baton on his own belt. He found it easily, but something prevented him from pulling it out. He was just turning his head to check what the obstruction was when a freight train connected with his left temple.

Everything went black for a second, and the next thing Korso knew he was laying on the floor with his back pressed against the wall. He had no idea how he got there. He glanced around the floor, but his taser was nowhere to be seen. The big guard was less than five feet away, shaking his head like a dog after a swim. Korso knew he must have used that forearm of his like a club. The man's body was as solid as a rock.

Korso knew he had to get to his feet right now, before the guard regained full control of his faculties. If he didn't, he was dead. With an effort, he somehow managed to get to one knee. Then, pressing an arm against the wall for support, he finally rose to his full height. He was reaching for the baton in his belt again when the guard said something guttural and suddenly lunged forward with a murderous glint in his eyes.

He saw the guard's right arm already swinging around towards him, and managed to duck his head just as the round-house strike swept past with millimetres to spare. Before he could get out of the danger area, Korso felt a hard blow in his side that knocked him back against the wall. He reached for the baton again, but the guard somehow got behind him and clamped his left arm around Korso's neck. He squeezed his arm tight, and Korso began choking as he fought to suck in oxygen that was no longer there.

The guard chuckled into his ear and began to squeeze his arm even tighter. Korso started to see black spots at the edge of his vision. He knew he couldn't take much more of this; the guard was too strong. Raising his right knee, Korso kicked back with all his strength and felt the heel of his shoe dig hard into the guard's shin.

He heard a sharp grunt of surprise at his ear, and the pressure against his throat relaxed enough for his to throw his head forward a few extra inches. It was enough. He brought his back in a reverse head-butt, slamming the back of his skull into the guard's face with every pound of force at his disposal. He felt the bone connect with something soft, and heard a cry of pain from behind him. He repeated the process again, and then again, and the man's chokehold loosened even more.

Korso gave him another reverse kick in the shin, even harder than before, and used the forward motion of his upper body to pull himself away completely from the man's clutches. Swivelling round to face his opponent, Korso took a step back and then brought his right leg up and kicked him hard between the legs. The man's eyes widened in shock and he gave a strangled grunt of pain as he doubled over. Korso noticed the man's nose was a bloody mess.

Without wasting a second, Korso reached down and yanked the tube of Mace from the guard's belt. He lifted up the safety catch, aimed the nozzle at the man's face and pressed down on the red button. Almost instantaneously, an intense stream of white gel shot out and splattered the man's eyes and what was left of his nose.

Effectively blind, the guard groaned loudly and brought his hands up to his face. He stumbled back against the wall and dropped to one knee. Korso looked down and considered tasering the guy with his own gun, but it would only delay things unnecessarily. The sooner this was finished the better. For both of them. From his shirt pocket Korso pulled out the flat tin and opened the lid. He extracted one of the hypodermics, popped the protective cap, and depressed the plunger to expel any air bubbles.

He approached the guard and kicked him in the side of the head. The guard collapsed silently to the floor, and Korso sunk the needle into his carotid artery, depressing the plunger all the way. As the powerful sedative sped its way towards his brain, the guard's movements lessened and his breathing became much shallower. After another ten seconds, he lost consciousness entirely. Korso noticed his name badge read *Osman*.

Korso wiped a hand across his brow and took a deep breath. Now that the adrenaline rush was over, it was all starting to catch up with him. But the fact that he was still alone suggested the other guard was still unaware of their altercation. Retrieving his cap from the floor, he got to his feet and tiptoed toward the end of the corridor, peering around the corner again. The second guard was still at his position at the terminal, listening to whatever soundtrack was playing through his earbuds.

Korso returned to the unconscious Osman and scanned the immediate area, and finally spotted his taser on the floor next to the toilet. He picked it up, pressed the trigger, and electricity crackled between the two prongs once more. After checking his uniform to make sure there was no blood on the material, he got another syringe ready and placed it back in his shirt pocket. He cupped the taser in his right hand and with his left, extracted the two-way radio from Osman's belt. He walked back to the end of the hallway, and holding the radio up to his face, entered the antechamber and began walking towards the cage.

The second guard noticed him when he was less than twenty feet away, and got up from his chair. He was shorter than this colleague — about five-ten — but looked to be in good physical shape. Korso kept walking and muttered some Russian into the radio, as though responding to orders from the other end.

'*Kakŭv e problema?*' the guard said.

'*Kŭde e Osman?*' Korso countered, hoping his asking after the other guard by name would allay any possible suspicions.

'*Toaletna.*'

'Uh huh.' Korso reduced the distance between them, and when he was close enough, he suddenly jammed the taser into the side of the man's neck and pressed the trigger. The guard's body trembled and his eyes bulged as the electricity surged through his system. After five more seconds, Korso dropped the taser, pulled the second hypodermic from his shirt pocket, stuck the needle in the carotid artery and depressed the plunger.

Ten seconds later, he was out for the count too.

Korso returned to the corridor, dragged Osman back to the cage, and laid him down on the floor. He removed the set of keys from the other guard's belt and stepped over to the steel door. The fifth key he tried unlocked it, and he raised the steel latch and pulled the heavy steel door open.

He saw only darkness beyond. Teodor hadn't been exaggerating when he said there were no lights in this section of the prison. He could also hear a faint groan coming from inside, coming from a rasping voice ruined by long-term shouting. Another one joined it briefly before fading away to nothing.

Korso went back to the guards' cage and found a heavy-duty flashlight on one of the desks. He looked for some paperwork relating to the inmates in solitary but there was nothing, and the monitor screen showed only a paused puzzle game. He grabbed the flashlight and returned to the open door.

Switching on the flashlight, Korso passed through the doorway and entered the Hole.

TWENTY-THREE

Korso found himself in another corridor, twice the width of the previous one, only this time the walls and arched ceiling were made from brick. He moved the flashlight around. Very old brick, by the looks of it. The air was dank and heavy, mixed in with an overpowering smell of decay and human waste. The temperature felt at least fifteen degrees lower than the room he'd just left. He looked down and saw the ground under his feet was covered in dark stains. It didn't take too much imagination to guess what might have caused them.

The hallway was about thirty yards long, with cells on both sides. Korso counted ten doors on the left and nine more on the right. They were all similar to the one he'd just unlocked, with a barred observation window at chest level, a heavy steel latch and a keyhole.

He walked over to the first door on the left. Raising the flashlight, he looked through the observation window and saw a small cell, about five feet square. The brick walls were covered in markings. All he could see was a worn mattress on the floor, with an underweight man lying on top, wearing just tracksuit bottoms and a ragged t-shirt. He had his arms wrapped around himself. The man stirred at the light, mumbled something under his breath.

It wasn't Teodor. That much was obvious. This guy looked as though he'd been there for months. Backing away, Korso called out, '*Teodor Yanev.*'

A clamour of shouting and screaming greeted him. None of it made any sense. Further back, somebody cackled loudly. He waited for the noise to die down, and tried again: '*Teodor Yanev. Call out if you're here.*'

'*Maĭnata ti,*' somebody yelled back, followed by that same cackling laugh.

This was bad. If the asset wasn't in one of these cells, then everything he and the others had accomplished to this point was for nothing. But he wasn't about to leave without getting a definite answer, one way or the other.

Korso kept to the left-hand side of the passage and peered through the observation window in the next cell along. He saw another mattress on the floor, along with an overflowing waste bucket in the corner. No sign of the occupant, though Korso could hear a consistent scratching sound on the other side of the door.

'Teodor Yanev?' he asked.

No answer. Just more scratching noises, and as regular as before.

He went through the same process at the next cell. This inmate just sat cross-legged on the floor and stared back at him, saying nothing. He tried the neighbouring cell with similar results, then repeated the process all the way down to the end. He always got some kind of response from the occupant, but never the one he wanted. He began walking back along the other side, repeating the same name at each door.

When he reached the fifth cell along this side, he shone the flashlight through the grille and saw a stocky man with close-cropped hair, lying on the floor in a foetal position with his eyes shut. He wore a dark tracksuit similar to the one Samara had described. His face was a mass of bruises, including one over his right eye. Most of the bruises looked recent.

'Teodor Yanev?' Korso asked. 'Are you awake?'

No response. No movement other than his breathing. Korso checked the other four cells, but none of the occupants matched the description. He went back to the room with the uncon-scious man and, one by one, tried each of the keys on the door.

The seventh key unlocked it. Korso raised the steel latch from its housing and opened the door.

Entering the cell, he spotted an empty steel bucket in one corner, which suggested this inmate hadn't been here that long. No mattress either, just the hard stone floor. Korso knelt down and shone the light in the man's face. A thin strand of saliva ran from his mouth to the floor. He patted the man's bruised left cheek. 'Time to wake up,' he said.

He kept tapping the bruise until he saw movement behind the eyelids.

The prisoner winced at the light, and raised one hand as he slowly opened his eyes. '*Koǐ…?*'

'I'm Korso. What's your name?'

'Korso?' The man coughed a few times, then used an elbow to raise himself up a little. He spat on the floor. 'What day?'

'It's Friday. Now tell me your name.'

'Huh? My name? Yanev. Teodor Yanev.'

'Good. I'm here to get you out. Can you move?'

Teodor made a harsh sound in his throat. 'Damn right I move… Help me.'

Korso got an arm under one shoulder and carefully helped the man to his feet. Teodor still looked dazed and unsteady. He placed the man against the wall, and said, 'Wait here a moment, get your strength back.'

He returned to the guards' cage and managed to get a grip on each of Osman's wrists, which were as thick as Korso's upper arms. With an effort he dragged the heavy guard into the Hole, and then into the cell. Teodor looked down at Osman, and then spat on his face.

'Son of whore,' he said. 'This one almost kill me yesterday. Likes to bust heads with bare hands. What you use on him?'

'Everything at my disposal.'

'Good.'

Once Korso had removed Osman's equipment belt, he left the cell and returned to the cage. He soon returned with the other guard, also sans keys and belt. He dropped him on the floor next to his partner. 'Okay, time we got out of here.'

'Not yet.' Teodor pushed off from the wall, raised his foot and brought it down hard on Osman's left hand. The unconscious guard didn't react at all, though he'd feel it when he woke up. Teodor did it again, and then did the same with the other hand, grinding his heel deep into the palm. Korso was sure he could hear bones breaking in there. Teodor turned to the other guard and kicked him in the scrotum with everything he had. The guard remained still. He was just pulling his foot back for another kick when he suddenly grimaced, clutched his chest, and stumbled to the floor. He muttered something Korso didn't catch, but it sounded like a curse.

'Okay, you've had your fun,' Korso said, and grabbed Teodor under his shoulders and pulled him upright again. 'Let's go.'

'Not fun,' Teodor wheezed, still holding his chest. 'Revenge. If I have more time I give them plenty more to cry about. But you the boss today. We go now.'

They exited the cell, and Korso locked and latched the door behind them. Teodor rested against the wall, still short of breath, and watched. He didn't look good at all. Those guards must have really done a job on him. Korso helped him down the corridor. As soon as they entered the antechamber, Teodor raised a hand to shield his eyes from the harsh lighting.

'Hey, good buddy, you got sunglasses for me? My eyes not so good right now.'

'You won't need sunglasses where we're going. Let me lock this door and we'll be out of here in no time.'

Korso found the key he'd used before and inserted it into the keyhole. As he was turning it clockwise, Teodor said, 'Hey, you bring partner too, huh? That him over there?'

'What are you talking about?' Korso turned to see him peering down the corridor ahead, his eyes narrowed. Korso swivelled round and saw two male figures emerging from the stairwell at the far end. They were about a hundred-and-fifty-feet away. One was motioning with his hand as he said something to the other. They began walking this way. They hadn't looked in this direction yet, but they would any second now. Korso grabbed Teodor's arm, and said, 'More guards. Let's move.'

'You the boss.'

Still watching the two approaching men, Korso helped the unsteady Teodor along the antechamber as fast he was able. They were just passing the cage when one of the approaching guards yelled something while fumbling at his belt. They'd been spotted. The other guard began running towards them, already pulling a stun gun from his belt.

'Oh, shit,' Teodor said.

'Time to pick up the pace.' Clutching Teodor's arm tightly, Korso pulled him into the corridor at their right and jogged with him towards the refectory door a hundred feet away. Already gasping for breath at Korso's side, Teodor couldn't seem to move any faster. Behind them, the two unseen guards were still yelling for them to stop.

'Where we go?' Teodor asked.

Korso ignored the question, and just kept dragging the slower man down the hallway towards the closed door at the end, urging him along as fast as he could. But not fast enough.

They'd just passed the toilet door when Korso shouted at the top of his lungs, '*Cole, Defcon one. Defcon one.*' Fifty feet ahead of them, he saw the refectory door being pulled open from the other side. Cole's head appeared momentarily. His eyes widened when he saw Korso and Teodor coming his way, and then he immediately vanished from sight. But the door remained open.

More shouts from behind them, the voices now clearer and more distinct. He could also hear the rapid pitter-patter of footfalls on stone. Korso didn't bother turning to see how close they were. All that mattered was what lay ahead. He picked up the pace even more, and practically dragged the puffing Teodor along with him. Fifty feet became forty, became thirty, twenty. The noise of footsteps behind them steadily increased in volume.

'*Sprete!*' a voice yelled back there. It sounded less than twenty feet away now.

The darkened doorway was just fifteen feet away, then ten. As they closed the distance to nothing, Korso practically threw Teodor through the dark opening, and dived through after him. He heard the door slam shut behind them, and quickly got to his feet and pushed his full body weight against the wood, while Cole knelt in front of the keyhole and busied himself with the lock.

'Just give me a few seconds,' Cole said.

'Get over here and help,' Korso called over his shoulder, and gave a start as something heavy launched itself at the door from the other side. It remained firmly closed. There was more muffled shouting from the guards, more threats.

Teodor appeared at his side and, still breathing hard, pressed his body against the door, which suddenly shuddered again as a guard rammed it again. But it held. Over the noise, he thought he could hear a tinny voice coming from a radio. Less than five seconds later they could all hear an emergency siren start up in the distance, its menacing banshee wail rising and falling in pitch as it steadily increased in volume.

'That's it,' Cole said, through gritted teeth. 'We're in lock-down. What the hell did you do in there?'

'Exactly what I came here to do,' Korso said, as something heavy slammed against the door again. 'How long?'

'Just a few more seconds. Almost there... Almost there.' There was a loud metallic click, and he grinned. 'Done.'

'That won't hold them for long.' Korso looked around, then pointed at one of the larger rocks that had previously blocked the door. 'We'll push this in front of it. Come on.'

The three men got behind the three-foot high concrete slab and carefully pushed it along the floor until it was placed right up against the door. Now the only way for them to get through was with an axe. Which they would, but not just yet.

'Now what?' Teodor asked.

Korso turned to Cole. 'Where's the gear?'

'I moved it back to the chamber entrance.'

As the prison siren continued to blare out on the other side of the door, Korso and Cole picked up a lantern each, and then led their Teodor back to the entrance to the sewers. In front of the hole were both sets of protective coveralls – one dirty, one clean – two respirators, and a pair of hard hats.

'Suit up,' Korso said to Teodor, who picked up the clean set of coveralls and inserted a foot into one of the legs. As Korso began pulling his dirty coveralls on over his guard's uniform, he turned to Cole. 'Everything else prepared?'

'All set and ready to go.'

'You better go first then.'

'Right.' While the other two got dressed, Cole crouched down before the opening and crawled into the small chamber beyond, taking a lantern with him.

Once Korso had finished gearing up, he stuck the cap into his work belt and quickly helped Teodor with his respirator. He could hear the hammering on the refectory door getting more and more frantic. Over the clamour of the siren, there was the sound of splintering wood, and then a beam of light suddenly appeared from that direction.

'They're almost through.' Korso passed Teodor his hard hat. 'Go on, follow Cole through that hole. I'm right behind you. *Move*.'

Teodor moved. Dropping to his knees, he clawed his way through the misshaped hole and into the little chamber, while Korso followed close behind with the other lantern. As he urged Teodor to move faster, Korso spotted the tell-tale jiffy bag taped to one of the aluminium shoring planks, along with the two electrical wires that ran from the envelope, along the roof of the shaft, and out to the sewer. Careful to keep his head away from them, he pushed Teodor along the short passage until Cole was able to help him out into the main tunnel. Korso emerged from the shaft seconds later, and Cole grabbed his hand and supported him until he was all the way out. The siren was still audible, but already sounded as though it was a mile distant.

'This no good,' Teodor said. 'We come this way, guards come this way too.'

'Give us some credit.' He grabbed Teodor's arm and led him back down the tunnel. Once they reached the two-way junction at the end, he pulled Teodor to a stop and turned back.

Cole was unwinding a large spool of electrical wire as he walked backwards towards them. He came to a stop a few feet away and knelt down. Korso watched as he took some pliers from his belt and snipped the a length off. Dropping the spool into the water, Cole carefully split the end of this wire into two parts and exposed the copper on each, and then pulled a small plastic box from his work belt. It was about the size of a pack of cigarettes, with two screw-on fuses at one end, and three switches on top. He carefully spliced one of the wires around one fuse, then did the same with the other. After some more fiddling and fine-tuning, Cole pressed the first switch and a little green LED light came on at the top of box. He placed his thumb against the third switch, and looked up at Korso.

'Do it,' Korso said.

Cole flicked his thumb. There was a muffled *whoomp*, and a huge wave of rock, dirt, mud and smoke erupted from the hole they'd just left. Dust motes glittered in the dank air from the light of the lanterns, and the smoke started to move in their direction.

'*Govno*,' Teodor said. 'What was *that*?'

Cole got to his feet and dropped the now useless detonator into the water. 'Just a small measure of Ammonium Nitrate fertilizer mixed in with a few teaspoons of diesel fuel, along with a few other essential household ingredients. I guarantee nobody will be following us through there.'

'We're not out of the woods yet,' Korso said. 'I'll take point. Cole, you take the rear. Teodor, you stay between us and call out if you need a hand.' Teodor waved a mock salute at this. 'We all set?'

'Ready when you are,' Cole said.

'Let's go.' Korso turned and entered the south tunnel, and the others followed.

in our own head through the . . . . Teodor waved a mock salute with . . .
. . . . We . . . . . .
. . . . Teodor, showing a real . . . Cole said
. . . Let's go then,' Korso turned and opened the sewer tunnel, and
the others followed.

TWENTY-FOUR

Even without any gear to carry, their final journey through the sewers was a lot more demanding than Korso had anticipated. Teodor seemed to still be suffering from whatever internal injuries he'd taken from the guards' beatings, so they were forced to stop every couple of minutes until he was able to get his breath back. Then a few hundred feet later, they'd have to stop again for the same reason. This constant stop–start to their progress soon began to wear on everyone's nerves. Even Korso wasn't immune.

Assuming the prison authorities were even halfway competent, they'd surely have alerted the city police to Teodor's underground escape within seconds of the siren going off. So it was essential they get where they were going before the cops had a chance to cordon off the surrounding area, both above and below. But so far they'd been walking for fifteen minutes, and they were still in the same damn tunnel.

As he trudged through the waste, Korso checked the sewer blueprints again on his phone's display. If his calculations were correct they should be coming to the first junction any time now. He held the lantern up even higher, and saw what looked like a fork two hundred feet in front of them.

'First junction's up ahead,' he said. 'Meaning just two more tunnels to go before we reach our exit point.'

'About goddamn time,' Cole said at the rear. 'Man, I want out of here like you wouldn't believe.'

Korso checked the time on his phone. It was 5.03 p.m. 'Won't be long now.'

They continued sloshing through the liquid waste. After a few moments, Teodor said, 'Where is girl, Samara? Why she not down here with us?'

'She's busy up top. Forget about her. Just focus on putting one foot in front of the other.'

'Ha. Telling Teodor to forget women same as telling eagle not to fly. This Samara, she got boyfriend, husband, what?'

'No idea. The subject's never come up.'

'I think no boyfriend. When she comes see me in prison I can tell she goes for me. I know what women like ever since I was boy. It's a gift.' He held his chest as he began coughing. Once he was done, he lifted up the mask and spat on the ground. 'Hey, we stop here for one second, okay?'

'No, we keep going. Time's running out, and we can't keep stopping every few hundred feet for you to get your wind back. You ever hear the phrase, "No pain, no gain"?'

'Yeah, I hear this. Nothing in life easy, huh?'

'Hold on to that thought, and keep on walking.'

They continued moving forwards through the sewer. When Korso finally reached the junction, he took the left fork and entered another tunnel, no different to the one he'd just left. He heard the other two wading after him. As he walked, he raised the lantern as high as he could. Every now and then they passed a set of vertical iron rungs bolted into the side of the tunnel, leading up to a dark shaft directly above. All useless to them. But the one they wanted couldn't be too far away now.

To his credit, Teodor stopped demanding rest breaks even though his breathing became noticeably louder and more strained. Nobody talked. There was little to say. They reached the final junction fifteen minutes later, and Korso led them into the right-hand tunnel. The last tunnel. As he continued onwards, he was counting off the feet in his head. He'd just reached seven hundred when he saw the ladder rungs in the wall up ahead. Exactly where they were supposed to be.

'There,' he said, pointing, 'that's the one we want.'

'Finally,' Cole said.

With the end in sight, Korso picked up his pace a little. He could hear the other two doing the same behind him. Upon reaching the ladder, he placed a foot on the lowest rung and when the others joined him, handed his lantern to Teodor.

'Keep the light on me as much as you can.'

Teodor nodded. 'Sure.'

Korso removed his respirator and hard hat, carefully slipped out of his coveralls, and dropped all three garments in the water. He retrieved the guard's cap from the work belt and put it on. That and the uniform would give him an extra level of authority should anyone challenge him. He climbed the ladder until he was in the dark shaft directly above, and kept going until he reached the manhole cover. Because of the tight space, and the shadows caused by his body, it was still hard to see much. But it didn't matter. Using both arms, he pushed up against the manhole cover for about a minute until he finally felt it shift in its housing. Clenching his arm muscles tighter, he kept the pressure on until the iron plate finally came free and a sliver of daylight fell onto his face. The sun was still out. The sounds of rush hour traffic and beeping horns filtered through the gap. Normal, everyday city sounds.

The steel cover was about fifty pounds heavier than the one at the other car park, and Korso could already feel his muscles straining at the effort. With one last push, he gave it everything he had, finally sliding the cover free of the opening, and pushing it to one side.

He peered out of the hole and quickly scanned the area. The shaft was situated right in the centre of the parking lot's main aisle, and he could see a line of bays on either side, with more bays beyond. The place looked filled to capacity. He couldn't see a single empty space anywhere. About fifty feet to his right was the hospital, a collection of large interconnected buildings that managed to take up an entire block. He could also hear the sounds of engines close by, and knew it was only a matter of time before a visitor entered this aisle, looking for a space.

Movement to his left suddenly caught his attention. A pair of headlights was flashing at him from about twenty feet away. They belonged to a silver BMW E90 sedan, parked between an old station wagon and a newer SUV. Korso smiled when he saw the Beamer's licence plate. He also recognised the face behind the wheel. He heard the engine catch and then watched as the driver gently pulled out of the space and steered the vehicle towards him. It came to a stop three feet from the manhole. Lucian, wearing tinted anti-glare driving glasses, poked her head out the window.

'How'd it all go down there?' she asked.

'We got what we came for. How does it look up here?'

'Bad. Ever since that prison siren went off, there's been a constant stream of flashing blue lights racing past this place. This whole town's stinking with cops on the hunt for you guys. You must have really lit a fire under them.'

'Exactly what I was afraid of.' Korso ducked his head back into the shaft, and called out, 'Okay, come on up. Fast as you can.'

Korso pulled himself up and out of the shaft, and then went over and opened the rear door of the BMW. As he waited for the others to appear, he could hear a faint police siren coming from the east. It seemed to be getting louder. Spotting movement out the corner of his vision, he turned and saw a family unit – a man, a woman, a boy and a girl in their teens – walking out of the hospital's rear entrance. They were less than thirty feet away, and moving in Korso's direction. Even worse, the girl was playing with her phone.

'Oh, shit,' Lucian said.

Korso turned back and saw Teodor had appeared at the manhole entrance. Only part of his head was visible, and he was squinting as he looked around. But that wasn't what Lucian was referring to. Fifty feet ahead, a dark grey sedan was slowly turning into their aisle. The vehicle continued moving forward before coming to a sudden stop.

Korso ran over to the manhole, grabbed Teodor's arms and helped him out onto his feet. 'Into the back of the BMW. Quick, before anyone gets a good look at your face.'

Teodor darted past him and dived into the rear of the car. Korso turned back to the manhole and could only see the top of Cole's head as he ascended the ladder. He was about halfway up. Meanwhile, the driver of the grey sedan stepped out of the car and began walking towards Korso. He called out, '*Kakvo stava tuk?*'

Korso held up a palm, and spoke in his most officious voice, '*Politsiya. Sprete.*'

The man paused, unsure of the situation before him. Korso turned in the other direction. The family of four was less than fifteen feet away and still coming this way. The man had already spotted Korso and the open manhole, and said something to his wife, who was now looking over as well. And if that weren't bad enough, that police siren was getting louder too. This was all escalating too fast.

'We need to vamoose, Korso,' Lucian said, and revved the engine for emphasis. 'Like right this second.'

'Way ahead of you,' Korso said. He turned back to the shaft and saw Cole was almost at the top. He reached down for his arm, and hauled Cole out onto solid ground. 'Get into the back with Teodor. Walk normally. Don't run.'

Cole understood the situation immediately, and stepped over to the car without another word. He got in the back of the car and slammed the door shut. Meanwhile, Korso moved around the front of the vehicle, and was just opening the front passenger door when he saw the young girl look up from her phone. The moment she realised something interesting was happening, she began raising the phone in his direction. Knowing what was coming, and powerless to stop it, Korso pulled his cap visor down low over his face, ducked into the front seat and slammed the door shut.

'You two keep your heads down,' he said, and saw that the guy out front was now talking into his phone, probably calling the cops. 'Lucian, get us out of here, fast.'

TWENTY-FIVE

Without a word, Lucian jammed the stick into reverse and backed the car up, then put it into second gear, swung the wheel to the right and hit the gas pedal. The vehicle bolted forward as she steered them away from the sedan and towards the four pedestrians. Keeping one hand on his cap visor to conceal his face, Korso could just make out the girl aiming her phone at the BMW as it swept past her and her family. Lucian coolly swung the wheel left and then right, narrowly missing three parked vehicles at the end of the aisle. Three more similar tight turns and then they were speeding past the rear hospital entrance, and hurtling towards the exit gates three hundred feet away.

'Seat belt,' Lucian said.

As Korso pulled his belt across and clicked it home, he paid closer attention to that police siren. Even with the windows closed he could hear it, but it sounded noticeably fainter than before. He hoped it wasn't his imagination.

Teodor was whooping for joy in the back, 'Happy days, good buddies. *Happy days.*'

'Yeah,' Cole said, 'it's actually starting to look that way.'

Korso knew better. He just kept his eyes on the approaching gates and the main road beyond. Traffic was passing by in both directions, but less than he'd hoped for. This was supposed to be rush hour. That's why he'd chosen this particular time to break into the prison. As soon as they were though the exit, Korso's head snapped forward as the vehicle screeched to a stop. Lucian looked both ways, then calmly turned right and joined the flow of traffic heading east, keeping their speed at thirty.

'Nothing behind us,' Cole said. 'I think we're okay.'

'Don't count on it,' Korso said. 'That kid back there was taking pictures of us, and that driver could have been calling the police.'

'Hey, driver lady,' Teodor said from the back, 'you real good back there. I like your style. After this is over you and me relax together, have some drinks, yeah?'

Without taking her eyes from the road, she said, 'Is he for real?'

Korso shrugged.

'Asshole,' she said under her breath. 'So we still sticking to the original plan?'

'It's still our best option, whether we're spotted or not. Is Samara in position?'

'Yeah, she called in ten minutes before you showed, and said that nobody—' Lucian's cheek muscles tightened. 'Uh-oh. Trouble.'

Korso had already seen it. Just up ahead on the right, a blue-and-white police vehicle had pulled up at the next junction. His left indicator was flashing as he waited for a space to join the traffic. Korso turned and saw Cole and Teodor still sitting upright. 'I told you both to stay low. Cole, get on the floor, *now*. Teodor, lie across the seats and stay there.'

They each moved in unison, without argument. Once both men were out of sight, Korso faced front again as they passed the junction. The police vehicle was still there, waiting patiently. Clearly in no hurry, which was a good sign. Korso turned and glanced back, and saw the driver finally join the traffic two cars behind them.

'Just what we need,' Lucian said.

Korso said nothing, and continued watching the cop car.

'Four-way junction coming up,' she said. 'I can take a left turn, or we can stay on this.'

Korso faced front and spotted the red lights at the next junction up ahead. The vehicles in front of them were slowing down, and Lucian lightly tapped her own brakes to match their speed. The BMW slowed to a crawl.

'Well?' she prompted.

'Take the left turn. I don't want to risk that cop getting any bright—'

The sudden, piercing crescendo of the siren behind them immediately cut off that line of thought. Korso saw the flashing blue lights, and watched as the driver suddenly began manoeuvring his vehicle past the car in front.

'We've been made,' he said. 'Go.'

Swinging the wheel hard to the left, Lucian hit the gas and they lurched forward. She swerved expertly around the car in front and continued down the median strip towards the crossroads up ahead. The oncoming cars swerved hastily out of the path of the BMW speeding towards them, with drivers hammering their horns as they swept past.

'What the hell?' Cole yelled, while Teodor shouted something in Bulgarian.

'Shut up,' Korso said, glancing out the rear window, 'and stay down.'

The pursuit vehicle was matching their speed exactly, sticking to them like glue as he followed them down the median strip. Korso could see two figures in the car. The passenger had a radio to his mouth, which meant they'd likely have company very soon.

As they tore past the traffic lights and entered the intersection, Lucian released the clutch while simultaneously slamming on the handbrake. The rear wheels momentarily locked and the back-end fishtailed. Lucian adjusted her grip and swung the wheel hard to the left and then right again, with the vehicle sliding into the sharp ninety-degree turn like it was the most natural thing in the world. Narrowly avoiding an oncoming SUV, Lucian released the handbrake, geared down, then stamped on the accelerator and the BMW took off again at speed, the engine screaming in response.

To Korso's right, a Honda driver panicked at the sudden intrusion of his space and swerved into the next lane, then braked to avoid smashing into an oncoming vehicle. The oncoming car also braked at the same time, and there was a barrage of horns as other drivers tried to avoid crashing into them. But Lucian was already past them all as she overtook the vehicle in front, keeping to the centre of the road as she increased speed. Pedestrians on both sides stopped and stared as they whizzed by.

Korso looked back and saw their pursuers had detoured onto the sidewalk to avoid the mess Lucian had caused. Then the driver got the vehicle back onto the road, and steadily increased speed as he continued after the BMW.

'Well, it almost worked,' Lucian said.

Seconds later, another police siren added its noise to the first. Still looking out the rear window, Korso saw an unmarked grey sedan much further back, its police lights flashing intermittently across the front grille as the driver weaved in and out of traffic to reach them.

'Where did they come from?' Lucian said, glancing at the rear-view.

'Does it matter?'

Lucian said nothing, and continued pouring it on as she overtook the cars in front.

'How far now?' Korso asked.

'Right at the next junction,' she said, her eyes glued to the road, 'then northeast for another twenty blocks until we get to the central terminal. But I'll need to get some space between us and them before we reach that turn we want, or it'll never work.'

'I know.'

Korso let her drive while he pulled his phone from his pocket and found Samara's number. He called it. The line rang. They were almost at the next junction. Lucian performed another sliding handbrake turn, and Korso's head hit the side window

179

as he leaned into the sharp turn. The call was picked up. Samara said, 'Talk to me.'

'We're on our way to you now,' Korso said, as Lucian evened the car out and stepped on the gas again. 'With company. You all set?'

'All good to go. How long?'

'Couple of minutes at most. We're getting to the crunch now. Keep this line open.'

'Copy.'

'Hey, what goes on up there?' Teodor yelled from the back seat. 'Where all these cops come from? You guys know what you're doing, or what?'

'Couldn't you have gagged him first?' Lucian said.

Korso saw there was another major intersection coming up, and another line of cars waiting for the lights to turn green. The cross-traffic looked heavy. Lucian accelerated and then swerved into the westbound lane and overtook them all, while oncoming vehicles veered out of the way in panic. Horns beeped incessantly. Behind them, both police sirens were still wailing like it was the end of the world. The unmarked sedan had closed the distance some, and was now just a couple of cars back from the blue-and-white, which was about ten car lengths behind the BMW.

Easing off the gas a little, Lucian steered them straight past the red lights and entered the intersection, letting the police sirens do the work for her as she manoeuvred between the cross traffic as though she were in a game of pinball. Drivers who'd already slowed at the sound of the sirens suddenly braked at the intrusion, honking their horns in impotent anger.

Then they were through and out the other side. Lucian stamped down hard on the gas. The engine roared as the car took off, gaining speed with each second.

'Nicely done.' Korso looked back and saw the two pursuit cars had fallen behind a little. They had breathing space. Not much, but enough. As long as nobody else decided to join the party.

Lucian drove as though she were the thinking part of the machine, showing almost no nerves or emotion, calmly beeping her own horn whenever she felt drivers weren't getting out her way fast enough. The speedometer climbed. A blur of apartment blocks, public parks, and industrial buildings rushed by them on both sides. Nobody spoke. The police sirens remained constant. They were still back there, but not gaining.

It wasn't long before Korso spotted the bus terminal building up ahead, with its instantly recognisable mirrored glass frontage. The three-lane thoroughfare became more clogged with traffic the closer they got. Without slowing, Lucien simply drove around, through, or past it all. Sweeping past the bus terminal with the cops still on their tail, she followed the road around as it curved to the left.

Coming up on the right, Korso saw the long cantilevered building that served as Sofia's central railway station. The large terminal building was set well back from the main highway, with a pedestrian-only shopping area out front containing numerous market stalls and boutique shops. Bisecting the pedestrian zone and the terminal was a huge D-shaped perimeter road for taxis and private cars to drop off travellers.

Lucian looked about to pass the entrance to this road when she stamped on the brakes and spun the wheel to the right. The car tilted and the tyres squealed as she drifted into the access road at high speed, barely missing a taxi about to enter the road from the opposite direction.

After checking to make sure the cops had seen where they were going, Korso raised his phone, and said, 'We just took the first turn on the perimeter road. You'll see us any second now.'

'I hear the sirens,' Samara said. 'I'm ready.'

Lowering her speed to fifty, Lucian followed the road around to the left in a burst of screeching tyres and kept going. Thankfully, there wasn't much traffic ahead, just a few taxis and private cars delivering their charges to the terminal on their right. Lucian overtook them all. There were fifty or sixty angled short-stay parking bays staggered along the left side of the road, most of which were full. Past the terminal building, Korso knew this perimeter road curved round to the left once more before finally joining up with the main highway again.

'Almost there,' Lucian said under her breath. 'Almost there.'

As they raced past the station building, Korso looked out the rear window and saw the blue-and-white less than fifty feet behind them, its siren still going at full blast. The unmarked sedan was right behind it.

Then they were past the terminal building entirely. As Lucian steered them into the left turn at the top of the D, she punched the horn three times.

That was the *go* signal.

As they came out of the turn and onto the short straight, Korso saw the last of the angled parking bays coming up on their left. There were only a dozen or so on this part of the road, and he watched as another silver BMW E90 suddenly pulled out of the fourth bay along and took off down the road ahead of them.

Meanwhile, Lucian downshifted to third gear as she passed the first two bays, then simultaneously depressed the clutch to lock the rear tyres, wrenched the wheel hard to the right and gave the handbrake lever a good yank. The BMW's tyres screeched as the car instantly spun to the right in a tight semi-circle, and Lucian released both the brake lever and the clutch, bringing the vehicle to an immediate stop. Depressing the clutch again, she pumped the gear stick into reverse, stepped on the gas and expertly backed the BMW into the space Samara had just vacated.

All in the space of a second.

Lucian killed the engine, and she and Korso ducked down in their seats in unison, as low as they could go. The two police sirens steadily increased in volume, and moments later he saw part of the blue-and-white racing past them in a blur, closely followed by its grey partner. As soon as they were past, he rose up and watched them racing towards the junction to the highway. He saw a momentary glimpse of the other BMW as it sped off to the right, and then the two cop cars vanished after it.

Lucian turned to Korso with a raised brow. She wasn't even breathing hard.

'You should turn pro,' he said.

She smiled. 'Wasn't sure it would work out, but Samara did her part just fine. Got it timed right down to the second.'

'Hey, why we stop?' Teodor moaned from the back. 'Why we not moving?'

'You two can get up now,' Korso said, looking over to their left. He could see the rented Nissan Infiniti parked three spaces along, exactly where it was supposed to be. 'We'll be changing vehicles now.'

'Seriously?' Cole asked, pulling himself up. 'We're free and clear?'

'Not quite yet.' Korso popped the glove compartment. Inside were the two licence plates he'd unscrewed from an old Skoda at an auto scrapyard north of the city, and the keys for the rental. He grabbed the keys and turned to Lucian. 'You clear on what to do next?'

'Don't worry about me.'

With a nod, Korso got out of the BMW and looked around. He could see several pedestrians in the distance, but with the excitement now past, none were looking in this direction. And they were also far enough away from the terminal to be out of shot of any security cameras. Just another reason why he'd chosen this particular location. Walking over to the Infiniti, Korso pressed the key fob and heard the locks disengage. Teodor and Cole soon joined him, and all three watched as Lucian slowly steered the BMW out of the parking bay and calmly drove off to her next destination.

Korso passed the keys to Cole. 'You drive. Teodor, you're in the trunk.'

Teodor's face grew red. 'The *trunk*? Go straight to hell, bro. No more small spaces for Teodor. I go up front with you.'

'Where everybody can see you as plain as day.' Cole snorted. 'That's real good thinking there, Teodor.'

'Yeah? Maybe you spend a day in Hole after being beaten to shit, and then see how you feel after, okay?'

'It's only temporary until we get to the safe house,' Korso said, and lifted the trunk lid. 'Don't make this any harder than it is. I'll say please, if that helps.'

Heaving a sigh, Teodor muttered something in his own language, then came over and placed one foot in the trunk. Korso helped him get all the way inside, and then carefully positioned him within the tight space so he was as comfortable as possible.

'I not happy people.' Teodor glared up at each of them. 'You better not forget me.'

'You'll always be in our thoughts,' Korso said, and closed the trunk.

TWENTY-SIX

Once Cole had lowered the garage door and sealed them in, Korso raised the lid of the trunk and looked down at their willing captive.

'We're here,' Korso said.

Wincing at the harsh fluorescents above, Teodor gripped Korso's hand and climbed out of the tight space. Once he was on solid ground again, he arched his back and stretched his arms out wide as he looked around. 'Where?'

'Back at the safe house. We've also got you some fresh clothes, right after you've treated yourself to a good long shower.'

'Definitely take that shower,' Cole said as he walked over to the connecting door and pulled it open.

Korso and Teodor each followed him into the house. As they passed the kitchen area, Korso pointed to a small pile of neatly folded clothes arranged on the kitchen counter, topped off with a brand new pair of black Nikes. 'For you.'

'Hey, my favourite.' Teodor grinned as he checked the soles. 'My size too. You guys mind readers or what?'

'We just do our research. Bathroom's upstairs, along with fresh towels.'

Teodor sniffed under his arms, and made a face. 'Yeah, okay, I take hint.' Grabbing his new clothes, he began climbing the stairs to the second floor.

Cole grabbed a beer from the refrigerator, popped the top, and collapsed onto the settee with a dramatic sigh. He turned on the TV and clicked the remote until he found a sports channel.

Meanwhile, Korso got himself a bottle of Coke and took a seat at the breakfast bar. He checked his watch: 6.07 p.m.

They'd made pretty good time, considering. Following Korso's explicit instructions, Cole had taken an extremely indirect route back to the house, constantly doubling back and retracing part of their route to make sure nobody was taking any undue interest in them. Nobody was. But Korso was still surprised that everything had gone as well as it had, especially that final chase through the busy streets of Sofia. Just one small error there could have cost them everything, with all their previous hard work counting for nil. But Lucian had more than earned her fee this afternoon.

Not to take anything away from Samara's role in the proceedings, of course. She and Lucian had spent hours working on their timing until each completely trusted the other, and that effort had paid dividends today. Since Korso had known that the cops wouldn't be taking notice of the second BMW's licence plate in the middle of a high-speed pursuit, he'd instructed her to drive as fast as she could but always within the speed limit. He wondered how long it had taken them to realise they were chasing a completely different car. He knew Samara could handle herself if they gave her any grief once they pulled her over. It also helped that her silver E90 – unlike Lucian's BMW, which had been purchased under a false name and ID – was totally legit, with all the relevant paperwork ready to present to the cops.

Listening to the sound of the shower upstairs, Korso took a long sip of his Coke and went back over everything that had happened over the last few days. He always did the same thing on every job. It was amazing what you could miss when you were caught up in the moment, and often a certain detail that might seem insignificant at the time could prove to be a game-changer later on. It had happened before, and more than once. It would again.

Never overlook anything. Just one more little rule to ensure he always stayed one step ahead of the pack.

Korso came back to the present the moment he heard a key turning in the front door. He turned and saw Samara entering the living room. Shutting the door behind her, she spotted Korso at the breakfast bar and walked over to him, exchanging a wave with Cole as she passed by.

'Any trouble?' Korso asked.

'Only what we expected.' She went over to the fridge and grabbed herself a beer. Popping the top, she took a long swig of the amber liquid, then said. 'The cops finally pulled me over a mile west of the train terminal. I'm telling you, Korso, I should have won an Oscar for my performance. They were confused, I was confused, everybody was confused. I told them I had no idea what they were talking about, that I'd just dropped off a friend at the station and couldn't figure out why these two police vehicles were chasing me, and that I just panicked instead of pulling over. I've been under a lot of pressure lately, and I've just lost my job *and* my boyfriend, and everything's too much right now and I got scared and I just lost it, and yada yada yada.'

'And they believed you?'

'Why wouldn't they? I even managed to shed a few tears during the interrogation, which was a bonus. The senior cop took down my contact details, and then let me go.'

'What about the BMW?'

Samara finished her beer. 'Left it a long-term parking lot, then got an Uber to drop me off three streets away. I walked the last part. What about you?'

'We just got back a short while ago. Our friend's upstairs taking a shower now. Once Lucian returns, I'll arrange some food and then we can all have a long discussion with Teodor with regards to our next move. You've contacted Belmont yet?'

'No, but I was about to. Why?'

'Hold off for a while, at least until we know more than we do now. Besides, he's sure to have heard about the prison break by now, and so he'll automatically assume we've been successful.'

She gave a shrug. 'Whatever you say. I'm gonna make some coffee. Want some?'

'Sure.'

Samara stepped into the kitchen and grabbed some filters for the machine, while Korso went over to the living area. Cole was still reclined on the settee, in front of the TV, but his eyes were closed. He didn't stir when Korso picked up the remote, and clicked through the channels until he found the country's premier news station, BNT 1.

On the screen, the studio anchor was currently conversing with the station's on-site reporter, standing outside the main entrance to Central Prison. She was making lots of excitable hand motions as she talked, as though this could well be the story of the year. In the background, Korso could see a number of police attempting to keep the crowds of onlookers back. Increasing the volume, Korso tried to concentrate on what was being said, but they were talking too rapidly and he could only understand about one word out of every ten.

He turned to see Samara standing nearby, also watching the screen. She said, 'They're taking about the breakout, but they still haven't been told who's escaped yet. Plenty of conjecture and not a whole lot else.'

That would change as soon as they got hold of the phone footage that girl took of the BMW, but Korso said nothing. After lowering the volume again, he placed the remote on the coffee table. He heard the sounds of footsteps coming from outside, then a key turned in the lock and Lucian entered.

She dropped the keys on the table, the jarring noise instantly jolting Cole out of his slumber. 'Hey, what...?'

'Relax,' she said. 'It's just me. So we all here?'

'All present and correct,' Korso said. 'Where'd you dump the Beamer?'

'I pulled into an alley and wiped everything down and switched the licence plates, and then I just parked it right outside a café in one of the busiest parts of town. I left the keys in the ignition, so it's probably already being broken up for parts as we speak.' She walked over to him. 'We got anything to eat? I'm ravenous.'

'There should be some cold cuts left in the fridge. But now you're back we can grab a takeout.'

'Fine, I'll wait.' Under her breath, she said, 'Uh, Korso, there's something else.'

'What?'

'After I left you guys at the rail terminal, I could swear somebody was still following me part of the way. I kept seeing this black Honda sedan every time I looked in my rear-view, and always about three or four cars behind. And it didn't feel like law.'

'A black Honda. Did you get the model?'

'An Accord, looked about three years old. Why, what are you thinking?'

'Balakin was driving a Civic when I last saw him, but he's bound to have more than one vehicle at his disposal. Or it could be another interested party. You said they only followed you part of the way. So you managed to lose them?'

'It wasn't hard. I took a few little detours through various side streets, and double-backed a few times until I was completely sure they were gone.'

'Good. And thanks for letting me know.'

Lucian shrugged. 'We're all after the same thing.'

Cole was looking up at the TV with a deep frown. 'Hey, what happened to the game?'

'You fell asleep,' Korso said. 'Turn it back if you want.'

'No, I mean, how long was I out?'

Korso checked his watch, and saw it was already 6.36 p.m. Which surprised him. He hadn't realised it was that late. Teodor should have joined them by now. Unless... He felt a cold tingling sensation down the back of his neck.

Ignoring Cole's questioning glance, Korso made his way through the house and climbed the stairs to the second floor landing. At the top, he turned left and rapped his knuckles against the first door on the right. 'You finished in there? We've things to discuss.'

No answer. He knocked again with the same result. 'Okay, I'm coming in,' he said, and tried the handle. It gave easily. He pushed the door open.

The bathroom was empty.

Three damp towels were lying over the side of the bath, while droplets of water ran down the shower's sliding door. Lying in a heap on the floor next to the shower cubicle was Teodor's old tracksuit top and bottoms, along with the sneakers he'd been wearing when Korso had found him in the cell. He noticed the single rear-facing window was partially open. He pushed it open all the way and looked out. All he could see was a section of the rear garden and part of the fence surrounding the property. But no Teodor. He glanced to his right and spotted a solid looking drain pipe less than two feet away, running from the roof guttering to the ground. He reached out and tapped the pipe. Cast iron.

He pulled his head back in, and listened to the others racing up the stairs towards him. Samara was the first to appear, with Lucian and Cole arriving a second later.

Sam's eyes widened when she saw the open window. 'You're kidding.'

'Let's not rush to conclusions,' Korso said. 'Check the other rooms.'

The three heads disappeared. Korso left the bathroom and waited in the hallway. All the doors were open, and he could hear noises coming from the various rooms as everybody searched for the missing man.

Moments later, Sam's voice echoed through the house, '*What the hell are you doing in here, you little shit?*'

Korso ran down the hallway and entered Sam's room at the end. The first thing he saw was a fully-dressed Teodor pressed up against the clothes cupboard, with Sam's hand clamped tight around his throat.

'Hey, chill,' he said, both hands clasped around her arm. He couldn't budge it. 'I just looking, that's all.'

'Looking for what?' Korso said.

'I like to know who friends are. I want check passports, make sure you all who you say. Hey, come on, lady, let go.'

'I can guess what this guy was really after,' Lucian said from the doorway. 'You might want to check your underwear, Samara.'

'Oh, gross.' Samara released her prisoner, backing away as though he were contagious.

'What was he doing exactly?' Korso asked.

Samara nodded at her open knapsack on the floor, by the open clothes cupboard. 'I found him kneeling down there, rooting around for something.'

'Check IDs.' Teodor rubbed his throat. 'Like I tell you before.'

'You could just as easily have asked,' Korso said with a sigh. 'Believe it or not, we're all on the same side here. But it means I'm now going to have to search you.'

'Hey, I not thief.'

'Then you've got nothing to worry about. But one way or another I'm searching you, so let's do it the easy way, okay?'

Teodor looked ready to make a scene, but after seeing how outnumbered he was, he simply gave his trademark grin and raised his arms wide. 'Okay, search.'

Korso patted him down expertly, but found nothing in his trouser pockets. Nothing in the pockets of his leather coat either. 'Okay, you're clean. Let's head downstairs.'

As they all made their way downstairs in single file, Korso asked Lucian to go and get them some takeout buckets and meals from one of the nearby KFC knockoff joints. She grabbed the keys from the kitchen counter and left through the side door, while Cole grabbed another beer and resumed his place on the settee. Samara poured herself a coffee in the kitchen, while Teodor took one of the stalls at the breakfast bar and smiled at her.

'You got good grip,' he said, 'like wrestler. I ever tell you I always like strong ladies, ever since I was kid? Hey, you and me, we pals now, or what?'

She gave a sigh. 'Sure, best pals.'

'Cool. Hey, pal, you maybe pour a coffee for me too?'

Korso just let the conversation go on around him as he made his own coffee and took it to the dining table. He already knew Teodor was lying about checking their bags for IDs, and wondered what the man had really been looking for. But short of torturing the guy, he couldn't see any way of getting to the truth. What he mostly wanted to talk about was the location of the prototypes, but he didn't want to get into that until everybody was present. And a conversation like that would go over much better on a full stomach anyway.

He drank his coffee, and waited for Lucian to get back.

TWENTY-SEVEN

'So now that we've fulfilled our end of the deal,' Korso said, 'maybe you could start by telling us where your brother secreted these White Nights of his, and we'll go on from there.'

Teodor shook his head as he placed a foot against the coffee table. 'Too fast, good buddy. Other things to talk about first, I think.'

They were all in the living area, having finished off their fried chicken a short while ago. Korso and Samara sat on one side of the L-shaped settee, while Cole and Teodor took the other section. Lucian remained standing by the front window, not looking at anyone in particular as she absently rolled a coin back and forth along the knuckles of her right hand.

'What other things?' Korso reached for his can of Sprite.

'Okay, where is my half million dollars US?' Teodor turned his attention to Samara. 'Your boss forget about this already?'

'Not at all,' she said. 'Like I told you before, a deal's a deal. Although I should also point out that Belmont's not actually my boss. "Partner" is probably a better word.'

'Sure, sexy lady. Whatever you say. So where is money?'

'Right now it's sitting in an anonymous account in the Seychelles, waiting for me to activate the transfer code. But before that happens I'm gonna need you to give us something solid, such as a general location for these pills. As a gesture of good faith, you understand.'

'Sure. Pills are right here, in city. Okay?'

'That's not exactly what I meant, Teodor.'

'Hold on,' Korso said, 'listening to you two going back and forth on a point of procedure isn't what I had in mind for this meeting. Samara, if Belmont agreed to give him the money, then I suggest you complete the transfer now so we can all get on with the main business at hand.'

'I agree,' Lucian said, still knuckle-rolling her coin.

'Okay, okay,' Samara said, 'I know when I'm outnumbered. Give me a few moments here.' She took her phone from her pocket, and began swiping the display.

'Somebody give me phone,' Teodor said. 'I check account.'

Korso got up and walked over to the dining room area, where he grabbed the laptop from a side table and brought it back to their guest. 'Use that instead.'

Teodor opened it up and began playing his finger over the trackpad. Less than a minute later Samara asked for an IBAN and an account number, and Teodor quickly recited both from memory. Samara keyed the information into her phone. After another minute or so, she said, 'There, the cash has been transferred over.'

Teodor just stared at the laptop screen, and then gave a slow smile. 'Okay, now I'm happy guy.' He logged out, and smiled at Samara as he placed the closed laptop on the coffee table. 'Maybe you and me celebrate later. Now I got money, I get us champagne and we go to your room. I got some special games we play together.'

Samara just rolled her eyes, while Korso said, 'Let's talk business. I just hope you weren't lying to us when you said you know where Darian hid the White Nights.'

'Hey, I'm *only* one who knows.' He gave a sad shake of his head. 'Poor Darian. My little bro was very bright boy with science and fractions, but in everyday things maybe not so smart. Not like Teodor. Ever since we were kids he has head in clouds, and nothing up there but thin air. So when he comes visit me in prison and he tells me about these special pills he make, I tell him he watches too much movies and he better start growing up, because I can't look out for him no more. But when guard's not looking he slips me pill he brought along and tells me to try it later that night and not say word to anyone. By next morning, I *know* he's telling truth.'

Samara sat up. 'Wait, he actually gave you a sample? You didn't mention that before.'

'You don't ask, lady. But Darian's my bro, trusts me better than anybody. Just like I trusted him.'

'So you took the pill,' Korso said. 'Describe the effects.'

'Okay, I wait for lights–out that night, and then I lie on bunk in darkness and listen for cellmate to fall asleep. When he starts snoring, I swallow pill and wait. So maybe twenty minutes later, everything slowly starts getting brighter and brighter until I think it's middle of afternoon, yeah? Like sun is shining on face, but without heat. I jump off bunk in panic, thinking guards turned on lights for some reason, and I see everything so clear like I see you guys now. But my cellmate still asleep like normal, so I know it can't be lights. I take his Qur'an from bookshelf, and I open it and read every word, no problem. Also, we got barred window that looks out onto courtyard, and I see everything over there clear as anything. I'm thinking this pill is like miracle drug, and my brother invented it. My baby brother. Man, I was so proud.'

'How long did the effects last?' Korso asked.

'Don't know time exactly. Because of light, I wrap pillow over my head to sleep, but I think maybe six or seven hours. Darian comes and visits me three days later, and I tell him he's gonna be rich man, but only if he plays it careful. I tell him to hide samples in very last place anybody ever looks for them.'

'And where's that?'

'In heart of enemy, of course. Right on third floor of Vercogen building where bigshots got offices, including the big bastard who killed him, Deleva. I got Darian to tell me everything he remembers about top floor, and right away I think of best location to hide pill container. Darian smiled and told me he would never think of that in million years, and he was glad he had me for a brother.' Teodor breathed a sigh. 'Last time I ever see him smile.'

Korso said, 'What does the container look like?'

'Thin tube thing with screw cap, like in pharmacy, but made of metal. Maybe four centimetres tall, one centimetre wide. Darian told me he put twelve more sample pills in there. He make fifteen altogether, but he use two himself to test, and he also give me one too. Leaves twelve.'

'And the container's current location?'

'Told you, room on third floor of Vercogen building.'

Korso narrowed his eyes, sensing trouble ahead. 'I mean the *exact* location.'

'Yeah, well, that's second thing we have to talk about, good buddy.'

'I *knew* it,' Cole said, jumping to his feet. 'Didn't I warn you this guy would try and screw us over somehow?' He pulled his Marlboros from his pocket, extracted a cigarette from the pack.

'No smoking in the house, Cole,' Samara said.

'Screw this house.' He lighted the cigarette, took a drag and blew a plume of smoke towards the ceiling.

Korso's focus remained on Teodor. In a completely neutral voice, he said, 'Let me remind you that not only did we just spring you from prison, but you're now half a million dollars richer. Now I hope you haven't decided to go back on your part of the deal, Teodor, because that would be a very bad mistake on your part. I can't stress that strongly enough.'

'Hey, relax, good buddy. Teodor always keeps his end. I give you exact location like I promise, but first just one detail I forgot to mention.'

'And that is…?'

'I go with you.'

There it was. The bolt out of the blue that turned everything on its side. Korso had known there'd be a spanner in the works at some point, but hadn't guessed it would happen so soon. 'You mean to the Vercogen building itself?'

Teodor nodded. 'Right.'

'You can't be serious,' Samara said. 'Once the authorities release your photo to the media you'll very quickly become the most wanted man in the country, and based on past experience, they'll also post a reward for information leading to your capture. Which means everybody and their mother will be on the lookout for you. And you want to parade around the city like it's just another day in paradise?'

Lucian crossed her arms. 'Maybe he thinks a false moustache and sunglasses will make him invisible.'

'Hey, I know everybody out there looking for me, but I gotta protect my interests, yeah? Maybe you guys all know each other from before, but you all strangers to me. I give you hiding place, where is guarantee I get rest of my money once pills are in your hands? I only ever trust one other person in my whole goddamn life, and he's murdered three weeks ago. Now Teodor don't trust nobody except Teodor. So that means when you guys bust into Vercogen building, I go with you. Only way I can be sure.'

Korso said nothing. The worst part was he could see Teodor's point. If the roles were reversed Korso would be demanding the very same thing from his rescuers. All that was left was to see if everybody else felt the same. He turned to Lucian, who'd so far proven to be the most reasonable and even-tempered member of his crew. 'What do you think?'

'I think he's about as crazy as a soup sandwich, but I can also kind of see where he's coming from. To be honest, I was half expecting something like this.' She splayed a hand. 'I guess we can work around it, but if he blasphemes again we're going to have problems.'

Teodor bowed his head. 'I just want to be friends, pretty miss.'

'Fat chance of that,' Cole said. 'Every time this scheming bastard opens his mouth this job takes another turn for the worse. I don't like it.'

'Nobody does,' Korso said, 'but it's what it is. Samara?'

She gave a shrug. 'I'll side with the majority on this one, assuming you're okay with it?'

'It seems the decision's already been taken out of my hands.' Korso turned back to Teodor. 'All I can do is urge you to reconsider. I haven't even begun to figure out how to gain access to that building yet, but I do know that it's significantly harder to get two people into a secured premises than just one.'

Teodor just smiled back. 'Samara says you real smart guy, Korso. Says you always plan everything so nothing goes wrong. You bust me out of prison today, and now here I am' – he spread his arms out wide – 'having good life, see? Guy like that will think of something, for sure. One hundred per cent.'

Korso sighed, knowing nothing he could say would make any difference. All he could do was accept it and move on.

'Okay, Teodor, since you're intent on making everything that much harder, then you'll have to follow my instructions every step of the way. That's the deal. And whatever I do decide, there'll be no arguments from you. Are we clear?'

Teodor grinned. 'Deal.'

'Fine. Now tell us about the Vercogen building.'

'Okay, so Vercogen headquarters is large three-storey building on Bulgaria Boulevard. Here, I show you.' Teodor opened the laptop again and went straight to Google Maps. 'According to Darian, place also has plenty of security inside and out.'

'Naturally,' Samara said. 'They're a pharmaceutical company, after all.'

Teodor found the location and switched to the street-view. He turned the laptop screen in Korso's direction, and said, 'This the place.' Samara leaned in for a better look. Cole and Lucian also came over.

Korso moved his finger along the trackpad to navigate around the building. The three-storey structure was situated at the corner of an intersection just off Bulgaria Boulevard, with only a small car park separating it from its only neighbour, a seven-storey apartment building on the west side. It faced Pinn Street to the east, with Ralevitsa Street at the rear. Ten-foot-high steel railings surrounded the entre perimeter except for the main entrance, which was left open, and the car park entrance, which was protected by an unmanned automatic barrier with a combo keypad and intercom next to it. A gap of ten feet separated the security fencing from the building itself on the east side, while at the rear on Ralevitsa Street, the building butted right up against the railings. He saw a fire exit door back there. There was also a roller door situated on the west side of the building, no doubt used for deliveries and the like.

The first floor mostly consisted of mirrored glass panels, while the upper floors were made up of plain white stucco with a few windows here and there. Korso noticed the spot-lights running all around the exterior and knew there'd also be a multitude of alarms on the grounds, including passive infrared detectors, motion sensors, door contacts, and vibration detectors.

'Not exactly a cake-walk,' Cole said.

'Looks like only three ways in,' Samara said. 'Either directly through the front entrance, the delivery entrance, or via the roof.'

'And you can bet that roof's alarmed to hell and back' Cole said.

Korso just grunted. Without more information, any opinion he had was essentially worthless at this point. He felt his phone vibrating and pulled it from his pocket. As usual, the caller was anonymous. 'This should be Dog,' he said, and got up and made his way over to the kitchen. He took the call. 'Yes?'

'Hey, K. It's you-know-who.' This time Dog's voice was young and female, not a million miles away from her real voice. 'You okay to talk?'

'You tell me.'

'Well, this line couldn't be any more secure, if that's what you're getting at. Put your trust in the Dog. So anyway, I've been listening to lots of reports about a certain prison escape this afternoon, and I was just wondering if you might know anything about it.'

'Anything's possible. Have they released his identity to the media yet?'

'Yeah, just a few minutes ago, complete with mugshot and everything. I have to say he looks distinctly untrustworthy to my eyes, although that's possibly down to the lighting. So how's our Mr Y handling his new-found freedom?'

'He's proving to be highly adaptable. We've been discussing our next step, and he's just informed us that the only way we'll be able to retrieve the assets in question is if he comes along himself. It's that, or no deal.'

Dog chuckled. 'Wow, couldn't see that one coming, could we? Why are jobs never straightforward? So has he given you a starting point, at least?'

'Yes.' Korso gave Dog the specific address on Bulgaria Boulevard, and said, 'Darian secreted the pills somewhere on the third floor, but that's as much as Teodor will admit to for now. So what I'm going to need from you are the blueprints of the building itself, along with whatever schematics exist for their internal and external security systems. Also, do you think you can gain access to their CCTV footage so I can get a look at the general layout of the building? There's bound to be some.'

'Well, the blueprints and schematics should be easy enough. But as for the CCTV footage, I've only got some of my equipment with me so I'll most likely have to get up close and personal in order to get through the firewalls, since they're sure to be using a midrange standalone server rather than a large mainframe network. Which means no remote access, such as coming in through the clouds. But I'm looking at the area now and I can see plenty of parking around there, so that shouldn't be too much of a problem.'

'I assume you've rented yourself a van from which to work then?'

There was a pause. 'Possibly. Why, you planning on paying me a visit, K?'

Korso smiled to himself. As much as he was tempted to see Dog up close again, he knew it would be the worst move either of them could ever make. 'I don't think so,' he said. 'After all, why ruin a good relationship?'

'Exactly how I see it. Okay, anything else you want from me?'

'Yes, I'll also need extensive personnel files for every employee in the building, from the lowliest technician right up to the top dog himself. I'm not entirely sure yet how we're going to get inside, but I've got one or two ideas formulating and that kind of data might prove to be essential. And see if you can find out if they ever employ temporary staff through an agency. That could be another avenue worth pursuing.'

'Sure, I'll get on it. Wait one.' Korso heard fingertips tapping on a silicone keypad. He waited patiently. After a minute or so, Dog said, 'Okay, so I'm using my own special translation service and it looks like Vercogen outsource all their HR stuff to a third-party company called PGF Konsult, which is good. But I'm not seeing any references to temp workers anywhere, so it looks as though their staff are all employed in-house. Anyway, I'm currently going through their database as we speak, so I should be able to email you the HR files shortly. What else do you need?'

'The other thing we talked about before, it should be up and running now. Check for me, will you?'

'Hold on… Yep, it's all activated and ready to go.'

'Good. Text me when you've got something to send over.'

'Right. *Ciao.*'

Korso returned to the living area, where the others were still discussing the images on the laptop screen. After he filled them in on his phone conversation, Teodor said, 'Why this Dog not here with us now?'

'Because they work more effectively in the shadows,' Korso said. 'They also told me the police have just released your name and photo to the media, so you might want to check out one of the news sites yourself.'

Teodor swore softly and went straight to a news website called Novinite. As soon as the home page loaded up, they all looked at the colour police mugshot at the very top of the screen. Teodor's head was tilted back slightly so he seemed to be looking down his nose at the viewer. His hair was significantly longer and greyer in the photo, but the face looked essentially the same, except for the dark shadows under his eyes.

'Not your best side,' Lucian said. 'Also, you look a lot more arrogant in real life.'

Cole chuckled. Teodor just shook his head as he read through the news item below the photo. Samara got up from the settee and came over to Korso, gesturing with her phone.

'Just got a text message from Belmont,' she said. 'Says he wants an update. Do I call him, or will you?'

Korso told her he'd take care of it and took a stool at the breakfast bar. He called the phone number he'd been given. It was answered after two rings.

'Yes?' Belmont said. 'Who's this?'

'No names. A mutual acquaintance said you wanted to talk, so let's keep it brief.'

'Oh, it's you. Well, you've made quite a splash. As expected, our friend's currently the top story on every channel, as well as every news site in the country. Very impressive.'

'That's not the word I'd use. The police got any leads yet?'

'Funny you should mention that. The Nova channel's somehow got a hold of a short video taken by an eye witness at the National Hospital of Cardiology today. It's only fifteen seconds long so they're just replaying it over and over, but it shows a silver BMW containing a pair of shadowy figures whizzing through the car park at high speed. They've even put a soundtrack over it for added effect, not that it needs it. It's dramatic enough as it is.'

The girl he'd seen with the phone. It had to be. 'Is the driver or passenger visible?'

'No, they're only indistinct shapes, so you can't even be sure if they're male or female. But the car registration's as clear as day, which means the whole country's gonna be on the lookout for that BMW now.'

'For whatever good it'll do. My guess is it's already been chopped up.'

'I was hoping you'd say that.' Belmont paused. 'Any progress with our friend?'

'Of a kind. He's been paid his first instalment, and he's given us most of what we want. He says he'll give us the remainder nearer the time.' Korso saw no point in bringing up Teodor's new demands. It would only complicate things.

'Nearer the time? What's that supposed to mean?'

'It'd take far too long to explain, but it's all in hand. You'll just have to trust me.'

'Easy for you to say.' Another pause. 'Look, is there anything I can do, or is there anything else you need from me?'

Korso shook his head at the too-eager tone in Belmont's voice; the last thing they needed was another amateur on the scene. 'Not right now. If there is, you'll be contacted. Don't call us again unless it's an emergency. Goodbye.'

He hung up. That conversation had gone on too long as it was. Looking down at the display, he saw a message had arrived while they'd been talking.

It was just a short one: *Check your email*.

TWENTY-EIGHT

For security's sake, Korso preferred never to use a phone to access his emails, but the others were still using the laptop so he had little choice this time. He went straight to his secure service and logged on. There was one new email, from an anonymous sender. The header read: *HR Files*.

Korso was impressed at Dog's speed. He opened the email. There was no message, just a PDF attachment that he downloaded to his phone. After logging out of his account, he opened up the file.

The whole document ran to a total of 176 pages, with two to three pages devoted to each employee. Even better, each file included a colour waist-up shot of the staff member in question. On the downside everything was in Bulgarian, but Korso's fluency in Russian helped him make sense of most of the commentary.

He sat at the dining room table and went through each file systematically, disregarding all of the female staff right from the off. That left him with a total of 54 male employees, including the CEO, Andrey Deleva, and his Operational Consultant, Yan Simov. The files for these latter two were the very definition of skimpy, lacking all but the most essential information, such as height, weight, eye colour, and the like. No employment history for either man, and no current home address. To all intents and purposes they appeared to have simply fallen out of the sky.

But he studied their photos carefully. Simov, with his bullet-shaped head, lined face and stern brow, had that look of the professional fixer to whom nothing was off limits. With his patented thousand-yard stare, his photo looked more like a mugshot than the one currently on display on the news websites. As for Deleva, he looked a second away from smiling in his shot, but it was clearly all surface-charm. Korso could spot the sheer ruthlessness behind the man's dark eyes as clear as day.

Korso went through the document again, this time paying special attention to the photos, the job titles and the employment start dates. By the time he'd reached the last page, he was down to two possible candidates. One was a member of the part-time cleaning staff, and the other was the janitor. Since they each had low-level positions, Korso felt they were far less likely to be noticed by the more senior level employees on a day-to-day basis. Added to which, each man had only begun working for Vercogen within the last three months. The most recent was the janitor who'd started just four weeks before. This guy was also the only one who shared more than a passing resemblance to Korso, which automatically pushed him to the head of the very short list. From what he could see they shared the same basic body shape, and at six feet tall, they were the same height too. There were other advantages too, the main one being that the janitor's regular shift was from 3 p.m. till midnight every day. Which meant that if everyone else generally left around five, there were far fewer chances that other employees would challenge him.

'What's all this?'

Samara was standing just over his shoulder, watching him go through the personnel files. Until she spoke, he'd been lost in his own world. He could see it was already getting dark outside. He checked his watch: 8.15 p.m.

'How long have you been standing here?'

'Not long. You looked pretty engrossed. Those are Vercogen employees?'

Korso nodded, passed her the phone. 'Give me your opinion on this one. He's the night janitor, been at Vercogen less than a month. Think I could pass for him, at a pinch?'

Samara studied the photo carefully. 'Just about, I guess. You both look about the same age and you've got the same dark hair, although his is much shorter here. He's got dark blue eyes to your grey, but contacts could solve that problem easily enough. And you've both got oval-shaped faces, although yours is easier on the eye.'

'I'll take that as a compliment.'

'What I mean is this guy's not exactly going to win any beauty contests, is he? You've got a fairly symmetrical face, but this guy's left eye is noticeably lower than the right and droops down, he's got heavy acne scarring on both cheeks, and only a mother could love that nose. You considering taking his place?'

'Just looking at all the options. Until I get word on the kinds of security measures they employ at Vercogen, I can't do much else at the moment.' He looked to his right and saw Lucian and Cole sitting together at one end of the settee, discussing something or other in muted tones while occasionally glancing up at the TV. 'Where's Teodor?'

'Went upstairs a while ago. Said his insides were playing up after his recent beating, and he wanted to get some rest. I gave him some ibuprofen for the pain.' She smiled with one side of her mouth. 'I told him he could use your room.'

'Thanks very much.'

'Well, you said you didn't care where you slept.'

'I should learn when to keep my mouth shut.'

She passed the phone back to him. 'How long do you think before this Dog sends over the rest of the information we need?'

'Definitely within the next twenty-hour hours, and probably a lot sooner than that.' He watched Samara for a moment.

'What?' She pulled out the chair next to him and sat down. 'Have I got a spot on my face?'

'No, I'm just thinking back to that question you started to ask me before, back in the sewers, before Cole interrupted you. Was it important?'

'Oh, that. No, it was just about that Paris job you told us about when we first went down there. You know, the one with the Picasso and the sub-basement vault.'

'What about it?'

'I just wanted to know how much of that story was true. If any.'

Korso let his eyes grow vague. 'There was probably about seventy-five per cent truth in there. Maybe eighty. Most of the events happened as I described them, although it ended up taking me a lot more than three minutes to find the safety-deposit box containing the Picasso. And I also glossed over the problems I had with one member of my team immediately after we gained access to the vault.'

'What kind of problems?'

'The terminal kind.'

'I see. So this team member's no longer around to tell his, or her, side of the story?'

Korso shook his head. 'Unfortunately I had to leave him down there. Things got a little messy, let's leave it at that.'

'Intriguing. I don't suppose you want to furnish me with a few more details?'

'What's the point? The past is dead, just as he is.'

'So why tell us that story at all?'

'You already know the answer to that.'

'Yeah, okay, it was pretty obvious you wanted to get our minds off our surroundings. I admit I wasn't having the best of times in that small tunnel.' She gave a mock shiver. 'It felt like the walls were pressing closer in on me with each step. You know that feeling?'

'Yes.'

'So that part about the two-foot wide sewer tunnel you guys had to crawl through in Paris. That actually happened?'

207

'It was like being stuck inside a drainpipe. I still have flash-backs about it to this day.'

'I kind of doubt that, Korso.' She narrowed her eyes as she looked at him. 'You're quite the manipulative son of a bitch, aren't you?'

'Whatever it takes to get the job done. It worked, didn't it?'

Samara gave a low chuckle. 'Okay, I'll grant you that.'

'While we're on the subject of motivation, you still haven't explained the reason behind your involvement in all this. I still think you're connected with one of those three-letter agencies, but you don't strike me as one of those super-patriots who put their country before all other interests. There must be a deeper reason why you're here. That is unless I'm completely wrong about you, and it's simply about the money.'

'Or it could be that I'm just an adrenaline junkie who gets off on the thrill of the chase.' She gestured towards Lucian, who had left the living area and was now climbing the stairs to the second floor. 'Like little Lucian over there. That girl plays it real cool but I can tell she's enjoying all this, probably even more than her racing. Some people don't feel truly alive unless they're constantly pushing the envelope and testing the limits of their own mortality. Maybe I'm the same.'

'Are you?'

'To a certain extent, maybe. I can't deny I've led an active life for much of my life, and that's a hard thing to just shake off. But that doesn't necessarily mean I'm a spook.'

'Doesn't mean you're not either.'

'You know, I get the feeling we could go around and around on this subject for hours, only to end up right back where we started.'

Korso was about to reply when he was distracted by the sounds of muffled footsteps coming from above. They sounded as though someone was moving from one room to the next in a rush. Fearing the worst, he got up from his seat and walked over to the staircase.

He was about to ascend when Lucian appeared at the top landing, glaring down at him.

'What's the problem?' he asked.

'The problem is I've just checked every room and they're all empty. Our boy's flown the coop.'

He was about to descend when Cav had appeared at the top of another staircase, down at heel.

"What's the problem?" he asked.

"The problem is I've just locked everyone out, and now I can't—Cav, let's fetch the cops."

TWENTY-NINE

Teodor pulled the visor on his baseball cap down a little more as he watched the familiar streets and buildings passing by outside. The cab driver had shown no recognition at all when he had gotten in the back seat a short while ago, barely even glanced at him, but that was no reason to start getting careless. Everybody in the country was on the lookout for him now, not discounting the very people who'd broken him out in the first place.

He smiled. It was nice to be wanted. But it was even better being back on the streets again. At least it was fully dark outside now, so he felt a little less conspicuous than before.

Back at the house, it hadn't been difficult to make out he was in worse shape than he appeared. He'd done the exact same thing in prison. Once he retired upstairs he simply continued doing what he'd been doing earlier, searching everyone's rooms for cash. He'd finally found what he wanted in Cole's room. Stuck in one of the interior pockets of his flight bag were a bunch of 100-leva notes, along with some fifties and a few twenties. Teodor pocketed all of it and then grabbed a navy baseball cap from the same bag. It was just a loan. Cole would get the money back, and the cap too. But Teodor's immediate need was greater.

After clambering down the iron drainpipe outside the bathroom window, he found a spot out of view from the rest of the house, and climbed over the fence and began walking north. Three blocks later, he'd spotted a yellow taxi approaching and hailed it. Once he gave the driver his destination and got in the back, he said nothing else for the rest of the journey.

They were currently heading north on Balsha Street. Traffic was fairly light. When Teodor spotted several of the university hospital buildings further up ahead, he said to the driver, 'Right here will do.'

The driver indicated and pulled over to the side of the road. Teodor glanced at the meter, gave the driver a twenty note, and stepped out onto the sidewalk. Once the taxi re-joined the traffic, Teodor crossed the street and began walking northeast towards Pencho Slaveikov Boulevard.

A few weeks before, he'd been talking with one of the recent arrivals at prison and enquired about his old hunting grounds. Among other things, the guy had assured him his three favourite houses were still open for business, as was his favourite bar, *The Icicle*. That news had given him all the incentive he needed to leave. If his luck held, one or two of his favourite girls might even still be working. You never knew.

He kept his head down as he walked, making no eye contact with any of his fellow pedestrians. Along the way he made a brief stop at a convenience store, where he purchased a cheap pre-paid phone and one or two other items that would come in useful. Once he reached Pencho Slaveikov Boulevard he kept walking northwest. Finally, he picked out the neon lights of *The Icicle* up ahead, just before the turn-off for Tsar Petar Street. His three favourite houses of ill repute were all located on that same street, right out in the open, but completely untouchable thanks to their underworld connections. Teodor also knew that if he showed his face in any of them, news of his presence would spread through the city faster than the speed of light. But there were other options.

When he reached *The Icicle*, he adjusted the bill of his cap and then he pulled open the door and stepped inside. The large interior looked the same as he remembered, except for the lighting, which seemed a little more subdued. But the bass-heavy dance music coming over the system sounded exactly the same as when he'd last visited three years before. Booths and tables took up most of the floor space, with the main bar running down the right-hand side. The place was about three-quarters full already, and would no doubt be packed to the rafters in another hour or so. Almost all of the booths were occupied by women of varying ages, mostly texting or checking social media on their phones. Some already had male company, while the rest either sat on their own or in small groups of two or three. More guys sat drinking either at the main bar or at the tables, usually in pairs, building up their courage to approach whichever girl took their fancy.

Teodor looked around but didn't see anyone he recognised, which was both good and bad. He'd built up a number of fantasies while inside, imagining that Sofija would still be here and would jump for joy the moment she saw him walk through the door. Or Ivana. Or Rosa, even. But he was well aware that reality never lived up to what you wanted it to be. But on the plus side, at least nobody here knew who he was. He didn't even recognise any of the bar staff. So as far as anyone was concerned, he was just another anonymous john looking for a hook-up. He'd already spotted one girl who looked interesting.

At the bar, he ordered a bottle of Zagorka from the nearest bartender. As Teodor waited for the change he noticed a man three stools down was watching him. Keeping his head partly turned away, Teodor grabbed his change and then took his bottle back towards one of the booths he'd just passed.

The girl was still texting, of course. She was sitting on her own and looked to be in her mid-twenties, with long frizzy brown hair down to her shoulders and the kind of full figure he liked on a woman. Even though she wore heavy make-up and false eyelashes, he could see she was still good-looking underneath. She was wearing tight jeans and a tanktop that showed off her attributes to their best effect. There was a single empty glass on the table.

'Buy you a drink?' he asked.

She looked up from her phone and gave him her best professional smile. Straight away, he could see the years of experience behind those large brown eyes. 'Sure. Make it a Menta and Sprite.'

Teodor placed his beer on the table and returned to the bar. Thankfully, the guy from before was no longer looking his way, but doing something on his phone instead. Moments later, Teodor came back with a tumbler of the green peppermint liqueur and a bottle of Sprite. He placed them in front of the girl and sat down opposite. They touched glasses and drank.

After a while, he said, 'What's your name?'

'Anna.' She added some more Sprite to the Menta and took another slug. 'And you?'

'Petar. You're real pretty, Anna.'

The smile she gave him didn't quite reach her eyes. 'Why thank you, Petar. You looking for some company tonight?'

'Am I ever. Although it kind of depends on what it might cost me.'

'One hundred and twenty leva for one hour, and that includes the room.'

Teodor nodded. At least the rates hadn't gone up since he'd been away. 'And where's this room?'

'Not far away. There's an apartment house in the next block that rents them by the hour. But they're clean if that's what you're worried about.'

'I wasn't. How much for the whole night?'

Her smile immediately grew wider as she took another sip of her mint liqueur. 'Well, I don't usually do that kind of thing, Petar, but for you I could maybe make an exception. Overnight will cost you five hundred leva, with another eighty on top for the room.'

'Five hundred and eighty, huh? That's a lot of money.' He pretended to think about it while he scanned the room again. He watched as a serious-looking older guy in a grey suit entered from the street and just walked straight over to the bar without looking at anyone. For a brief moment, Teodor thought he recognised him. He'd always had a photographic memory when it came to faces, and rarely made a mistake when it came to placing somebody. But the moment was only a brief one. It quickly became obvious that he'd never seen the guy before. He was sure of it. Still, there *was* something about him…

He realised Anna had spoken, and turned to her. She was looking down at her phone again. 'What was that?' he asked.

She looked up at him. 'I was saying that you get what you pay for, and I happen to be worth every penny. I've never had any complaints.'

'Well, I'll tell you what, Anna. Make it five hundred for you and the room combined, and you've got yourself a deal.'

She pursed her lips for a few moments, and then shrugged. 'Okay, but only if you pay for dinner as well.'

'Sounds reasonable.' He wasn't particularly hungry, but saw no reason to spoil the mood now. If she wanted to eat, they'd eat.

'Good,' she said. 'You want to go now?'

'What's the rush? We've got plenty of time, and I haven't even finished my beer yet.' He pointed at her glass. 'Want another one of those?'

'Sure, why not.'

Teodor went back to the bar and ordered her another glass of that green stuff. He noticed the stern guy who'd just come in was in deep conversation with the other bartender. He never even looked Teodor's way. Taking the drink back to the table, Teodor relaxed and started asking Anna about herself, where she came from, where she lived, and so on. This was all part of the process for him, having learned long ago that delayed gratification always offered greater reward. And he'd also discovered that the more he knew about his companion's life, the more enjoyable the sex afterward. At least, for him. He doubted the women he slept with gave it any thought at all, other than a wish for it to be over. But that was okay too. It was all part of the game.

They talked, they drank. The time passed quickly. Any time Anna asked him about himself he'd give her one of his stock answers he'd used countless times before, and then quickly turn the conversation back to her again. Teodor could feel himself getting increasingly aroused with every minute that passed by. He was just finishing up his third beer when he decided it might be a good time to move on.

'Just need to visit the men's room,' he said, getting up from his seat, 'and then we'll go grab a light supper somewhere.'

'I'll be here.' Anna gave him her best professional smile. 'Don't be long, Petar.'

'Count on it, baby.'

He turned and walked towards the rear of the room. As he passed the bar he noticed the serious looking guy was no longer there. He hadn't noticed the man exit the bar, but then he hadn't really been paying too much attention. He stepped through the open doorway at the back of the room, and entered a corridor that still smelled of ancient urine and stale food. Some things never changed. Forty feet away was the fire exit, while running down the right-hand side were three more doors. The second one had the universal male icon above it.

Teodor pushed this door open and stepped into the men's room.

When he saw the lights had been turned off, his guard went up almost immediately. An image of that serious dude outside immediately came to mind and he spun round, ready to bolt, when he heard a scuffling sound coming from his right. Before he could even turn his head, a pair of strong hands grabbed both his arms from behind and pulled him back into the toilet, and then slammed him face-first into the wall.

Somebody punched him hard in the left kidney, taking all the breath out of him in an instant. The pain was tremendous. Teodor heard what sounded like an angry voice behind him as he desperately tried to suck in air, and then without warning his legs gave way and he felt himself falling.

But strong hands held him upright, and then those same hands spun him round so he was facing his assailant. Somebody else switched on the lights again, and Teodor found himself face to face with the last person he'd expected to see here.

'And I thought you were supposed to be the smart one,' Korso said.

THIRTY

'*You*,' Teodor said, his voice barely above a whisper. He glanced over at Cole by the door, still looking pissed, then turned back to Korso. 'Why you hit me like that?'

'Blame Cole. He's not very happy with you, and he struck before I could stop him. I can see his point of view, though. You've caused us a lot of problems tonight.'

Teodor winced as he pressed a hand against his side. 'Hey, after two years inside I want sex with lady, okay? Samara and your driver always say no, so I go find somebody else instead.' He jutted his chin towards the door. 'She waiting out there for me right now.'

'We know. She can carry on waiting.'

'Shit, man. She—' Teodor stopped as he finally noticed the long thin package Korso was holding in his right hand. The plain brown wrapping paper did little to conceal the true shape of the object within. 'Is what I think it is?'

'More than likely.'

'Hey, chill. I go quietly… Wait, how you guys even find me?'

'It wasn't difficult. I planted a micro GPS device in the sole of your left sneaker.'

And if that one malfunctioned for whatever reason, then there was also one secreted in the collar of Teodor's leather jacket, as well as the collar of his shirt and in the buckle of the belt he was wearing. Korso was nothing if not thorough, but Teodor didn't need to know that part. He'd long suspected that their captive might feel the need to spread his wings once he'd regained his freedom, which is why he'd asked Dog right from the start to get hold of the smallest GPS trackers she could find and drop them at his self-storage mailbox in Sofia. Each tracker was no larger than the size of a micro sim card, and so it hadn't taken long for him to conceal them within the clothes he would give to Teodor once he was on the outside.

All of which meant Korso hadn't been too surprised when Lucian searched the house and told them their man was no longer on the premises. After a full search of the place, they'd discovered the missing cash from Cole's bag along with a navy blue baseball cap he'd brought along. Meanwhile, Korso had already called Dog up to explain the situation, and Dog then activated her special tracking app, relaying to him Teodor's gradual progress through the city streets. It was Samara who'd figured out where he was most likely headed. During an earlier prison visit, Teodor had brazenly boasted of his fondness for brothels and easy women, and had even mentioned the specific places he liked to frequent, including the area around Pencho Slaveikov Boulevard.

Lucian had driven them out to that general location, with Dog guiding them every step of the way. When she gave Korso final confirmation that their mark had entered a bar called *The Icicle*, Lucian found a parking spot with a good view of the front and killed the engine. Korso, Cole, and Samara made their way to the narrow alley at the rear and found a place next to one of the parked cars back there. It only took twenty-five minutes before a bartender pushed open the bar's fire exit, slipped a wedge under the door, and lit up. Samara approached the man and using all her feminine charms, asked him to help her with some problem she was having with her phone. When he walked over to her, Korso and Cole quickly slipped inside behind him and made their way to the men's room further in.

The toilet wasn't large, with just two cubicles and a long urinal against one wall. Koros silently handed Cole the Mossberg that Samara had found for them, then pulled a baseball cap from his jacket pocket and put it on. Pulling the visor down low, he slipped out to the bar area out front and gave the place a once-over before anyone took any notice of him. He quickly spotted Teodor in one of the booths sharing a drink with a young lady.

The last thing they could afford was a scene, especially with so many witnesses. Far better to simply wait for Teodor to take a leak, and then handle him quietly and with the minimum of fuss. So Korso returned to the men's room and waited in the other empty cubicle. So far, so silent. But for how much longer, it was harder to guess.

'Please tell me nobody recognised you in there,' Korso said.

Teodor snorted. 'Hey, after two years away I'm stranger here, same as you.'

But Korso had seen a frown quickly pass across his features as he said it. 'What? Tell me.'

'Well, guy in there I thought maybe I recognised, but now I don't think so. About my age, with very serious face. Grey suit. Never even looked at me, so I don't know. When I leave girl I don't see him no more, so I'm thinking it's him punching me when I come in here. But no, it's my good friends instead.'

'You wanna be friends,' Cole said, 'we gotta be able to trust you first.'

But Korso was already thinking about this mysterious guy in the bar. Could it have been Balakin, back on their trail somehow? Or maybe it was Deleva's security man, Simov. It might even be a cop. Whoever it was, the sooner they were gone from this place the better.

Korso's phone vibrated in his pocket. He brought it out and took the call.

'Storm warning,' Lucian said. 'Vehicle just pulled up and parked two spaces in front of me. Driver and another guy got out. Driver's thirtyish, other guy's about Cole's age. Both look like players. Older one's definitely packing. Younger one, too, I think. They're looking over at the bar right now as they talk… Okay, the older guy's walking towards the bar now, while the driver turns and veers off to the left. Looks like he might be heading for the rear of the bar. Older guy's just waiting by the front door, calm as anything.'

'Call Samara,' Korso said. 'Warn her company's coming. And keep the engine running.'

'Way ahead of you.' Lucian hung up.

Cole and Teodor were both looking at him. 'What?' Cole asked.

'Unwanted guests. Time to leave.' But Korso was thinking about the older guy out front. He sounded like someone to be avoided if possible. 'Cole, take Teodor back to the fire exit door and wait for me. But don't even think of opening it until I tell you.'

'Where will you be?'

'Right here, watching your backs. Go. Now.'

Cole pulled open the door and poked his head outside. He looked both ways, and then pulled his head back in. He whispered, 'Two girls just left the head, and are making their way back to the bar.' He waited a few more seconds, then took another peek. 'All clear. Let's go.'

Cole pushed Teodor out first, and then followed close behind. The door closed gently behind them. Korso stood next to it, not moving. Just listening. Waiting for the inevitable.

It came less than fifteen seconds later, when he heard a man's deep voice shout out, '*You two. Stop or I shoot.*'

Korso gingerly pulled open the toilet door an inch or two, and peered to his right. Standing less than ten feet away, with his back to Korso, was a man in a grey suit. He was pointing a pistol at the two men at the other end of the hallway, both of whom had their hands raised. The gunman said something else in Bulgarian, and Korso opened the door a few more inches and slipped out through the gap. Teodor said something else in the same language, and Korso used the distraction to tiptoe towards the gunman, gripping the concealed shotgun tightly in both hands.

He'd closed the distance to just three feet when the gunman sensed something and began to swivel round, gun first. Korso didn't let him finish the move. He darted forward, Mossberg raised, and slammed the butt into the side of the gunman's head with full force.

The man dropped to his knees as though pole-axed, and Korso raised the shotgun again and clubbed him on the back of the neck for good measure. The man collapsed to the floor in a heap. Korso reached down and took the gun – a 9mm Glock 26 – from the unconscious man's grip and was finally able to see his features clearly. The lined face was the same as the one he'd seen in those personnel files Dog had sent over.

Cole and Teodor ran back. Teodor reached him first and peered down at the man's face. 'This same guy I see in bar before. Who is he?'

'Deleva's security man, Simov. Just hoping you'd be dumb enough to show up here.'

'We're right out in the open here.' Cole turned back towards the fire exit. 'Let's get a move on.'

Korso heard a *ping* and said, 'Wait.' He pulled out his phone again, then read the brief text. 'We're not leaving that way.'

Cole frowned. 'Why not?'

'Because Samara says there's a guy with an automatic weapon on the other side of that door, just waiting for it to open. She says she can't get anywhere near him. We'll have to leave by the front.'

'Shit, just what we need.'

Korso had already prepared for this possibility. He reached into his jacket pocket and pulled out a pair of folded flesh-coloured stockings he'd brought along, just in case.

'Take these.' He passed one to Cole, who immediately understood and began pulling the thin elasticated material over his head until his facial features were completely distorted. Korso handed the second stocking to Teodor, who frowned back at him.

'What the hell, man?'

'As far as anyone else is concerned we'll look like we're robbing the joint. Put it on. Don't argue.'

While Teodor grudgingly stretched the stocking over his own head, Korso held out the Glock to Cole. 'Better take this. Keep it ready, but don't use it unless you have to.'

Cole took the piece. 'What are you going to do?'

'Make sure you don't have to.' Korso traced his fingers along his package until he felt the Mossberg's trigger guard under the wrapping paper. He ripped away two small sections of the packaging so that the trigger and ejection port were both clear. He inserted his index finger into the guard, and then used his other hand to pull his cap visor down even lower. 'I'll go first. You two stay close and follow my lead. You ready?'

Both men nodded without a word. Korso turned and led them down the hallway towards the bar. He opened the door at the end and stepped through into the bar area. The music was a lot louder now, and there were more customers and even more girls. The place wasn't packed yet, but it was starting to get busy. The two bartenders were already hard at work behind the bar, mixing drinks. Nobody paid their little group any undue attention. A girl and a guy drinking at the bar frowned when they spotted Teodor and Cole behind him in what looked like stocking masks, but that was all.

Eyes darting in all directions, Korso carefully led his two charges through the room towards the front entrance. All around him the bar's clientele drank, laughed, and made their arrangements for the evening. Some stood, some danced, but most sat in the booths on either side of the room. Focusing on the huge front window directly ahead, Korso watched the minimal traffic on the street outside and the occasional pedestrian walking past. Everything out there looked normal.

He was less than twenty feet away from the entrance when the front door opened, and a single man in a trenchcoat stepped into the bar. Korso halted in his tracks. So did the man. Korso recognised the craggy face straight away.

Balakin.

The Russian's eyes widened in recognition, his right hand instinctively reaching for something inside his raincoat. At the same time, Korso brought up the shotgun with both hands and aimed at his centre mass. Balakin saw what was coming and dived to the floor at his left just as Korso pulled the trigger. The shotgun *boomed*, and a large ragged hole appeared in the door where Balakin had been standing. At the sound of the explosion, everyone else in the bar froze. Korso pumped the forestock and the spent shell flew out of the port. Even over the blaring sound system, he could hear it land on the floor.

Then the screams and shouts started, the whole place erupting as everybody moved at once.

'*Get him to the car,*' Korso yelled to Cole as panicked people swept past them towards the exit. '*I'll cover you.*'

'*Right.*'

Cole grabbed Teodor's arm and started waving his Glock around as he pulled Teodor towards the entrance with the rest of the clientele. Korso looked around until he could make out Balakin crawling at speed along the floor towards the booths on the other side. He didn't look injured. Korso aimed the Mossberg in his direction, ready to fire again, but couldn't get a clear shot. Too many moving people in front of him.

Cursing under his breath, Korso thought quickly. As much as he wanted to stay and finish Balakin for good, his ultimate objective was to get Teodor out of the vicinity before the cops showed up. Then there was Balakin's armed partner at the rear exit, who could also appear at any moment. He'd undoubtedly heard the shotgun blast, and was probably already on his way. And an SMG against a shotgun wasn't even worth thinking about.

Over the blaring music, Korso heard the unmistakeable crack of a gunshot. He ducked down as a running man in front of him screamed out and fell to the floor, blood spraying from a wound in his shoulder. Through the legs of panicking men and women, he could just make out Balakin kneeling by one of the booths, aiming his pistol for another shot.

Korso didn't give him another chance. He aimed at the roof directly above Balakin and squeezed the trigger. The shotgun roared, and chunks of plaster erupted from the ceiling in a huge cloud of dust and dirt. Korso racked the forestock, the spent shell flew out, and he fired again in the exact same spot. More pieces of plaster fell from above. More dust. Korso used the distraction to run for the front door with the last of the stragglers.

Once he was outside, he turned both ways and saw his fellow patrons running off in all directions. Thanks to the gunshots, the rest of the street was now empty of bystanders. He could also see the Inifini was still parked in the same spot on the other side of the street.

Lucian flashed her headlights once, and then quickly accelerated out of the space, did a smart handbrake turn until she was pointed in the opposite direction, skidding to a stop right next to Korso. The passenger door flew open. Korso saw three pairs of eyes staring back at him from the rear. Lucian just looked straight ahead as she revved the engine once, twice.

Korso dived in and slammed the door shut. Lucian stamped on the gas and got them out of there.

224

THIRTY-ONE

'All I know is I'm surrounded by incompetence,' Deleva said, glaring at Balakin and Simov in turn, 'everywhere I look. On all sides.'

Balakin shook his head as he studied the abstract tree sculpture at the other end of the large office. Deleva letting off steam was a pitiful sight. But Balakin knew better than to let it affect him. As for the sculpture, he decided it wasn't his kind of thing it all. It seemed to be made entirely from interconnected metal rods, and resembled something out of a drug addict's nightmare. Balakin appreciated most forms of art, but this mess just hurt your eyes. He wondered vaguely how Deleva could stand it.

'Balakin, are you listening to me?' Deleva yelled across the room.

'Only sporadically. Let me know once you've finished ranting, and I'll be happy to rejoin the conversation.'

He watched as Deleva carefully reined in his anger, and then quickly busied himself with a fat cigar from his humidor. Once Deleva learned about the shootout, he'd called Simov and Balakin and demanded an emergency summit at his office. Balakin couldn't exactly refuse. The man was right about one thing, though. The events at the *Icicle* had been a complete debacle, though that was hardly Balakin's fault. He left the sculpture and approached the other two men. Simov was still seated in front of the desk, anxiously waiting for his boss to cool down. Deleva lighted his cigar with a match and blew out smoke.

'Are you calm again?' Balakin asked. 'Can we talk seriously now?'

'Watch how you speak to me, Balakin. I'm not one of your ex-KGB goons. So talk. Explain to me what the hell happened tonight.'

'What happened, Mr Deleva, is that the two of you decided to go behind my back, and Korso and his people made you pay for it. Had I been kept abreast of the particulars ahead of time, we would have had Teodor Yanev in this very room right now, telling us everything we could possibly want to know, but instead you went and blew our only chance by going it alone.' He sneered at Simov. 'God protect us from amateurs.'

Simov jumped to his feet and glared at Balakin, his face a picture of smouldering rage. 'I don't have to take that shit from you.'

'You'll take everything I throw at you, Simov, and more besides. If my driver hadn't found you unconscious in the hallway and hauled your useless carcass out of there, you'd be in police custody right now, probably singing like a canary. The placement of those bruises tells me everything I need to know. Only amateurs allow themselves to be taken from behind. I'm only surprised you've managed to live this long.'

Deleva winced at that. 'Cold-cocked from behind, Simov? *You?*'

'It wasn't like that, boss. I—'

'Shut up. Let me think.' Deleva closed his eyes and took a deep breath. 'Okay. First, explain to me how you knew Teodor was there.'

Simov said, 'I was finishing up another lead last night when I received a call from my man, Ferad, saying that a guy matching Teodor Yanev's description was chatting up a freelancer in a booth at *The Icicle*. So I raced over, entered the bar and walked straight over to the bartender, never once looking at Teodor or Ferad. I got the bartender to take a photo of him on my phone. It was Teodor all right. So I ducked into a nearby booth just as he headed for the toilets, leaving his woman at the table. It was clear they were about to leave together so I waited there and called for backup. After about a minute he hadn't returned, so I headed back there myself and spotted him and another man I've never seen before heading for the fire exit. I pulled my piece and ordered them both to halt. Then I heard movement behind me, and as I was turning someone clubbed me in the temple, then again on the back of my neck. This Korso must have been hiding in the toilet.'

'You forgot to mention he also took your gun,' Balakin said, shaking his head. 'If Korso wasn't armed before, we can be sure he is now. Brilliant.'

'Never mind all that,' Deleva said, turning to Balakin. 'How did you learn that Teodor was at this particular bar at that particular moment? That's what I want to know.'

'Oh, that part was easy. I bugged your phones.'

'You did *what*?' Deleva jumped to his feet, his face red. 'Who the hell do you think you're dealing with here, Balakin? What gives you the right to plant—?'

'Oh, please,' Balakin interrupted, 'let's forego the dramatics, shall we? I'm a professional, and a professional always covers his bets whenever he gets the chance. I suspected the two of you might get greedy at some point and try to keep me out of the loop, and so I planted some intricate spyware in each of your phones, just as a precaution. And it turns out my instincts were right. The moment I heard Ferad call Simov here I sped over to *The Icicle* as fast as I could, but it was still too late. Had I been involved from the start, we could have had Teodor in our hands right now, and Korso and his crew would no longer be an issue, but you had to do it your way.'

It also meant that any chance of a side deal between himself and Korso was now out the question. Not that he'd really believed Korso would go for it, but still… He sighed. 'I warned you Korso shouldn't be underestimated, but did you listen?'

Deleva ignored the question, and took a long drag of his cigar. 'What about the police? Did they—?'

'We were gone before they arrived.'

Deleva nodded grimly. 'Well, that's something, at least. So Teodor gets sprung from prison this afternoon, and then just a few hours later he somehow escapes his rescuers and goes hunting for an easy lay. That's some feat. How do think this Korso managed to track him down so fast?'

Balakin shrugged. 'It's not difficult. If it had been me, I'd have inserted a small GPS tracker into the man's clothing as a backup. I imagine Korso did the same.'

'How many of his people were present at the bar, do you know?'

'I saw Korso and the second man with my own eyes, and I have to assume somebody drove them there and got them out. So at least three. Beyond that I'd only be guessing.'

'And you didn't see their car?'

'They were gone before I managed to exit the bar. My man, Vlad, said he saw a light grey sedan speed off in an easterly direction, but it was dark and he couldn't get the make or model.'

Deleva grimaced. 'So we're right back where we started.'

'There are still one or two avenues to explore yet.' Not to mention further discussions with other interested parties, as well. But Deleva didn't need to know that. 'After tonight I believe I'll start handling things my way, if that's okay with you. But don't worry, I'll make sure to update you the moment I find something useful. Now is there anything else? Because the sooner I leave here, the sooner I can get started.'

There wasn't anything else. Without another word, Balakin left the two executives to their little schemes and went his own way. As always.

THIRTY-TWO

Korso closed the laptop, and sat back in his chair at the dining table. He stretched his arms out wide until he felt his shoulders crack, and checked his watch. 12.33 a.m. Saturday morning already. He hadn't realised it was so late. Friday had been a long and exhausting day for everybody, in more ways than one.

He was the only one still up, the others having retired to their respective rooms not long after their return. Once they'd reached the house safely nobody had said very much, but Teodor had clearly sensed the animosity directed towards him and didn't even try flirting with the two women. Which showed he had brains, after all.

But Korso remained downstairs, knowing there was no way he was going to get any sleep until he figured out how Balakin *and* Simov had known Teodor was going to be at that particular place last night. In the car, Teodor had admitted seeing another guy in the bar texting on his phone, and that it hadn't been long after that when Simov had come in and walked straight over to the bar without looking at Teodor at all. Which suggested that Simov had either planted his own men at various establishments around the city, or bribed the staff thereof, in the hope that Teodor would eventually show up at one of them. Then all it would take was one call and Simov could show up himself to make sure.

But Balakin's appearance at the bar had been unexpected. Was he working with Deleva, or were they competitors? Either option was possible. Korso knew Balakin had eyes and ears everywhere, so it wouldn't have been too hard for him to keep close tabs on Deleva and Simov if he wanted to. But if he were working with them to recover the prototypes, it would make things even easier for him. Not that he'd ever stick to their deal, of course.

One thing was for sure, they'd been very fortunate to get away clean tonight. But Korso couldn't afford to rely on luck again, and Balakin and Deleva clearly couldn't be underestimated either. If they'd managed to figure out Teodor's location once, then they could conceivably do it again. Balakin, in particular, was one of the shrewdest and wiliest adversaries Korso had ever known. No matter how careful he thought he was being, the Russian was sure to be looking for any kind of advantage to second guess his next move.

On the plus side, Dog had come through once again by sending over the architectural blueprints for the Vercogen building, as well as providing extensive details of the security systems they currently had in place. He didn't know how she accomplished it all so fast, but it did explain why she was always in such high demand.

The building blueprints didn't really tell him very much, other than to reveal how many executive offices were on the top floor – sixteen in total – and their relationship to each other. The largest office was Deleva's, located at the very rear of the building. Naturally, it was the only one with an en-suite executive bathroom. Simov's was the second largest, situated right next to his boss, although he doubted Simov used it much. Research and development laboratories took up most of the second floor, while the first floor housed the various administration departments as well as the in-house production facilities.

As for Vercogen's security situation…

Korso was brought out of himself at the sound of footsteps coming from above. Moments later, he watched Samara slowly descend the stairs. She was barefoot, wearing just a baggy t-shirt and long pyjama leggings. When she saw Korso, she greeted him with a nod and padded into the kitchen, and then opened the refrigerator door and pulled out a carton of grapefruit juice.

'Don't you ever get tired?' she asked, pouring some juice into a glass tumbler.

'I do my best thinking in the early hours. And I've got plenty to keep my mind occupied.'

'Yeah, that sounds like our Korso.' She brought her drink over and took a seat next to him. 'Always scheming, always looking for that extra edge that'll take him over the finish line.' She ran a hand through her sleep-tousled hair and looked at him. 'Cole told me you've barely changed in seven years, at least physically. What's your secret?'

'Work keeps me young. How come you're up?'

'Dry throat.' She took a sip of her juice. 'Forgot to take some water up with me.'

'Did you happen to check on Teodor on your way down?'

'I did. He's still in your room, sleeping the sleep of the dead. Looks like maybe he's finally learned his lesson.'

'I wouldn't count on it.'

She gave a snort. 'I don't. So what else is occupying your thoughts at the moment?'

Korso told her about the intel Dog had sent over, and gave her a quick summary of the building's layout. 'But you were essentially correct earlier when you said you saw only three plausible entry points. There *is* a fourth, a fire exit at the rear of the building, but the steel door's triple-alarmed to prevent any unauthorised access or exits, so I don't see us using that. Also, it's right out in the open.'

Samara leaned in closer. 'What other security arrangements do they have over there?'

'Externally, they've got motion sensors situated all around the place, with the alarms set to go off if anything larger than a pigeon sets down in that space between the building and the steel fence. According to Dog, there are no smoking areas anywhere on the premises, which means anyone with a tobacco habit has to leave by the front entrance and smoke on the sidewalk. They've also got motion sensors and vibration detectors on the roof, and if you can somehow get past those, the only way inside is through a steel access hatch protected by a keypad and a nine-digit key code, which changes daily. Inside, they've got contact sensors on every window, none of which can be opened from the inside anyway. Passive infra-red detectors also protect the research and development laboratories on the second floor, so if Darian secreted his samples in there we might have some real problems.'

Samara frowned. 'From what I've heard of the man, it seems unlikely he'd hide the prototypes on the same floor as his own workspace.'

'I agree. It's too obvious, and it's also the first place Deleva would have looked anyway. As for the front entrance, anyone can get past the outer doors but that only gets you to the main reception desk, where there's always an armed security guard on duty, day and night. All employees have to go past him and then swipe their specially issued key card on the inner doors before they can get to the rest of the building. As you'd expect, each pass is also programmed with the specific employee's ID number. As soon as it gets swiped the user's details show up on the guard's terminal, and if by chance those details don't match up with the person in front of them, then it's game over right there.'

'All in all, about what we expected. No sewer access, I suppose?'

'Not this time,' Korso said, suppressing a smile. 'For one thing, they don't have a basement. Anyway, it's always a good idea to avoid using the same methods twice on the same job.' He began tapping his forefinger against his lower lip. 'No, I'm thinking those HR files might be the way to go on this one. And one file, in particular.'

'You mean that janitor you told me about earlier?'

Korso nodded thoughtfully. 'I really don't see any other way inside other than to temporarily assume his identity, which naturally opens up a whole new set of obstacles.'

Samara shrugged. 'Ain't that always the way? Find a solution to one problem and straight away ten more crop up. You want a piece of advice?'

'Always.'

'Sleep on it, give that brain of yours a rest for a few hours. You need some quality downtime. We all do.'

She was right, of course. He glanced over at the huge settee. It did look very inviting. He was very tired, and just a few hours' sleep would make the world of difference.

'Korso.'

'Hmm?' He turned back to see her looking directly at him, her lips parted slightly.

'I mean in an actual bed.'

'Well, thanks to you I don't actually have one of those any more.'

'Now you're being deliberately obtuse.' Taking another sip of her juice, she gave him the kind of lascivious smile that would have made Teodor's heart miss a beat. Korso had never been slow on the uptake, and received the message loud and clear. He smiled back at her. She got up from her chair, and said, 'You do remember where my room is, don't you?'

'It's imprinted on my brain.'

'Good. Don't forget to turn off the lights before you come up.'

She ambled off towards the stairs without looking back, Korso watching her all the way. Once she'd disappeared upstairs, Korso got up and began turning off all the lights.

THIRTY-THREE

'I'm not sure that was a good idea,' Korso said, glancing up at the ceiling. It was the first time either of them had spoken in quite a while, conversation having been the last thing on their minds.

'Too late for regrets.' Samara was lying on her side next to him, absently tracing her index finger up and down his right arm. 'Anyway, you're the one who started it.'

'I did?'

'That lovers act we put on outside the prison on Tuesday, remember?'

'Well, the situation kind of called for it. And I have to admit I enjoyed it at the time. I can still remember how you smelled that day: primarily cherry blossom with a hint of vanilla, if I'm not mistaken.'

'Giorgio Armani: now there's a guy who never lets a girl down. A rare quality in an Italian male.'

'I'll take your word for it. But I'm curious. Other than Bulgarian, how many other languages do you speak?'

'Well, I'm fluent in French, German, and standard Arabic, and I can also make myself understood when I'm in Italy, as long as I stick to the main cities. You?'

'Just Spanish, and a little Russian.' This wasn't exactly true, but she didn't need to know that. 'You've always had a talent for languages and dialects?'

'Since I was a small girl. Could never get my head around Latin at school, though. I mean, who wants to learn a dead language? Unless you're a history professor, that is.' She paused.

'So I gather you've been doing this kind of thing a fair few years now, right?'

'What kind of thing?'

'This covert salvage business, or whatever you call it. Locating and recovering valuable items for people. You sure act as though you've been doing it a long time.'

'Long enough.'

'So what were you doing before?'

'Marking time mostly. The less said about that part of my life, the better. I'm not one who enjoys talking about the past much, which seems to be a characteristic we both share.' He turned to look at her. 'Don't you think?'

Samara reached up and traced a finger along his cheek. She brushed her lips across his, then said, 'I take it that's another not-so-subtle reference to my supposedly shadowy CIA back-ground? You still don't fully trust me, do you, Korso?'

'I might never. Call it psychological body armour. I've seen human beings at their very worst, and so I find a healthy distrust of my fellow man keeps me alert and ready for anything. It's partly why I'm still in one piece after all these years.'

'And what's the other part?'

'I'm a survivor, I guess. Knock me down and I get up again, as sure as the sun sets in the west.'

'Like the Energizer Bunny.'

'If you like. As for your shadowy background, you've got CIA written all over you, no matter how much you might deny it. I've had dealings with enough of their people over the years to be able to tell.' He frowned. 'Although now that I think about it, you strike me more as the freelance contractor type rather than a full-time agency employee.'

'Really? How's that?'

'Because you were a Navy SEAL once, probably Special Ops. And to go from that kind of adrenaline-fuelled existence to a dull embassy posting in Eastern Europe doesn't fit in with your character. Besides, you already admitted that you carry an unofficial status at the embassy, only getting called in for special assignments, or "consultancy work," as you call it. Or was that not the truth?'

'It's close enough.'

'What caused you to leave the Navy SEALS anyway? Black Ops not exciting enough for you?'

'I just came to realise I was pushing my luck, that's all. I lost the faith, so I quit.'

'I can relate. So was it a specific event that caused the change of heart, or was it more a gradual process?'

'Half and half, I guess. There were plenty of little niggles over a period of time, all culminating in a shitstorm of epic proportions that ultimately made my decision for me.'

'What kind of shitstorm?'

She was silent for a while. Finally, she said, 'It was a hostage situation in Belize. A VIP had been kidnapped from his hotel in Belize City by an extreme far-right fundamentalist militant group desperate for both money and recognition.'

'A bad combination.'

'Tell me about it. I was part of a seven-person unit assigned to extract him. We knew where their hideout was – a dilapidated office block in the worst part of town – and we made the usual preparations for an insertion. We went in during the early hours, but they somehow knew we were coming and ambushed us. What should have been a straightforward snatch and grab turned into an absolute massacre. My whole team were wiped out, with me as the only survivor, and that was only because they thought I was already dead from a head wound. Somebody high up must have talked, there's no other way it could have happened. When I eventually woke up in a Stateside hospital, I was informed each of my teammates had been tortured to death over a period of days. I felt sick, angry, and disillusioned. As soon as I was able to walk, I walked away. From all of it.'

'You ever find out who betrayed you?'

'Never even tried.' She blinked her eyes at him. 'Didn't really see much point. The ones at the top are all the same, all as bad as each other. It seems we've been both seen humans at their very worst, doesn't it? But then, I guess it's those experiences that make us what we are.'

'For better or worse.' Korso remained silent for a few moments, thinking. 'Before, you mentioned you and Belmont have worked together several times in the past. Care to enlighten me about those times?'

'What makes you think I've worked with him more than once?'

'Well, when I asked you before if Belmont planned to pay Teodor off as promised, you said he always keeps up his end of the deal. And that "always" implies plural rather than singular. Ergo...'

She pinched his nipple. 'Nobody likes a smart ass, Korso. Hasn't anyone ever told you that?'

'I believe it's been mentioned.'

'Why do you ask anyway?'

'I'm just interested to know what brought the two of you together. But it's up to you.'

Silence. Just the sound of two people breathing. Korso wasn't sure she was going to give, but finally she said, 'Belmont and I only worked together on two previous occasions. Neither assignment was particularly illegal, although they weren't sanctioned by the State Department either. One involved a senior diplomat at the embassy suspected of leaking national defence secrets to one of his Bulgarian mistresses. Belmont got me to set up a fairly complex surveillance network at both their homes, and then I had to listen to everything they said to each other for the next month. Real interesting work, as I'm sure you can imagine.'

'And was he leaking secrets?'

'Yeah, but not the national defence kind. Let's just say the intel I eventually gathered could well have turned out to be very beneficial to Belmont, in more ways than one.'

Korso smiled in the darkness. 'They call that blackmail. And the second job?'

'Belmont was placed in charge of security for a set of highly secret trade negotiations between the US and… an unfriendly nation, and certain payments had be made to certain individuals in Sofia to ensure everything went as smoothly and as quietly as possible. I was put in charge of making sure those payments went exactly where they were supposed to go.'

'They call those people bagmen.'

'That's what I was, all right.'

'And you acquitted yourself well and didn't make any waves, thereby earning Belmont's trust and gratitude, thus ensuring that you'd be his first choice anytime he needed similar covert work done in the future.'

Samara stretched her arms out and yawned. 'Something like that.'

'You still haven't told me what you're getting out of all this, Samara. I don't believe it's the money that interests you, not completely anyway. It's got to be something else.'

She chose that moment to clamber on top of him and place her arms around his neck. 'Maybe I just wanted to get you into bed. Life can be that simple sometimes.'

'Rarely, in my experience. And I'm far from irresistible. Which just leaves two other possibilities.'

Samara looked down into his eyes. 'Only two?'

'That occur to me right now, though I'm sure there are others. One: there's a personal element in this for you that I've got no chance of even guessing at this stage. Or two: somebody's got something on you – something very bad, I imagine – and getting your hands on these White Nights is your only way out. Am I close?'

She chuckled. 'That's quite the imagination you have there, Korso. It really is.'

Korso was about to speak again when Samara pressed her fingers against his mouth, shutting off all further conversation. He also couldn't ignore the fact that a beautiful naked woman was currently lying partially spread-eagled on top of him. She pulled her hand away, leaned in and brushed her lips against his. Giving in, he reached up and cupped her cheek and kissed her back.

At some point she started moving her body, and after a while so did he.

THIRTY-FOUR

Korso paid the driver and waited for the taxi to leave before joining Samara and Teodor at the front gate. It was Saturday afternoon. The trio had just completed a very necessary errand in town, the success of which was mostly down to Teodor and his talent for finding what they wanted in a very short amount of time. After last night's events, he'd also made sure to be on his best behaviour all afternoon. Korso could only hope this new attitude would continue throughout the rest of the mission.

Unlocking the front door, Korso let Samara enter first and followed right after. He saw Cole leaning against the breakfast bar, while Lucian stood in the living area and flicked through the TV channels with the remote.

Teodor removed his 'disguise' of flat cap and dark glasses as he walked straight over to the kitchen area. He opened the refrigerator and extracted a bottle of Zagorka. Popping the cap, he took a large slug of the beer and belched loudly. 'Lucian, you looking real good again today,' he said. 'Share beer with me.'

'Thanks, but I think I'll pass.'

'Hey, no problem, baby.' He walked over to her. 'We forget all about beer and go straight upstairs. I know how to make you forget everything except Teodor.'

Lucian just looked at him contemptuously, while Cole said, 'You need to start learning some manners, boy. Keep on going and maybe I'll teach you a few.'

'Big man, huh?' Teodor turned to him with a grin. 'Think you can take me, big man?'

So much for the new and improved Teodor, Korso thought, as he shut the front door. It had been good while it lasted. 'Enough,' he said, walking over to them. 'We've got more important things to discuss. Cole, what's the situation with the van?'

'Well, it's back in our possession again. I spent the best part of an hour searching every inch of that parking lot and didn't see a single soul watching the vehicle. No sign of surveillance, no cops, no nothing. Which means we could have stuck to Plan A yesterday after all, and avoided all that racing around the streets during rush hour.'

'Everything's obvious in hindsight.' Samara said.

'Ain't that the truth? So once I felt it was safe, I got in and started her up, and then drove on over to the garage you got us on Knyaz Boris Street, which is actually perfect for us. The street's all one-way so you don't get too much traffic passing by, and the garage is totally enclosed with more than enough room for me to do the work that needs to be done.'

'Glad you like it,' Korso said.

Even though there was ample space for the van in the double garage next door, Korso hadn't wanted to take a chance of somebody following Cole back to the safe house. Fortunately, he'd already planned for that contingency back in London, by leasing them a separate garage space from the same real estate agent who'd supplied them with the house. As ever, it was always best to prepare for the worst in any given situation.

'By the way,' he said, 'that design place called me earlier and said the stencils are ready to pick up, so do that tomorrow morning. They're open Sundays. You've already got the cobalt blue and emerald green spray paint canisters?'

Cole nodded. 'Picked up two canisters of each along the way, which should be more than enough for our purposes. I'll get to work on it tomorrow morning. What about you guys? You manage to find somebody who fit the bill?'

'Amazingly, we did,' Samara said. 'The first candidate we approached turned out to be perfect in almost every way. And smart as a whip too, which was equally unexpected.'

'Why you look surprised?' Teodor said. 'I told you before, whatever you want Teodor gets for you. Supply and demand is my business.' He tapped his temple. 'All up here. Brain like computer. Since I was little kid I never have to write down nothing. I need somebody for something, phone number appears in front of eyes.' He snapped his fingers. 'Like this.'

'You're truly a walking miracle,' Samara said. 'If you'd only use that power for good, what a world this could be.'

Korso turned to Lucian. 'Did you manage to get out to the rental place and look the plane over?'

'Yeah, and it's perfect. The manager spoke pretty good English too. He said as soon as we wire over the deposit and rental fee, we'll be in possession of a fifteen-year-old single-engine Piper PA-46 Malibu for the next seven days. I gotta hand it to them, the plane looks damn good for its age, inside and out. It's got a solid 350 horsepower Lycoming engine and can reach altitudes of 25,000 feet, with a range of almost 1000 nautical miles on a full tank of fuel. Once I showed the guy my pilot's licence he even let me take it up for a quick spin, and it handles beautifully. I took a short video on my phone if you want to see it for yourself.'

'I'll take a look after I make the money transfer. How many can fit inside?'

'There's room for one pilot and five passengers.'

'Sounds good. Let's just hope we won't need it.'

'Speak for yourself. I can't wait to get up in the sky again; it's been far too long. Speaking of which, any updates about the plane's new home?'

'All taken care of,' Samara said. 'I spoke with my guy this morning, and we've agreed a straight cash fee for the temporary use of his company's backup hangar at Sofia West Airport. Actually, it's not so much an airport than it is a landing strip located about twenty klicks southwest of Sofia, in a town called Radomir. And the hangar itself isn't much more than a large wooden shed, but it should suit us just fine. Lucian, you and I can fly the Malibu over there tomorrow morning, when he'll be there to hand over the keys.' There was a sudden chirping sound, and Samara reached into her jeans pocket and pulled out her phone. She swiped the display with a finger and frowned at a text message on the screen.

Cole said, 'Wait, what guy, what plane? And what's this airport you keep talking about? Did I miss a conversation somewhere?'

'We were discussing it this morning before you were up,' Korso said. 'The rented plane's just there for backup, in case things go badly wrong and we quickly need to vacate the area and head for the Greek border to the south of us. But we clearly need a safe place to store the plane, so I did a little research and found out there's a small skydiving company based out at that airstrip in Radomir. It's fairly remote, and they're the only business out there. They've got a main hangar they use to keep their own two aircraft, and a much smaller one they use mainly for storage. Samara's been in contact with the owner. It seems business is slow at the moment, and he's agreed to let us use that one to house the Malibu for a week.'

'While still charging us the earth,' Samara said, putting her phone away. 'One thing about Bulgarians, they sure know how to bargain from a position of weakness.'

'Why you not talk with me first?' Teodor said. 'I find you perfect place, and for good price too. Teodor can get you anything you want.'

Lucian snorted. 'Naturally. Is there anything that you can't do?'

While the others talked, Korso turned to Samara. 'Who was that on the phone? Our girl? I thought it wasn't for a couple of hours yet.'

She returned his steady gaze, although he noticed she started blinking more rapidly than before. 'No, it was just another text from Belmont, requesting a further progress report. Look, I need to go to the nearby drugstore for something. You need anything while I'm out?'

Korso shook his head, and watched her grab the keys from the kitchen counter and slip out to the garage. He continued watching the connecting door once she was gone, wondering what had really been on that text message, when he remembered he was supposed to call Dog. Pulling out his phone, he speed-dialled her number as he entered the dining area and opened the sliding door to the backyard. He stepped out just as the call was picked up.

'Hey, hey,' Dog said. The artificial voice this time was that of an elderly man. 'I thought you might be calling around now. So how are things progressing at your end?'

Korso gave her a brief recap of the day's developments, as well as the dramatic events of last night. Once he'd finished, she gave a chuckle. 'Good thing we'd prepared for that little possibility, huh? I tell you, K, sometimes it gets depressing how predictable people can be. Although I guess it does make our job that much easier.'

'Don't get used to it. Have you made any headway in accessing Vercogen's CCTV systems yet?'

'Yep, you'll be glad to know I finally found a way in through the back door about an hour ago. I'm currently parked about fifty feet from the building as we speak. So on a scale of one to ten, just how impressed are you?'

'Imagine I'm giving you a virtual pat on the back.'

'I thought I felt something brushing against me back there. Anyway, I'm still feeling my way around their server, but you'll be happy to hear that I've got access to all the live video feeds currently being transmitted from their internal security cameras – there are sixteen in total – as well as access to most of their internal communications and emails too. On the down side, I can't seem to locate any saved recordings of previous footage like you wanted. I expect all that data gets automatically saved to an external hard drive somewhere onsite, in which case there's no way for me to access it remotely.'

'Don't worry about that part of it. Having access to their live feeds is my main concern. Tell me, do you actually have admin access to the cameras, or is this a "read-only" situation?'

'No, I've got full security access so I can deactivate any of the CCTV cameras as and when. I can even record transmitted footage and upload it as a loop if you need me to, though I wouldn't advise it. If there's a guy in a little room watching the monitors full-time, then he'll see straight away that something's buggy and check into it.'

'I didn't see a security control room marked on any of the schematics you sent over.'

'Doesn't mean there isn't one. As it turns out, there's a likely contender on the first floor. Just after you get through reception there's an unmarked door to the immediate left, leading to a small room with no windows.'

'I recall seeing that on the specs. I thought it might be a cloakroom or something.'

'Well, I've been keeping an eye on that room and the only people who go in and out are the security guards. I can't see what's behind that door, but my gut tells me that's the security control room in there, especially as it's the only door on that floor with a keypad next to it. The guards all key in a six-digit code to get in. Which I now have, before you ask. Now I can't be sure yet if they've got someone assigned to that office full-time or not. I'll know the answer to that once I know how many guards there are to each shift.'

'Okay, let's assume it is the control room then. And that's good news about the video surveillance. You've done well, Dog.'

'Thought you'd be pleased.'

'Now what about the other thing?'

'Already taken care of. I added a backdated order to their database just before you called, so it's right there in the system should anyone decide to check the paperwork. The order's for one replacement floor polisher and one wet & dry vacuum cleaner, and delivery's scheduled for Monday at four.'

'Perfect.'

'Don't jinx it,' Dog said. 'Speak later.'

Ending the call, Korso went back inside and saw Cole watching one of the sports channels on TV, while Teodor was making a ham and salami sandwich in the kitchen, humming to himself as he worked. Lucian wasn't anywhere in sight.

Korso sat down at the breakfast counter, and then told Teodor what he wanted from him on Monday.

THIRTY-FIVE

'My secretary said you wanted to speak with me,' the cultured voice said in its familiar clipped English. 'Do you have good news?'

'I do indeed.' Balakin put his phone on speaker, and set it down on the table. As he spread some more Beluga Royal Caviar onto a cracker, he glanced out his suite window at the city's skyline and the mountains in the far distance. It was a beautiful view, as well it should be. The rates for his Personal Spa Suite in the 5-star Grand Millennium Hotel, complete with its own private sauna room and jacuzzi, were astronomical. But if you wanted the best you had to pay for it. It was as simple as that. Balakin had learnt to appreciate the finer things in life over the years, otherwise what was the point of living?

'I'm listening,' the Chinese minister said.

'Okay, not only do I now know where the opposing team is based, but I made contact with someone on the inside yesterday, and they responded very positively to my overtures. As ever, money was the great persuader. In fact, I had the distinct feeling that this person had been waiting for my approach, and so was only too happy to make me an offer.'

'Which was?'

'Twenty million Euros. In cash. Payment to be made on delivery. Along with a provision that only €500 notes are to be used, so that everything can fit into two large suitcases. Naturally, I accepted.'

There was silence at the other end of the line. Balakin took a bite of the cracker, and chewed silently. It was excellent caviar, but at these prices he expected no less. He washed it down with a sip of his imported Italian white, and waited.

Finally, the minister said, 'That was very presumptuous of you, Mr Balakin. Twenty million Euros is a vast amount of money. I'm not sure I can raise that much so soon.'

Balakin snorted. 'Minister, you represent one of the richest and largest nations on this planet. And you and I both know that your people would willingly spend twenty times that amount to get their hands on these prototypes, so let's stop playing games, shall we? Now I've given you the terms my Judas relayed to me. Is it achievable, or isn't it?'

A brief pause. 'All things are possible. When would you need this cash?'

'Tomorrow morning.'

'That soon? Well, I suppose it could be done. But you'd have to collect it personally, and you'd have to bring some protection with you. I don't have to tell you how seriously we would take it if this money were to suddenly go missing. You do understand what I'm saying?'

Balakin sighed. 'I get the general drift. Believe it or not, I'd rather not have an entire nation after my blood if I can at all avoid it.'

'Very wise of you. Now let's go back to this man, or woman, on the inside. Clearly, we're not talking about the planner, Korso?'

Balakin took another bite of the cracker. 'No. He'll never deal with me again. That branch is dead.' *Especially after the events of last night*, he thought.

'So who is this insider of yours?'

'I believe I'll keep that information to myself for the time being. No offence, but I'd prefer not to reveal my whole hand too early. I'm sure you understand.'

'But the deal is all set with this new candidate?'

'In stone. As soon as Korso gets his hands on the prototypes, my Judas will appropriate them and then hand them over to me. For the agreed fee, of course.'

'So you plan to keep up your end of the bargain? That is to say, *our* end of the bargain?'

'I'll see how it plays out.' Balakin took a sip of the wine. 'When the time comes, if I feel there's an opportunity to get the prototypes without handing over the twenty million, then I'd be a fool not to take it. After all, that's simply good business practice.'

'Just be absolutely sure before you act. We wouldn't want any mistakes. Do you know when they'll make their move?'

'Definitely tomorrow. I don't know what time exactly, but most likely late evening. That's all I know right now.'

'Very well. In that case, unless there's something else you need from me, I'll see you at the embassy in the morning.'

'Until tomorrow then.'

Hanging up, Balakin finished his snack and thought about Monday. Everything was gradually coming together, and far quicker than he'd hoped. By this time tomorrow, he'd conceivably have more money than he could spend in three lifetimes. Maybe even with a €20 million bonus on top, depending on the circumstances. And wasn't that a nice thought?

He picked up the phone, called a number. It was answered after two rings.

'What's the situation over there?' he asked in Russian.

'The usual comings and goings, sir,' Vlad said. 'That Infiniti of theirs has really been racking up the mileage today. The American woman took it out almost an hour ago, and arrived back at the house just before you called. Before that, it was the other woman behind the wheel. It definitely looks like they're getting ready for something.'

That much I already know, Balakin thought with a smile.

Yesterday morning, Balakin had personally conducted interviews with every tenant and business owner located within a hundred yard radius of *The Icicle*. He finally struck gold when he questioned a group of kids playing in the stairwell of a nearby apartment house, and one of them admitted to recording the drama outside on his phone. The police hadn't even talked to him, didn't even know he existed. When Balakin handed the boy enough cash to buy twenty new phones, the kid happily gave him his Samsung in return.

The footage was brief, but there was one very interesting segment where a Nissan Infiniti pulled out of a parking spot in the street and performed a neat handbrake turn before picking up an unidentified man on the sidewalk. Even better, just before the driver sped off, Balakin could clearly make out the car's registration. After that, it didn't take too long to trace the vehicle to a certain two-storey house on a quiet street in the Pavlovo district, in the southern part of the capital.

Vlad was currently installed in another house whose master bedroom boasted an excellent view of the gated entrance to Korso's rented property. The owners were a middle-aged couple who hadn't been too enthusiastic about a group of strangers taking over their home, which was unfortunate. Balakin didn't have time for niceties and decided it would be more convenient to simply remove them from the equation entirely. As a result, the couple were now consigned to an eternity crammed together in the large freezer in their garage.

'What about Korso?' Balakin asked. 'Any sign of him today?'

'Not yet. But when the bastard shows his face, I'll know it.'

Balakin could plainly hear the threat in the other man's voice. 'Remember what I said, Vlad. You will make not make contact with him under any circumstances. I'm not interested in your petty vendettas, and if he sees your face or you screw this up for me, I'll have you castrated and dragged naked through the streets, are we clear on that?'

'Yes, sir.'

'Good. I'm coming over now to see things first hand, so I'll be with you shortly.'

Balakin took a last sip of his wine, and went to get his jacket. Everything was moving along nicely now, with the endgame not too far away.

Life was good. Very soon it was going to get even better.

THIRTY-SIX

Georgi Ninov smiled at the stunning girl dancing opposite him, and she beamed right back at him like it was the most natural thing in the world. She had long black hair, and wore a skin-tight sleeveless bodycon dress that showed off every inch of her thin, lithe figure. Even amongst the numerous other dream girls in the nightclub she was a standout. He still couldn't quite believe that she was his date.

They'd only met for the first time yesterday. Faced with another dull Saturday evening at home playing video games, he'd just been leaving his apartment house to get some cigarettes from the store when this beautiful girl had bumped into him on the sidewalk. She'd been doing something on her phone at the time, but he apologised anyway and she apologised back, and then they'd started talking and the next thing he knew they were both walking towards her favourite coffee shop three blocks away.

Her name was Tanya. She told him she'd just moved to Sofia and was working as an IT support analyst in a small firm in town, that she was addicted to Instagram, and she loved comedies and horror movies. That was about as much as he knew about her, because as soon as they sat down with their lattes at the coffee shop she seemed to only want to talk about him. Which was a whole new experience for Georgi. She asked him about his life, his family and friends, and then moved onto his job and his place of work, and asked what his duties were there, and what his colleagues were like, along with a host of other questions about himself, even laughing at his feeble attempts at humour. For the first time in his life Georgi was the centre of attention, and he relished every second of it.

It took another hour and a half before Georgi was able to build up the courage to ask her out for dinner. She happily accepted, and they went on to a steakhouse he knew where she continued to ask him questions about himself for the rest of the evening.

He knew he was smitten. This Tanya was perfect in every way. At the end of the meal, right after she'd booked an Uber for herself, she'd surprised him further by asking if he wanted to go to clubbing tomorrow night. He couldn't say yes fast enough.

All Sunday long Georgi had been in a partial dream state, wondering if Tanya was actually going to go through with it. He was no oil painting, he knew that much. Nor was he particularly witty. So what could a girl like that possibly see in him? It didn't make sense. But when the time came, she not only met him outside the club exactly at nine like she'd promised, but she immediately dragged him to the front of the long queue where she whispered something to the bouncer, who then nodded and waved them both inside.

It was now well past two in the morning, and he was still buzzing from the ecstasy he'd taken hours earlier. She'd brought two pills along, and they'd each taken one as soon as they entered the place. He knew he had work tomorrow, but he didn't care. Screw those guys. You only lived once, and this girl was worth it.

Tanya stopped dancing suddenly, and leaned in close to him and put her arms round his neck. She gave him a long smouldering kiss, her body writhing in time with the deafening beat, while Georgi wrapped his arms around her waist and pulled her even closer to him. He felt like he'd died and gone to heaven. When they finally parted, she said, 'I'm feeling horny, Georgi. How about we head back to your place, what do you say?'

Georgi grinned back at her. 'I say I'm ready when you are.'

'Let's beat it then.'

Once they were outside, Georgi soon grabbed them a taxi and gave the driver directions back to his apartment house. Tanya dragged him into the back and they began necking as the driver pulled away. That he was in a state of bliss all through the journey was only partially down to the chemical stimulant in his system.

When they finally arrived at his Podkrepa Street apartment house, located in the less-desirable Moderno Predgradie district, Georgi paid off the driver and led Tanya up to his single-bedroom flat on the third floor. He'd spent much of the day tidying the place up in case he got lucky tonight, and was now glad of his foresight. The place wasn't much to look at, but it was clean.

Not that Tanya seemed to care. Giving the place a quick once-over, she motioned towards the kitchenette. 'Got any beers? My mouth feels like a desert.'

'Coming up.' Georgi opened the refrigerator and pulled out two Budweisers. He popped the tops and gave one bottle to Tanya, who took a large slug of the drink. Georgi went to the bathroom to relieve himself. When he came back, Tanya handed him back his beer and clinked her bottle with his. They each finished their drinks.

Tanya then led him into the bedroom, where they undressed quickly and got under the sheets. And for the next twenty minutes or so, life was everything he'd ever hoped for. Tanya may have been the sweet new girl in town, but she was anything but shy in the sack. Her hands were everywhere, and so were his.

But at some point during the excitement Georgi started to feel himself drifting away. Thinking it was connected with the ecstasy he'd taken earlier, he focused harder on the girl on top of him, but despite his efforts his eyes began to feel heavy and the cloudiness kept threatening to take over. It seemed the harder he concentrated, the fuzzier everything became and the weaker he felt. He couldn't understand it. It wasn't long before the blurriness took over entirely, and he found himself closing his eyes more often in a futile attempt to clear the cobwebs, but nothing he tried worked.

After a few more attempts his eyes closed of their own accord. And they stayed closed.

–

At the third floor landing, Samara and Korso turned right and walked down the short hallway until they reached flat 3B at the end. Samara rapped her knuckles against the door. Korso checked his watch again. 3.34 a.m. Outside, the city was as close to silent as it would ever be. The streets had been practically empty on the drive over.

Moments later the door opened to reveal their recent recruit, Tanya. Her hair was pulled back in a ponytail, and she was wearing a man's t-shirt that just reached past her hips. She looked a lot prettier without make-up, but he thought that true of most women. She beamed at Korso, but got serious again when she saw Samara behind him. She opened the door wider, and Korso followed Samara into the apartment's living space.

'Everything go as planned?' Samara asked in English.

Tanya gave a yawn. 'Sure. I spike beer with drug you give me, and he go to dreamland. How long he stay like this, I dunno.'

'That depends,' Korso said. 'Did he take anything else tonight?'

She shrugged. 'We both take ecstasy pill when we go to club. Six hours ago, I think.'

'Well, the amount of Propofol I gave you usually lasts for twelve hours, but the ecstasy will likely reduce its strength by at least half. Keep a close eye on him. If he shows signs of coming round too soon, just give him some more propofol. I'll give you some extra vials before we leave.'

'We need him out of action for the whole day, Tanya,' Samara said.

'Yeah, yeah, you tell me before. You have rest of my money?'

Samara smiled. 'You'll get the full amount in your account tomorrow, as we agreed.'

'Along with a fat bonus on top,' Korso said, 'but only if you're a good girl.'

'Ha. You want good girl, you come to wrong place. How much bonus?'

'Five thousand dollars, US.'

Her eyes widened. 'Five thousand? No shit? What I got to do for it?'

'Just what you are doing. Make sure Georgi's out of action for the rest of the day, then just leave him here and go home. I assume he's taken a real liking to you?'

'Pfft. He *crazy* about me, same as every other guy I ever meet.' She gave a weary shake of her head. 'Men.'

'Tell me about it,' Samara said. 'Did you manage to get the information out of him that we wanted?'

'Sure. I record it on phone yesterday at coffee shop. But no talking tonight. Too loud.' She tilted her head at them. 'You know we speak in Bulgarian, yeah? Not English.'

'Let me worry about that,' Samara said, reaching into her jacket pocket. 'You want to send the mp3 to my phone now?'

'Sure.' Tanya began scrolling down her phone screen.

Korso said, 'Did Georgi tell you what clothes he wears to work?'

'Yeah,' she said, without looking up, 'dark blue shirt, dark blue trousers. Same every day. Also, black baseball cap. Sometimes face mask and gloves if he working in toilets.'

Korso left them to it and turned and stepped into the small bedroom. He switched on the light and went over to Georgi, who was lying face-up on the bed with the sheets covering his lower body. His mouth was parted and he was snoring lightly. Korso leaned in and carefully studied his face, his hair, his general build.

The man's black hair was about an inch long all round. Tanya had already sent them a good shot of Georgi yesterday while they were at the coffee shop, and as a result Korso's own hair was now cut to the exact same length. It was also dyed the same shade of black. The acne scarring around Georgi's cheeks posed a slight problem, but in reality it wasn't as bad as it appeared in the two photos he'd seen. Korso had stopped shaving two days before in preparation, and his dark beard stubble now covered much of that area, so hopefully that would be enough. The man's fleshy nose was a more serious obstacle, however, as it was completely unlike Korso's Greek nose, with its straight bridge. But he'd picked up a theatrical make-up kit and some modelling wax on Saturday, so he felt confident that with a little work he could make his nose temporarily resemble Georgi's. He'd done this kind of thing before on numerous occasions.

Pulling out his phone, Korso snapped a few close-ups of Georgi's face from a variety of different angles. He used a thumb to pull Georgi's left eyelid back, and a dark blue eye stared sightlessly back at him. Good. It was almost exactly the same shade as the colour contact lenses he'd bought from the same supplier.

Raising himself up, he looked around the room. There wasn't much to see: just an old dresser set against one wall, and a tatty wooden cupboard next to the sole window. He opened the cupboard and rummaged through the clothes hangers until he found three long-sleeved plain navy-blue polo shirts. All three were identical. Next to these were two pairs of navy-blue work trousers. Korso took one of the shirts and hung it over his arm. He also extracted one pair of trousers and held it up against his own leg. Same length. They joined the shirt. At the bottom of the cupboard were three pairs of sneakers and one pair of suede shoes. He left them there.

He went through the dresser next, and found what he wanted in the bottom drawer: a plain black cap with no logo on the front panel. It joined the shirt and trousers. No face masks, though. Hopefully, Georgi kept a packet of disposable masks at work. Next, Korso picked Georgi's trousers up from the floor and went through the pockets until he found the man's wallet.

He opened it up and looked through it, finding nothing of any use. But when he checked the rear pockets, he found a plastic entry card connected to a lanyard. He pulled it out. Underneath the Vercogen logo was a headshot of Georgi, and next to it his name in Cyrillic lettering. He put the items in his own pocket and returned to the living area, where Tanya was now sitting cross-legged on the floor, watching TV.

Samara had her phone to her ear, listening to something. She noticed the clothes on Korso's arm, and said, 'So are we good?'

'I've got everything I came for. How's the recording?'

'Not bad at all. Tanya's asking all the right questions, and she's quite the talented little actor too. She's almost got me believing her.'

'Men always believe everything I tell them,' Tanya said, turning round.

'I don't doubt it,' Korso said. 'If things go well today, Tanya, I might have more work for you in the future. Skilled actors can be hard to find in my business, especially those who don't ask questions.'

She smiled at him again. It was a very seductive smile. He could see how most men would fall under her spell. Even he wasn't immune.

'You call me any time, mister, and I come.' The smile grew wider. 'Serious. *Any* time at all.'

Korso smiled back at her. 'I'll make a note,' he said.

THIRTY-SEVEN

Samara cut the Infiniti's engine, while Korso released his seat-belt and glanced at the Vercogen building on the other side of the street. It was 2.27 on Monday afternoon. The day was bright and sunny, the temperature in the low twenties. Pedestrians passed in front of the three-storey building without noticing it, some of them returning from lunch and heading back to their own workplaces in adjacent streets. As Korso watched, an exec carrying a laptop bag and a Subway exited the small fenced parking area at the side of the building, passing the guard stationed at the gate. He then turned right on the sidewalk, climbed the three steps to Vercogen's front entrance and disappeared inside.

Korso absently felt his new nose again. The wax had hardened a little since he moulded it over an hour ago, while still retaining its overall pliability. As long as it remained that way for the rest of the day. He turned to Samara. 'How do I look? Be objective.'

Samara studied him carefully before slowly nodding her head. 'It's a damn good resemblance, I have to admit. Seriously, it's amazing how much a nose like that can alter a person's facial features. And that two-day beard stubble also helps a lot. As long as you keep the cap on and say as little as possible, you should be okay.'

'Speaking of which…' Korso pulled a small, flesh-coloured wireless earbud from his shirt pocket, pressed a button on the side, and inserted it into his left ear. He also pulled out a small voice activated recorder, about the size of an iPod shuffle. He switched it on and put it back in his shirt pocket. 'One last test run.'

Inserting her own wired earpiece, Samara raised the small mic to her mouth and said softly, '*It is a truth universally acknowledged, that a single man in possession of a good fortune, must be in want of a wife*. Want me to go on?'

'No. As opening sentences go, that one's hard to top.' As before, every word had come through clearly, with zero distortion. He removed a small manila envelope from the glove compartment and then looked out the side window again. 'I wouldn't have thought Jane Austen was your kind of writer.'

'Well, she's kind of timeless, isn't she? I minored in English Literature at college, and even now I've got whole sections of *Pride and Prejudice* memorised. I'm still reading you loud and clear, by the way. What are you looking for?'

'Someone I can tag along with on the way in, possibly returning from a late lunch.'

He kept watching. Although he hadn't been blessed with an eidetic memory, he still had excellent recollection when it came to faces. He'd already recognised the exec from the HR files. If he spotted anyone else from those same files, he'd know it immediately. Turning in his seat, he looked through the rear window and studied the dozen or so vehicles parked behind them. He spotted two work vans back there, along with another one parked four spaces in front of them. He felt it highly probable that Dog was in one of them right now. But as to which one, he had no idea.

Turning back to the street, he saw a man and a woman turn the corner from Bulgaria Boulevard and start walking this way. The woman wore a blazer and business dress, while the man wore a shirt and tie, and whatever she was saying to him was making him smile. The man was also sipping from a Starbucks cup as he walked. Korso recognised them both as lab technicians, probably working on the second floor.

Knowing he probably wouldn't get a better opportunity, Korso reached for the door handle. 'Time to see if I can hold up to close scrutiny.'

'Break a leg,' Samara said.

Korso exited the car and shut the door. After making sure his windbreaker covered the gun in his waistband he crossed the street, timing it so that he arrived at the front steps just a few feet behind the two lab technicians. They were just started up the steps when the woman noticed they had company. She turned to Korso and said something brief and unintelligible, although he had heard Georgi's name at the start.

In his ear, Samara's voice said, 'She just asked if you had a good weekend. Say "Okay. *Makhmurluk.*" It means hangover.'

'*Da,*' Korso said to the woman, and touched his head gingerly, '*Makhmurluk.*'

She gave an understanding smile in response while the man opened the front door and held it open for her. They each went inside. Korso followed them in, and found himself in a small reception area containing a single security guard in his fifties. He was sitting behind a desk, watching his monitor. The huge Vercogen logo was pasted across the wall next to him, while to his right was a revolving door with a touchless entry pad next to it.

The guard nodded impassively at the three of them. Korso just nodded back and watched the other two approach the inner door.

The woman pulled her entry card from her pocket and waved it at the pad. A small green light flashed at the bottom. There was a faint electronic *click*, and she pushed through the revolving doors and entered the building proper. The man then did the same. Once he was through, Korso faked a yawn as he removed the lanyard from his neck and touched Georgi's entry card to the pad. He waited for the light to go green.

Nothing happened.

He tried again, this time waving the card across the pad more slowly. Again, nothing happened. Out the corner of his eye, he could see the guard start to rise from his seat. Korso ignored him, and faked another yawn as he waved the card back and forth across the pad.

This time the light flashed briefly. There was a click, and Korso let out a breath as he pushed the revolving door and stepped into the Vercogen building.

Korso walked at a slower-than-usual pace, making a note of everything around him, especially the security cameras dotted around the ceilings. He'd spent much of Sunday memorising the building specs, so he knew where the all cameras were located, and where each department was. Dog had also made recordings of some of the security footage and forwarded them on to him as well. Those both helped, but it was Samara's translation of the conversation between Georgi and Tanya that provided the most valuable intel, especially in regards to who he reported to and what his daily duties consisted of.

Ahead of him was a long, wide corridor with various doorways running down the left side, opening out into a large open-plan area at the far end. To his immediate right was an elevator car, currently on the third floor, and past that was a large stairwell leading upwards. The two technicians he'd followed were nowhere in sight, but there were plenty of other employees, either walking with purpose or just milling around. The air was thick with chatter coming from all directions. He could also hear phones ringing somewhere in the distance.

On his left was the unmarked door that Dog had told him about, the one with the keypad that most likely gave access to the security control room. She'd also confirmed how many security guards there were to each shift. During the day there was the one stationed outside at the gate, and three more inside the building. There was a shift change at 8 p.m., at which point the outside guard went home and three night guards took over from the three in the building. Dog also confirmed that none of the guards were assigned to this control room full-time, although one of them would check in on a fairly regular basis during their shift.

Korso kept his head lowered and kept moving down the corridor towards the rear of the building, looking as though he knew where he was going and avoiding eye contact with everybody, hoping nobody would feel the need to engage him in conversation. Above all else he wanted to avoid any contact with a lady called Maya Yakova, who worked on the second floor and served as Georgi's immediate supervisor, assigning him new tasks as and when they were brought to her. Korso knew if he came into contact with her, it was all over. She'd see through his disguise in a microsecond. All he could do was keep his head down and hope that there were no emergencies in the next few hours that required Georgi's services.

He was halfway down the hallway when a female employee darted out of the doorway to his left, holding a phone to her ear and almost colliding with him. Korso stepped back before they could make contact, and she halted and goggled at him. '*Kheĭ!*' she said.

'*Kheĭ!*' he said, offering a faint smile, and kept moving down the hallway. He knew what Maya Yakova looked like, and thankfully that hadn't been her. 'What did I just say to her?' he asked without moving his lips.

'That's just their version of "Hey,"' Samara said in his left ear. 'Like an informal greeting between friends or colleagues. Did it seem as though you were friends?'

'No idea. And I didn't hang around to find out.'

A few feet further on he saw a set of double doors to his left and slowed. He'd been counting his steps so far, and so he knew the shutter entrance for collections and deliveries was on the other side. Not caring if anyone was watching, he pushed open the door and entered a medium-sized storage room. There were about a dozen floor-to-ceiling racking units arranged about the area, with plenty of manoeuvring room in between each unit. Most of the cages contained boxes and cartons of varying sizes. There was nobody else in sight, although he could hear an electric forklift moving along one of the aisles to his right.

He walked past each rack, making a mental note of the few empty spaces here and there. Halfway down, he saw the forklift operator carefully pulling out a large carton on the top shelf. The workman saw Korso, who gave the man a mock salute. The man nodded back and returned to his work. The steel roller shutters were currently closed, and seemed to be controlled by a keypad set into the wall. The keypad contained just three clearly signed buttons: up, down, and stop. He also spotted two upright hand trucks over by the left wall, along with three sturdy ladders and a pump pallet truck.

Satisfied, Korso exited the room and turned left down the hallway and kept on in the same direction as before. He made it the rest of the way without coming into contact with anybody else, and when he entered the open-plan area at the end he was glad to see about half of the work cubicles were currently unoccupied. He saw a few people at their workstations, but they paid him no attention. Two women and a guy stood grouped together at one desk, drinking from cups as they talked about something. He heard feminine laughter from over there. One of the women spotted Korso and waved at him. Korso waved back, and then turned towards a small row of offices to his right.

There were five doorways spread out in front of him. He knew the door in the corner led to the rear fire stairs, while the next three were for a meeting room and two offices. All these doors were closed. The fifth doorway was the one he wanted. He walked over to it and turned the handle. It was unlocked. He opened the door, stepped into the darkened room and pressed the light switch on the wall. As he shut the door behind him, three fluorescent tubes in the ceiling flickered on.

The room was small and narrow — less than ten feet wide — and windowless. In contrast to everywhere else in the building, the room looked neglected and ignored. Which was all to the good as far as Korso was concerned. There was a small work-desk at the end, with an ancient PC and monitor on it, along with a desk phone. Set against the left wall were large shelves containing all kinds of cleaning equipment and supplies, along with a stack of faded yellow safety signs. Neatly arranged under the wall shelves were the larger appliances, including a house-keeping trolley, a steam cleaner, a floor-buffing machine, an industrial vacuum, and several other items he didn't recognise. He searched the top shelves again, and smiled when he found a large keychain containing about twenty keys of varying sizes and shapes nestled against some cleaning rags. Taking the keychain back to the door, he tried each key on the lock under the handle until he got lucky with the twelfth one. He tried turning the key clockwise, and nodded to himself when it turned freely and he heard the tumbler pins fall into place. Good.

Unlocking the door again, he took the keychain back to the desk. Taking off his jacket, he sat down on the plain office chair and switched on the PC. There was a cork notice board on the wall in front of him, containing various flyers, checklists, notices, invoices, and so on. All in Bulgarian, of course. There was also a clipboard full of paperwork hanging off a large nail set into the wall.

'I've made it to Georgi's workspace,' he said as he waited, 'if you can call it that. It looks more like a converted janitor's cupboard.'

'Welcome to the lowest rung of the ladder,' Samara said in his ear. 'Georgi should count himself lucky they didn't just stick him in one of the toilets instead. You alone?'

'For the moment. I'm booting up his PC now. I just hope Tanya was right about him not needing a password. Wait, here we go.' The screen now showed the usual Windows background. Korso moved the mouse and clicked on the Outlook icon at the bottom. There was no password prompt. The app simply opened up, instantly displaying Georgi's inbox.

There were no new emails. No new emails for the past month, in fact.

'Anything?' Samara asked.

'I'm in, but it seems Georgi's so low on the totem pole he doesn't even receive regular company-wide emails. So much for that approach.' Korso reached up and pulled the clipboard from the wall. The front page was some kind of delivery note, but the page underneath looked a little more interesting. It was a printout of an Excel spreadsheet, with five headings running down the left that were clearly Monday to Friday. The words were spelled practically the same in Russian. Next to these headings were various bullet points, about nine or ten for each day. Korso recognised a few words here and there, but not enough to make sense of it.

'It looks like I've found his weekly rota. I'll send you a snapshot so you can translate Monday's duties for me.' Korso pulled out his phone, took a shot of the page and sent the file to Samara's number. 'On its way.'

'Hold up,' she said.

'What?'

'The Man's just arrived back from lunch. He's parking his luxury Mercedes Coupe as we speak.'

'Is he alone?'

'Looks like it. Okay, I'm opening up the photo now... Yeah, it's a duty roster, all right. Not sure if they're in any particular order, but I'll read out today's tasks for you. First, you've got to thoroughly clean the men's and women's first floor restrooms, including all cubicles and urinals...'

She continued to list out his duties while Korso keyed them directly onto his phone. Once she'd finished, she said, 'So, plenty there to keep you occupied.'

'I'll do the restrooms first,' he said, 'or pretend to. People are less likely to make conversation with me in there.'

'Especially the female members of staff. Just a thought, but you might want to do the men's room first.'

'Good point.'

Also, there were no security cameras in the bathrooms. Korso checked the time and saw it was already 2.53 p.m. He rose from the chair and turned to the shelves. He pulled out three of the bright yellow, double-sided safety signs and placed them on the floor.

He looked around and considered what else he'd need for the unenviable task ahead.

THIRTY-EIGHT

Korso was leaning against the wall of one of the men's cubicles, making noises to indicate he was working, when Samara spoke for the first time in almost an hour: 'Just been informed the van's on its way to you. ETA roughly ten minutes from now.'

Korso gave a grunt of affirmation as he checked his watch: 3.48. Right on schedule. He wasn't alone right now so he couldn't really talk. Instead he just continued making tapping and sloshing sounds like he'd done for much of the past hour, while listening to the unseen visitor zip himself up by the urinals. On the plus side Georgi had managed to keep this place fairly spotless already, and as a result the place smelled a lot fresher and cleaner than he'd anticipated.

Once he heard the man open the door and leave, Korso opened his cubicle door and checked that the restroom was completely empty. It was. 'I'm on my way,' he said, placing his tools on the floor. He left the safety signs where they were. He'd be back here again pretty soon. 'No problems with Teodor?'

'Not as far I know. He's actually been as good as gold recently.'

'That's what worries me. It's like the calm before the storm.'

Samara didn't answer, and he heard the familiar beep that indicated she'd turned off her mic again. Korso exited the restroom, and walked quickly back down the corridor towards his cubbyhole. The faster you walked the busier you looked, and people were far less likely to talk to a preoccupied man than an idle one.

Once he reached his workspace, Korso opened the envelope he'd brought in with him and removed the letter within. It was a printout of the invoice for the cleaning equipment about to be delivered, printed on an official Vercogen letterhead. Another gift from Dog. He attached this sheet to the front of his clipboard, and then sat down and waited.

At 4.01, Samara spoke into his ear: 'Here we go, the delivery van's just arrived… It's turning left into the gate entrance, and the security guard's just stopped it… Okay, he's talking with the driver now… And he's just been handed some paperwork. He'll probably be calling you any second now… Yep, he's pulling his phone out.'

The desk phone rang moments later. Korso answered on the second ring and put it on speakerphone. 'Georgi,' he said.

A man with a guttural voice threw a stream of words at him. The rising inflection at the end made it sound like a question. In his left ear, Samara said, 'He wants to know if you're expecting a delivery. By the way, cleaning equipment is *pochistvashto oborudvane*.'

'*Da*,' Korso said into the speaker, '*pochistvashto oborudvane.*'

The security guard spoke some more, and then ended the call without waiting for an answer. Samara said, 'He'll meet you at the delivery entrance.'

'On my way.'

Korso grabbed his clipboard and made his way back to the storage room, passing various other employees along the way. None of them paid him any attention. A janitor was the closest thing to being invisible, except when something suddenly needed fixing. He reached the double doors, pushed them open and entered the storage area as though he owned it. As he walked towards the roller shutters, he heard a radio playing loud pop music and saw two guys in overalls in the far corner, stacking a pallet with boxes. They both stopped what they were doing and turned to him.

The youngest one called out, '*Exo, Georgi. Kavko stava?*'

Korso figured the guy didn't really care how he was doing, so he just pointed at the shutters and said '*Dostavka*.' *Delivery*. The word was the same in Russian. The young guy just nodded back at him and they both returned to work. Korso went over to the keypad on the wall and hit the up button. There was a moment's pause and then both shutters began rising up into the ceiling. Korso put down the clipboard and walked over to the two hand trucks against the wall. He grabbed one and wheeled it back to the loading area.

The shutters were already halfway up, and he saw the driver carefully backing the vehicle into the opening. The generic *MAXXIClean* logo pasted across the side of the van in blue and green lettering looked very professional. Cole had done a good job. The gate security guard was also standing nearby, watching everything with an eagle eye.

The driver braked and cut the engine, and then got out of the van, carrying his own clipboard. Cole looked convincing in plain blue overalls and a green cap, the visor pulled down low to partially shield his features. As he walked back, he nodded wordlessly at Korso as he unlocked and opened the rear doors. Inside, Korso saw about a dozen large boxes arranged about the cargo area. He also knew that all but two of them were empty.

Cole moved in closer to Korso, and said under his breath, 'All good here?'

'So far. You?'

'It got a little tense when I showed up at the gate. The guard back there threw a bunch of questions at me, but I just played dumb and kept repeating *Dostavka* over and over — did I say that right? — while showing him my paperwork, until he gave up and let me through.'

'That usually works. How's Teodor been holding up?'

Cole gave a sigh. 'He's been pissing and moaning for most of the journey, so about as expected. I'm just glad I can finally get rid of him.'

'And Lucian? She back from the airfield yet?' Korso had suggested she take a cab out to the hangar that morning in order to get a few more hours in the air, since you could never be too prepared. She hadn't needed much persuading to go.

'Yeah, she called about an hour ago and said she's on her way back.'

'Good. You got something for me to sign?'

'Right here.' Cole handed him his clipboard, pulled a pen from his pocket and passed that over too. He pointed at a space on the form on the top. Korso scribbled something unintelligible there and passed the pen back to Cole, who tore off the sheet underneath and gave it back to him. It all looked very official to those watching, which was all that mattered.

Cole then climbed into the back of the van and found one of the boxes that weren't empty. It had a photo of a rotary floor polisher on the side. He began dragging the box towards the open doors. When it was close enough, Korso grabbed hold and lifted the box out of the van and onto the hand truck ledge. He whispered, 'Wait while I find a space for this.'

Cole nodded, and Korso tilted the truck backward until the weight was balanced over the wheels, and then turned and pushed his load towards the racks. He entered the fifth aisle from the left, stopping when he came to the empty cage he'd spotted earlier. It was at floor level and large enough to take the box if turned on its side. Once Korso had placed the carton into the space he wheeled the empty truck back to the van, where Cole was waiting for him.

Korso climbed up into the rear of the van, and they both walked over to the box with a line illustration of a wet & dry vacuum cleaner on the front. The box was basically a cube, measuring four feet square. Teodor had to be pretty uncomfortable in there, but it had been his decision to come along. Korso leaned down and said, 'We're about to move you now. There are people nearby, so whatever happens don't make a sound. Got it?'

The only response was the sound of a knuckle tapping the side of the box, twice. Which was encouraging. Teodor clearly knew when it was in his best interests to shut up.

Korso and Cole pushed the heavy carton along the floor until it could go no further, and then they jumped out of the van and onto the ground. Once they each got a good grip under the box, they slid it out and gently lowered the two-hundred pound weight until it was resting securely on the ledge of the hand truck. As Cole shut the van's rear doors, Korso picked his clipboard up off the floor and placed it on top of the box.

The security guard came closer for a better look. He gave the large carton a withering glance, and then said something while slapping the side of the van with his palm. Clearly, he wanted Cole to hurry up and get the vehicle out of there.

'Okay, okay,' Cole said, and gave Korso one last glance before returning to the driver's side door.

Not wanting to push his luck any further, Korso stepped over to the keypad and pushed the down button. Machinery whirred as the roller shutters began to descend. With an effort Korso slowly tilted the hand truck back, feeling Teodor's body shift from one side to the other. Once it was at a forty-five degree angle, he started wheeling it slowly towards the double doors. He pushed them open and wheeled his load into the main corridor. Once he'd closed the doors he continued down the hallway in the same direction as before.

Nobody stopped him. Nobody asked what was in the box. So far, so good.

Keeping his head down, Korso wheeled his load past the desks in the open-plan work area, and gently steered it in the direction of his cubbyhole. He was less than twenty feet away from the door when a grouchy looking man in shirtsleeves and tie emerged from one of the small offices directly ahead, and barked an order at one of the phone operators in the main work area. The man gave a thumbs-up and went back to his work, while the manager turned his attention to Korso.

Frowning, he called out, '*Georgi, kavko pravish po dyavolite?*'

'Samara,' Korso said under his breath, 'help me out.'

'Rough translation,' she said quickly into his ear, '"What the hell are you doing?" You could try using *dostavka* again. Or if

271

you want to tell him to mind his own business, say *ne e tvoya rabota*, but be sure to smile when you say it.'

Korso made a snap decision. Without pausing in his task, he gave the manager a sardonic smile and said, '*Ne e tvoya rabota.*'

The manager narrowed his eyes for a brief moment, and then he snorted once and just waved Korso away dismissively. The phone in his office started ringing at that moment, and he went back to answer it. Korso let out a breath and carried on towards Georgi's office. He opened the door and pushed his heavy load inside. Kicking the door shut behind him, Korso gently tilted the hand truck forward until the carton was flat on the floor, and then slid the ledge out from under it. Pulling a penknife from his pocket, Korso carefully cut through the protective plastic covering and then opened the top two flaps of the box.

Inside, a forlorn Teodor winced up at him, one hand raised to shield his eyes from the harsh light. 'Hey, get me out of this thing.'

'Careful not to damage the box,' Korso said, helping him to his feet. He was still wearing the same leather jacket as before, and didn't seem to be in too bad shape, all things considered. But then Cole had only sealed him into the thing two hours ago.

Once he was fully out of the packaging, Teodor stretched his arms out wide and cracked his neck muscles. 'Oh, yeah,' he said. 'Feels good. So how is my good friend, Korso? Everything goes like clockwork?'

'For the moment.' Korso looked down into the box and saw three plastic 500ml bottles of Evian at the bottom, one of which was now empty. He pulled them out and placed them on the desk. 'If you need to go, use that empty bottle.'

'Huh? Why? Where you go now?'

'Back to work. I'm supposed to be the night janitor, remember? So I have to at least give the appearance that I'm doing my job for the next few hours. It also means I'm going to have to leave you here on your own, and that troubles me.'

'You mean you don't trust Teodor?'

'You haven't given me any reason to. Bad enough that I could be exposed at any second by someone who knows the real Georgi, but now I've got you to worry about as well. I shouldn't even have to say this, but on no account are you to leave this room until I get back. Are we clear on that?'

'Shit, you think I want go back to prison again?'

'You'd never get the chance to reach prison, Teodor. Don't you get it? Unless Deleva's a complete idiot, he already knows you're the key to locating these pill prototypes. If you're caught, he and Simov will make you talk and then simply dump your body in the gutter afterwards, just like they did your brother.'

Teodor's face darkened. 'You don't gotta remind me about Darian. I know what these bastards did to him. I never forget.'

'Good. Just so you understand what's at stake. If either of us gets caught in here, we're both dead.' Korso looked him squarely in the eye. 'While we're on the subject, I don't suppose you've changed your mind about giving me the exact location of the pills, have you? It'd simplify things greatly if you just told me now. Assuming they're secreted in an accessible place, I can go and get them right this minute. Then I come down and get you, we bluff our way past the guard at the front reception and jump into the waiting car and Samara drives us away from here. Job done.'

Teodor gave him a humourless smile. 'Sure, I tell you where they are, just as soon as everybody in building go home, okay? You don't trust Teodor, so why should he trust back?'

'Because unlike you, my word means something.'

Teodor slowly shook his head. 'Sorry, my friend, but I think first plan is best. Anyway, I am here now.'

'Well, it was worth a try.' Korso stepped over to the door, pointed at the key in the lock on this side. 'As soon as I leave make sure you lock this door. I don't know why anybody else would want to come in here, but no sense in getting careless now that we're so close to—'

The ringing phone on the desk took them both by surprise. They each turned and looked at it. The tone was very loud in the enclosed space.

Korso quickly considered his options. He'd been expecting the first call, and knew the reason for it. But if the person on the other end of this one asked him very specific questions, he'd have to rely on Samara for a fast translation and she might not be fast enough. And if he let it ring out the caller would come looking for him, and that would be even worse.

'You planning on answering that?' Samara said in his left ear.

Korso turned to Teodor. 'You answer it. Put it on speaker, and keep your voice neutral and your answers short. Just act like an overworked janitor. Think you can do that?'

Teodor gave a casual shrug. 'No problem, my friend. I be anyone you want.'

'Prove it. Your name's Georgi, by the way.'

Teodor sat down at the desk and calmly picked up the handset. 'Georgi.'

The answering voice coming through the speaker was female, and she talked fast. Had Korso answered, he would have had real trouble keeping up. He understood the odd word here and there, but most whizzed past him like the cars on a racetrack. In his ear, Samara said, 'It's Georgi's supervisor, Miss Yakova. Sounds like she's got something for him in one of the labs on the second floor.'

'*Da, da,*' Teodor said while Miss Yakova finished giving him her orders. Finally, she came to a stop and Teodor said, '*Nyama problem, az shte se spravya.*' Without waiting for a reply, he carefully replaced the handset and turned to Korso. 'Lady got job for you on second floor, research lab number two. Somebody smash bunch of specimen things, broken glass everywhere. I tell her I go take care of it right now.'

'There were a few more details in there,' Samara said softly into Korso's ear, 'but he gave you the gist of it. You better go.'

'On it.' Korso grabbed hold of the janitor's cart and checked that it contained everything he'd need for the clean-up job. He added two pairs of rubber gloves, and pushed the cart towards the door.

Teodor looked around the spare, dingy room. 'What you want me to do for next few hours? Stare at walls?'

'Play some solitaire on the PC, or grab some shuteye. I don't care what, just don't leave this room. Got it?'

'*Da, da.*' Teodor sighed as he came over and opened the door for him. 'I hear.'

THIRTY-NINE

Taking the elevator to the second-floor, Korso turned into the large hallway and saw all the doors were marked with just numbers. He approached the number two lab, where a serious looking lady in a white coat met him at the door. She spoke a few words as she led him over to the area in question. It seemed some clumsy person had upturned a large box of glass beakers, the shattered contents of which were now sprayed over one whole section of the lab. The woman said something else and then left him to get on with it.

Korso donned his gloves and began carefully clearing the tiled floor of glass fragments, making sure not to miss any tiny shards. He did the same with all the other work surfaces in the immediate area. It wasn't exactly strenuous work, though Korso managed to string it out to almost a full hour. The other fifteen or so technicians in the room were all so involved in their own research work they barely paid him any attention at all. Which was exactly how he wanted it.

It was almost five o'clock when he finished, whereupon he took the cleaning cart back to the first floor to continue his 'work' in the men's restroom. He figured this was the most convenient method of keeping out of everybody's way for another thirty minutes or so, when the majority of Vercogen's employees would finish for the day and head for home.

At 5.30, Samara whispered into his ear: 'Folks are starting to leave the building now, mostly in groups of three or four.'

'Good,' he said. He was now the only person in the restroom, the last visitor having departed five minutes before. 'Keep me updated, especially with regards to Deleva.'

'Copy that.'

Korso waited an additional ten minutes before packing everything up and pushing the cleaning cart towards the women's restroom next door. He knocked first, and when he got no reply, placed a yellow safety sign outside the door. He pushed the cart inside, and left it there while he went back to check on Teodor. He only saw two other employees on the way back, each working on computers in their offices. What had been a bustling workplace just minutes before was now quiet as a library.

When he reached his cubbyhole, he knocked lightly on the door. 'It's me. Open up.'

Moments later he heard a key turn in the lock, and the door opened. Korso entered the room, and Teodor quickly closed the door behind him.

'Man, I dying of boredom in here. When we go?'

'When I know the third floor's completely empty. Maybe another hour, maybe three. We'll only get one chance at this, so we do it right.' Korso looked over at the PC monitor and saw a tile-matching puzzle game, on pause. 'Any more phone calls while I was gone?'

'No calls, only four walls and dumb kids' games. This same as prison.'

'Just imagine you're on an island somewhere in the tropics or something.'

Teodor snorted. 'Sure, desert island with coconuts and pirate treasure.'

'That's the ticket.' Korso told him which restroom he was in if there was an emergency, and added, 'Don't forget to lock the door behind me.'

'*Da, da.*'

Korso left the cubbyhole and waited for the click of the lock behind him before walking back to the women's restroom. At the other end of the hallway ahead, he saw one of the security guards slowly making his rounds. Korso gave him a friendly salute, but the guard just turned away and stepped into an office at his left. It seemed Georgi was so far down the career ladder that even security guards ignored him.

He entered the women's restroom and perched against one of the sinks. All he could do now was wait, and look busy every now and then for the cameras. He absently looked around the room, realising he'd never been in a women's toilets before. Other than one notable difference, he didn't feel he'd missed anything.

He pulled out his phone and called Dog's number. Once she'd picked up, he asked, 'How's it looking from your end?'

'Well, the building's emptying out slowly but surely.' This time she was using a gruff man's voice. 'I'm logged into the building's security access system and can see a hundred and twelve people have already swiped themselves out. Other than yourselves and the guard on the gate, that leaves thirteen people inside the building, including the other three security guards. And the CEO's still in his office on the third floor, although his PA's gone for the day.'

'Hold on,' Samara said. 'Something's happening outside.'

'One second, Dog. What is it, Samara?'

'An SUV just pulled up outside the main entrance, and three more guards got out and are heading for the main door. They're going inside now.'

Korso frowned. 'Dog, are you seeing this? You told me the evening shift change is at eight p.m. every night.'

'It has been up till now. I don't what this is. Maybe Deleva suspects something's up and decided to bring in some extra manpower.'

'That's what I'm thinking,' Samara said.

Korso shook his head as he stared up at the ceiling. Unbelievable. As if things weren't bad enough. 'Just tell me what you see, Dog.'

'Okay, I don't wanna get your hopes up, but it might not be as bad as you think. There's some kind of discussion going on between the newbies and the guard at reception, and I'm watching that guy gathering up his stuff like he's about finished for the day. And now he's talking to someone on his radio while he puts on his jacket... Come on, come on. Okay, he's zipping his jacket and headed for the front door, while one of the newbies takes his place behind the reception desk and the other two swipe themselves into the building. It looks like a shift change, after all. Just a little earlier than usual.'

'I'm watching the guard exit now,' Samara said in his other ear. 'He's walking down the steps while doing something on his phone. Definitely looks like he's done for the day. Yeah, he's just turned right, and now he's walking away from me. And the guard by the gate looks like he's getting ready to take off too.'

That was promising, but Korso wasn't about to start counting his chickens yet. 'Dog, what about the two day guards still inside the building?'

'Yeah, they both look as though they're through for the day. One of them just left an office on the first floor. He's putting on his jacket as I speak. Hold on.'

'What?'

'Deleva's just left his office, and shut the door behind him. He's carrying a briefcase and heading for the elevator. Looks like it's home time for him, as well.'

'How many others left on the third floor?'

'He's the last. We've still got seven worker ants spread around the second floor, and two more with you on the first. Wait... I'm watching one of the replacement guards keying in the code to that control room we talked about... And now he's gone inside.'

'Let me know when he leaves. And anyone else, for that matter.' But with the third floor empty, it meant he no longer had to worry about Miss Yakova calling him up for another emergency. And there was nobody else left to check up on his work routine.

'The two day guards are leaving the building now,' Samara said. 'And here comes Mr Deleva right after them.'

'Right.' But mention of that control room keypad reminded Korso of something else he'd meant to ask before. 'Dog, when I viewed the footage you sent me of the third floor I counted twelve rooms up there, and four of those also had keypads next to the doors.'

'That's right. Deleva's office and three others. I think the one next to Deleva's suite is probably Simov's office, but I've never seen him go in there. Never seen him at all, actually.'

'Have you got the codes for those? Because I've got a sneaking suspicion the prototypes are going to be behind one of those four doors, and time might be of the essence when we get up there. I'd prefer not to have any last minute surprises if I can help it.'

There was a pause on the line. 'Damn, you got me there, K. I'll have to check some of the old CCTV footage I saved and see if I can zoom in whenever somebody enters, like I did with the control room. I'll get back to you, okay?'

'I'll be here.'

As Korso waited, he spent the time musing on the myriad other problems that might crop up in the hours ahead, and possible ways to resolve them. The time passed slowly.

At 7.53, Samara told him that three more employees had just left the building. Thirty minutes later, he felt his phone vibrate in his pocket. He took the call.

'Just spotted a guard making his rounds,' Dog said. 'He's just entered the men's room right next to you. My guess is he'll be checking the women's next, so look busy.'

'Understood.' Korso pocketed the phone and dashed over to the last cubicle, where he'd already laid some cleaning equipment on the floor in case of emergencies like this. As he picked up the commercial grade plunger and entered the cubicle, he heard the outer door open and the sound of someone entering the room.

Korso knelt down and inserted the rubber ring of the plunger into the drain opening, and began pushing and pulling on the handle with fast, concentrated trusts. He saw a shadow fall over him, but didn't look back, just kept on working in the hope that the guard would get bored and leave him alone.

The shadow didn't move.

Pretending not to notice, Korso kept working the plunger. After a few more seconds a hand tapped his shoulder. Korso couldn't ignore that. He had to react. He stopped what he was doing and slowly got to his feet, already working out his next move. As he began to turn, he extended the already tightly compressed fingers of his left hand straight out, preparing himself for a thrusting spear-hand strike to the guard's throat or neck. But he saw the guard had backed up so that he was out of Korso's reach. The moment the guard saw his face, he immediately pulled his weapon from his belt holster and aimed at Korso.

'*Kŭde e Georgi?*' he said.

'Huh?' Korso frowned, then tapped his own chest. '*Ya Georgi.*'

'*Ne mŭrdaĭ,*' the guard said, pulling the walkie-talkie from his belt with his free hand.

He was just raising it to his mouth when Korso noticed another shadow moving behind him. Then he saw a man's hand suddenly appear, raising what looked like a wooden mop handle. A split second later the wooden handle struck the back of the guard's head with great force, and the guard grunted as he dropped the radio and fell to his knees. Korso dashed forward and yanked the pistol from his grip. The guard looked at him in confusion for a moment, and then his eyes closed as he collapsed to the floor on his face.

'Lucky for you I want proper toilet for once,' Teodor said, placing the mop back on the janitor's cart.

'For once, I'm happy to see you,' Korso said. Kneeling down, he removed the guard's cap and saw an ugly gash in the back of the man's head. His hair was matted with blood, but he was still breathing. With any luck, the concussion would keep him out for hours. He just hoped the guard in the control room hadn't spotted Teodor on the CCTV.

'What now?' Teodor asked.

Korso handed him the black cap, while looking him up and down. Teodor and the guard had slightly different builds but they were more or less the same size, and both were clean shaven. 'Better start changing clothes. It won't take long for the other two guards to notice they're down a man, so you'll have to take his place instead.'

'Hey, good thinking.'

Teodor slipped off his leather jacket and started removing stuff from the pockets, while Korso inspected the weapon he'd taken. It was a black Smith & Wesson .38 with a 2-inch barrel, and fully loaded. He stuck it in his pocket and then knelt down and checked the guard's trousers. In the rear pocket, Korso found a vinyl wallet and inside was a photo of a smiling woman and two kids in swimming gear. The wedding band on the man's left hand told him the rest. According to his credit cards, his name was Ilian Petkov.

'I heard most of what was going on there,' Samara said in his ear. 'So are we still good?'

'So far,' Korso said, as Teodor started unbuckling the guard's utility belt. He moved away to give him space. 'Just an additional complication, that's all.'

The walkie-talkie squawked suddenly, and both men froze. The slim device was still lying where the guard had dropped it. From the speaker, a tinny voice said, '*Ilian, Kŭde si?*'

Korso turned to Teodor, pointing at the unconscious guard. 'That's Ilian. You remember what his voice sounded like? Because you'll have to tell this guy something.'

'Sure, I remember.' Teodor picked up the radio and clicked the transmit button. In a slightly lower register, he rattled off something that Korso couldn't quite catch, and the other guard gave a loud cackle in response and clicked off. 'Told him to leave me alone,' Teodor said. 'Ilian busy taking a crap break.'

'Good.' Korso pursed his lips as he pondered his next few moves. Finally, he said, 'Okay, finish getting dressed while I get back out there with the floor buffer. There's a pack of zip ties on that cart. Use them to bind the guard's hands behind his back and then gag him and leave him in the cubicle. Don't leave this room until I get back. I mean it. You got lucky once, but if either of the other guards actually meets you in person we're both done for. Are we agreed?'

Teodor shrugged. 'Hey, you the boss man. Before you leave, give me gun you took from guard, yeah? Empty holster looks suspicious, I think.'

'That's a chance we'll have to take. The gun stays with me.'

'You still not trust Teodor, huh?'

Korso assumed the question was rhetorical and said nothing. He took a set of earbuds from his pocket and inserted them in his ears, the left one atop the earpiece already in there. It was the best way he could think of to deter the remaining staff from talking to him. After inserting the lead into his phone, he turned back and said, 'I'll come get you once that other guard leaves the control room. We can't move until he's away from those monitors.'

'Uh huh,' Teodor said sulkily, and unzipped the guard's black windbreaker and slipped it off his body.

Korso left him there and returned to the janitor's office. Once inside, he grabbed the upright rotary floor buffer and extended power cord, and dragged the machine out into the main hallway. After plugging the cord into the nearest outlet, he adjusted the motor to its lowest setting and pressed the on button. The circular brush pad whirred into motion and he began sweeping the thing along the floor like he would a vacuum cleaner. As he worked, he slowly began moving it in the direction of the fire stairs at the rear.

A few minutes later, his phone chirped in his earpiece. He took the call. Dog said, 'Okay, I'm watching my screens and the two remaining staff members on your floor look like they're both getting ready to go.'

'Good. We better keep this line open from now on. How's it going with those door codes?'

'So, so. I got two complete codes, and one partial. Simov's office is the missing one, since nobody ever goes in there. The five-digit code for Deleva's office is the partial. Anytime he enters his combo, his head's in the way of the keypad. Except for lunch time today, when he turned to talk to his secretary and I saw him press the first three numbers: 7, 3 and 1. I think the fourth number might be zero, but I can't swear to it.'

'Okay. Keep on it.'

Korso continued cleaning the floor, making sure he always had a good view of the main corridor. More time passed. He'd almost reached the fire stairs door when he spotted motion at the other end of the hallway. The other guard was finally leaving the control room. Korso watched him shut the door, and then he turned and walked towards the stairs at the front of the building.

Once he was gone, Korso turned off the machine and quickly made his way back to the women's restroom. He opened the door and saw Teodor leaning against the sink, scrolling through a phone. Teodor looked up in surprise, then relaxed when he saw who it was. He was now wearing the guard's black jacket, black cap, black utility belt. The fit was pretty good. From a distance, he looked no different from any of the other guards. It would have to be enough.

'Where did you get that phone?' Korso asked.

'From guard. He don't need it, so I take. So what now, good buddy?'

'Coast's clear,' Korso said. 'Let's move.'

FORTY

After a quick check to make sure the unconscious guard was gagged and bound securely in the cubicle, Korso led Teodor back to the fire stairs where he'd left the floor buffer.

He opened the stairs door, and saw a small dimly lit area containing a narrow set of stone steps leading up, with half-landings between each floor. To his left was the steel fire exit door leading to the outside. More importantly, there were no cameras anywhere in sight.

Korso raised the earbud mic to his lips: 'Dog, you got eyes on the guard who just left the control room?'

'Yeah, he's on the second floor talking with one of the female technicians still up there, and showing her something on his phone. The third one's still at his station in reception. You're clear.'

'Let me know if anyone goes up to the third floor. We're heading up there now.'

'Roger.'

Korso turned to Teodor. 'Bring that buffer along, will you? I still need it.'

Teodor glanced at the heavy cleaning appliance. 'Why I have to carry?'

'Because I asked you to. You agreed to follow my instructions every step of the way, without any arguments. Or have you forgotten?'

'Why we not take elevator then? Easy.'

'And risk one of the other guards meeting you coming down? I don't think so.'

Teodor made a face, but he picked up the machine as instructed and coiled its long lead over his shoulder. Korso began climbing the stairs, Teodor following close behind. Minutes later they reached the top landing, with Teodor already breathing heavily from the climb. Korso pulled the door open, and peered out into the hallway. Even though the lights were dimmed, he could see it was completely empty up here. He saw offices lining both sides of the corridor, although none of the doors were marked or labelled. He could also make out Deleva's large suite right at the other end, with a small reception area out front. He closed the door and turned to Teodor.

'Well, we're here. You going to tell me where Darian hid the pills now?'

Teodor met his gaze squarely as he lowered the cleaning apparatus to the floor. 'Of course, my friend. I told you before my brother was one smart cookie, yeah? So what you think he does? He go hide his pills in very last place Deleva would ever look.'

'Let me guess. They're secreted somewhere in the man's own office.'

Teodor looked hurt. 'Hey, you ruin big surprise.'

'I kind of saw it coming. Where in the office, exactly?'

'When we get inside, I show you where. No problem.'

'I don't suppose Darian gave you the keypad code as well?'

'Sorry, good buddy. My bro only tell me this info as backup, yeah? He never think his boss find out about pills and torture him to death.' He shook his head sadly. 'Darian smart in some things, but maybe not so quick in others, like staying alive.'

Korso pulled the door open again. Nothing had changed; the third floor was still completely deserted.

He took the rotary buffer and extension lead from Teodor, and began walking down the hallway with it. Teodor kept pace at his side. As they passed one office Korso stopped for a moment and tried the door. It opened easily and he peered inside. The room itself was plain and sparsely furnished. There was a large L-shaped desk by the window, and through the blinds he could see night had already fallen on the city. Headlights from passing traffic briefly lit up the room before fading away to nothingness.

'This not boss's office,' Teodor said.

'I'm aware of that.'

Shutting the door, Korso and Teodor continued making their way down the hallway towards the large office suite at the end. They'd made it about halfway when the sound of the elevator in motion stopped them both in their tracks.

'Dog, somebody pressed the elevator button,' Korso said. 'What's happening?'

'It's that control room guard on the second floor,' she said. 'He's finished talking with that woman, and just standing in front of the elevator doors. He must have called it up from the first floor when I wasn't looking.'

Korso heard the elevator stop below. Teodor said, 'What goes on?'

'A guard's on his way up. I'll continue cleaning, but you need to get out of sight.' Korso turned to the nearest door and saw a keypad on the wall next to it. No good. Instead, he turned to the office opposite. There was no keypad for this one, and the door opened freely. The room was similar to the previous one, with the standard L-shaped desk by the window, and a small round table in the centre of the room for one-to-one meetings. Not much in the way of hiding places, but you could only work with what you were given. Teodor came over, and Korso pointed towards the main work desk. 'Hide behind that. Move.'

Teodor dashed inside and Korso shut the door after him. He could already hear the elevator starting to move again. Only seconds to go. Grabbing the buffer's power cord, he spotted an electrical outlet about ten feet away and ran over to it. He inserted the plug, then ran back to the machine and pressed the on button. Gripping the handles, he'd just started to move the polisher around the floor in a circular motion when he spotted the guard step out of the elevator fifty feet away. Korso didn't look up. It would have been out of character. He was a janitor doing his job, just like he did every other night.

Out the corner of his eye, he watched the guard turn away and then stroll over to Deleva's suite and check the door. Then he came back and began checking the rest of the floor. He opened the nearest door, switched on the lights for a few seconds, looked around the room, and then turned them off and backed out. He casually crossed over to the opposite office and went through the same routine. Korso continued polishing in the same general area, in order to stay close to Teodor.

The guard continued his rounds as though he had all the time in the world. When he eventually came within a few feet of Korso, he stopped and said something to him. Korso continued polishing the floor and gave a shrug, pretending not to hear through his earbuds. The guard shook his head in annoyance and said something else, and then he finally moved off towards the office where Teodor was hidden. As the guard gripped the handle and opened the door, Korso stopped and moved his right hand to his rear waistband until his fingers brushed against the Glock he'd taken from Simov.

Korso watched the guard turn on the lights and scan the room. He looked over to his left, where the large desk was located, and took one step into the office. Then another. Korso gripped the handle of the Glock, waiting for the man's next move. If he took one more step forward or even just tilted his head a little, it meant he'd spotted something that shouldn't be there. And then Korso would have no choice in the matter.

But the guard didn't move. He just stood there looking around the room. After what seemed like an eternity, he finally he took a step back, turned off the light, and shut the door. Letting out a breath, Korso took his hand away from his gun and began sweeping the polisher across the floor again. The guard walked past him to check the other offices, while Korso carried on in the opposite direction. It took the guard a long five minutes before he finished his tour of the floor and returned to the elevator.

Once he was gone, Korso turned off the machine and opened the office door. 'He's gone.'

Teodor rose from behind the desk, and came over. 'Too close, bro.'

'Get to Deleva's office. I'll be right behind you.'

Teodor strode down the hallway towards the front of the building, while Korso unplugged the power cord and pushed the machine ahead of him in the same direction. The reception area outside Deleva's suite was partitioned off from the corridor by a glass screen, and contained a large work desk and a fancy ergonomic chair, both of which undoubtedly belonged to Deleva's personal assistant. Teodor was perched against the desk, staring at the keypad next to the office door. The buttons were labelled 0–9. Luckily, there were no hash or star buttons, which would have complicated matters greatly.

'You got password?' Teodor asked.

'Part of it.' Korso raised the mic. 'Dog, any progress on the access code to Deleva's office? Because that's the one we need.'

'Yeah, so I heard. Unfortunately I haven't found any more footage of Deleva entering his room, so those first three numbers are all I got. Possibly with 0 as the fourth number, or maybe a 9. It was around that area. As for the fifth number, your guess is as good as mine. And don't even think of breaking down that door. It's wired into the building's security system, with the alarm rigged to go off if anyone tries to force their way in.'

'Naturally.' Korso focused on the problem in front of him. Since the access code contained five digits, that left him with a hundred possible combinations to try out. Figuring he might as well be methodical about it, he pressed 7-3-1-0-0. The digital readout at the top remained dark. He tried 7-3-1-0-1 next. Again, nothing. He kept going…

He'd just keyed in 7-3-1-0-9, and gotten no response for that one either, when Dog said, 'K, that same guard's heading back to the control room again. Look busy.'

'Keep me posted,' Korso said, and looked up to the ceiling and saw a CCTV nearby, with an almost perfect view of the office door. Turning to the work desk, he spotted the electrical outlet in the wall, and told Teodor about the guard down below. 'Start making a slow patrol of this floor in case he's watching, but keep your head down.'

Teodor nodded, and started strolling back the way they'd come as though he owned the place. Korso grabbed the buffer's power cord and plugged it into the socket.

'He's just entering the control room now,' Dog said.

Korso pressed the on button under the handle, the machine hummed into life, and he began moving it around the floor. As the minutes passed, he kept one eye on Teodor as he made his tour of the floor. He had to admit, the man sure looked and acted the part.

He figured another seven minutes had gone by when Dog spoke into his earbud again: 'He's just leaving the control room, K. You're good to go.'

'Copy that.' He pressed the off button and called out to Teodor, who began strolling back unhurriedly. Korso returned to the door, and remembered what Dog had told him about the fourth number being a 0 or 9, and keyed in 7-3-1-9-0 on the keypad. But the screen remained stubbornly dark. He moved onto the next number sequence…

When he got to 7-3-1-9-7, they both heard a soft click and *OKAY* suddenly appeared in green lettering on the little display. Teodor turned to Korso with a raised eyebrow, while Korso turned the handle and gently pushed the door open. 'We're in,' he said.

'Yeah, I see you,' Dog said.

Korso let Teodor enter first, then followed him in and shut the door behind them. He switched on the lights, and his gaze immediately fell on the large abstract steel tree sculpture on their left. It was kind of hard to miss. The thing almost reached the ceiling, and seemed to made out of interconnected steel rods. But the rest of the spacious office was a little more conventional in appearance. There was a large kidney-shaped desk by the window, with a leather settee against the wall just a few feet away. Next to the settee was a partially open door. Through the gap he could see a sink and part of a shower. In the centre of the room was a conference table with eight chairs positioned equally around its circumference, while a huge LCD screen took up part of the west wall.

'So I've got you inside as promised,' Korso said, turning to Teodor. 'Now you can do your part. Where did your brother hide the prototypes?'

Teodor smiled with one side of his mouth and pointed at the strange metal tree sculpture. 'Inside there. Boss looks at it every day and he don't even suspect. I told you Darian was smart kid.'

Frowning, Korso approached the sculpture for a better look. The steel rods were about an inch in diameter and bent into a huge variety of shapes and angles, depending on what part of the sculpture they had to represent. Every rod had a plastic cap at each end. He tapped a fingernail against one bar and confirmed they were hollow, meaning a small tubular pill container could easily fit inside one. But which one? Korso figured there had to be at least two or three hundred rods embedded into the sculpture.

He was about to ask when Samara spoke into his left ear: 'Uh oh, we've got company. Deleva's Merc just pulled into the parking lot, with somebody else in the passenger seat. It could be Simov. I can't see from here.'

'Deleva, here? Are you sure?'

'As sure as I'm sitting here talking to you. I'm looking at his car right now. Wait, another vehicle's just pulled up outside the building, and a man's just gotten out. I can't see his face, but it looks like he's waiting for Deleva to join him. No pressure guys, but you might want to get a move on.'

Korso shook his head at the news. This was just what they needed.

Then he suddenly felt his Glock being plucked from his rear waistband. He swivelled round and saw Teodor now standing a few feet away, pointing the barrel at his chest.

'Seriously?' Korso said. 'Look, I don't know what you're planning, but I've just been informed that Deleva's downstairs, and on his way up here. With company.'

'I know,' Teodor said. '*I* told him to come.'

Korso just stared back at him, his mind speeding through a dozen possible reasons for Teodor's betrayal. But out of all the viable motives there was only one that made any real sense, and it was also the one he was powerless against.

'Okay,' Korso said. 'So what's on your mind?'

Teodor motioned with the gun. 'Earbuds, earpiece. Get rid.'

Korso removed both earbuds and the earpiece, and stuffed them in his right trouser pocket. The voice-activated recorder in his shirt pocket was still transmitting, though, meaning Samara should still be able to hear everything they said.

'Now other gun, in pocket. Be slow.'

With his right hand, Korso gingerly pulled the guard's .38 from his left pocket and showed it to Teodor, holding it between thumb and index finger. 'Now what?'

'Kick over to me.'

Dropping the gun on the floor, Korso punted it towards Teodor, who then kicked it over to his left, where it came to a stop underneath the steel sculpture.

'Now sit in big boss's chair, behind desk.'

Korso made his way over to the large desk and took a seat. He noticed two drawers hidden under the desk, one on either side of him. There might be something in those drawers he could use. Like a lighter, for instance. Even a steel ruler would be better than nothing.

'You mind telling me what this is all about? I think I deserve that much.'

'You find out soon, good buddy.' Teodor moved backwards until he was positioned next to the hinge side of the door.

'I'm still trying to figure out how you managed to contact Deleva in the first place.'

'Very easy. I spend long time in janitor room, and I always pretty good at finding things. After searching database, I finally find phone number for Deleva. When I take phone from guard, I get text message ready, saying he and his best boy should come to office if they want night vision pills they search for. Then when you come get me, I send text.'

'So you had this all planned from the start?'

'For long time, sure. I think about this every minute of every day since I get news of Darian's murder. He's only family I ever have and only one I ever trust. I look out for him my whole life, make sure he's okay. And those two bastards downstairs kill him, like this.' Teodor snapped his fingers. 'Like rat in sewer.'

'I guess revenge is something I can understand, even if I don't see much point in it.'

'Yeah? Somebody important to you is murdered, maybe then you think different.'

'Maybe I already did lose somebody, Teodor, a long time ago. And violently. But I also learnt that revenge never really satisfies, especially when it's followed through to the exclusion of all else.'

'Except something you don't know about Teodor, good buddy.' He gave another sad smile. 'Something that changes *every*thing.'

Korso pondered on that statement for a moment. A number of possibilities occurred to him straight away as to its meaning. But one leapt out above the rest. 'You're dying.'

The Bulgarian slowly nodded his head. 'Pretty good guess, my friend.'

'What is it? Cancer?'

Teodor nodded again. 'Lungs. Stage four. Maybe got six months left, but I think less. Prison doc found out year ago. I pay him plenty to destroy X-rays and stay quiet.'

Korso knew he was telling the truth. It explained why he'd acted so weak during their escape through the sewers, why he'd needed to stop every few seconds to get his breath back. The beatings from the guards, combined with the cancer slowly eating away at his insides, would have been enough to slow any man down. It also explained why he'd been so insistent on coming along on the mission in the first place. All he cared about was making sure his brother's killers died before he did.

'So all this talk about the prototypes doesn't really mean anything to you, does it?'

'What do I care about stupid pills? Thanks to your American, Belmont, I got half million in bank now. Enough to last me. Don't need more.'

'What about Darian? Did he know you were sick?'

'Never. I keep secret from *every*body.'

'So now what? You planning on killing me too?'

'Not if I don't got to. You got me out, so maybe I let you go after. I think about it.'

Except Korso had a major problem with the passive approach when it came to his own wellbeing. In any life or death situation you could only rely on yourself. He shifted in the chair, crossing his legs until part of his left shoe was touching the underside of the drawer to his right. Without glancing down, he added pressure to his foot and used it to slowly slide the drawer out, millimetre by millimetre.

At the same time, he said, 'So were you telling the truth about the pills' location? The container really is hidden somewhere in all that junk over there?'

'Sure, I don't lie about that. Darian even marked special rod with pen.' Teodor edged over to the sculpture and after a quick glance, said, 'Yeah, I see it there.'

Teodor then sidled back to the door and listened for a moment. 'Elevator coming now. Hands on desk.' Korso placed both palms flat on the desktop, while using his foot to slide a little more of the drawer out. 'You don't say nothing when they come in, understand? I don't want have to kill my good buddy.'

'I don't want that, either.'

They waited in silence. Korso soon heard faint mutterings coming from the other side of the door. He figured Deleva and Simov would come up without security guards, if only because they'd want as few people to know about the pills' existence as possible.

The handle turned and the door was pushed open. The stocky Andrey Deleva stepped into the room, his dark eyes focused on the man sitting in his office chair. He looked very much like his file photo, with grey receding hair and large jowls, and he was wearing an expensive navy blue suit. Right behind him was the taller figure of Simov, wearing a dark suit with a slight bulge under the left armpit. Korso could see they were alone. Which made him wonder where the third man was, the one Samara had seen arrive earlier.

'You must be Korso,' Deleva said, a deep furrow across his brow. 'It was you who sent me the text message? What do you want? How did you get into this building?'

Deleva's English was perfect, with barely a hint of an East European accent. But Korso said nothing in reply. He didn't even nod. He was still trying to edge the drawer out a little further while keeping an eye on Teodor, who was standing behind the door, aiming the Glock at the two men in front of him. Three, if you counted Korso. Simov quickly took his position on Deleva's left side, and just glared down at Korso as though he'd like to perform a surgical experiment on him.

'Look, I asked you questions,' Deleva said. 'I want answers, and I want them now.'

Korso just watched as behind them, Teodor gently pushed the door until it clicked shut. Both men turned instantly at the sound, and Teodor made sure they had a good view of the gun in his hand. His right arm remained perfectly steady. 'Put up hands.'

Both men raised their arms in the air.

'You know me, boss man?' Teodor asked, a faint smile on his lips.

296

Deleva said something in Bulgarian that indicated he knew exactly who he was, but Teodor interrupted him before he'd finished. 'Talk English. My buddy back there don't speak Bulgarian so good, and also I like to practice.'

'English is fine with me, Mr Yanev. I was just about to say that I was hoping you and I would meet at some point.'

'Uh-huh. You armed, boss man? Tell truth. I find out you lie, I put a bullet in you.'

After a brief pause, Deleva said, 'I'm not armed, but my associate here has a 9mm semi-automatic in his shoulder holster.'

'Good. You reach in, take it out and drop on floor. Then kick over to me. Be very slow. I very nervous man.'

As Deleva painstakingly followed Teodor's instructions, Korso used the distraction to continue sliding the drawer out as much as he could. Without moving his head, he looked down at the contents of the drawer. Inside, he saw numerous legal pads, a desk calculator, and various stationery items. There was no steel ruler in sight, but he did spot something even better. Half covered by some papers was an ornate, antique silver letter opener with an engraved blade and a tassel at the top. It looked very old, and very expensive.

Korso was proficient with a knife when he needed to be, except this barely qualified. The blade was little more than a joke, nor did it look heavy enough to be much of a threat in the air. But the tip looked dagger sharp, and anything was better than nothing. Raising his eyes, he saw that Teodor's attention was still on the two men in front of him. Korso waited patiently for Deleva to finally pull the gun free of Simov's holster. He held it up for Teodor to see. The moment he dropped it to the floor, Korso casually passed his right hand across the open drawer until his palm was directly over the letter opener.

'Now kick gun to me,' Teodor said. 'Slowly.'

While Deleva punted the gun with his foot, Korso, using just his fingers, quickly slipped the letter opener into the sleeve of his shirt, blade first. As he pulled his arm away, he began sliding the drawer shut again with his shoe. He looked up. Teodor watched the gun stop a few inches from his foot and left it there, keeping the Glock pointed at the two men.

'Now turn and face window. Keep hands up.'

Both men turned so they were facing Korso. Meanwhile Teodor crouched down and picked up Simov's 9mm. He looked at it briefly before sticking it in his rear waistband. Then he stepped forward and with his free hand, began patting down Simov's body from the shoulders down. Simov just glared at Korso without expression. Finding nothing, Teodor searched Deleva next, with the same result.

Korso continued watching everything before him in silence. Just waiting.

Meanwhile, Teodor stepped back and said, 'Okay, boss man, one last thing. I want you call other two guards and tell them stay on first floor, while Ilian stays up here with you. Ilian is name of other guard. Use his radio here.' He pulled the walkie-talkie from his belt and lobbed it underhanded to Simov, who caught it and handed it to Deleva.

Deleva pressed the transmit button. After confirming that it was their boss on the line, he then gave them a few brief commands in Bulgarian. Almost immediately, he received two affirmatives in response.

'Good. Now kick radio back to me.' Deleva did as he was ordered. Teodor left it where it was, and said, 'Okay, now we talk. So how come you want meet jailbird like me, boss man? Maybe you want collect fat reward, yeah?'

'That's the farthest thing from my mind, Mr Yanev. In fact, I was hoping that you and I could do some real business together.'

'Yeah? What kind of business?'

'You know what kind. Your brother Darian worked for me for a long time, and I know he recently developed some glaucoma pills with very unique side effects. And I also know that he managed to manufacture some prototypes and hide them before his untimely death three weeks ago. And I also believe that during one of his prison visits he told you exactly where he'd hidden them, which I imagine is why you're here today.'

'Yeah, Darian one smart cookie, for sure.' Teodor shifted his glance to Simov. 'Cops think heart attack happened because of mugging gone wrong. What about you, mister man? You think dumb muggers kill my baby brother?'

Simov made a vague hand gesture, and said nothing.

'You know what I think?' Teodor aimed the gun at Deleva's chest. 'I think Darian too scared to walk anywhere without streetlights and no people around. He always scared of own shadow, ever since he was kid. No. Forget about mugger story. I think when you find out about magic pills, you take him into dark room somewhere and then your man here tortures my baby brother until his heart gives up. I think this what happened.'

Deleva was already shaking his head. 'No, you're wrong, Mr Yanev. Sure, I admit I was angry when I discovered Darian wasn't planning on sharing his discovery, especially as he developed it on the company's time and on company premises, but there's no way I'd ever risk damaging him in any way. He was far too valuable. In fact, rather than start a long protracted legal battle over ownership rights, I'd already instructed my lawyers to draw up a partnership agreement between Darian and myself, guaranteeing the two of us an equal share in all future profits, but he died before I could even present it to him. Had he lived, we could have made billions together.'

Teodor's eyes became hooded. 'You real smooth talker, Mr Deleva. I know plenty people like you, people make you believe sun rises in west instead of east. But *you* killed Darian, I know this for fact. You and your boy here. I don't show up at your work now because I want to do business. I come to make you pay.'

Korso noted the droplets of sweat at the back of Deleva's neck as he spoke. 'If you pull that trigger you'll be killing an innocent man, that much I can promise you.'

'Sure, you plenty innocent, just like stone-face bastard next to you.' The Glock was still aimed at Deleva's chest. Korso could see Teodor index finger begin to squeeze the trigger. 'Time to go now. You got last words?'

'Just one,' Deleva said. '*Now!*'

FORTY-TWO

The word was barely out of his mouth when the office door suddenly burst open, and a third man charged into the room, gripping a pistol in his right hand. It was Balakin.

Then everything seemed to happen at once.

As Balakin continued racing towards Korso's position, he half-turned to his left and fired off a brief volley of shots at Teodor before diving to the floor close to the wall, where Korso lost sight of him.

The gunshots sounded like firecrackers going off. They all hit their mark.

Korso had time to see Teodor's body convulse from the bullets' impact, and as he fell back his own trigger finger twitched and the Glock fired twice. Simov had already dropped down out of the line of fire, but the slower Deleva had remained where he was. His body immediately slammed back against the desk as one of Teodor's rounds got him in the neck. Globules of blood spattered onto the desk as he crumpled and fell.

Then Korso was busy diving off the chair and onto the floor behind the desk. Yanking the letter opener from his shirtsleeve, he quickly scrambled around the right side of the desk for a better view.

He saw Teodor lying on his back near the door with both arms outstretched, the Glock a few inches from his right hand. His chest was covered in blood. He wasn't moving. At the base of the steel sculpture five feet to the right of him, Korso could see the .38 on the floor where he'd thrown it, looking like a Christmas present for the damned.

Simov was just a short distance away from Korso, and already on his feet. He began moving towards the fallen Teodor, towards his own Glock that had been taken from him.

Korso couldn't let that happen.

Without conscious thought, he rose to one knee and raising his left arm for balance, pulled his right arm back with the letter opener blade gripped tightly between thumb and index finger. He swung his arm forward, letting go of the weapon at the last possible moment. The blade flew from his grip like a bullet, and a split second later it was lodged deep in Simov's right shoulder blade. Simov immediately dropped to one knee, one hand on the floor for support. But he got up again and kept moving towards Teodor and the Glock.

Conscious that Balakin was still somewhere off to his left, Korso jumped to his feet and flat-out sprinted for the tree sculpture on the right side of the office. As he ran he heard Balakin yelling, '*Stop*,' but Korso ignored him as he passed the wounded Simov. He heard one firecracker go off and then another, expecting to feel pain at any second as the rounds entered his flesh. But there was no pain. Just the goal directly in front of him. When he was just a few feet from the sculpture he dived to the floor with both arms at full reach, and as he landed, managed to grab the .38 with his right hand.

Gripping the revolver tightly, index finger resting against the trigger like it belonged there, he swivelled his body round, gun first, and took in the situation in a microsecond, his mind momentarily slowing everything down so that it felt like he was looking at a still life.

He saw Simov crouching in front of Teodor's corpse, right arm extended as he reached down for the Glock. The antique paper opener was still sticking out of his shoulder blade. In another second, the Glock would be back in his hand. Less.

Deleva was lying in front of his desk, not moving. There was a huge pool of blood around his head and under his body, and a large messy bullet hole in the side of his neck, right where the carotid artery was located. Blood pumped steadily from the wound, glistening brightly under the ceiling lights. If he was still alive, he wouldn't be for much longer.

Balakin was still on the other side of the office, crouched down next to the desk as he readjusted his aim. Or tried to. Korso could only see part of him, which meant the reverse was also true. Simov was currently between the both of them and blocking each man's view. At this exact moment in time, neither man had a clear shot at the other.

Left hand supporting the right, Korso aimed the .38 at Simov's centre mass at the same time the other man picked up the Glock. Just as Simov was in the act of turning round to face him, Korso squeezed the trigger. Once. Twice.

Both shots found their target. Red roses suddenly bloomed on the man's chest, and Simov fell to his knees and swayed for a moment, before he fell back to the floor, his upper body landing messily on Teodor's outstretched legs.

Which just left—

'*Wait*,' Balakin yelled, his own gun now aimed in Korso's direction as he slowly got to his feet again.

Korso kept the .38 pointed at Balakin's chest area, his finger still resting on the trigger. But he didn't squeeze it. Yet. Balakin was clearly in the more advantageous position, while Korso, lying flat on his stomach, was little better than a sitting duck. But he still had four rounds left, and he wouldn't die easy. If he went, he'd make sure Balakin went with him.

'Wait a moment,' Balakin said, more quietly this time. 'I don't want to kill you.'

'I wouldn't mind killing you,' Korso said, 'but that doesn't mean I won't listen. I'm going to raise myself up now. Don't try and stop me.'

'I won't stop you. But I'd advise you to do it very slowly.'

With the barrel of the .38 never wavering for a second, Korso slowly managed to get his feet under him and then carefully pushed himself up to a kneeling position. From there he just as carefully raised himself up until he was once again on equal standing with the Russian.

Keeping the .38 pointed at Balakin's chest, Korso darted a quick glance towards Deleva. Blood was no longer pumping from the neck wound. His heart had stopped. An equally quick glance towards Simov told him he'd no longer be a problem either. And Teodor was still lying in the exact same position, with several small bullet holes in his chest. So it was just the two of them now.

Korso looked down the muzzle of the gun Balakin was pointing at him. The hand holding it was very steady. Just as Korso's was.

'We seem to be at an impasse,' Korso said. 'What do you want?'

'What I've wanted all along, of course. The prototypes. But with Teodor Yanev no longer with us, that presents me with a very large problem. I'm assuming he told you where they're hidden?'

Korso nodded. 'Just before you came in, as it turns out. You can probably guess my next question.'

'Naturally, I didn't *plan* to kill him. I only meant to wound, but the idiot moved at the last second, and I was running at the time...' Balakin shrugged using just his eyebrows.

'You probably did him a favour anyway,' Korso said. 'Look, before we go any further I need to speak with a colleague first. For both our sakes.'

'Very well. Continue.'

With his left hand Korso carefully pulled his phone from his pocket and, without looking, put it on speaker. 'Are you still there?' he asked.

'I'm here,' Dog said.

'Did anybody else in the building hear anything?'

'Not as far as I can tell. There's nobody left on the second floor now, and the two remaining guards are still on the first floor, and I doubt the shots carried that far. One's currently working a computer in one of the offices, while the other one's still in reception playing on his phone. It all looks like business as usual.'

'Good. Let me know if that changes.'

'Will do.'

'So back to the problem at hand,' Balakin said. 'You're saying you know where the prototypes are hidden?'

'I didn't before. I do now.'

'Somewhere in this building?'

Korso shook his head. 'Not even close. Teodor originally told me they were located on this floor, but only in order for me to get him inside the building so he could get close to his brother's killers. That was the main reason he wanted out of prison. Plus he was dying of cancer, which I didn't learn until just now.'

'Really? I didn't know that.'

'Nobody did. Teodor kept things a lot closer to his chest than I would have imagined. He only had a few months left, at best. But as payment for getting him this far he did finally tell me where the pills are hidden, about three miles from this location. I've got the exact coordinates memorised, in case you're wondering.'

'That doesn't surprise me. So, how do we play this?'

'*We* don't. You turn around and leave, that's all. Once I get word you're out of the building, I'll make my own exit.'

'And why should I allow you do that?'

'Because you've got no other choice. I'm now the only person on the planet who knows where those prototypes are hidden, and there's no way I'll reveal that information to you or anyone else. If I die, their location dies with me.'

'The information could be forced out of you,' Balakin said. 'There are methods to persuade people to open up, as I'm sure you're aware. Nobody's invulnerable.'

'That's true. But if you were to go the torture route, I'd make it a matter of your having to kill me outright, knowing full well

305

that you can't afford to let that happen.' Korso smiled. 'Or we can both start shooting now, and go out in a blaze of glory. Your choice.'

Balakin chewed his inner cheek. 'This isn't the end of it. You must know that.'

'I know it.' Korso jutted his chin at the mess around them. 'But this is neither the time or the place. Decide now.'

Balakin paused in thought for a few moments. Then he began to slowly move sideways towards the door, his gun never straying from its target. Likewise, Korso followed him closely with the .38. Once he reached the door, he pulled it open with his free hand and said, 'I'll be seeing you, Korso.'

'I don't doubt it.'

Then he left, shutting the door behind him. Korso waited a few more seconds, then raised his phone. 'Dog, is he leaving?'

'Yeah, he's going, all right. Heading for the stairs as we speak.'

'I doubt he'll set the guards on me, but keep an eye on him anyway.'

'You got it.'

Korso looked down at Teodor's body. *And it could have all gone so smoothly*, he thought. Except it rarely did when amateurs were involved. He glanced at the lifeless figure of Deleva, slumped next to his desk, his head lying at an odd angle. Teodor had finally gotten his revenge, and with his very last breath. For what it was worth. Turning back to Simov, Korso reached down and plucked the Glock from his grip, stuck it his waistband.

Now for the main attraction.

Pursing his lips, Korso carefully studied the steel pipes that made up the strange sculpture, focusing on the specific area where Teodor had been looking earlier. Finally, his eyes fell on a four-foot-long steel tube, one of a dozen identical pipes that had been bent and welded together to form a thick L shape set at a fifteen-degree angle near the base of the sculpture. The special rod was in the middle. It had a small splotch at one end as though made from a black marker pen, and was only really noticeable if you were looking for it.

Korso reached in and grabbed hold of part of the section and tried shaking the pipes back and forth, but there was no give at all. The sculpture barely moved a millimetre. Every piece in there was welded tight. He traced his finger down the pipe in question until he reached the plastic cap at the end. He inserted a thumbnail under the edge, and after jimmying it a little, eventually managed to pry it free. Activating the flashlight on his phone, he aimed the light down the tube and tried to get a good look. But the pipe was too long and he couldn't see anything that far down.

He frowned in thought. Darian was clearly a highly intelligent man. Not only had he managed to somehow create these wonder pills in the first place, but he'd then found the perfect hiding place for them. If he'd thought that far ahead, it seemed logical that he would also have figured out an easy way to retrieve them again. Otherwise, what was the point?

Then he remembered Teodor's description of the pill container itself: a thin tube with a screw-on cap, about four centimetres long, and one centimetre wide.

And most important of all, made from metal.

Figuring Teodor wouldn't have come all this way unprepared, Korso crouched down next to his body and searched through his trouser pockets. He found a few hundred leva in the left pocket, while the right contained a small, heavy, circular item. He reached in and pulled it out. It was a thick, heavy stainless steel disc with a simple keychain attached. About the size of a medium-sized coin, but much heavier.

He held the disc close to the sculpture and could fell the strong magnetic pull even while it was still a few inches away. Crouching down, he placed the pocket magnet against the special rod with the black marking, right at its lowest point. The disc immediately stuck to the steel on contact, as though glued there. Korso gripped the keychain tightly and began slowly dragging the magnet along and up the steel cylinder.

As it neared the end, Korso saw something cylindrical inside the pipe also rising up towards him. As soon as the top part emerged, he grabbed the item with his free hand and pulled it all the way out.

It was a thin metal tube with a screw-on cap. Exactly as Teodor had described.

Korso shook the container. Nothing rattled, but there was definitely something in there. He could already feel his pulse quickening as he studied the plain metal container in his hand. It was like this every time he reached the end of an assignment and laid eyes on the prize he'd been chasing for so long, regardless of what that item might be. It was one of the few things left that made him feel truly alive.

Korso unscrewed the cap and saw a white cotton wall ball inside. He pulled the ball out and saw the pills at the bottom of the container. Holding out his left hand, he tapped the container gently with his index finger and two white tablets fell into his palm. They looked completely ordinary, like aspirin or paracetamol, or even sugar pills. He picked one up and slowly rotated it. One side was without any kind of marking, while the other side was imprinted with a simple crescent moon symbol. Just as Belmont had described it.

So this was it.

Hard to believe that something that could so easily crumble into dust with a little pressure could be worth so much to so many. But that's often how it worked out. Somebody, possibly Sir Francis Drake, once said that 'big things have small beginnings', and truer words were never spoken before or since. That's assuming these pills were genuine, of course. Korso kept staring at the small tablet between his fingers, turning it this way and that as he viewed it from a variety of different angles. He was almost entranced by it. Although in truth it was less the pill itself that fascinated him, but more what it represented. He was essentially looking at the ultimate bargaining chip.

It was a few minutes later when Dog's modulated man's voice suddenly blared out from the phone speaker, 'Hey, K, I don't mean to rush you, but are we any nearer to getting what we came for?'

Korso looked down at his phone. He dropped the now sealed pill container into his shirt pocket, turned off the speaker and held the phone to his ear. 'I've got it,' he said.

There was a short pause. 'Well, goddamn. That's astounding news.'

'Tell me about the guards. Where are they now?'

'Okay, one's still at his station in reception. The other's in the kitchen on the first floor, making himself a coffee while he plays on his phone. Balakin's gone too. If you're gonna head downstairs, I'd say now's the time to do it.'

'Copy that.'

Korso dashed over to Deleva's private restroom and looked around until he found a box of Kleenex on a shelf above the sink. He grabbed half a dozen sheets, then went back to Deleva and carefully daubed two of the thick tissues against the wound in his neck. Both came away bloody. He folded these tissues carefully within the clean ones so that none of it touched his hands, and then took one last look round the office. Satisfied he had everything he needed, Korso stepped over to the door, unlatched it and pulled it open. He stepped out and then gently shut the door behind him, hearing the lock click home. Then he retraced his steps down the long empty corridor towards the rear fire exit stairs. Once inside the stairwell, he silently descended the steps until he reached the first floor. He pulled open the door and walked back across the open work area.

After a brief visit to the janitor's closet to retrieve his jacket, Korso continued down the corridor towards the front of the building. As he walked he unfolded the Kleenex until the bloody tissues were on top, and raised them near to his face. He also adopted more of a sloping posture, slumping his shoulders and stooping forward more. To complete the picture, he started coughing and hacking into the tissues in his hand. Retrieving Georgi's ID card from his pocket, he swiped himself into the outer reception area. He approached the night guard sitting at the desk while coughing violently and pointing at the exit door.

The guard got to his feet with a frown, and sidled around the desk towards him.

'*Bolna*,' Korso spluttered between coughs, displaying the bloody tissues in his hand.

The guard's eyes widened and he stopped in his tracks, keeping his distance. He asked a question, but Korso just continued hacking while gesturing for him to unlock the main door. The guard said something else, which Korso also ignored. He'd already told him he was sick. It was obvious he had to leave. Finally, the guard pulled a set of keys from his belt and approached the doors. He keyed a ten-digit code into the alarm keypad on the wall and then inserted a key into the lock on the door itself. He said something else while pushing it open, and then took a step back.

'*Blagodarya*,' Korso croaked, and shuffled past him and out the door, still coughing.

Standing on the top step, he looked both ways and saw the street was almost empty of traffic. The windows in the commercial buildings opposite were all dark. He couldn't see any other pedestrians around. The Infiniti was still parked across the street, about a hundred feet to his left. Its nearest neighbour was a Ford station wagon, parked about fifty feet away in front, and then two generic panel vans beyond that. The Infiniti's tinted windows made it hard to see inside, especially as there were few streetlights along this road, but he could just about make out Samara's face watching him through the windshield. But she would have heard everything that had happened through the receiver, so she knew he was coming.

Suspecting the guard was still watching him, Korso remained in character as he descended the steps to the sidewalk. He then turned left and shuffled off down the street, still coughing into his hand. Once he felt he was safely out of view, he scrunched up the tissues and dropped them on the ground. He waited as a car passed by, and then crossed the street and approached the Infiniti's passenger side.

After looking both ways, he opened the front door and got in. He gently clicked the door shut, then turned to Samara in the driver's seat.

She had both hands on the wheel, and was still looking out through the windscreen with a slight frown on her face. Other than her breathing, she didn't move a muscle. She blinked and slowly turned her head towards him.

Korso could already feel the snakes writhing in his stomach. Something was badly wrong here. But she didn't seem injured in any way, so what was it?

'Something's happened,' he said, reaching for the Glock in his rear waistband.

'*We* happened,' a male voice whispered from behind him, as something cold and hard touched the back of his neck.

FORTY-THREE

Korso froze, not moving a muscle. Head still turned towards Samara, he watched as Lucian, wearing all black clothing, rose up from the rear footwell and placed the barrel of her gun against Samara's neck. She was so small he hadn't spotted her back there, especially with the interior light turned off.

She looked over and raised a finger to her lips, slowly shaking her head from side to side. Korso got the message. They clearly didn't want Dog listening in and getting any ideas about coming to his rescue. Which he wouldn't have expected anyway.

Lucian gently prodded Samara's neck with the gun, and Samara reached across and placed her fingers in Korso's shirt pocket. She arched her eyebrows at what was in there, and slowly pulled out the little micro voice transmitter. The pill container she left where it was. She passed the transmitter back to Lucian, who lowered the window and threw it out.

'Now we can talk,' Cole said from behind him. 'I see you started reaching for that Glock of yours, so keep on going and pull it out, but do it very slowly. One wrong move and it'll get messy in here, understand?'

'Perfectly.' Korso leaned forward, slowly pulled the 9mm from his waistband and held it up by the barrel.

Cole reached past his shoulder and plucked the gun from his hand. 'That's real good. But then you always were smart.'

'Not always, it seems,' Korso said, making eye contact with Samara.

'Sorry,' she said. 'There was no way to warn you.'

'I can see that,' Korso said, pointedly glancing at the door release handle at her side before looking back at her. He did it again. Samara saw where he was looking, then returned his gaze and blinked twice. She was a pro, and understood what he was saying. When the time came, she'd know what to do. 'I wouldn't have suspected this of you, Cole. Nor Lucian, for that matter. Are things really that desperate?'

'More than you can know, old buddy. See, I may have left out one or two details when I told you about my situation before. To be honest, the kind of trouble I'm in back home you can't buy your way out of, not for any amount of money. So I figure with the huge payday we'll get from these prototypes, I can disappear to a small point on the map where nobody can ever find me.'

'There's no such place.'

Lucian turned to him, smiling faintly. 'To hide from you, you mean? Well, there's an easy solution to that.'

'No need for that,' Cole said. 'So, Korso, we were listening in to that party of yours on the third floor, and once again it looks like you're the last man standing. Well, you and Balakin, who we saw leave a short while ago. Man, how the hell do you do it?'

'By keeping my eyes peeled, and my guard up.' *And also by taking the best advantage of my immediate surroundings*, he thought but didn't say. 'It doesn't always work. Out of interest, when did Balakin approach you?'

'Saturday afternoon, right after I dropped the van at the underground garage. After the cab dropped me off a few blocks away from the safe house, I was walking back and this guy Balakin came up to me and said he knew who I was and that we should have a private talk somewhere. No gun, no threats. Just a friendly talk. So I went with him to this plain house about a stone's throw from ours, and we talked. And when we finished talking, I returned to the safe house and talked with Luce here, and we both agreed that twenty million Euros is a hell of lot of money. Far too much to turn down, old buddy.'

'You'll never see a penny of it,' Korso said. 'I know Balakin, and I know how he operates. Like most sociopaths he can charm the skin off a snake, but it's all surface. He only wins if everybody else loses.'

'That's not a bad philosophy to have. But don't you worry about it, boyo. We can take care of ourselves just fine. After all, we handled you two easily enough.'

'And where's Balakin now?'

'How do I know? He left here in kind of a rush. But I'll call and arrange a meet once we've finished our business here.'

'Come on, come on,' Lucian said, 'let's wrap this up.'

'Yes ma'am,' Cole said. 'Okay, Korso, we know you found the special pill container up there, so why don't you pass it back to me nice and slow, just like before.'

Korso snorted. 'And then you'll just let us go, right?'

'We can put two in the back of each of your heads right now if you want,' Lucian said. 'At least this way, you get a few extra seconds of breathing time. Now hand over the pill container. That's the last time I ask nicely.'

'Well, since you asked nicely…' Moving slowly, Korso reached into his shirt pocket and using just thumb and index finger, pulled out the small metal tube. He glanced at Samara as he held it up, and noticed her left hand was almost at the door latch. She looked back at him, and he gave the minutest shake of his head. *Not yet.*

Cole snatched the container from his hand, and said, 'Watch them.'

'Uh huh.'

Korso looked at Cole in the rear view as he unscrewed the cap. A moment later he held one of the pills up to his eye, gently rolling it between thumb and index finger.

'Don't look like much, do they?' he said.

'It's what inside that counts,' Korso said, resuming eye contact with Samara again. With one of their assailants occupied, he knew they wouldn't get a better chance. As he slowly moved his right hand towards the door latch, he glanced down at his left hand and then back up at Samara. She looked down too and saw his first three fingers clearly extended.

'So are we golden?' Lucian asked.

'You know what?' Cole said quietly. 'I think we are.'

On that last word, Korso tucked his ring finger into his palm, leaving two. A second later he tucked away the middle finger, leaving one.

Korso tensed his muscles. It was now or never.

'*Wait,*' Cole said, and Korso froze as the cold steel of the gun barrel pressed into his neck again.

'What's the problem?' Lucian asked.

'I don't like it. This is all too easy. I know Korso and he always thinks two or three steps ahead. And now I'm remembering back at the house last Friday, when he asked Teodor what the pill container looked like.'

'That's right.' Lucian nodded her head in understanding. 'And it can't be that hard to find duplicate metallic containers in a city this size. We managed to grab ourselves two black market guns practically without trying, and we barely speak the language.'

'That's what I'm thinking.' Cole paused. 'And I don't like how there's no markers on these things, either. That Darian guy would definitely have stamped or branded them somehow, or how could he ever tell if they were the real thing or not?' In the rear-view, Korso watched as Cole raised a pill to his mouth and took a small bite. He rolled the contents around his mouth for a few seconds. 'Shit, nothing but sugar pills.' He crumbled the rest of the pill between his fingers, and flicked the remaining powder at the windshield. 'You get points for trying. Now where's the real stuff?'

Korso held back a sigh. It had almost worked. 'In my back pocket.'

'Bring it out, nice and slow. You know the drill.'

Korso knew the drill. Arching his back, he slowly reached into his rear trouser pocket with his left hand, and pulled out the same pill container he'd found in the steel sculpture. The one containing the real prototypes. He raised it up and Cole quickly snatched it from his fingers. The moment Korso felt the gun barrel disappear from the back of his neck, he casually lowered his left hand to his stomach, out of Lucian's line of sight. Extending his first three fingers again, he glanced over at Samara, who was still watching his every movement.

'Okay,' Cole said, 'now this is more like it.'

Korso tucked away his ring finger again, leaving two.

'Yeah,' Cole went on, 'they even taste medicinal too.'

Korso tucked away his middle finger, leaving one.

'And look, dude even marked each one with a crescent moon. How cute is that?'

Korso made a fist of his left hand, pulled the door latch with his right, and shouldered the door open and fell out of the car, all in one fluid movement. Landing on the pavement, he looked back and had enough time to see Samara doing the same before he kicked the door shut. Then he was on his feet and sprinting down the sidewalk, towards the parked station wagon fifty feet away. He'd done what he could. Now she was on her own. *Elementary Survival Tactics 101: When in doubt, run like hell.* As he pelted down the street, zigzagging as he went, he heard a gunshot from behind, quickly followed by another. But he felt nothing. He wasn't hit.

He reached the cover of the Ford seconds later without hearing any more gunshots, and hugged the ground next to the front bumper, out of sight of the Infiniti. Then the whipcrack sound of another gunshot behind him. Pulling the .38 from his pocket, he peeked round the headlight.

The street back there was still empty of traffic and pedestrians. He couldn't see Samara anywhere, and hoped she'd had time to make it to cover safely. There were still a few vehicles parked on the Vercogen side of the street, and she could be hiding behind any one of them. Cole was standing beside the Infiniti, gun in hand, looking down at the wheels. In the background, Korso could just make out a small female figure dressed in black running back towards Bulgaria Boulevard. A second later, she turned the corner and was gone. Meanwhile Cole aimed his piece at the rear wheel on the passenger side and pulled the trigger. The gun boomed, and the car rocked immediately, tilting to the left as all the air left the rear tyre. Then Cole turned and raced after Lucian. Seconds later, he was gone from sight too.

Korso knew without looking that the third gunshot he'd heard was Cole shooting out the front tyre. He would have known it was pointless chasing after Korso and Samara when the cops could show at any moment. Better to just cut their losses and hobble the enemy, and then head off to the meeting with Balakin, wherever that was supposed to be. That's what Korso would do, were he the double-crossing type.

Sticking the .38 in his waistband, Korso got up and ran to the other side of the street. Once on the sidewalk, he saw the figure of Samara crouched down behind one of the parked vehicles with her back to him.

He inserted thumb and forefinger into his mouth and gave a short whistle. Samara swivelled round, saw him standing there and ran over. She appeared unharmed.

'Man, I really thought that was it,' she said. 'How about you? You okay?'

'I'll live. But we need to get after them fast, preferably before they hand those pills over to Balakin.'

'How? We don't have a vehicle, and even if we did we've got no idea where they'll be meeting Balakin. Assuming that's where they're going right now.'

'I know Balakin, and he'll want to get his hands on those pills as soon as possible. So he'd have insisted the exchange be tonight or early tomorrow morning. As for the where, that shouldn't be too hard to guess. And we may not have to.'

'What does that mean?'

'We're too exposed out here. Let's find some cover before the cops show up.'

FORTY-FOUR

Korso led her away from the Vercogen building to the other side of the street, passing the station wagon he'd hidden behind. He kept going towards the two panel vans he'd spotted earlier, an old Mercedes Sprinter that had seen better days and a badly scuffed VW Transporter that looked even older. When he reached the Sprinter, he stopped to pull out his phone and speed dialled a number.

'Who you calling?' Samara asked beside him.

He ignored the question, and began peeling off the layers of modelling wax covering his real nose. When the call was picked up, he said, 'Which of these two vans are you using? The Merc or the VW?'

There was a brief pause. Dog said, 'Uh, neither?'

'Look, we don't have time to play around here. You already told me you'd need to park close to the Vercogen building in order to get through their security firewalls, so I already know you're in one of these vans. And if you heard those gunshots just now, then you've probably already connected the dots yourself. Cole and Lucian went rogue and snatched the assets, while Samara and I barely got out with our skins intact. Now they're off to meet with Balakin, and we need wheels if we're going to catch them. *Your* wheels.'

'Uh, look, K, I'm real sorry to hear that, but you know the rules. My survival depends on my anonymity. I broke that rule once for you, for a very specific reason, but I won't do it again for anybody else. Not for anything.'

'If you're in the Sprinter, you won't need to. The cargo cabins in those things are completely self-contained. We can get in the front while you remain out of sight in the rear, and we can continue communicating by phone. It's only if you're in the other van that we might have a problem. Now where are you?'

There was another pause, longer this time, followed by a sigh. 'In the Sprinter. And since I'm currently hearing your voice in stereo, I'm guessing you're standing not a million miles from me right now, right?'

'Correct.'

'Shit… Okay, wait one. Don't move.' As Korso waited, he peeled the last of the wax from his nose and removed both contact lenses from his eyes. Then there was a brief chirp as the central lock was activated up front. 'Okay, you can both get in the cab now. I dropped the keys on the driver's seat.'

'Thank you.' Korso walked to the front of the van and opened the driver's door. Inside, he saw the cramped cab area was indeed separated from the rear cargo area by a steel partition, which contained a small hinged panel in the centre, at shoulder height. Dog must have used it to reach through and drop the keys. Korso leaned in and picked them up, and then motioned for Samara to get in. 'Slide across. I'll drive, you point the way.'

She got in and clambered across to the other side. Korso got in after her, and inserted the key into the ignition. 'My guess is they're making for that hangar you rented us for the Malibu, out at that landing strip. But we can do a little better than guess.' He set his phone down on the centre console and put it on speaker. 'Dog, you might want to activate that special tracking app of yours. Tell me what you see.'

'Okay, wait while I turn that phone on again.' This time, the voice coming through the speaker was female. Korso recognised it as her own voice.

'You've stopped using the modulator,' he said.

'Doesn't seem much point now that you can hear the real me through the partition. I'm female. So what? So's half the population. But I've latched the service panel on my side, just in case you were thinking of peeking.'

'Don't worry, we'll be good,' Samara said. She raised an eyebrow at Korso. 'So you planted a bug on Cole and Lucian. Like the one you planted on Teodor.'

'Guilty as charged.' Korso spotted a pair of lightly tinted driving glasses poking out of the twin cup holders under the dash. He unfolded them and tried them on. Not a bad fit. 'I had a few micro GPS bugs left over, so I thought it might be prudent to cover my bets just in case things went south. Last night I planted one in the sole of Cole's left shoe, and then did the same with Lucian.'

Samara pointedly glanced down at her own boots, then back up at him.

'Yes, you too,' he said. 'I told you before I've got trust issues, and tonight's events only reinforced that.'

'Can't really argue with you there, can I? Doesn't mean I'm not pissed at you, though.'

'You'll get over it. See anything, Dog?'

'Yeah, I'm showing three readings here. One's right inside this vehicle, which I've now deactivated, while the other two are practically on top of each other. They're currently about two kilometres away and heading in a general south-westerly direction.'

'And is there a town called Radomir along that route?'

'Hold on, just zooming out... Yeah, there it is. Along with a little landing strip optimistically known as the Sofia West Airport. So you think they're heading out there?'

'It's what I'd do in their shoes. Lucian's a trained pilot, and I can't think of a better place to make the exchange than out there in the boonies, with a light single-engine plane in a nearby hangar, all fuelled and ready to go. I think they'll head out there first and get themselves ready as much as they can, and then call

Balakin to come and meet them with the cash. As soon as they get the money, they'll figure they can just take off and fly down to Istanbul, or maybe even one of the Greek islands.'

'But you don't think that will happen,' Samara said.

'It *won't* happen.' Korso turned the key in the ignition. The diesel engine immediately coughed into life. 'If it were anyone but Balakin, they might have had a chance. But with him in the equation they're essentially driving to their own graves. They just don't know it yet.'

'What about us? Are we going in unarmed?'

'We've still got a few tricks up our sleeves.' Korso pulled the .38 from his pocket and showed it to her, then put it back. 'As well as the element of surprise, although we can't count on that.'

'You think Balakin will be expecting us?'

'I would, so he will. Unless he's completely lost his edge, which I doubt.'

Korso still couldn't hear any approaching police sirens. Not wanting to push their luck any further, he crunched the gear stick into first and gently swung the van round until they were facing Bulgaria Boulevard.

'Don't forget your headlights,' Samara said.

Korso had forgotten. He flicked them on, and then stepped on the gas.

FORTY-FIVE

Less than five minutes later they were heading southwest on the E871 expressway, which would take them down towards Pernik, a heavily populated province situated in the high plain between the Vitosha, Lyulin and Golo Burdo Mountains. From there it was only another five or six kilometres before the much smaller town of Radomir, and then another four kilometres to the little landing strip that used to be an airport, right out in the middle of nothingness.

Samara didn't have a chance to do much navigating. Korso was taking an alternate route to the one she'd used on Sunday, with Dog feeding him directions as and when required. Dog also confirmed that Cole and Lucian were still moving in the same general direction as them, but using the slightly longer Highway 1 route. They were currently about four kilometres ahead. Korso kept the van's speed at a steady 120 kph, with the diesel engine fighting him every inch of the way. Thankfully traffic was sparse, but then it was late on a Monday. *22:13* according to the dashboard clock. The weather was on their side too: a heavily overcast sky with no visible moon. Korso couldn't really ask for more favourable conditions for what lay ahead.

He glanced down at his phone. 'Still with us, Dog?'

'Now and always. What's up?'

'I don't suppose you've got any additional firearms in this van, do you?'

'As it happens, I did pick up a little something not long after I landed, courtesy of my many contacts on the deep dark web.

For personal protection, you understand. I assume you'll want to borrow it when the time comes?'

'No time like the present.'

'Okay, face forward and I'll pass it through. That goes for both of you.'

Korso kept watching the road ahead while Samara turned and looked out the window on her side. A dark-skinned slender hand soon appeared at the corner of his vision, holding a small black semi-automatic. Korso took the weapon from her grip and set it down next to the phone, while she pulled her hand back and locked the panel again.

'Thanks.'

'*De nada*,' she said through the phone's speaker.

Samara turned back again, and looked down at the gun on the console. She picked it up and inspected it. 'Kel-Tec P-32. Haven't seen one of these in a while. Nice little sub-compact, though. Good for close-up work.' She ejected the magazine. 'Seven round mag with one in the chamber. This all the ammo you got, Dog?'

'Like I said, it's just for personal protection. I didn't see the need for any more.'

Samara turned to Korso. 'Wanna swap for the .38? I prefer something a little heavier.'

Korso took the Smith & Wesson from his pocket and passed it over. Samara handed him the Kel-Tec in return, which he stuffed back in his pocket. As long as the weapon was reliable, he didn't care what size it came in.

'There, that's *much* better.' Inserting the gun into her waistband, Samara faced front and said, 'So what's the deal between you two?'

Korso squinted at the harsh beams of an oncoming truck in the other lane. 'Deal? I don't get you.'

'I just get the impression you and Dog have been working together for a while. I sense an aura of trust between the two of you, which generally only comes with time. Or maybe it's more than just a work relationship?'

Dog snorted through the speaker. 'Forget about it. With K and me, what you see is what you get, although in my case it's more what people don't see. No, what it is, K helped me out of a very bad situation a short while back, so now I kind of owe him big time.'

'How bad of a situation?'

'Well, it mainly involved spending the rest of my natural life looking through thick steel bars while wearing an orange jumpsuit. And I hate orange.'

'So what, you're working for free now?'

Another snort. 'I don't do nothing for nothing, sweetheart. Mama always needs a new pair of shoes.'

Samara turned to Korso. 'So as a specialist at finding things that are well hidden, you've never felt the urge to uncover Dog's real identity at any point?'

Korso shook his head. 'I don't get those kinds of urges. Besides, why ruin things?'

'Exactly,' Dog said. 'If it ain't broke, leave it the hell alone. Cole and Lucian are still headed in the same direction, by the way. And moving way past the speed limit.'

'Lucian must be driving,' Korso said.

Samara was looking out the windshield again. 'I can just about make out some tall buildings in the distance. Looks like we're nearing Radomir.'

Korso just nodded. He'd already spotted the buildings quite a while back.

She said, 'Are you thinking what I'm thinking?'

'Be more specific.'

'Well, if I were in Cole's shoes and I was heading out to a remote location to meet with a ruthless ex–KGB agent who's got a reputation for double-crossing his partners, then I'd be thinking this is the perfect time to try one of those see-in-the-dark pills for myself. You know, as a safety precaution?'

'Ordinarily I'd agree, but this is Balakin we're talking about, and he's been one step behind us all the way. So I think it's a good bet he already knows that there are supposed to be exactly twelve pills in that container, in which case he'll have made it a main stipulation that Cole only gets the money in return for all twelve pills. In a situation like this, it has to be sole ownership or nothing. And I know Cole. With him money always come first, with security and peace of mind a very distant second. So I think he and Lucian will hand over all twelve pills as per the agreement, and try and protect themselves as best they can some other way.'

Samara didn't look convinced. 'You sure about that?'

'I'm not sure of anything at this point. But based on what I know of each man's character, I'd say that's the most likely scenario.' Not that it would stop Korso from being prepared for the worst, of course. He wasn't about to change the habits of a lifetime over a theory, no matter how reasonable it sounded.

'I just hope you're right,' she said. 'Road sign up ahead.'

'It's just for a furniture warehouse.'

'Really? You can see that far?'

Korso said nothing and just drove. The conversation soon lapsed and silence took over as they drew ever closer to their destination. They passed through the town of Radomir. There wasn't much to see, just a cluster of generic apartment buildings and a few public parks, interspersed with one-storey houses and small businesses. There was barely any traffic either. Just before they reached the town borders, Dog said the turnoff for Route 604 was coming up and Korso took a left at the next junction. It wasn't long before their surroundings became more rural again. The landscape gradually flattened out around them, with endless barley crops to the left of them and cornfields on the right. And always with the mountains overlooking them in the far distance.

Not much to see. But Korso saw it all.

A couple of kilometres later, they passed through a little village made up of two bus stops, a convenience store and a few scattered residences and farmhouses. Then they were out the other side and back in farm country again. There was no other traffic at all. No streetlights, no pedestrians, no signs of life. Two more kilometres after that, Dog said, 'Okay, we're almost there. In approximately three hundred yards, you'll be coming up to the turnoff for the airstrip, on your left.'

Korso glanced over at Samara. 'What can we expect? Give me the general layout.'

'Well, there's a blue arrow sign just before the turnoff, and then once you turn in there's a small stone structure on the right, with the school's logo spray-painted on it. About two hundred yards further in you come to a rickety steel gate leading to a small grouping of buildings. Only two are still in habitable condition and they're both used by the school, while the rest are all basically empty shells just waiting to be demolished. I'll give you the rest once we're there.'

Korso drove. It wasn't long before he could make out the small arrow sign in the distance, and he took his foot off the accelerator and gently tapped the brakes. He switched off the van's headlights as well. No sense in advertising their presence. And they were unnecessary now anyway.

'Jesus,' Samara said, 'It's like entering a coal mine. I can't see a damn thing except the dashboard lights.'

'That's the whole idea,' Korso said.

He pulled the van off the road and onto the grassy verge just before the turnoff, and killed the engine. He could see the small windowless concrete monolith exactly where Samara had said it would be. It looked as if it might have been an electrical sub-station back when the airport was a going concern; now it was just a mostly forgotten remnant of the past.

'This is where we get out,' he said to Samara. 'Dog, the van's yours again. I want you to drive back to that little village we just passed through and find a place to sit this out. Last thing we need is Balakin noticing this van and getting funny ideas.'

'Consider it done,' Dog said. 'Make sure to keep in touch, y'hear?'

'I'll do my best.'

Samara made sure the dome light above their heads was switched off, and then opened the passenger door and got out. Korso got out his side, and gently closed the door after him. He and Samara padded over to the little road that led to the skydiving school.

Korso crouched down next to a bush next to the turnoff. He heard the sound of the van's engine start up behind them, followed by the crunch of tyres on tarmac as Dog made a U-turn and headed back the way they'd come. He faced front and took a good look at what lay before them. He could see the ramshackle gate two hundred yards away, with a small guardhouse next to it. Beyond that, he could also make out the various two-storey buildings that Samara had mentioned. There were no lights anywhere, not even in the night sky. Except for the faint sound of rustling leaves in the gentle night breeze, all was quiet.

Samara was crouched next to him, the .38 gripped in her right hand. She looked at him, and said, 'What do you see?'

Korso smiled. 'Everything.'

FORTY-SIX

There was a moment's pause. 'Everything?' she said. 'Does that mean what I think it does?'

'That depends,' Korso said, turning to her. He could make out every line in her face, as well as the small mole above her left eyebrow, and the tiny black flecks in her light brown pupils. He could see it all in perfect clarity. 'What do you think it means?'

'That you took one of those night sight pills for yourself just before leaving Deleva's office. Which tells me you knew this was going to happen all along.'

'I knew something was going to happen. I just didn't know from which direction it would come, so I thought it best to be prepared for anything.' He decided not to mention that he figured it would be Samara who'd turn out to be the Judas, rather than Cole or Lucian.

'Yeah, that sounds like the Korso I know. So if there are supposed to be twelve pills in that container, what did you replace the missing one with?'

'One of the spare sugar tablets I brought along. After I found a penknife in the office, I also engraved a little crescent moon on one side. The difference is only noticeable if you look closely, which Cole didn't. But Balakin will.'

'So does Darian's pill actually work? You can really see everything now as though it were day?'

'Pretty much. The only real difference is most of the colours have been leeched out, so the world looks a lot more greyer than before.' He raised his hand and looked at his open palm. 'But

328

everything's still in sharp focus. I can see every line on my hand, for example.'

'What about approaching headlights when you were driving? Didn't they blind you?'

He shrugged. 'Truck headlights were too strong to look at directly, but normal car headlights aren't too bad. It's hard to explain, but they're like soft circles of whiteness surrounded by a slightly blurry haze. But even those I didn't want to be looking at for too long.' He looked at the buildings two hundred yards away. 'But as far as I'm concerned these are absolutely perfect conditions for a field test. You ready to move?'

'Just lead the way.'

'Stick close. I'll make a noise if I spot anything.'

Keeping to the field that paralleled the little road, Korso led Samara though the overgrown grass, his eyes and senses alert to any kind of movement around them. He saw nothing. Heard nothing. As they got closer to the gate, he noticed a chain-link fencing surrounding the entire property. It was only four feet high, so clearly more for show than anything. It looked old and rusted. He saw large holes in some sections. Grabbing Samara's arm, he led her over to the largest one, and they each crouched down and slid their bodies through the gap.

To their right were five buildings. The guardhouse looked in fair condition, and there was another two-storey structure set further back that looked like it could be the school admin building. But the three other buildings were in very bad shape, with missing doors and windows. One was also missing a whole section of its front wall. Straight ahead, he saw the airstrip itself as it trailed off to the east. About five hundred yards away was a low building that had to be the main hangar. It looked big enough to house three small planes. Next to it was a much smaller structure, which would be the surplus hangar Samara had rented. Korso also saw a single vehicle parked next to the airstrip, close to the hangars. He couldn't tell the make from this distance. The landscape was generally flat for the most part, although he did notice a number of small hills and knolls to the left of the airstrip.

They could be a problem.

Keeping low, Korso led Samara over to the small guardhouse. They crouched down on either side of the door, and Korso tried the handle. Locked, of course. 'Open it.'

Without a word, Samara pulled a snap gun and tension wrench from her pocket and got to work on the lock. Less than ten seconds later, there was a *click* as the tumblers fell into place. She opened the door, and they slipped inside.

'What did you see out there?' she asked.

Korso told her about the car. 'I wouldn't be surprised if it's that BMW you dumped in that long-term parking lot on Friday. Did you happen to tell Lucian where you'd left it?'

She frowned. 'I probably mentioned it, yeah.'

'There you go. Saves stealing another one. I also noticed a number of knolls and small hills overlooking the airstrip, which I don't like at all. Any one of them would make a great vantage point for a sniper, particularly one armed with a night scope.'

'Is Cole proficient with a rifle?'

'I don't know. But he knows handguns, so we have to assume he knows rifles too.' He looked around the cramped room and saw all four walls were covered with promotional posters for the skydiving school. In front of the sole window was a work-desk with two drawers on the left side, while over in the opposite corner were two metal storage cupboards. 'A place like this is bound to have a supply of field glasses on hand. You check the desk drawers, see if you can find some. I'll check these two cupboards over here.'

Samara approached the desk, while Korso walked over and opened the first cupboard. It contained spare work boots, hi-vis jackets and overalls, and various other items of clothing. The second cupboard was much the same, except for a large plastic box at the bottom, filled to the brim with various odds and ends.

'Nothing over here,' Samara said. 'You?'

'Still checking.' Korso reached down and rummaged through the box. He found five single gloves, an old gear bag, three helmets, two pairs of goggles, a weight belt, and right at the bottom, an old pair of field glasses. 'Bingo.'

He pulled them out of the box and returned to the east-facing window. He raised the glasses to his face and immediately saw why they'd been kept at the bottom of a cupboard. The left lens was cracked in about seven places. He closed his left eye and aimed them at the vehicle anyway. At least the magnification was decent. 'It's a BMW, all right,' he said. 'The exact same model as the one you drove on Friday.'

'No surprise there.'

Perching on the desk, Korso turned the field glasses towards the small hills along the left side of the airstrip, and stopped when he came to the far one that directly overlooked the two hangars. He stayed focused on that general spot for at least a minute, his right eye barely blinking, looking for the slightest—

'*There.*'

Samara started at the sound. 'What?'

'Movement. Behind that low hill at the end, the one over-looking the hangars. Only for a second, but it looked like a man lying on the ground, reaching back for something. It's gone now, but there's definitely somebody on watch over there. And armed with a rifle, no doubt.'

'Shit. And it's wide open out there. With a night scope they'll spot anyone who comes within a mile of those hangars.'

Korso nodded. 'Which means one of us will have to go out and circle round and take him, or her, from behind. And do it as quietly as possible.'

'One of us…?'

'I guess it's me. Have you got a knife?'

Samara looked at him for a moment, then reached down and pulled up the left leg of her combat pants. Wrapped around her ankle was a thin Velcro belt containing a push dagger, with its

331

familiar T-handle at the top. The three-inch-long, diamond-shaped blade was serrated on both sides. 'A little something I keep for close encounters.'

'You're more lethal than I thought. Better give me the whole kit.'

Samara unfastened the strap, and passed the belt and knife over. After affixing the strap to his own ankle, Korso grabbed the field glasses and said, 'We'll communicate by phone from here on in.'

'And if you don't answer?'

'Then I'm probably dead. See you soon, I hope.'

Still crouching, he opened the door and exited the guard-house. He retraced his steps as far as the front gate, and then he kept on going through the field in a northerly direction, quickly upping his pace to jogging speed. After another two hundred yards of this, once he was well past the hilly terrain, he began to turn northeast in a gentle curve. He covered the first two hundred yards at the same jogging speed as before and then slowed it right down to a fast walk.

He was now heading east with the low hills and mounds about a hundred yards to his right, completely blocking his view of the airstrip. The terrain was tough going with overgrown grass and thick weeds everywhere. His pace suffered as a result. It took another five minutes before he reached the specific hill he wanted, at which point he'd slowed his pace to a crawl. Then he stopped, raised the field glasses to his face and slowly panned across the small hill. He wasn't even halfway across when he spotted the human figure lying prone, near the top. The figure was about a hundred yards away. Maybe a little more. Even with the magnification of the field glasses, he couldn't tell yet if it was male or female.

Ignoring the Kel-Tec in his waistband, Korso reached down and silently extracted Samara's push dagger from his ankle belt. Whatever happened next had to be done quietly. Gripping the T-handle in the palm so the short dagger protruded out from between his middle fingers, he lowered his body to a half-crouch and began making his way through the field on a diagonal course, never taking his eyes off the figure at the top for a second. He was conscious that sounds carried much further at night, so his progress was slow. Footsteps on dry grass couldn't really be mistaken for anything else. If the figure turned to look behind him, all Korso could do was freeze and hope they weren't equipped with night-vision goggles. The irony of this didn't escape him.

He reached the bottom of the slope minutes later, without incident. The figure was now only a hundred feet away. It hadn't moved at all in all that time. Whoever it was up there was good. Had Korso not seen definite movement before, he might have mistaken the shape for a bunch of old rags. Korso began climbing the shallow hill, one careful step at a time. The grass still reached his knees, but there was still a gentle breeze coming from the west, which should cover any rustling noises he might make. He hoped.

Fifty feet away now. Then forty. Thirty.

The figure shifted position, and Korso froze. He saw the person's head turn to the right, looking at something towards the gate. It was a male head, he could tell that much. The body was too large to be mistaken for Lucian's. The man, possibly Cole, casually raised what looked to be night-vision goggles to his eyes and scanned the area over there for a few moments. Then he set them back down on the grass in front of him and faced front once more. Korso resumed his slow, painstaking passage up the hill, towards him.

When he was twenty feet away, Korso was able to see the man was gripping a thin rifle, with a large night scope mounted on top. The rifle was currently aimed at the largest hangar down below. Korso kept moving towards him, closing the distance step by step.

He was only ten feet away when the man suddenly sensed something. He turned his head, saw Korso bearing down on him with a knife in his hand, and immediately started bringing the rifle around in his direction. But Korso was already sprinting the rest of the way up the hill, and before the man could complete the move Korso was on him.

Korso landed on the man's lower body like a sack of rocks, and heard a muffled grunt of pain from beneath him. He pulled his right elbow back to jab with the knife, but the man somehow managed to swivel his upper torso in time and quickly thrust the butt of the rifle up towards his attacker's face, the steel stock slamming against Korso's lower jaw with the force of a jack hammer. He felt his brain rattle in his head as he fell back onto the grass, stunned.

Shaking his head, Korso forced himself up to a sitting position, surprised to see he was still gripping the push knife. He saw the other man on his knees and already bringing the rifle round again. Korso immediately recognised that face. It was Balakin's man, Vlad. The one he'd cold-cocked in the hypermarket restroom. Ignoring the searing pain in his jaw, Korso scrambled across the grass on all fours and jabbed the knife at Vlad's ankles.

Vlad saw him coming and forgot all about the rifle as he tried to back away, but Korso kept jabbing repeatedly until finally, the tip of the blade sunk deep into Vlad's right shin. Vlad's eyes widened in shock and he grimaced in pain as Korso released his grip on the knife and scrambled forward and launched an elbow strike at the side of the Russian's head, the hard bone slamming into Vlad's temple and knocking his head sideways like a rag doll's. Without missing a beat, Korso extending the first knuckle of his middle finger and punched Vlad hard in the throat, just to the left of his Adam's apple. As Vlad tried desperately to take in more oxygen, Korso reached back with other hand and extracted the dagger from his shin. Blood was already spurting from the deep wound.

Pressing his left forearm hard against the man's mouth, Korso thrust the pointed blade deep into Vlad's abdomen, in the right lumbar area. The man tried to shout, but the material of Korso's jacket muffled his screams. Korso pressed down harder anyway, and plunged the blade another inch into his right side and held it there.

Vlad's eyes were wild and he was struggling frantically, still trying to push Korso off him. He couldn't see the blood yet, but he knew bad things were happening down below.

'Talk or die,' Korso said in Russian. 'I remove this knife from your abdomen and you'll bleed out in seconds. Your choice. What'll it be?'

Korso took his forearm away from Vlad's mouth. 'Talk,' he said in a breathless whisper. 'I talk.'

'Good. Are you alone?'

Vlad glanced down at the knife sticking out of his body, and grimaced. 'How deep?'

'Deep enough. Answer the question. Are you here alone?'

'Yes. Alone. For now. But—'

'But Balakin's on his way. I know. How long till he gets here?'

Vlad winced in pain. 'Five… five minutes. Less, maybe. You'll kill me.'

'Not if I don't have to. How did Balakin know this would be the location for the exchange?'

'He didn't… for sure. But he found out about the plane and the rented hangar… You know him. Boss has sources… all over. Sent me here two hours ago as backup, in case your people chose this site for the handover.' As Vlad talked, he was staring down at the knife in his side, at the blood seeping into his shirt and jacket. 'That's everything, I swear.'

'Not quite. How does Balakin communicate with you?'

'By text. Boss will arrive with the money any time now, then when he's ready he gives me a hand signal and then I'm supposed to do what I do.'

'Take them both down.'

Vlad nodded once.

'How many more are on their way?'

'Two. Boss and one other guy.'

From past experience, Korso thought that unlikely. He tried to think of any other intel he might need, but nothing else came to mind. 'Okay, that's it,' he said, and got himself into a crouching position. Then he moved out of the way and yanked the knife out of Vlad's stomach in one quick motion.

Blood immediately started gushing out of the wound like a river, completely saturating the grass underneath the hit man. Vlad didn't even have to time to scream. In a panic, he reached down with both hands and applied pressure to the wound in a frantic attempt to stem the flow. But it was futile, the wound was too wide and too deep. Korso hadn't lied. He'd said he wouldn't kill him if he didn't have to, but leaving him alive was no longer an option either.

Korso stood there and watched the life leave the man's body. It took another twenty seconds before Vlad ceased his final struggles, and another fifteen before he stopped breathing altogether. Korso used Vlad's jacket to wipe the man's blood off his hand, and then picked up the rifle and scanned the ground until he finally spotted the phone in the grass a few feet away. He turned it on, and quickly went to the settings to reduce the brightness before it blinded him. Once he was able to view the display clearly, he saw there was a new message – '4 minutes.' It had been sent one minute before, from an anonymous number. Korso scrolled quickly through the chat history. Vlad had replied to most of the previous texts with 'OK'. Korso did the same this new one and sent it off.

He found a new position a few feet away from the body, and lay down on his stomach with the rifle in front of him, setting the phone face down on the grass close by. The rifle was a bolt-action Bergara with a solid aluminium chassis and stainless-steel barrel, equipped with a five-round magazine. Korso detached the magazine and counted five steel-tipped .308 Winchester rounds in there, along with a sixth in the chamber. He replaced the magazine again. The night-vision scope was currently switched on, which was the last thing he needed. He turned it off and then peered through the scope at the area below.

He could see everything clearly, as though it were daylight. The magnification was decent, about x10. Maybe a little more. He saw the smaller hangar was still closed-up, but Cole had partially opened the shutters to the much larger building next to it. He saw the wheels of two single-engine prop planes inside, but couldn't make out much more than that, even with his improved vision. It was too dark in there. The BMW was parked next to the airstrip, about twenty feet away from the largest hangar. Korso aimed the scope at the windshield and saw a human shape in the driver's seat. He couldn't see too many details, but it was most likely Lucian. He slowly scanned the area again, and stopped when he reached the small gap between the two hangars. He thought he'd spotted movement in there. There it was again. A flash of something metallic, most likely a pistol. So that accounted for Cole.

Pulling his own phone from his pocket, he called Samara's number. She picked up almost immediately. 'Any news?'

'Some.' Korso quickly updated her on the events of the last few minutes, and said, 'Balakin's due any second, so you better make your way towards the hangar now and then stay low, out of sight.'

'So what's the plan? *Is* there a plan?'

'We watch, we wait, we see what happens. Nobody knows we're crashing the party, so let's keep it that way for as long as possible. Balakin will already be feeling pretty secure, thinking he's got his pet sniper up on the hill to cover his back, and I want him to keep feeling secure and in control. Once things go south, which I guarantee they will, we'll let them fight it out amongst themselves and then go in and pick off the stragglers.'

She snorted. 'So much for the honourable approach.'

'Honour's for the movies. This is reality. You better get moving.'

'Already on my way.'

The line went dead. Korso picked up the rifle again. And he waited some more.

FORTY-SEVEN

It was only another minute before Korso saw distant headlights approaching from the west. He swivelled his body around and aimed the rifle at the oncoming vehicle. It was a black Mercedes sedan, moving at a crawl down the access road. The vehicle stopped at the gate. The driver got out. Looking in every direction, he pushed open the gate and then got back in and steered them through. Korso followed the Merc all the way down the airstrip until it came to a gradual stop thirty feet from the BMW, its headlights pointing away from Korso.

He kept his scope on the rear of the Mercedes. Although the windows were tinted, he could make out two people inside. There would be another man somewhere else, though. One thing about Balakin, he always had a Plan C. A sniper on a hill wouldn't be enough for him. He'd want additional backup. He had to figure there was a third guy already approaching the area on foot. Maybe even a fourth and a fifth too.

The Merc's front doors opened at the same time, and both driver and passenger got out. Korso recognised the back of Balakin's head straight away. The driver he didn't know. He'd never seen him before. Balakin made a vague hand motion, and called out something. Korso tried to listen but couldn't make out the words. Too far away.

After a few moments, Cole emerged from the gap between the two hangars and began walking towards the Mercedes, a semi-automatic in his right hand. He came to a stop a few feet from the BMW and said something in response. The conversation went on for another thirty seconds, and then Balakin said

339

something to his driver, who went back and opened the rear door of the Merc. He reached in, pulled out a huge aluminium suitcase and set it down on the ground. It looked very heavy. The driver wheeled it over to Balakin, who crouched down and laid the case on its side. He released the latches and then opened the front shell to reveal the contents. Korso saw the interior of the case was packed tight with what looked to be bricks of cash, all shrink-wrapped in plastic.

Balakin pulled out a single brick. He was about to stand when Cole said something, and he shrugged and replaced the brick of cash. Then he slowly moved his hand over the rest of the suitcase's contents, waiting for the next command. Cole spoke again and Balakin's hand stopped moving. Balakin grabbed the brick directly beneath his hand and pulled it free. He lobbed this brick towards Cole, who reached down and picked it up off the ground. He used a switchblade to cut through the plastic, and extracted a few samples.

As he checked the banknotes with the aid of his phone's flashlight, Balakin spoke again. Now that he'd shown Cole the money, he was probably demanding to see the prototypes. In response, Cole pointed at the rear wheel on the BMW's passenger side, and said a few more words Korso couldn't hear.

Korso aimed the rifle at the spot where Cole was pointing. When he finally spotted the little metal tube wedged tight under the rear wheel, he gave a slow nod of appreciation. Either Cole had more foresight than he'd given him credit for, or this was Lucian's idea. Probably the latter. Cole would now be explaining that if there were any tricks, Lucian would simply release the handbrake and crush the priceless prototypes under two tons of steel. Balakin raised a hand, no doubt reassuring him that was the furthest thing on his mind, and Cole went back to checking the money.

Balakin turned and said something to his driver, who nodded back and casually pressed something on his watch. Seconds later, Korso spotted movement at the rear of the car and re-aimed his scope. He watched as the Merc's trunk lid began to slowly rise up a couple of inches. A gloved hand protruded from the darkness within and lifted it up further. With the vehicles' headlights ruining everyone's night vision, neither Cole or Lucian would be able to see back there until it was too late. When the lid was only halfway open, a male figure dressed in black emerged from the trunk and dropped silently down onto the hard clay of the airstrip. Kneeling next to the rear bumper, he reached back into the trunk and pulled out a SMG. It looked to Korso like a Heckler & Koch MP5, with its curved thirty-round magazine sticking out the bottom. The man slowly closed the trunk lid and then moved a few feet back from the car, away from the rear lights. The man just stood there, waiting for the signal to move. Which would probably come any minute now.

So this was Balakin's Plan C. Not bad. Simple and effective. Or it would be if his pet sniper hadn't just been replaced by a ringer.

Korso moved the scope around, rechecking the positions of the players down below. Cole was still inspecting the watermarks on the notes, while Balakin just stood next to the open passenger door, waiting for the right moment. Samara was still nowhere to be seen, while Lucian was still inside the BMW.

Korso refocused his attention on the dark figure at the rear of the car again. While he didn't really care if his ex-team members survived the night or not, he wasn't much for wholesale slaughter either. It might be time to even the odds a little.

Breathing in through his nose, exhaling through his mouth, Korso sighted down the rifle until the gunman's head completely filled the night scope. The man was almost motionless. So was Korso. His hands were steady, his palms dry. He listened to his pulse beating slowly and softly in his ears. He felt calm. In control. As always. He picked his spot, just above the man's right ear, and caressed the rifle's trigger with his index finger.

341

Korso took a breath, and held it. He gently squeezed the trigger.

And nothing happened.

No click. No sign of resistance. Nothing. Dead trigger.

Without altering his body position, Korso looked down at the ejection port. It looked fine. No sign of damage at all. He slammed his left palm up against the magazine's base to make sure it was firmly seated. It was. But he knew that was unlikely to be the cause. It had felt like a light primer strike, when the firing pin fails to strike the cartridge primer with the force needed to ignite the gunpowder. He could only think that the firing pin must have been damaged during his scuffle with Vlad. Whatever the cause, he didn't have time to fix it now.

Which left him with no other choice. He'd have to go down there himself, and work close-up. The stakes were simply too high to allow Balakin to win this one outright. The moment he and his crew got their hands on the prototypes, they'd be gone forever. He couldn't allow that to happen.

Dropping the rifle, Korso got to his feet and pulled the Kel-Tec from his waistband. He checked the magazine again. Seven rounds, plus one in the chamber. Not much, but it was all he had for now. He briefly considered warning Samara about the change of plan, but discarded the idea. There wasn't time. In situations like this, you had to be prepared to improvise at a second's notice. Samara would know that, and be prepared for it.

He stuck the gun back in his waistband, and took the push dagger from his ankle strap. Stealth was key right now. Gripping the knife in his right hand, he began descending the hill towards the Mercedes. Even though he was a part of the darkness, he kept low. No sense in getting careless. Keeping his eyes away from the harsh beams of the headlights, he focused solely on the gunman by the Merc's trunk. He hadn't moved. He was still in the same pose. Still waiting for the signal.

Once he reached level ground again, Korso calculated he was still about thirty feet away from the Merc. The gunman's concentration remained solely on the drama in front of the vehicle. He never once checked behind him. Korso just kept on moving stealthily towards his target. He closed the distance to twenty feet. Then ten. The gunman still hadn't looked this way. Out the corner of his vision, he could see the two figures of Balakin and the driver in front of the car. He could hear snatches of conversation coming from over there, but tuned it all out. He kept his focus on the man ahead of him. Nothing else existed.

He'd closed the distance to less than five feet when he saw Balakin say something to his driver, and he in turn did something to his watch. Just like before. Then he saw the gunman ahead of him touch his right ear, as though listening to something.

The *go* signal. It had to be.

The gunman flicked the safety off the SMG and took a single step forward. Before he could take another, Korso crept up behind him until he could smell his sweat. Without pausing, he reached around and clamped his left arm against the man's mouth in a chokehold. The gunman started in surprise, and lost his footing. Korso kept him upright by pulling him hard against his chest. At the same time, he brought his right hand around and thrust the dagger deep into the man's side, just below the right kidney. Blood started to gush from the wound, and Korso plucked the MP5 from his grip and threw it on the grass behind them. It landed with barely a sound. The gunman convulsed from the sudden pain, and Korso clamped his arm harder against the man's mouth to silence the screams threatening to erupt from his throat.

Shrouded in darkness, the two men struggled on in near silence, the only sounds the scuffling of feet on dry clay. The gunman reached tried to loosen Korso's chokehold with both hands, but it was no good. Korso's grip was too strong. In panic, the man kicked out with both legs, forcing Korso to drag him back so he wouldn't make contact with the vehicle. Wanting to finish this quickly, Korso reached down with his free hand and extracted the dagger from the man's side, and then brought it up to his jaw line. He jammed the blade up into the man's neck and then brought it straight across, slicing his throat in one fluid motion.

A stream of blood sprayed from the wound, and Korso quickly backed away as the gunman collapsed to the ground in a growing pool of his own blood. With his vocal chords now severed, the man thrashed about silently, both his hands clasped to his neck in a desperate attempt to prolong his life an extra few seconds.

Korso didn't have time to wait. Turning, he rushed over to the spot where he'd thrown the gun and plucked it from the grass. He checked the mag was fully loaded, made sure the safety was off, and set the fire selector to three-shot burst mode. He turned back and saw the gunman had ceased his thrashing about, and was now barely moving at all. Up ahead, he could see Cole next to the BMW thirty feet away, still checking the bank notes. Balakin was still stood by the open suitcase, with his driver waiting in front of the open door of the Merc. Korso stepped over to the dying gunman, and was just about to reach down to check his pockets for extra mags when a hoarse shout filled the air.

He looked up. Balakin's driver had turned round and was staring back at him with open mouth and wide eyes, his hand already reaching for something under his jacket. Balakin had also turned to see what the noise was about.

When he saw the figure of Korso, he yelled, '*Kill him. Kill them all.*'

Voices filled the air as everyone reacted at once. Dropping the money, Cole raised his handgun and fired it directly at Balakin. At the same time, Balakin dived to the ground and fired back twice. Both shots missed Cole, who turned and immediately began sprinting back towards the large open hangar.

Meanwhile, the driver had extracted his handgun from his shoulder holster. Before he could take aim, Korso raised the

MP5 and squeezed the trigger. The driver ducked down behind the door, and glass smashed as a burst of 9mm rounds tore through the window.

Korso could hear more gunshots coming from somewhere near the large hangar, their cracks echoing in the night. But he had more immediate matters to deal with. He aimed under the open car door and squeezed off another brief burst, hoping to get the driver's legs. But he was no longer there. Korso looked up and saw him running towards the BMW. As he ran, he half-turned and fired twice at Korso, who ducked down behind the trunk again. A lucky round ricocheted off the rear wing just a few inches from his position. By the time he raised himself up again, the driver was no longer in view.

Pulling the Kel-Tec from his rear waistband, Korso aimed the little gun at the BMW's left headlamp, squeezed the trigger and shot out the light. He did the same with the right. Then he reached into the Merc and pulled the keys from the ignition. The Merc's headlights died as well, instantly plunging the whole area into complete darkness.

Now Korso had the advantage again.

As he slipped the little Kel-Tec into his jacket sleeve, he heard two distant gunshots coming from somewhere beyond the small hangar, well away from the action. It was answered by a brief burst of automatic gunfire, then another, this followed by another lone gunshot. Which suggested he'd been right about another of Balakin's men approaching on foot. It also sounded like Samara was on the case.

Korso ran towards the BMW at a low crouch. He'd only covered half the distance when there was another shot from just up ahead. He dived to the ground out of habit, and listened to a further exchange of gunfire over there. None of it seemed to be aimed at him. He got up again and continued on the same course. When he reached the front of the BMW a few seconds later, he lowered himself to a crouch and peered round the vehicle, weapon extended out in front of him.

Lucian was lying on the ground, her left hand pressed against a large wound in her chest area. There was a lot of blood. There was also a hole in her right shoulder, and a much larger one in her stomach area. A Colt semi-automatic lay on the ground, just out of reach of her right hand. Ten feet away from her, Balakin's driver was down on one knee, one hand on the ground for support. There was a large dark stain on his left shoulder and he was breathing heavily. In his right hand was a semi-automatic.

'*Kuchka*,' he hissed, and raised the pistol in Lucian's direction.

Korso aimed his MP5 at the man's head and squeezed the trigger. Three 9mm rounds instantly peppered his face, and he screamed out briefly and fell back to the ground, arms and legs akimbo. Korso ran over and put another three into his chest, just to make sure. The man didn't move again.

He walked back and glanced down at Lucian, who was wincing from her chest and stomach wounds. Either one looked fatal. There was blood everywhere. He found it hard to feel anything for her now, though. She'd chosen her path, for good or ill.

She looked up at him, her breath coming in short rapid bursts. 'Korso… That you?'

'It's me. The driver's dead. By the looks of it, you're not far behind.'

She tried to smile with one side of her mouth. 'By the… feel of it too.' Then she grimaced again as another jolt of pain hit her. 'Ooh… Jesus, that stings.'

It seemed blasphemy was no longer a priority for her. He decided not to mention it.

'We really… got screwed,' she said with a sigh.

'I warned you about Balakin,' Korso said. 'Twice. You didn't listen.'

'Thought I… I knew better. Hey, Korso? Kill that… bastard… for me.'

'I plan to. But not for you.'

Knowing he couldn't do anything else for her, even if he wanted to, Korso picked up her Colt and stuck it in his

346

waistband. You could never have too many weapons in these situations. He walked over the driver and searched the man's pockets until he found his phone. Once he confirmed it wasn't password protected, Korso turned the brightness all the way down to its lowest setting and then checked the clock settings for what he wanted. He nodded, satisfied, and then stuffed the phone in his pocket.

Turning away from the dead and the dying, Korso began jogging towards the large hangar. Towards Balakin and Cole.

347

FORTY-EIGHT

Korso reached the corner of the hangar, and then kept moving along the front of the building until he reached the huge entranceway. The shutters had only been partially raised, leaving a gap of about four feet at the bottom. He held back and just stood next to the opening for a moment, listening. Somewhere in the far-off distance he could hear a pair of barking dogs, but that was all. No sounds coming from within the hangar itself.

Frowning, he pulled the driver's phone from his pocket and activated the dimmed screen. The time was now 22:53:13. He opened the clock app and went to the alarm settings. He paused for a moment, and then set it for 22:56. It should be enough time. He programmed the alarm to cancel itself after sixty seconds, and raised the ringer volume to its highest setting before putting the phone back in his pocket. Then, gripping the MP5 in both hands, he lowered his head to avoid the shutters and slipped inside.

It was extremely dark in the hangar, with very little external light filtering through the opening. Even with his enhanced vision, Korso had trouble making out details. But the four single-engine turboprops in front of him were clear enough. The two smaller planes in the middle looked like Cessna 182s, while he recognised the much larger Cessna Caravan on the far left. To the far right was another large turboprop that looked like a Pilatus PC-6 Porter. It was in a major state of disrepair, and was missing not only its cockpit door but a large section of the starboard wing as well. And probably more besides. All around him, Korso spotted large crates and boxes lining the walls, any one of which could make a decent hiding place.

Breathing only though his mouth, Korso lowered himself to a crouch and scanned the entire room from left to right. He did it slowly, missing nothing. But he couldn't see any sign of Balakin or Cole. No signs of movement anywhere. He listened out for tell-tale signs of breathing, or rubber soles squeaking against concrete, and heard nothing at all. But he could sense both men's presences nearby. They were in this room somewhere, each man waiting for the other to give himself away first.

Korso studied the planes lined up before him. He thought it unlikely that the owner would bother locking the doors, meaning Cole could currently be hiding in any one of them. Not Balakin, though. Like Korso, he was on the hunt. So he'd be on the floor somewhere, waiting for Cole to make a mistake and give himself away. It's what Korso would do.

He'd been counting the seconds since setting his alarm, and figured he now had about ninety left. Time to stoke the fire, and see what sparked. Korso got up and using just the balls of his feet, started making his way towards the remains of the Pilatus on the far right of the hangar. As he moved cautiously down the room, he kept his eyes and ears alert for any signs of movement on either side of him, ready to fire at a moment's notice.

Thirty-five seconds later he reached the turboprop without incident. He'd seen nothing, heard nothing. Pulling the phone from his pocket, Korso went over to the cockpit and reached in and placed the phone on the floor, right in front of the pedals. Then he continued walking down the length of the plane, only stopping when he reached the rear wall of the hangar. To his immediate left were three large crates arranged in a loose group, along with a rusted rotor blade and an old pair of wheels still attached to their tricycle undercarriage. Once he'd assured himself nobody was hiding in the spaces between the crates, Korso lowered himself to his haunches next to the nearest one, and waited.

Korso relaxed his gaze, focusing on nothing in particular, allowing his peripheral vision to take in everything around him. He counted the seconds, and waited.

Even though he'd been expecting it, the alarm when it came made Korso start. The standard Apple opening was very loud, echoing throughout the cavernous hangar.

Korso remained where he was, not moving. Patient.

Five seconds passed. Ten.

Then movement.

To the right, Korso spotted a dark figure detach itself from the wheels of the furthest Cessna 182. He must have been there all this time. The man walked towards the rear of the place at a crouch and then turned right, towards Korso's position. Korso turned his head for a better look, but couldn't make out the man's identity yet. It was still too dark over there. But he was holding a gun in his right hand. That much was clear.

Korso mentally tuned out the blaring alarm, faced front again, and waited.

Moments later, the man passed in front of him, moving slowly, cautiously. Korso recognised the man's profile. It was Cole. He was about ten feet away from Korso's position, his head partly turned away from him as he looked towards the Pilatus's cockpit. As he walked past, Korso followed his movements with the MP5. It wasn't Cole he wanted right now. Balakin was the far more immediate problem.

Over the sound of the alarm, there came a sudden high-pitched squeak somewhere to Korso's right. Cole immediately halted in his tracks, swept his head round in Korso's direction, and fired blind. The boom was thunderous. The shot went somewhere above Korso's head, hitting the prefabricated steel wall panel behind him. Cole fired again, the gun flash lighting up the space for a split second. That shot had been even closer.

Korso couldn't allow to him to try again. He squeezed the trigger of the MP5 and let loose a brief three-round burst. The rounds took Cole high in the chest, and he grunted and fell back to the ground, his gun clattering loudly as it slid across the concrete floor. Shaking his head, Korso edged forward and peered around the crate next to him. Nothing.

He was just getting to his feet when there was a sudden blinding light in his face. The world flashed white and Korso instinctively raised his free arm to cover his eyes. As he did so, he felt the MP5 being kicked out of his right hand. He heard it clatter on the ground somewhere to his left.

Faked out. Balakin had faked them both out. Cole was dead, and Korso knew he was next. Effectively blind, Korso waited for the final shot that would end it all.

But none came.

After a few more seconds, the harshness of the light dimmed a little as the flashlight was moved away from his face. The alarm timed out at that moment too. The resulting silence came as a welcome relief.

The Colt was plucked from his rear waistband, and he felt Balakin search his body for other weapons before he was pushed back against the wall. But Balakin hadn't felt along his arms or wrists. That was a mistake. Korso just hoped he'd live long enough to make him regret it.

'Interesting,' Balakin said. 'So it seems the prototypes really do work as advertised.'

'They work,' Korso said, his left arm still covering his eyes.

'And when did you take the tablet?'

'Shortly after you left the Vercogen building. Darian hid the pill container in that tree sculpture in Deleva's office. There were twelve pills inside, so I took one for myself and replaced it with a sugar pill. Apparently, it lasts for six or seven hours before your vision returns to normal.'

'I see. Describe the effects to me. I want to know everything.'

Anything to buy a little more time, Korso thought. He could already feel his vision starting to return, slowly but surely. He said, 'It's kind of similar to the standard thermal imaging you get on night vision goggles, but without the green. I can see just about everything as though it were daytime, except with most of the colours leached out.'

'What about artificial lighting? How does that look to you?'

'I try to avoid harsh lights where possible, but they're still okay if you don't look at them directly. Car headlights are like soft circles of whiteness at the edge of your vision, but shining that flashlight in my face completely blinded me.'

'Yes, I thought it might. And how is your sight now? Is it improving?'

'Not sure.' Korso removed his arm from his face and made slits of his eyes. Everything was still far too bright, but he could now make out vague shapes. He could see the figure of Balakin standing in front of him, gun in hand, although the details were still fuzzy. At the same time, he angled his right arm until he felt the little Kal-Tec slip down his elbow and drop into his cupped palm. 'Not much improvement yet,' he lied. 'I can just about make you out, but you're essentially a silhouette, still very blurry at the edges.'

'Good, good. You know, I think my buyers will be very happy with their purchase tomorrow. Very happy indeed.' He paused. 'You know, Korso, you really should have killed me back in Mexico City.'

'I was just thinking the same thing.'

Balakin snorted. 'You were always too soft, you know. Never leave witnesses behind, Korso. That's the first and only rule in this business.'

'If you say so.' Meanwhile, Korso carefully extended the fingers of his right hand until the gun was fully in his grip, and his index finger was resting against the trigger.

Balakin said, 'So, my friend, this is where we must finally go our separate ways.'

'I'm not your friend.'

'Disagreeable to the last, I see. Still, I can't deny it's been an experience.' He began to raise his gun. '*Do svidan*—'

Korso didn't let him finish. He brought his right arm straight up until the Kel-Tec was pointing directly at Balakin's centre mass, and squeezed the trigger and kept on squeezing. There were five loud cracks, one after the other like a machine gun, and he saw the Russian's arm drop back down and heard the gun fall from his grip onto the floor. Balakin's head swayed back for a moment, and then his lifeless body slowly collapsed to the ground like a sack of wet towels.

'*Do svidaniya*,' Korso finished for him.

FORTY-NINE

Korso had almost reached the BMW, his vision noticeably improving with each step, when he saw Samara walking down the access road towards his position. She looked unhurt. She was also carrying an SMG, which explained a lot. As she came closer, she gave him a single nod of acknowledgement and then looked down at the bodies of Lucian and Balakin's driver.

'Poor little Lucian,' she said, shaking her head. 'So what happened here? They kill each other off?'

'No. He killed her. Then I took care of him.'

'Uh-huh. And what about Balakin and Cole? They dead too?'

Korso nodded. 'You can find them in the large hangar if you're interested.' He pointed at the SMG in her hands, which he recognised as one of the newer CZ Scorpion machine pistols. 'I see you've been busy too. How many were there?'

'Two,' she said. 'Obviously Balakin's men. The first guy I took care of without too much exertion, but his partner led me on a merry chase through the admin buildings back there. I only just caught up with him a minute or two ago.'

Korso furrowed his brow. 'I didn't hear any shots.'

'I was quiet.'

Korso smiled as he knelt down by the rear wheel of the BMW and inspected the small pill container wedged under the tyre. The metal looked a little squashed but still in one piece. He tried to free the tube with his fingers but the thing was wedged in too tightly, with no give at all. They'd need to move the car forward to free it fully.

'How do you want to do this?' Samara asked.

'You put the car into neutral and release the handbrake, I'll push. But not until I give the word. This car only needs to roll back a few millimetres and it's game over.'

Samara nodded and went over and carefully got in the driver's seat, while Korso placed both hands against the top of the trunk. He placed his left foot forward, with his right set a little further back for support.

'Ready?' Samara called from inside the car.

'Ready,' Korso yelled back, and immediately began pushing with all his weight. At first it was like pushing against a wall, and then all of a sudden the vehicle began to slowly roll forward, inch by inch. After a few feet, he called out, 'Okay, that should do it.'

The car came to a sudden halt as Samara pulled the hand-brake. Korso reached down and picked up the pill container and looked it over. The bottom half of the tube was partially crushed from being wedged in so tightly, but there were no cracks or holes in the thin metal. He unscrewed the cap and looked inside, and saw that most – if not all – of the pills were still intact.

'Drop your weapons, please.'

Korso looked up. Samara was standing a few feet away, her expression serious. She was still holding the Scorpion in her right hand, although it wasn't pointed at Korso. Yet.

'Not you, as well. And if I choose not to drop them?'

'Then you won't like what comes next. But notice I did say *please*.'

'That's right. You did.' With his free hand, Korso pulled the MP5 from his waistband and let it fall to the ground. He also took the almost empty Kel-Tec from his pocket and dropped that too. 'Now what?'

'Now kick them along the ground towards me. But not *at* me.'

Korso did as he was told.

'Good. Now toss me the pill container.'

Korso screwed the cap back on and lobbed the little tube underhanded towards her. She caught the container in her free hand, and then rattled it to make sure.

'That's quite the haul,' he said. 'Your CIA bosses will be pleased; you might even wrangle yourself a promotion. Or maybe this was all part of your original deal with Belmont, and you're simply making sure all loose ends are tied up?'

'I told you before, I never was a part of the CIA, although I have done the occasional job for them through intermediaries. Not that I knew it at the time, of course. And as for Belmont, he'll be majorly disappointed when I tell him we failed to recover the pills, but he'll get over it. Guys like him always do.'

'So who's your actual buyer?'

'Now that's the real question, isn't it? Here, I'll show you something.'

Using just her free hand, she slowly unscrewed the cap. Once it was free she flipped it away, then upended the container and all twelve pills fell to the ground in a loose pile. Korso just watched, puzzled. He was even more bemused when she raised her right leg and then began to methodically grind the pills into dust under her boot. All of them. It took less than a minute. Once she was done, she took her foot away and kicked the last of the powdered remains in all directions until almost nothing was left. Korso just looked at her, his mind working overtime as he tried to figure it out.

'There,' she said, throwing the empty container away. 'And all the king's horses and all the king's men couldn't put Humpty together again.'

Korso looked down at the few grains of white powder still remaining. 'Okay, that I didn't expect. So clearly, this *was* something personal.'

'Yes,' she said, 'but not in the way you're thinking.'

'I'm all ears.'

'It all comes back to what we talked about the other night. You and I have each seen human beings at their very worst,

Korso, or at least we think we have. With me, the last straw was that hostage mission in Belize five years ago. There was clearly nothing to be gained from those terrorists torturing my fellow team members to death. We were all just grunts, none of us knew anything of any tactical value. But those fundamentalist assholes went to town on them anyway, and they took their sweet time over it. Because they enjoyed it. Just like all these drug cartel scumbags in South America. They all get off on torture and death, even when there's no need for it. And the more gruesome the death, the better.'

Korso said nothing. He knew about the drug cartels' methods. More than he wanted to, in fact.

'So cut to five years later, and I get a call from Belmont raving about this new medical breakthrough he's learnt about, this prototype pill that grants people perfect night-vision. As soon as I heard the sheer elation in his voice, I knew there was nothing else I could do but tag along and make sure those prototypes never got a chance to go into mass production.' She shrugged her shoulders. 'Other than offering the worst people on earth new opportunities to kill and mutilate each other, I can't see what other benefits they would have provided. The world's got problems enough already. Why throw more fuel onto the fire?'

Korso nodded to himself as the last piece of the jigsaw slotted into place. Samara's exact role in all this had been bugging him for some time now, and now that itch had been well and truly scratched.

'I am kind of surprised, though,' she said.

'About what?'

'Well, you don't seem too cut up about my destroying the very assets we've been chasing after for so long. All that planning, all that work, all for nothing.'

'Maybe I agree with you about the prototypes,' he said. 'Some medical discoveries should never see the light of day, regardless of how revolutionary they might be. But don't think it was all for nothing. Incidentally, are you planning on letting me have that pistol back? It belongs to Dog, not me.'

'Sure.' Samara reached down and picked the little gun up, and lobbed it back to him.

Korso caught the gun, and said, 'Now, as to the matter of my fee...'

'Yeah, I thought that subject might come up. Well, Balakin did bring all that cash with him, so maybe you could take that as payment instead. After all, twenty million Euros isn't exactly chump change.'

Korso snorted. 'There's no twenty million in those suitcases, that I guarantee. But we'll look anyway.'

He walked back to the Merc, and crouched down next to the aluminium suitcase on the ground. The top layer was made up of seven shrink-wrapped packages, all neatly arranged on their side. There was a gap near the centre where Balakin had removed one for Cole to inspect. Korso removed one of the other bricks, and ripped part of the plastic wrapping away. He extracted several notes from the middle, and saw straight away that they were all genuine €500 bills. He placed the brick to one side, pulled out another from the bottom and ripped it open. This one contained nothing but scrap paper, which came as no surprise at all. He tried another brick. Meanwhile, Samara had already found out a second suitcase in the rear of the Mercedes and placed it on the ground nearby. After opening it up, she grabbed one brick from the top layer and used a knife to cut through the wrapping...

Ten minutes later, they were finished.

As Korso had expected, most of the bricks were made up of nothing but newspaper cuttings and scrap paper, while the lowest layers were simply chunks of wood covered in plastic. But there was enough real money in there to make it worth their while.

The final tally came to €3,426,240. Which was less than twenty per cent of what Balakin had promised Cole, but more than enough for Korso's purposes. He placed his and Dog's share into one of the suitcases, and dumped it in the rear seat of the BMW. He pulled out his cell and called her number.

When she picked up, he said, 'It's me.'

'Boy, am I glad to hear your voice. So how did it all go out there?'

'About as expected. I'll fill you in on the details in a few minutes time, after I drop off your share of the fee.'

'You mean you've got it in your hands already? All of it?'

'Down to the last penny.'

Dog gave a soft chuckle. 'Man, you are without doubt my most favourite client of all. Seriously, no one else even comes close.' She gave him her current location and said she looked forward to seeing him soon, and then hung up.

He walked back to Samara, who was looking down at the last remaining brick of cash. It was less than half full now, since Korso had used most of it to make up the three million.

'What do you think Balakin did with the rest of the money?' she asked.

'You're assuming he had it all in his possession in the first place, which I have my doubts about. But even if I'm wrong, you can be sure he hid it in a place nobody will ever find it. Let it go. It's not our problem.'

'And what about the remaining money here?'

'Give it to Belmont. He's already out that half million you transferred to Teodor's account, which he'll never see again. Plus our expenses. He played straight with me, so I see no reason not to pay him back in kind. Can I trust you with that, at least?'

'No need to be nasty, Korso. He'll get it. I don't burn my bridges either.'

'Very wise. And don't forget to return the Malibu we rented either.' Korso frowned as something else occurred to him. He reached down and extracted a small wad of Euros from the package on the ground. He counted out forty notes and stuffed them in his pocket. The rest he put back in the brick.

'What's that for?' Samara asked.

'None of your business.'

But Korso was thinking of the promise he'd made last night to the delectable Tanya, back at Georgi's apartment on Podkrepa Street. About the bonus she'd get if she were a 'good girl'. He recalled that flirtatious smile she'd given him before they left, and thought he might deliver the money to her personally. She'd more than earned it, and there were worse ways to mark the culmination of an assignment than in the company of an attractive woman. He'd have to give her a call shortly. As Korso turned and started walking towards the BMW, he smiled at the possibilities that lay ahead.

The night was still far from over. And that was good enough.

ACKNOWLEDGEMENTS

As ever, huge thanks goes to my editor, Kit Nevile, for his sage advice during the final stages of the writing of this novel.

Thanks also to Krzysztof Kolodynski for his codebreaking talents.